Solovyov and Larionov

Solovyov and Larionov

EUGENE VODOLAZKIN

Translated from the Russian
by Lisa C. Hayden

A Oneworld Book

First published in North America, Great Britain and Australia
by Oneworld Publications 2018
Originally published in Russian as *Соловьев и Ларионов*
by AST, Eleny Shubinoi imprint
The publication of the book was negotiated through Banke,
Goumen & Smirnova Literary Agency (www.bgs-agency.com)

ISBN 978-1-78607-035-7
ISBN 978-1-78607-036-4 (ebook)

This publication was effected under the auspices of the Mikhail Prokhorov Foundation
TRANSCRIPT Programme to Support Translations of Russian Literature

Published with the support of the Institute for Literary Translation (Russia)

ИНСТИТУТ ПЕРЕВОДА

AD VERBUM

Typeset by Palimpsest Book Production Limited, Falkirk, Stirlingshire
Printed and bound in Great Britain by Clays Ltd, Elcograf S.p.A.

Oneworld Publications
10 Bloomsbury Street
London WC1B 3SR
England

In memory of my great-grandfather

1

He was born by the train station bearing the unprepossessing name *Kilometer 715*. The station was not very big, despite the three-digit numeral. There was no movie theater, no post office, not even a school. Nothing but six wooden houses stood along the railroad bed. He left that station shortly after his sixteenth birthday. He went to Petersburg, was accepted at the university, and began studying history. This was to be expected, considering the surname—Solovyov, just like the famous historian—with which he had been born.

Solovyov's advisor at the university, Professor Nikolsky, called Solovyov a typical *self-made man*, who had come to the capital with a string of sledges bearing fish, but of course that was a joke. Petersburg had ceased being the capital long before Solovyov's arrival in 1991, and no fish was ever to be found at *Kilometer 715*. To the adolescent Solovyov's great regret, there was neither a river nor even a pond there. Reading one book after another about maritime journeys, the future historian cursed his landlocked existence and decided to spend the remainder of his days—a rather considerable number at the time—at the place where land and sea met. The attraction of large bodies of water, along with his thirst for knowledge, settled his choice in favor of Petersburg. In other words, the comment about the fish sledges would have remained a joke if not for its emphasis on overcoming one's initial circumstances; something elegantly stated in the English expression. Say what you will, but the historian Solovyov was a most genuine *self-made man.*

General Larionov (1882–1976) was another matter. He came into the world in Petersburg, in a family where being a military officer was hereditary. All of his relatives were officers, with the exception of the future general's father, who served as the director of the railroad department. As a child, Larionov even had the good fortune to know his great-grandfather (there was a penchant for longevity in the family), who was, naturally, a general, too. He was a tall, straight-backed old man who had lost his leg back in the Battle of Borodino.

In the eyes of the young Larionov, every movement his great-grandfather made, even the very knock of his peg leg on the parquet floor, was filled with a special dignity. When nobody was watching, the child loved to lift his right foot up, traverse the room on his left leg, and recline on the sofa with a deep sigh, resting his arms on the back of the sofa like great-grandfather Larionov. Larionov's grandfather and his lush-mustached uncles were not really any worse than his great-grandfather, but neither their gallant officer's appearance nor their talent for eloquence (his great-grandfather was not a talker) could even begin to compete with the absence of a leg.

All that reconciled the child to his two-legged relatives was their abundance of medals. He liked a medal one of his uncles had received, *For the suppression of the Polish rebellion*, more than anything. The melody of the word combination fascinated the boy, who did not have the faintest idea about Poles. In light of the child's obvious affinity for the medal, his uncle finally gave it to him. The boy wore this medal—along with the medal *For the conquest of Shipka*, which he received from another uncle—right up until the age of seven. The word *Shipka* certainly lost out to the word *rebellion* in terms of sonority but the beauty of the medal itself made up for its phonetic shortcomings. The child's happiest moments were spent sitting among his officer relatives with the two medals on his chest.

These were still Russian officers of a bygone time. They knew how to use cutlery (including the fish knife, now forgotten), effortlessly kissed ladies' hands, and performed numerous other courtesies unimaginable for officers of a later epoch. General Larionov had no need to overcome his circumstances. Quite the opposite: he needed only to absorb the qualities of his environs, to brim with them. Which is, in fact, what he did.

His inclination to become a general manifested itself in early childhood, when he began lining up wooden hussars in even rows on the floor before he had fully learned to walk. Seeing him engaged in this pursuit, those present uttered the only possible combination of words, 'General Larionov.' Ponder the naturalness of the union of those two words: they were made for one another, they were pronounced without a pause and became a united whole, flowing from one to the other, just as a rider and his horse become a united whole in battle. General Larionov. This was his first and only name among the family, and he became accustomed to it immediately and forever. General Larionov. Whenever the child heard that form of address, he stood and silently saluted. He did not learn to speak until he was three and a half years old.

What, one might ask, unites two such dissimilar individuals as the historian Solovyov and the General Larionov, if of course it is permissible to speak of uniting a budding young researcher and a battle-weary commander who, furthermore, is no longer of this earth? The answer lies at the surface: historian Solovyov was studying General Larionov's activity. After graduating from St. Petersburg University, Solovyov began his graduate studies at the Institute of Russian History, where General Larionov became his dissertation topic. Based on entries in reference books, there is no reason to doubt that by 1996—that being the time under discussion—General Larionov already belonged wholly to Russian history.

Needless to say, Solovyov was not the first to devote himself to studying the famous general's biography. Over the years, a couple of dozen scholarly articles had appeared at various times. They were devoted to various stages of Larionov's life and, above all, the mysteries associated with him that have yet to be unraveled. Although the number of works appears considerable at first glance, it seems completely insufficient if compared to the interest that General Larionov has always inspired, both in Russia and overseas. The fact that the number of scholarly research works is significantly fewer than the number of novels, films, plays, etcetera, in which the general appears—either as a figure or as a prototype for a character—does not appear to be accidental. This state of affairs symbolizes, as it were, the predominance of mythology over positive knowledge in everything concerning the deceased.

Beyond that, critical analysis by French researcher Amélie Dupont has shown that the mythology has even penetrated various scholarly articles about the commander. Which explains why the topic of research becomes a minefield, to a certain extent, for anyone just beginning work on the subject. However, even those articles (and Dupont writes about this, too) in which the truth comes across, thanks to all the splendor of scholarly argumentation, shed light on such narrow problems and episodes, that the significance of the extracted and argued truth is reduced to nearly nothing. It is remarkable that Dupont's work (*The Enigma of the Russian General*, a book published in French and Russian) is still the sole monographic research dedicated to General Larionov. This circumstance emphasizes, yet again, the dearth of sources on the subject. The fact that the French researcher managed to collect material for a monograph is due exclusively to her selflessness and particular treatment of her topic, which she has called the topic of her life.

In reality, it is no exaggeration to say that Dupont was born to research the Russian commander. In her case, this was not a matter of the historian's external features, something the scholarly community permits itself to mock, due to her height (187 centimeters) and the emergence of a mustache after the age of forty. It is known, after all, that barbs and jokes behind a prominent specialist's back (Dupont is called *mon general* in certain narrow circles) are usually nothing more than a form of envy. Consequently, mentioning Dupont's destiny for her designated topic is, above all, a reference to her unusual persistence, something without which it would essentially have been impossible to discover the tremendously important sources she subsequently published. And, truly, those who surmise that the emergence of the mustache that caused the inappropriate reaction in scholarly circles could be attributed, first and foremost, to the researcher's fascination with her topic, were not far from the truth. For the sake of objectivity, however, it must be noted that General Larionov himself did not have a mustache.

In all the preserved photographs (see the insets in Dupont's book), there appears before us a carefully shaven person with his hair cut short and parted. The part is so even and the quality of the shaving so flawless that one unwittingly detects the scent of eau du toilette when contemplating the photographs. With regard to his appearance, General Larionov made the only possible valid decision, just as he did in most other situations. Thinking that his ideally proportioned facial features needed no framing, he did not style himself after Alexander III, as did the officers around him. What is interesting is that his face did not look handsome, despite its proportions. His face became livelier at a mature age, particularly in elderliness. It is not uncommon to contemplate a photograph of a person in his youth, marveling at its blatant insufficiencies and almost embryonic look when compared to what came later. In cases of this sort, one experiences regret regarding the existence of that stage in the life of the person portrayed. Needless to say, feelings of this sort are very highly ahistorical. As far as the general goes, his face looked more chiseled thanks to wrinkles that appeared, with age, under his eyes, and the bump that emerged on his nose. During one period of his life, between the ages of thirty-five and forty, his appearance was reminiscent of Cardinal Richelieu because of his facial expression and that bump, though not because of all his features. The peak of the general's activity—as well as the mysteries connected with him—dates back to this period. Perhaps his resemblance to Richelieu was the resemblance of people possessing mysteries? Whatever the reason, that resemblance departed with time, too.

Even a fleeting glance at Dupont's illustrative material attests to the undeniable prevalence of photographs from the final period of General Larionov's life. The old man never made a point of having his picture taken but he also never put on airs by turning away from any cameras that greeted him: he regarded them with utmost indifference. That regard gave portraits of the general a naturalness rare for the genre. Perhaps the triumph of two photographic portraits of the general in international competitions at various times should be ascribed, above all, to that naturalness?

There is no doubt that even those who are not at all familiar with the general's activity and have not heard his name would recall the black-and-white photograph of the old man sitting on a folding chair at the very edge of a jetty (Yalta, 1964). It became a classic of world photography, rather like the locomotive falling out the window of a Paris train station, rather like the lighthouse among raging waves, etcetera. Despite the summer heat, the old man is dressed in a white service jacket. He is sitting under a partially transparent awning, his legs crossed. The toe of a light-colored shoe is stretched before him, parallel to the ground, and almost blends in with the jetty, making it seem as if the lighthouse standing close by is balanced on the toe of that elegant shoe. The old man's gaze is directed into the distance and filled with the particular attention of one not interested in anything closer than the horizon. That old man is General Larionov. One cannot deny that all previous photographs pale in comparison with that shot of the general, that they have grown to feel inexpressive and, to some extent, unworthy of this outstanding person. That the general remained in his descendants' memory in his most, so to speak, mature form, could be considered his indisputable success. However, the biggest success of his life was, most likely, simply that he was not shot at the conclusion of the Civil War. This has always been considered inexplicable.

What is consequential, though, is that historian Solovyov decided to concentrate on that very enigma. Here, one might foresee objections of the sort that question whether historian Solovyov is, say, a figure capable of untangling this very complex historical snarl. And is it even worth placing hope on a very recent graduate who is, moreover, a *self-made man*? These objections do not seem well founded. It is sufficient to point out—and Dupont was the first to establish this fact—that Arkady Gaidar was commanding a regiment at the age of sixteen and a half. As far as *self-made man* goes, well, under a broad understanding of the term, anyone who has ever succeeded at accomplishing anything in life should be considered one.

It is sufficient to mention just one detail with regard to Solovyov's work on self-improvement: he was able to change his Southern Russian pronunciation to aristocratic Petersburg pronunciation. Needless to say, there is nothing about the Southern Russian pronunciation, in and of itself, that is shameful or belittles the dignity of its speakers (just as, say, deficient Moscow speech is incapable of discrediting residents of the capital). Mikhail Gorbachev, after all, led perestroika in Russia using Southern Russian pronunciation. Unlike Solovyov, Gorbachev was not a historian—he himself made history without taking particular care about the orthoepic side of matters, a tendency that continued even after he left his post and retired. As far as Solovyov goes, when he murmured Russian tongue twisters in the dormitory kitchen, he was working on something that went beyond simply training himself in pronunciation: he was, as he characterized it, eliminating the provincialism within himself.

Solovyov's thesis advisor, the eminent Professor Nikolsky, played an important role in Solovyov's development. After reading his student's first important paper, which was devoted to Russia's conquest of the Far East, the professor invited Solovyov to his office, where he said nothing for a long time, blowing on the paper tube of a *Belomorkanal* cigarette all the while (he had taken a liking to those cigarettes while working at the forced labor site bearing the same name).

'My friend,' said the professor after lighting the cigarette, 'scholarship is dull. If you don't get used to that notion, it will not be easy for you to pursue it.'

The professor requested that Solovyov delete from his paper the words *great, triumphant,* and *only possible.* He also asked his student if he was familiar with the theory according to which Russians squandered the energy granted to them by conquering expanses of inhuman dimensions. His student was not. Prior to acquainting Solovyov with this theory, Prof. Nikolsky requested that he delete the phrase *phenomenon indicating progress,* too. The author of the paper was

asked to pay special attention to the formatting of bibliographical and persuasive footnotes. A careful look at this
aspect of the paper revealed that the only properly formatted
footnote was 'Ibid., 12.'

To be utterly candid, the majority of what Prof. Nikolsky
said seemed like nitpicking to Solovyov, yet it was this very
discussion that formed the basis of a friendship between
professor and student. The professor was at that age when
his quibbles could no longer be offensive to the young man
and Solovyov's own history, which was anything but simple,
did its part in forcing his advisor to show more leniency
toward his student.

Prof. Nikolsky never tired of repeating to his mentee that,
as a rule, pretty phrases in scholarship are misguided, and
the beauty of those phrases is based on their alleged univer-
sality and an absence of exceptions. But—and here the
cigarette in the professor's hand would trace a smoky
ellipsis—that absence is spurious. No exhaustive truths exist
(hardly any exist, the professor corrected himself, bringing
the statement into accord with his own theory). For each a
there is always a b and a c to be found, as well as something
that no letters can convey. An honest researcher takes all
that into account, but his pronouncements cease being beautiful. Thus spoke Prof. Nikolsky.

At some point, Solovyov's blue-eyed romanticism gave
way to a pronounced inclination toward precision, so this
was a time when he discovered a particular beauty: the
beauty of reliable knowledge. This was a time when the
young man's papers started to be mottled with enormous
quantities of exhaustive and meticulously formatted footnotes. Footnotes became for him more than an occasion to

express respect for his predecessors. They revealed to him that there was no one realm of knowledge where he, Solovyov, would be first, and that scholarship is, to the highest degree, a process that is bequeathed. They were representatives of great, all-encompassing knowledge. They watched after Solovyov and educated him, forcing him to rid himself of approximate and uncertain assertions. They blew open his smooth school-based exposition, because a text, just like existence itself, cannot exist without conditions.

Solovyov inserted footnote after footnote, marveling that he had managed to get by without them at the beginning of his scholarly career. When footnotes began accompanying nearly every word he wrote, Prof. Nikolsky was forced to stop him. He announced to Solovyov, in passing, that scholars usually get by without footnotes at the end of their careers, too. The young researcher felt disheartened.

Despite Solovyov's expectations, the Pacific Ocean—to which he fought his way in his first important paper—did not become his primary topic. Prof. Nikolsky was able to convince his student that the most important part of history takes place on a continent. Only a strong familiarity with that part of history gives a researcher the right to leave dry land from time to time. After a wrenching internal struggle, Solovyov decided to postpone setting sail.

Solovyov came to appreciate Petersburg fully during his five university years. He began wearing high-quality but unostentatious clothing (clothing becomes more colorful when advancing south, and not only in Russia), referenced the powers that be with the short word *they*, and took a liking to evening strolls on Vasilevsky Island. His habit of taking strolls continued later, after renting an apartment on the Petrograd Side (Zhdanovskaya Embankment, No. 11). He would walk home after finishing his work at the library. Sadovaya Street. Summer Garden. Troitsky Bridge. In the winter, when the Summer Garden was closed (in accordance with its name) and its statues were boarded up in boxes, Solovyov would choose another route. He would reach the Neva River via Griboedov Canal and then turn on to Dvortsovy Bridge, after walking past the Winter Palace (which was open year-round, unlike the Summer Garden). At home, he would place his soaked boots on the radiator. By morning they would turn white, from the salt scattered by the yard workers.

Solovyov came to love the Public Library's special winter coziness: Catherine the Great's figure in a half-frosted window, pre-war lamps on the tables, and the barely audible whispering of those sitting behind him. He liked the indescribable library scent. That scent united the aromas of books, oak shelves, and worn runner rugs. All libraries smell that way. The snow-covered, one-story village library where the young Solovyov had borrowed books smelled that way. It was an hour and a half's walk from the *Kilometer 715* station; Solovyov stopped by the library after school before heading back to his station. He would sit, half-facing the elderly librarian Nadezhda Nikiforovna's desk, while she searched for his books some-where behind the cabinets. As he awaited Nadezhda Nikiforovna's return, Solovyov would examine his violet fingers, which he sank into his rabbit-fur hat. Her voice would emerge from behind the cabinets from time to time.

'*Captain Blood: His Odyssey?*'

'Already read it.'

He read everything. The village library became his first

true revelation and Nadezhda Nikiforovna was his first love. Unlike the houses by the railroad, the library was very quiet and did not smell of railroad ties. Mixed in with the fabulous library potion was the smell of *Red Moscow* perfume. This was Nadezhda Nikiforovna's perfume. If there was anything Solovyov felt was missing later, in his Petersburg life, it was likely *Red Moscow*.

'*In Search of the Castaways?*'

Her quiet voice made goosebumps slowly descend down Solovyov's spine. After licking a fingertip, Nadezhda Nikiforovna would pull his library card out of the drawer and enter the necessary notation. Fascinated, Solovyov followed the movement of her large fingers, with their dulled nails. A cameo glistened on her ring finger. When she placed a book on a shelf, Nadezhda Nikiforovna's ring grazed the wood and the cameo produced a muffled plastic sound. That sound took on an extraordinary elegance, almost an elite quality, in Solovyov's ears because it was so unlike the clanging of train carriage couplers. Later, he would qualify it as world culture's first bashful knock at the door of his soul.

More often than not, Solovyov did not come to the library alone: he was with a girl named Leeza, who lived in the house next door. Leeza was not allowed to walk home by herself and was ordered to wait for Solovyov at the library. She would sit some distance away, silently observing the book exchange process. Sometimes she would borrow something Solovyov had already read. Solovyov immediately forgot about Leeza after coming home. He would recollect all the details of his visit to the library, indulging himself in dreams of married life with Nadezhda Nikiforovna.

It should be emphasized that he was eight years old then

and his dreams were fully virtuous. Remote as he was from civilization's hotbeds (and based on Nadezhda Nikiforovna's expression, from those hotbeds' settled ashes, too), Solovyov vaguely imagined the tasks of marriage, as well as the ways it takes its course. As it happened, that village library was his sole link to the outside world, ruling out the availability not only of erotic publications but of suggestive illustrations in periodicals as well. Nadezhda Nikiforovna censored new acquisitions in her free time, ruthlessly cutting those items out.

There is nothing surprising in the fact that five years later, when their instincts were awakening, Solovyov and Leeza were deprived of all manner of guidance in *that* sphere and progressed by groping along, in the literal sense of the word. Nevertheless, when the adolescent Solovyov engaged in sex in later years, he did not consider himself unfaithful to Nadezhda Nikiforovna. The idea of marriage, which had so warmed his heart as a child, lost no attraction for him then, either. The change took place only upon recognizing that certain things should not be demanded of Nadezhda Nikiforovna.

Leeza's surname—Larionova—does not lack interest in this present narrative. This present narrative is inclined to accentuate various resemblances and coincidences because there is meaning in any similarity: similarity opens up another dimension and alludes to a true perspective, without which one's view would certainly hit a wall. In taking on research into General Larionov's life and work, Solovyov bore in mind his own previous familiarity with that same surname. He placed significance on such things. Needless to say, the young researcher could not yet explain the role of the Larionovs in his life, though even then he felt the role would not be secondary.

As happens more often than not with events that are intended to occur, Solovyov's research topic came to him by chance. Another graduate student, Kalyuzhny, had worked on the topic before Solovyov. Yes, this pleasant fellow lacked all manner of scholarly energy and, really, most likely any energy whatsoever. His efforts were sufficient for him to make his way to some academic beer joint and settle in there for the entire remainder of the day. Kalyuzhny regarded the general sympathetically and experienced an undeniable curiosity regarding his fate. The primary thing he did not understand was that (and here Kalyuzhny's index finger slid along a glass) the general had remained alive. Over the course of several years, Kalyuzhny retold Dupont's classic research to everyone who sat down at his table. This long retelling obviously wore him out in a real way because he did not write a single line during those years of unending narration. Gathering his last strength, graduate student Kalyuzhny unexpectedly did what the general had not brought himself to do in his day: he left the country. Kalyuzhny's further fate is unknown.

Solovyov's fate is known, however, and, according to the unanimous opinion of his colleagues, it was up to him to replace his drop-out associate. Only a few months after entering graduate school, Solovyov delivered a paper at a conference: 'Studying the Life and Activity of General Larionov: Conclusions and Outlooks.'

The conclusions that Solovyov drew and the outlooks he summarized made a most favorable impression on the scholarly public. The paper testified not only to the young researcher's well-organized mind but also, in equal measure, to his deep insight into the topic. The climax of the paper, which evoked extraordinary animation in the hall, was his introduction of corrections to data in Dupont's monograph that had been considered unshakable until that day.

And so, it turned out that there were only 469 soldiers on record in the 34th Infantry Division of the 136th Taganrog Regiment, not the 483 soldiers Dupont asserted. It also emerged that the French researcher had, on the other hand, reduced the number of soldiers in the 2nd Native Division of the Combined Cavalier Brigade to 720 (the true number was 778). Dupont did not shed full light on the role of Colonel Yakov Noga (1878–?) in the Crimean campaign; however, the officer's level of education had clearly been overstated: the French researcher mistakenly indicated that Noga graduated from the Vladimir and Kiev cadet corps, though he graduated only from the Vladimir (named for Saint Vladimir) Kiev Cadet Corps. Solovyov set forth a series of more minor quibbles with the French monograph, but in this case one must think it permissible to limit discussion to the examples cited above. Even they are enough to characterize the quality of the young scholar's work and his unwillingness to blindly trust his predecessors' authority.

This was Solovyov's finest hour. Dupont hid behind a marble column in the conference hall as she listened to Solovyov's paper. According to the accounts of those who saw her at that moment, the French historian's eyes were brimming with tears. A person less dedicated to scholarship might have been offended by all the corrections that Solovyov introduced. That person might have become embittered or, who knows, shrugged their shoulders and snorted with disdain. Or said, let us suppose, that the specified clarifications held an extremely relative value in explaining the Crimean events of 1920. But Dupont was not that sort of person. At Solovyov's 'Thank you for your attention,' she ran out from behind the column and embraced the presenter. Was that ardent scholarly embrace— which combined sobbing and smudged mascara and a prickly mustache—not a triumph of sincere values and evidence of the sanctity of the great international solidarity of researchers?

Standing behind the lectern, her faced streaked with mascara, Dupont recalled everyone who had devoted themselves to researching the post-revolutionary period at various times. She referred, with particular emotion, to Ieronim A. Ratsimor, who had conceived of, but not managed to complete, the monumental *Encyclopedia of the Civil War*.

'He died on the letter *K*,' Dupont said of the deceased, 'but if he could have held on for just one more letter, our level of knowledge about General Larionov would have been different, completely different. But now we see,' and with these words the researcher once again drew Solovyov to herself, 'our worthy successor. Now we can feel calm about leaving.'

The polite Solovyov initially wanted to object to what Dupont had said, to ask that henceforth she continue engaging in the work that was so important to everyone, but she would not allow it. With a sweep of her huge hand, she seemed to conjure out of thin air her monograph about the general, which she then forcefully pressed to Solovyov's chest. After kissing him again in parting, she marched across the conference hall and vanished into the duskiness of a corridor.

She called him from Paris. Positively everything about the young researcher interested her: his views on history overall, his biases in terms of methodology, and even—this was completely unexpected—his material standing. Unlike all the other areas, Solovyov found no intelligible answer to her question about the matter. Dupont herself deduced the reality of the Russian scholar's material standing: it was simply lacking.

Stunned by that circumstance, Dupont delved into the reasons for such a somber state of affairs. Standing firm on determinist positions, the representative of French historical scholarship lined up a long cause-and-effect chain. There is no point in citing it in full: the events Dupont referred to are well known to any Russian schoolchild, though perhaps it is worth dwelling on several fundamental principles that are characteristic of this chain.

According to Dupont, several factors determined our society's advancement, with key roles played by an insufficient propensity for labor, an inclination for appropriating another's property, and a heightened sense of justice. The cause-and-effect chain that had formed within the French researcher's head finally coiled into a circle that she recognized, on second thought, as vicious.

The state of affairs she depicted did not, in fact, seem rosy: appropriation of another's property intensified—to an extreme—a sense of justice within society, which in turn sharply reduced the society's propensity for labor. Needless to say, the latter circumstance could not help but stimulate an inclination for appropriating another's property and that automatically led to an even more heightened sense of justice and even less propensity for labor. It was within this context that Dupont examined the destructive Russian revolutions, the many-year rule of Communists (no less destructive, according to her assessment), and a whole series of other events.

That combination of factors was combustible on its own ('*Molotoff cocktail!*' Dupont sighed), and was aggravated by a personal factor. A series of figures proceeding along Russian history's teetering stage had managed to push the contradictions to extremes. In the French scholar's view, president Boris Yeltsin occupied a special place among them and had obviously misused his skills as an orchestra conductor. The success of his Berlin performance made him so giddy that he thought of nothing but the conductor's baton from then on. Under that baton's light stroke, the appropriation of another's property finally reached the point where the sense of justice was no longer intensifying and the propensity for labor was no longer decreasing. As far as Yeltsin's decisive manner for problem-solving went, Dupont characterized it in her article 'The Headless Horseman', published in *Sobriety and Culture* in 1999, as a typical cavalry charge.

There is no doubt that Dupont became entangled in a whole series of questions while forming her chain of cause-and-effect. For example, she demonstrated an overt exaggeration of the role of the individual in history (it probably comes as no surprise that Dupont's political views were staunchly de Gaullist), most likely brought on because the history she herself was working on was the history of a general. Beyond that, the dialectic of the necessary and the accidental—which is so important for a correct assessment of historical events—became a stumbling block for her. She simply could not figure that out by using Russian history. At some point, she began to see that necessity was accidental in our country to a certain degree. In other words, she could not manage to distinctly formulate the reason behind Solovyov's squalid existence. And so Dupont transferred all her irrepressible energy to something more consequential. She replaced her search for answers to Russia's accursed questions with a search for funds for the young scholar's needs.

After brief reflection, the French researcher made an appeal to the All-Russian Scientific Foundation, with the vague hope that this particular institution was counterbalancing the government's shortchanging of its scholars. After a short conversation in Moscow—people in the know had advised her to get in touch with the fund's employees only in person—the foundation's experts regarded the proposed research topic as insufficiently all-Russian. In saying their goodbyes, ('There was a shadow of something left unsaid at our meeting!' Dupont complained afterwards), they recommended their guest approach the Russian Foundation for Scientific Workers.

They heard out Dupont more favorably at the Foundation for Scientific Workers, and even fed her tea with biscuits of the *Stolichnye* brand. Along the way, they asked if she was an employee or at least an expert at any kind of French foundation. Upon learning that Dupont had nothing to do with French foundations, they inquired of the researcher who exactly at the All-Russian Scientific Foundation had recommended she approach the Foundation for Scientific Workers, and asked what that person had said. Surprised by the question and, above all, the questioner's unusual tone, Dupont choked and they pounded her on the back until an ill-fated shard of one of the *Stolichnye* biscuits emerged from the Parisienne's throat. They asked no further questions after that, helped her on with her coat, and gallantly kissed her hand. In Moscow, by the way, they do that no worse than in Paris.

Dupont undertook a further attempt to help the Petersburg graduate student: she got in touch with the S.M. Solovyov Foundation by telephone. In Dupont's mind, a foundation named for the great Russian historian could not refuse to support another historian, one who was both still young and bore the same surname. Oddly enough, in this case it was precisely the surname that became the stumbling block. Afraid of being accused of nepotism, there was a refusal on the other end of the line to even review an appeal of this sort. Astonished at the scrupulousness of Russian foundations, a pensive Dupont hung up the receiver.

Finally, at the suggestion of colleagues, she appealed to some famous entrepreneur or other, allegedly a man of contradictions who mixed market speculation with philanthropic activity. It is entirely possible that the contradictions were exaggerated since, according to information that reached her later, philanthropic activity inexplicably turned out to be one of the most profitable income items of his entrepreneurship. Whatever the case, Dupont approached him with a long letter, in which she noted the thoroughness of the scholar's work and enumerated, among other things, the corrections the latter had entered with regard to manpower in the subunits.

To the addressee's credit, he did not force Dupont to wait

long for an answer. His letter offered the highest appraisal
of Solovyov's industriousness and attention to detail. The
philanthropist then went on to point out that data for 1920
offered no relevance for him since he was predominantly
interested in information about armies currently in operation.

Needless to say, even such a gallant rejection could not
suit a person whose colleagues had nicknamed her *mon
general*. Dupont set off on another attack and wrote the
patron a far more voluminous letter. This letter examined,
in the most detailed fashion, the essence of each of the
adjustments Solovyov had entered, with historical parallels
and brief statistics regarding comparable subunits of
European armies. As for the relevance of the data, the
enterprising philanthropist was introduced to an extremely
ancient point of view, according to which all history repeats
itself. After subjecting the designated theory to constructive
criticism, Dupont nonetheless stipulated that she certainly
did not exclude the possibility of certain recurrences. The
only point with which the French researcher categorically
refused to agree was the possibility (even theoretical) that
a second General Larionov could appear on the peninsula.
In concluding her letter, so there would be no omissions,
she even specified that people of the general's sort are born
only once every thousand years.

It is unknown what had the greater effect here—the digres-
sion into the territory of the philosophy of history, the French
researcher's resoluteness in standing up for her position, or
the actual volume of the letter—but the entrepreneur-philan-
thropist answered with approval. He even joked agreeably in
his response that the researcher's observation regarding a

general of Larionov's sort might exclude the possibility of such a general appearing in the near future but it instilled certain hopes for the period following the year 2882. In expectation of that blessed epoch, he was designating that Solovyov receive, throughout his graduate studies (i.e. for three years), a stipend that was small but adequate for a modest life. This was a genuine victory.

Solovyov was stunned by the news of the stipend. He knew nothing of the efforts being made by the French woman on his behalf and felt genuinely happy when he heard about the gift. The phrase saying the stipend was designed for a modest life could not cloud his joy. On the one hand, Solovyov's life had always been modest, but on the other, he supposed, justifiably, that his notions of modesty differed mightily from his benefactors' notions. As informed as they were, they could not even guess the extent of the modesty of a scholar's life in Russia.

'You should go to Yalta,' Dupont told the scholarship recipient. 'I've looked high and low at everything in the capitals, but I've never made it all the way to Crimea. If there's something new to be found anywhere, it'll be in Yalta.'

She said that at the beginning of July. Solovyov spent about three weeks systematizing his papers. During that process, it emerged that there would be a conference (that, by some strange coincidence, was supposed to be funded by the S.M. Solovyov Foundation) in Kerch in August— *General Larionov as Text*—and so, despite the event's quirky title, Solovyov sent in his topic for a paper.

Feeling prepared for work under Crimean conditions, Solovyov appealed to the director of the institute for permission to travel for his work. Judging by the director's pensive chewing at the temple of his eyeglasses, Solovyov grasped that such work-related travel was not being granted to him uncontested. And here the young scholar began feeling awkward when he remembered, for the first time in three weeks, that Yalta was a resort city. Solovyov began explaining his motives for the trip with a vehemence unusual for an academic institution (in his agitation, he even forgot to mention the conference) but the director relaxed his toothy grip on his glasses and waved them in the air in agreement. After all, in recent years, work-related travel had been unfinanced due to lack of funds and involved nothing more than permission to be absent from the institute. Solovyov received that permission.

He left the institute's ostentatious building and headed, unhurried, in the direction of Tuchkov Embankment. On a whim, he turned down a side street, and ended up in a café. Solovyov could not remember when he had last been in a café and ascertained, with some surprise, that his life was becoming less modest. Solovyov viewed the dinner he ordered for himself that evening as a farewell meal. He already had a train ticket and could feel it (not without pleasure) when he put his hand into his jacket pocket. Without a doubt, August was the most apt month for work-related travel to Yalta.

2

Solovyov traveled south the very next day, on a train from St. Petersburg to Simferopol. Needless to say, trains were not the young historian's usual means of transportation. His life had taken shape in such a way that anyone capable of reading palms would have seen a railroad line parallel to Solovyov's lifeline. The trains that streaked past the small station called *Kilometer 715* were the first to reveal to him the existence of a large and fancy world beyond the station's limits.

Solovyov's first recollections of smells and sounds were attached to the railroad. Locomotive whistles woke him up in the mornings and the rhythmic clacking of wheels lulled him to sleep at night. His bed vibrated slightly when trains went by and his ceiling was streaked with the reflections of the lights in the compartments. As he dropped off to sleep, he stopped distinguishing exactly where that smooth but loud movement was coming from—here or outside. The iron knobs at the head of his bed jingled rhythmically and the bed slowly gathered speed, carrying Solovyov off to cheerful childhood dreams.

Solovyov learned to read using the placards on long-distance trains. It is worth noting that it was the trains' swiftness that brought about his speed-reading skills, which later eased his perusal of publications about the general: those publications were just as numerous as they were fantastic. It was from those same placards that Solovyov first learned of the existence of a series of cities to which the rails under his own windows ran, leading due north on one side and due south on the other. The station called *Kilometer 715* lay in the middle of the world.

Solovyov watched the trains with Leeza Larionova. After walking up the steps to the platform, they would sit down on a bench that had lost its color long ago and begin their observations. They loved it when the long-distance trains reduced their speed near the station. Then they could discern not only the placards but also rolled-up mattresses on bunks, tea glasses in special metal holders, and—most important of all—passengers who represented the mysterious world from which the train had come. It was not that they were glad for the trains because they were longing for a world unfamiliar to them; more likely, the very idea of 'long-distance' captivated them.

Their regard for the electric local trains and freight trains that occasionally streaked past the station was calmer. The people on the locals were more or less familiar to them, but as far as the freight trains went, well, there were no people on them at all. These were the longest and dullest of trains. They consisted of tank cars filled with oil, flatcars burdened with lumber, or just closed-up boxcars.

By a very early age, Solovyov knew the schedule for all the trains that went by the station. This information, which some might think capable of becoming a useless burden, played a considerable role in the future historian's life. For one thing, Solovyov was inculcated with a taste for valid knowledge—this may be why the young historian's regard for the mythology surrounding General Larionov was subsequently so unforgiving—from the very beginning of his conscious life. For another, a faultless mastery of the schedule cultivated in Solovyov a heightened perception of time, a real necessity for a genuine historian. The schedule used numbers that were never round. Nowhere in those figures were there approximate denotations such as *after lunch, in the first half of the day*, or *around midnight*. There were only 13:31, 14:09, 15:27. These unkempt fringes of time were as tousled as existence itself and possessed a very specific sort of beauty: the beauty of verity.

Solovyov's mastery of the schedule was not accidental. His mother worked as a controller at a crossing adjacent to the station. And though there was not much of anything to control there (the crossing could go unintersected by cars or trucks for days), Solovyov's mother would lower the crossing gate three minutes before any train appeared, put on her uniform jacket, and step out onto the control booth's little balcony. There was something captain-like in her unnaturally straight figure, her motionlessness, and her stern facial features. Sometimes the din of a train would wake Solovyov up in the middle of the night and he would look out the window at his mother. Her resolute standing, baton raised, held him spellbound. It was like that, in profile, that she imprinted herself upon his memory, amidst the train's rumbling and its flickering lights. When Solovyov read later about churches in abandoned northern villages and how a priest in that area ministered to an empty church, he thought that referred to his mother, too. Her selfless service, without any visible goal, continued, unvarying, like the sunrise. Regardless of changes in government, time of day, or weather conditions.

It was weather conditions, however, that turned out to be fatal for her. One frosty winter night, she was chilled to the bone and contracted pneumonia. She initially treated it with vodka and honey. From time to time, her mother, granny Solovyova, would take the baton and head out to substitute for her daughter at the crossing. Some time later, when the patient became worse, the old woman massaged her back and chest, spreading the suffocating smell of turpentine through the house. A few days later, Solovyov's mother announced unexpectedly that she was dying. Exaggeration was not the norm in his family, so the old woman grew worried. There was no point in sending to the nearest village, since there was nobody there but a drunken doctor's assistant. The old woman ran to the control booth to stop a train. Solovyov's mother died, but the old woman kept on waving her daughter's baton. Not one train stopped.

The trains almost never stopped anyway. Only rarely, predominantly in the summer, when the tracks were over-loaded, did trains pull up to the station, sighing heavily. The carriage attendants would step out onto the pock-marked slabs of the platform as if they owned the place. Behind them were fat men in T-shirts and women in tight-fitting exercise pants. And more rarely, children. Children were usually allowed no further than the vestibule, where they burst from their pensive grandmothers' hands. Adults smoked, drank beer straight from the bottle, and crushed mosquitoes with resounding slaps. When the children managed to make it to the platform, little Solovyov would run off, but continue to follow the proceedings from the bushes. During those moments, he was not the only one keeping an eye on the train that had arrived: the six houses surrounding the station were all eyes and ears, too. The residents pressed themselves against windows, stood in doorways, or cast quick glances at the arrivals as they pretended to dig in their kitchen gardens. It was not the done thing to walk up to the platform.

Only Solovyov's mother—when she was alive—was within sight of the passengers. The passengers, whose appearance seemed even more idle when compared with the railway worker's focused, solemn standing, made no attempt to call out to her. It was obvious right away that this motionlessness was of a specific type. Paying no attention to the passengers, Solovyov's mother gazed at the point where the rails met, as if watching for the arrival of her impending death. When reading later about the elderly general's famous gaze, Solovyov imagined it without the slightest effort. He remembered the way his mother had looked into the distance.

Solovyov's grandmother did not watch in that same way. Gazes into the distance were not really characteristic of her. Most often, she would sit, propping up her cheek with the palm of her hand and looking straight ahead. She outlived her daughter by several years and died not long before Solovyov graduated from high school. Her death pushed him to move to Petersburg. It was in Petersburg that he first heard about General Larionov.

Broadly speaking, it was not accidental that both Solovyov and Larionov were children of railroad workers. Perhaps it

was exactly this that determined certain similar characteristics, despite all their external differences. Railroad workers
in Russia have a special mission because the role of the
railroad in our country is not the same as in other places.
The time that we spend traveling is measured in days. That
time is enough not only for a good conversation but—in
successful cases—even for making marriage plans. What
marriage could be planned on the *Munich–Berlin* express in
seats lined up one after the other, with radio jacks in the
armrests? Most likely, none.

People who are somehow involved with the railroad are
all predominantly even-tempered and unhurried. They know
about conquering an expanse. These people know how to
listen to the sound of the even clatter of wheels and will
never start rushing around: they understand that they still
have time. This is why the most serious of foreigners also
choose a week or two, once a year, to take a ride on the
Trans-Siberian Railway. There is little need to mention that
these people resolutely prefer a train to an airplane, other
than for transatlantic situations, at any rate. The Americans
leave them no choice at all.

General Larionov's father had no choice, either. Airplanes
were simply not flying at the time he decided to associate
his life with the railroad. Strictly speaking, at that time, even
the railroad itself had not yet become a truly day-to-day
matter. Using it demanded of passengers not only a certain
degree of courage but also a progressive mindset. Possessing
these qualities in full measure, Larionov, director of the
railroad department, spent half of his on-duty hours on
wheels. He was entitled to use a special first-class lounge
carriage that was hitched to the end of the train. It was in

that carriage that he would set off to Crimea, for his vacation. As a scrupulous person, the department director paid
for his family's passage in that carriage, notwithstanding the
persuasion of railroad employees who considered that his
privileges should extend to his family. The governess rode
in second class on the same train and the servants in third.
This latter circumstance served later as cause for various
forms of speculation and even conclusions regarding the
openly undemocratic character of relationships within the
Larionov household.

In answer to accusations of that sort, one might cite the
opinion of Ieronim A. Ratsimor, who pointed out in his
1992 article 'Sprouts of Democracy in the Russian Military
Environment from the Late 19th to Early 20th Centuries',
that, for a number of reasons, class ideology prevailed over
democratic ideology at the end of the nineteenth century.
Ratsimor also put forth the supposition that democracy is
not a universal concept and is generally not obligatory for
characterizing all times and peoples. When established in
countries not prepared for it, democracy is capable of
bearing the saddest of fruits. According to the historian's
convictions, the distinctness of Russia's class divide regulated
social relationships far more effectively than democratic
procedures. Using material from the general's biography, he
convincingly demonstrated that, while still a pupil and junior
cadet, Larionov was obligated to ride second class but after
becoming a senior cadet, he could only ride third since
senior cadets were already considered to have attained a
low army rank and were not admitted into the two other
classes.

Less radical points of view were also expressed with

regard to democracy in the Larionov family. The graduate
student Kalyuzhny surmised, verbally, that the defining traits
of the seating arrangements of those riding south were
determined not so much by the opinion of Larionov, department director, as by the presence at the station of the elder
General Larionov, who was allegedly incapable of coming
to terms with scorn for Russia's class divide. The latter man
was, to be sure, known for his conservatism, which he
expressed in part through a disdainful regard for the railroad.
To him, the realm of the railroad seemed unworthy of their
family line—in the veteran's watery eyes, it presented something akin to a circus attraction. Only the post of department
director brought a certain seriousness to his grandson's work
and partially reconciled the old man with this odd choice
of profession. And though the hero of the Battle of Borodino
considered train travel inappropriate for himself, he invariably came to the train station at Tsarskoe Selo to see his
family off on their travels. As he made his way along the
row of carriages on his peg leg, he would stop by the locomotive with unexpected timidity and spend a long while
watching the steam bursting out of the boilers. Then he
would shrug his shoulders for effect, hurriedly make the
sign of the cross over his family members, and resolutely
hobble toward the exit, an echo resonating under the
station's metal arches. One might suppose the last thing on
his mind at those moments was the passengers' seating
arrangements.

Those trips were preserved in the future general's
memory as one of the brightest pages of his childhood. In
Notes for an Autobiography, which Dupont found and
published, General Larionov describes in detail the railroad

journeys of his childhood. The carriage itself evoked the greatest delight for him; with brass handles polished to a shine, oak paneling, and—most importantly—a glass rear wall that displayed the entire expanse of road already traveled. To the juvenile Larionov, it seemed as if the carriage at their disposal was a giant spider capable of producing two steel threads that ran out from under it at high speed and converged on the horizon.

The child was particularly keen on watching sunsets that lent enchanting colors to the forest on both sides of the railroad bed. The colors dimmed with every minute and the trees darkened, approaching the railroad bed ever closer. For the future general, who had first-hand familiarity with Russian folk tales, the train's motion was reminiscent of an escape from a spellbound forest. Clutching at the nickel handle on the bunk, he anxiously observed the rocking of fir crowns, from which, to his mind, it would be most opportune for an unseen adversary to attack. Only after some time had passed, when it was completely dark and the small glass wall had begun reflecting the carriage's cozy luxury, would the child calm down, unclench his numbed fingers, and let go of the nickel handle. General Larionov caught himself making that motion later, when he let go of a handle on the hatch of an armored train one summer evening in 1920. The scent of wormwood wafted from a stilled field. Sudden silence had replaced the sounds of battle, with the only exception being the brooding metallic noises that carried from somewhere below, deep underneath the carriage and inaccessible to the eye.

His Crimean battles ended just as abruptly as they had begun. These battles took place while traveling and were just as unpredictable as the movements of the general's armored train around Crimea. Larionov was often reproached—justifiably so, one must deem, albeit with a certain qualification—for excessive use of railroad transportation. The qualification is the fact that the railroad network in Crimea is not overly developed to this day. As is common knowledge, central Crimea is linked to only three cities on the coast: Kerch, Sevastopol, and Yevpatoria. It thus follows that the general's excessiveness, even in the worst case, could have had only an extremely limited character.

There did exist, however, a positive side to the general's predilection. Constrained by the lack of railroad track, General Larionov actively worked toward its construction. Even in his pre-Crimean period, he put together a narrow-gauge railroad in the forest near Kiev, as a test. He entered Crimea's railway history first and foremost as the person who built a fully fledged railroad bed from Dzhankoy to Yushun.

The general's childhood impressions turned out to be so strong that he even chose an armored carriage as his place of residence in Crimea. A host of legends has formed about that carriage, but all that is known and confirmed documentarily is that it was home to four birds (a crane, a crow, a raven, and a starling) and that Alexander Vertinsky visited the hospitable carriage and sang the well-known anti-war song 'I Don't Know Who Needs That And Why' for the general. According to Alexei Ravenov's *In the Blue Train Carriage*, those present said General Larionov's distinctive, unearthly gaze was noticeable even then; it was reflected, in particular, in the photograph from 1964 that reminded historian Solovyov of his deceased mother's gaze.

Solovyov thought back to that gaze yet again as he was speeding past railroad crossings, booths, and controllers with batons. He was standing by an open train window, the curtain flittering to his right like a bird that had been shot. Sunlight illuminated waves of fine hair along his arm, which felt the window frame's metallic coolness. Solovyov thought the hairs were coarsening in the sweltering August wind, that their bright glistening was a sign of a gradual transformation to copper. He pressed his lips to the hairs for a minute, as if to assess their wiriness, but they turned out to be surprisingly soft.

Solovyov was a most genuine passenger of long-distance trains. He drank tea from a glass in a metal holder without pulling out the spoon, went to the lavatory with a towel on his shoulder, and sauntered around stations in a Petersburg University T-shirt. But the important thing was that he was riding in a compartment carriage for the first time in his life. After closing the compartment door for the night, he took a passing, admiring glance at his reflection in the mirror. The bulbs from the light in the lower bunk were reflected behind his back, too, as were some bottles with little plastic cups on them, a taciturn gentleman in a track-suit, and two young female students. In short, there was everything that created the railroad's aching coziness; a brief unity before parting forever. As he lay down in his upper bunk, Solovyov enjoyed listening to the students' whispers. He did not even notice himself falling asleep.

He was awoken by light falling across his face. The train was standing still. Solovyov's window was under a station streetlamp. Slowly, so as not to awaken the sleepers, he lowered the snug-fitting window and a warm, night breeze wafted into the compartment. A central Russian breeze, it abstractly occurred to Solovyov, who did not know where the train had stopped. The name of the deserted station was hidden in the darkness: apparently, it was a lone street-lamp burning in the window. But the lack of people in that expanse was illusory. In the depths of the station, where window glass meekly gleamed against the building's dark contours, a quiet conversation was taking its course between two people. After sliding into the shaded part of his bunk, Solovyov discerned their unmoving figures on a bench, facing one another. He saw, in their bentness and in their chins that rested on their hands, something extraordinarily familiar that he could not, however, call to mind.

They were having a conversation that was utterly connected to the place in which the train was standing. The people they were naming were undoubtedly known only here and the details mentioned were also not likely to be understood without the preliminaries of living here a long time, but even so, Solovyov was unable to shake off an agonizing sense of déjà vu. In an attempt to determine where he had seen these same figures, Solovyov recalled all the stations and substations he had ever traveled through, but nothing similar came to mind. It turned out that situations varied at each of the stations he had seen. There were completely different people sitting everywhere (and even, perhaps, at the very same time), and it followed from that, in turn, that if the train were to stop at one hundred stations during the night, he would hear one hundred different stories. The diversity of existence made his head spin.

Meanwhile, the talkers fell silent. The one sitting on the right took out cigarettes, which he shared with his conversation partner. Two small fires appeared in the dark, one after the other, bringing to mind the lights at a crossing.

'That's all crap,' said the one sitting on the left.

Solovyov suddenly recalled where he'd seen figures like these. They were chimeras from Notre-Dame Cathedral, on the cover of a history textbook.

The train arrived in Simferopol at three o'clock the following afternoon. It was raining in the Crimean capital. The rain had most likely just begun—steam was still rising from the hot pavement. Solovyov purchased a trolleybus ticket to Yalta after a short wait at the ticket window. He decided to travel between the two cities using this unusual trolleybus connection, perhaps the only one in the world. The route from Simferopol to Yalta had surprised even General Larionov in his time: he lived to see the launch of the trolleybus route, and, by then, nothing had surprised him in a long time. His fantasies, which were historically limited to the railroad, had never hinted at the possibility of an intercity connection of this sort.

The general remembered carriage connections (the office was located on the first floor of the Oreanda Hotel) perfectly, just as he remembered carriages with rubber tires and the changing of horses in Alushta. He did not immediately grasp why the trolleybus had become a replacement for all that. He was soberly aware that, unlike the railroad, a trolleybus line was not suitable for transferring heavy armaments or any significant number of troops. Even so, despite the absence of strategic significance for the trolleybus line, the general began regarding the innovation fairly positively after all and rode the trolleybus to Gurzuf one spring.

After the trolleybus had driven up, Solovyov settled into

a window seat in the back row, in keeping with the ticket he had purchased. Passengers entered through the front door and heaped their luggage up on the back platform, resting it against a door that was not open for boarding. The passengers on the trollybus were almost entirely vacationers. They reclined noisily in their seats and wiped away sweat with the edges of their T-shirts. The only exception, by all indications, was a workingman with a girl who was about ten. They sat near Solovyov and had almost no belongings.

Despite the rain, the stuffiness had not subsided. It eased only when the trolleybus left the city and worked up a speed that was unexpected for such a vehicle. As if on command, the florid nylon curtains were pulled out the windows and knocked against the glass from the other side. This synchronized flapping lent the trolleybus a festive, somehow even nuptial, look. As the trolleybus climbed Chongarsky Pass, the workingman's daughter began feeling nauseous. Her father took a match out of a box and suggested she put it in her mouth. This folk remedy proved ineffective. The little girl looked at the match, then at the calloused fingers extracting it from the box, and vomited.

The weather changed completely after Chongarsky Pass. The rain clouds remained beyond the northern side of the ridge and the sun beat through the windshield of the trolleybus as it began its careful descent along the winding mountain road. Nature did everything it could to stun Solovyov that day. The sun, which replaced the rain so suddenly, was not simply shining in a flawlessly blue sky. Both the sun and the sky were reflected, mirror-like, somewhere far below, like an unending mosaic that shimmered through the cypress trees floating in the windows. That was how Solovyov saw the sea for the first time.

Needless to say, General Larionov's childhood reminiscences—which were found in an émigré's archives and published by the very same Dupont—were already known to Solovyov by this time. Despite the fragmentariness of the text and the author's stated intention to touch on his more mature years—this was the basis for Dupont's confidence that the subsequent chapters which had been lost still existed—it is here that a description of the general's first encounter with the sea is preserved. It follows from that description that the future commander's family also traveled from Simferopol, although even then the opportunity existed to arrive in Sevastopol by rail and ride from there along the coast to Yalta.

Five-year-old Larionov managed to remember that his family was traveling in carriages with two springs. He remembered the word *springs* very well because he repeated it the whole way (as has been noted already, the child did not speak until he was three and a half years old, but he vigorously made up for lost time afterwards). The younger Larionov's carriage was driven by an elderly Tatar, a handsome, smartly dressed man whose mastery of Russian was, without exception, inferior to all his passengers. Being sociable by nature, he reacted animatedly to the word *springs* and leaned on the coach box each time, showing the location of the spring with his whip handle. The coachman remained like that in the memoirist's consciousness: inclined to the side with fine drops of sweat on his forehead and a benevolent smile.

Like Solovyov, the future general was surprised by the

sharp change in the weather at Chongarsky Pass. The published notes also reference flecks of sunlight playing on the waves and viewed through the slow motion of cypresses. Special mention was given to the freshness of a wind, blowing not from dusty roadside groves but from that chilly turquoise expanse where the sky imperceptibly came together with the water. His mother's light dress, locks of his English governess's fair hair, and multicolored ribbons braided into the horse's mane fluttered in the wind.

The general's associative memory also forces him to speak of a piercing wind on Chongarsky Pass on November 1, 1920, when Crimea's remaining defenders retreated to the ports, worn out after one-sided battles. According to Dupont's supposition, a more detailed description of the evacuation was located in the part of the reminiscences that has not reached us. A faint hint cast by the general in passing, which may be seen as an intention to return to a theme he had broached superficially, speaks in favor of that. The general touches on those November events only because when watching from blizzardy Chongar as the White Army retreated (it was whiter than ever at that moment), by Larionov's own admission he saw nothing but two landaus descending, in a leisurely fashion, toward the sea.

The trolleybus turned along the shore. Now the passengers not only saw the sea but sensed its briny freshness, too. At the request of the police, all cars on the highway stopped twice to let government motorcades through. The preoccupied faces of those government ministers were more likely guessed at than seen in cars rushing past at vast speeds. They were riding to their holidays and thinking about the significant decline of the peninsula's funding. This mani-

fested itself most of all in the condition of the palaces of
the Russian aristocracy. The condition of the roads was no
better, though. The summer sun and winter rain, coupled
with the process of erosion, had produced a multitude of
ruts and cracks in the Crimean roads. If the cracks had been
patched up anywhere, it was on the government highway,
though even that repair was only partial, or so Solovyov
surmised, jolting in his seat every now and then.

The sun was already hiding behind Mount Ai-Petri when
they pulled in to Yalta. A cloud had drifted across the mountain's peak, where it was mingling with rays that shone so
unusually straight that they appeared to be beams from a
spotlight. Mountains clustered around the station from three
sides, leaving open only a boulevard that ran toward the
sea. An evening freshness was already beginning to make
itself felt in Yalta, along with a restlessness that touched
Solovyov's heart. A sense of light alarm. The ancient feeling
of a person about to spend the night in an unfamiliar place.

Solovyov stepped off the trolleybus and found himself
surrounded by women. They vied with one another to offer
him lodging and there were so many possibilities that the
young historian felt lost. He could choose between a bed,
a private room, or a cottage. He was invited to stay near
the Spartacus movie theater, by the Chekhov museum, and
even on Leningrad Street. Solovyov did not know the city.
Pressured by the agitated landladies, he agonized over the
location of his future lodging. The Petersburg graduate
student's soul leaned toward being Chekhov's neighbor, but
that offer was for an entire cottage that even his whole
stipend would not cover. 'Leningrad Street' sounded unacceptable given that the city's original name had been

returned. After some wavering, he settled on the Spartacus movie theater: the proposed apartment was right next door, on Palmiro Togliatti Street.

Solovyov remembered how Nadezhda Nikiforovna had solemnly taken Giovagnoli's novel *Spartacus* from a shelf that her cameo ring had touched and presented the book to him. In the course of subsequent discussion of the book, it emerged that Nadezhda Nikiforovna—like the adolescent Solovyov—had shed tears over make-believe, too, and turned out to sympathize with the gladiator very much. This had decisively strengthened Solovyov's decision to enter into marriage with her. As far as Palmiro Togliatti went, Solovyov appreciated his lovely name despite suspecting him of communist ties.

Solovyov and the woman rode to the Spartacus by trolley-bus. They crossed the road and ended up on Togliatti Street, which was narrow, quiet, and green. Solovyov liked the courtyard where his lodging was located. Just like the street name, everything about it was Italian: the terraces that had been added on and the intricate stairs that led up to them, the clotheslines hanging between the windows, and the branchy plane tree that was over everything. This, at any rate, was how Solovyov imagined Italy to be.

As he walked up a steep wooden staircase behind his hostess, he examined her unshaven legs. Those legs (like Solovyov's legs, too) elicited from the steps a knocking, creaking, and squeaking of unbelievable force. The deafening stairs spawned in the young man's mind the image of a huge out-of-tune instrument. After walking along a terrace covered with flower pots, Solovyov and his guide ended up in a dusky hallway. Once Solovyov's eyes had adjusted to the darkness, he discerned several gas burners and thought he had landed in a communal apartment. It truly had once been a communal apartment but it had managed to separate itself from Solovyov's lodgings through complex architectural solutions. The entry was hidden behind a small ledge in the wall, making it invisible at first glance. The woman took a key from her purse, winked at Solovyov, and opened the door.

The apartment consisted of two connected rooms and a glassed-in veranda. The door to the far room turned out to be locked. Solovyov was told there were things in there that the owners did not intend for lodgers to use. The first room, which led to the veranda, was at his full disposal. The veranda was also the kitchen, with a stove, counter, and cabinet containing dishes. In the far corner of the veranda was a structure reminiscent of a telephone booth covered with plywood.

'It's the bathroom,' said his escort, flushing the water to prove her point.

She wrote down Solovyov's passport information, took money for two weeks in advance, and disappeared through the door, winking just as enigmatically as she had earlier. When her clomping footsteps had faded, Solovyov flicked the door lock from the inside and began unpacking his things. He took his swimsuit out of his travel bag right away and put it on. Then he pulled out a towel and neatly placed it in a small rucksack. He shoved the key he had received into his shorts pocket and looked around. He was completely prepared for his first encounter with the sea.

3

As we know, Crimea was transferred from Russia to Ukraine in 1954, under an order from Nikita Khrushchev. It should be noted that this circumstance drew General Larionov's attention in its day. The unexpected addition to Ukraine made no less of an impression on him than the launch of the trolleybus line. And yet the aged general was not at all inclined to dramatize this circumstance.

'Russians, do not regret Crimea,' he announced, sitting on the jetty one May day in 1955.

Public statements were a great rarity for the general and a crowd quickly gathered around him. Flashing his erudition, the general reminded the listeners that Crimea had belonged to the Greeks, Genovese, Tatars, Turks, etcetera, at various times. And though their dominion was fleeting in historical terms, they had all left their own cultural traces here. In touching on Russia's traces, the general sketched out, in brief energetic strokes, an impressive panorama, from elegant parks and palaces to the lady with the lapdog. His speech concluded with military clarity: 'As a person who has defended these places, I am telling you: it is impossible to hold your ground here. For anyone. That is characteristic of the peninsula.'

The general knew what he was talking about. He had needed to hold the line in Crimea twice in 1920, in January and November. The events of October and November ended up being the final collapse of the White Movement. He was unable to hold on to Crimea.

Even so, the first defense (which nobody considered possible at the time) in January ended up being successful. It was this defense that held off the Reds' capture of the peninsula for nearly a year. Researchers assess the situation that took shape toward the beginning of 1920 more or less identically. The decline of the White Movement was becoming more obvious at this time.

'After all, we're not going to the fair, we're coming back from the fair,' is what General Larionov whispered in his horse's ear one sunny January morning.

For everyone observing that scene, the general's words took the form of a small cloud of steam. In the absence of witnesses, it remains a mystery how that phrase could have reached the public domain. There is no denying the multiple references in the historical literature to the trusting, nearly human relationship between the horse and General Larionov, who called the animal *my friend* and addressed lines specifically to the horse. And yet it would be ridiculous to imagine that the horse could respond to the general in kind, even more so that the horse was chatting right and left about what had been whispered in her ear.

The general, however, addressed the exact same words to a British envoy in November of that same year. The text arrived by telegraph because the general himself was securing his army's evacuation from Crimea and heading up the last line of defense. Needless to say, in the telegram to the British envoy (it has been preserved) there is not a word about the phrase not being addressed to him alone. Be that as it may, in scholarship—as, for example, in Vitaly Romanchuk's *In Decline*—the text in question is quoted with a reference to January. What is more, it is quoted fairly frequently in scholarship, yielding in popularity only to the well-known explanation of the reasons for the Whites' defeat. This explanation, which the general formulated with disheartening directness, is in the introduction to the reminiscences that Dupont discovered. It reads, 'A clod of dung, of medium size, began rolling through Russia. It grew with incredible speed due to the adherence of similar material, of which, alas, there turned out to be very much in Russia. We were crushed by that clod.'

And so the situation that had taken shape by January 1920 was anything but simple. The lethal clod depicted so elegantly by the general was rolling through Northern Taurida, which was the threshold to Crimea, and no one envisioned a force capable of impeding it. In fact, the supreme command of the White Army did not intend to defend Crimea. The Whites' primary forces were retreating and there were battles in those two directions, the Caucasus and Odessa, from where a counterattack was subsequently planned, after respite and regrouping of forces. If events developed favorably, they intended to force the Reds from Crimea with the return of troops that were encircling the peninsula in two streams rushing north. But that was a matter for the future. In January 1920, Crimea was tacitly destined for surrender. The limited forces sent to defend it shattered everyone's last doubts about that. Everyone's but General Larionov's.

As we know, Dupont's article, 'Leonidas and His Children', presents a rigorous enumeration of troops at the general's disposal during the defense of Crimea. So as not to force the reader to chase down this work, which is generally difficult to find, we will reiterate, in brief, the data cited in the article:

13th Infantry Division	800 bayonets
34th Infantry Division	1,200 bayonets
1st Caucasus Rifle Regiment	100 bayonets
Slavic Regiment	100 bayonets
Chechen Regiment	200 sabers
Don River Cavalry Brigade	1,000 sabers
Headquarters Convoy Corps	100 sabers

The troops enumerated had twenty-four light and eight horse-drawn weapons at their disposal. In the course of organizing the defense, General Larionov also succeeded in procuring six tanks (three heavy and three light) as well as eight armored trains. Despite all the armored trains turning out to be defective, they became a big source of moral support for the son of the railroad department's director.

For anyone with even the slightest knowledge of military matters, the above enumeration leaves no doubt: the White Army had decided, at the highest level of command, to relinquish Crimea. Only 3,500 fighters were sent to protect the front, which stretched for 400 versts. The general was aware that it was impossible to defend Crimea in Northern Taurida. And so he did not even begin to do so.

Without a doubt, General Larionov was inspired by a brilliant idea from Spartan king Leonidas, who decided to fend off the Persians in a narrow gorge. As we know, Leonidas's military contingent was extremely limited (a tenth of what General Larionov had at his disposal, not to mention the complete absence of armored trains), but that did not prevent him from fighting in the worthiest manner. This battle was analyzed in depth during tactical lessons at the Second Cadet Corps, where the future general studied back in the day. King Leonidas's feat made an indelible impression on cadet Larionov.

As life would have it, the general took part in battles that unfolded on emphatically open terrain. These were flood plains, boundless rye fields, or steppes that were parched until they cracked. During World War One, Larionov happened to fight in the mountains for a time, but those mountains turned out to be the Carpathians, which by 1914 had become thoroughly weathered and were not at all suitable with respect to defense. General Larionov mentally thanked fate that it was not the Persians opposing him in these tactically unsuitable circumstances. Only in January 1920 did he sense that his hour had come. Like the renowned Spartan, the Russian general was visited by the abrupt realization that the only chance for a successful defense was to narrow the front. He decided against defending Northern Taurida and moved his troops toward Perekop.

The Perekop Isthmus was probably the most joyless place in Russia's south. It was difficult to breathe there in the summer heat because of fumes from the dead waters of the Sivash, lagoons often referred to as the Putrid Sea. A wind would come up from time to time, rolling dried-out seaweed along salt-splotched soil but bringing no feeling of freshness. The wind became an utter disaster in the winter.

It drove stinging drifting snow over an uninhabited icy expanse where there were not even any shrubs to stop it. The wind carried away all hope of warming up. It crept behind the lapels of army overcoats and froze fingers to gun barrels, extinguished campfires made from cart debris and strewed Perekop's lunar landscape with ash. It is not surprising that territory of this sort made a most unfavorable impression on General Larionov. And so he decided not to defend it.

After familiarizing himself with the history of the defense of Northern Crimea, the military commander noticed that a common mistake of defenders each time was their absolute determination to stand firm on the Perekop rampart. Meanwhile, in light of the climatic conditions already described, simply being on the Perekop Isthmus sapped a huge amount of strength, resources, and morale because there is nothing more ruinous for an army than sitting in trenches in the bitter cold. The road to Crimea was opened after defenders were thrown from the Perekop ramparts. The resourceful general acted differently so as not to repeat his predecessors' mistakes. He decided to grant his adversary this expanse drifted with snow and deprived of any form of habitation. They did not wait for the Reds on the Perekop Peninsula; only a small outpost was left there and its role boiled down to informing the main forces of an attack. They waited for the Reds at the exit from the isthmus.

The Red Army lived up to the general's expectations. Their cavalry, reinforced by the infantry, was drawn onto the isthmus immediately after the White Army's troops abandoned it. The Red Army soldiers began feeling anxious at sunset, after walking along the icy desert the entire day and not encountering an enemy with which to do serious battle. Advancing so late at night seemed dangerous to them. They thought they were choosing the lesser evil by deciding to spend the night on the frozen steppe.

Many researchers consider that as early as January 1920 the commander of Red troops in the Crimean zone was Dmitry Zhloba (1887–1938), the son of a peasant and a graduate of the Moscow Aviation School (1917). There is an opposing opinion, too, according to which, by January 1920, Dmitry Zhloba was still continuing his training because of his failure to complete his flight hours under the school's program.

Everyone familiar with this aviator's story, of course, also knows of the vexed relations that developed between him and the other students at the aviation school. On the whole, they were far younger than Zhloba and indulged themselves in mocking the peculiarities of his appearance (the nearly complete absence of a forehead plus the presence of two extra upper teeth) and kept him away from the flying machines however they could. Bullied by his younger comrades, the aviation school pupil only had the opportunity to fly at night, thus restricting his qualification. Night flights were not scored as flying time for Zhloba. As a result, it was recommended he fly the required number of hours again—now in the daytime—something he undertook with varying success until 1920. In the end, he was appointed commander of the First Cavalry Corps and ceased his dangerous experiments in aerial expanses.

Zhloba the cavalryman turned out to be more fortunate than Zhloba the aviator. He was able to exert his influence over the personnel of his corps, particularly the horses. The animals unquestioningly obeyed the peasant's son's booming voice, which was intolerable at close range, and rushed to attack at his first shout. As he charged to attack the enemy with his unsheathed saber, Dmitry Zhloba imagined that it was his former fellow pupils from the Moscow Aviation School before him. The frenzy he displayed in battle did not just make an impression on the adversary; after a certain point in time, it even began causing apprehension within the corps subordinate to him.

Nobody objected when Zhloba announced they would spend the night on Perekop. Even if another, more accept-able plan had existed, it is unlikely that anyone would have dared contradict the commander. There was no such plan, though, and there could not have been. Everything that happened with Zhloba's troops after that hour was helping to realize General Larionov's strategy. The Red forces spent the night under a chilly Perekop sky. And then another night. Their overwhelming numerical superiority went untapped. Without the opportunity to fully deploy their battle forma-tions, they could not resolve to attack the Whites first. The longed-for battle seemed to have evaded Dmitry Zhloba.

After spending a third night on Perekop, half the corps' personnel were sick and the aviation school alumnus realized he risked losing his troops without a battle. He decided to act. At dawn on the fourth day, the Reds moved toward the exit from the Perekop Isthmus and came under brutal fire to their flank, from the Yushun side. Their attack ended with a messy escape and the capture of prisoners. It should be noted that prisoners were the primary source of replenish-ment troops for the White Army. Those taken prisoner were placed on active duty again and began moving in the exact opposite direction. They fought with just the same inflexibility as before captivity. Such was this war.

Dmitry Zhloba left in order to return. After gathering his forces, he once again attempted to burst into Crimea but—just like the first time—did not succeed in moving further than Perekop. The White general had built lines of defense that seemed insurmountable. Larionov, however, knew that they, too, were vulnerable. According to the Russian battle captain, General Winter had rendered an invaluable natural service by freezing the Red attack but was now threatening to switch to the enemy side. The winter of 1920 was so harsh that something unexpected happened. The Sivash, which is as briny as a barrel of salted cucumbers, began to freeze. On the days when Dmitry Zhloba was stubbornly hitting at the isthmus's stopped-up exit, General Larionov was sending men to the Sivash to monitor the formation of ice.

Initially, thin glass-like layers covered the gulf's water in the mornings. The general grew anxious when it stopped thawing under the daytime sun. Only a few days later, the ice was so solid it could hold a lightly armed infantryman. The general began sending loaded carts to the Sivash to test the firmness of the ice at night, so as not to give away the object of his apprehensions. The general's Thermopylae plan would crumble in an instant if the ice were to freeze a little more firmly, because the infantry and cavalry and all the Reds' available heavy weaponry could cross over the Sivash's ice. In fact, it appeared to have been frozen for several days but Dmitry Zhloba, distracted by yet another storm of the Perekop Isthmus, was paying no attention whatsoever.

The panic that began mounting in Crimea after the Reds' occupation of the isthmus gradually subsided. Institutions unpacked the paperwork they had hastily tossed into plywood crates. Everything was prepared for evacuation in those days. Thousands of refugees from central Russia, who had broken free of the Bolsheviks and were deathly afraid of landing back there, were planning to evacuate with the army. 'Deathly' is what they said, and they were not far from the truth. Only a very few of those who were not able to join the evacuation to Constantinople survived.

It is interesting that the establishment of Soviet power in Crimea was the topic that Prof. Nikolsky assigned to Solovyov in his fourth year of study. Solovyov did not know then that he would study the general's fate, but from then on, the topics he cultivated grew ever closer to what would become the main focus of his research in the future. Solovyov approached his work with all possible meticulousness and found several unpublished reminiscences in the archives, which would serve as the basis for a paper at the end of his fourth year.

It concerned primarily Sevastopol, which turned out to be a harbinger of the Communist spring. Solovyov described how notices were hung up in the city, inviting all *formers* to gather at the city's circus for job placement. Despite his efforts, the researcher was unsuccessful in clarifying why the circus had been chosen. Whether that would become a portent of prevailing absurdity, whether the gathering place hinted at ancient tearing to shreds by wild animals, or whether the circus was simply the only hall the Bolsheviks knew . . . none of the *formers* sensed a ploy. These were noncombatant *formers*; those who had been in combat were already in Constantinople. *Former* accountants, secretaries, and governesses all arrived obediently at the square in front of the circus. When the square was filled, troops encircled it and strung up barbed wire. So many people had come that they could not even sit down. Several thousand *formers* stood in the square for two days. On the third day they were taken outside the city and shot.

And that was only the beginning. After collecting data for all Crimea's cities, Solovyov reached the conclusion that around 120,000 people were put to death on the peninsula during the first months of Soviet power. This exceeded the data cited in Ratsimor's *Encyclopedia of the Civil War* by 15,000. The data on the elderly, women, children, and injured who were killed by firing squad diverged seriously and needed to be increased.

The paper was written very capably, using abundant factual material attested to by 102 footnotes. Prof. Nikolsky saw the paper's narrative style—which seemed excessively emotional to him—as a minus. He requested that Solovyov remove rhetorical questions as well as passages that expressed the researcher's attitude toward the Reds' actions. From the professor's point of view, the figures were the most eloquent part of the paper. In the final reckoning, they needed no detailed commentary.

In his fifth year of study, Solovyov wrote his diploma thesis on 'The Role of Latvian Riflemen in the October Coup and Latvia's Loss of Independence in 1939'. In his account, the two events reflected in the title turned out to have both a cause-and-effect relationship as well as, even more so, a moral and ethical relationship. According to Solovyov, by fighting on the coup plotters' side, the Latvian riflemen were supporting a regime that also subsequently devoured Latvia, its independence, and the riflemen themselves. This time, his paper was not accompanied by rhetorical questions. There was minimal commentary.

Despite the young historian's paradoxical thinking (or perhaps, actually, thanks to it), Prof. Nikolsky published the paper in the journal *Past and Present* in 1996. Several months later, a brief but forceful review of Solovyov's article, signed by 'The Council of Veterans', appeared in *Der Kampf*, a popular Riga publication. Its authors saw no connection between the specified events and, for their part, discussed the possibility of an alternative course of history in 1939. They saw Latvia's hypothetical future in the rosiest of hues.

Prof. Nikolsky considered it essential to stand up for his student under the circumstances and so published his own 'Response to the Riga Veterans' in *Past and Present*. He began with a theoretical introduction that validated the importance of the moral factor in history. In the scholar's opinion, moral inferiority deprived states of the energy they needed for a trouble-free existence. The professor showed how this ravaged them from within, transforming them into empty shells flattened by the very first wind. Within this context, he examined the fall of the great empires of the ancient world and the modern age.

True to his theory regarding the absence of all-encompassing scholarly truths, the professor also indicated that it is only possible to speak of tendencies, not of rules. By way of exception, he offered the example of the English and Americans, who conducted separate talks with the Bolsheviks behind General Larionov's back during that same year, 1920, and did not suffer in the least as a result. In the Petersburg professor's opinion, distance, and the fact that both Anglo-Saxon states were surrounded by water, turned out to be the decisive factors in the matter's happy outcome. The geographical factor also allowed those states to bide their time entering World War Two, until the circumstances had been clarified to some extent. Water played a deciding role in these cases; Nikolsky met Solovyov halfway here.

In making his conclusions, however, the professor admitted that his view of things might be excessively gloomy and Latvia's big future really had been taken away from it. From Prof. Nikolsky's point of view, his skepticism could be explained by the fact that historians deal primarily with the deceased and so are, for the most part, pessimists. The Russian professor concluded his essay unexpectedly, saying history is the science of the dead and there is little room there for the living.

Needless to say, the aphoristic form of that statement was intended, first and foremost, to underscore the necessity of maintaining a certain distance from the material under study. Even so, Solovyov's advisor's remark made an indelible impression on Solovyov. He was in a rather dejected condition when he entered the graduate program at the Institute of Russian History. The marble in the Large Conference Room, where he took his entrance exams, reminded him of an anatomical theater. Solovyov was able to come to terms with the historical figures awaiting his study only because they were still alive during the period of their activity.

Graduate student Kalyuzhny's departure definitively saved Solovyov from a crisis in his worldview. Solovyov inherited from the general's melancholic admirer not only a scholarly topic, but also one single bibliographical card and a fundamental research question: why did the general remain alive? The card contained—but of course!—data on Dupont's book. Solovyov read the book and found the topic interesting and little-studied. On top of all that, General Larionov was absolutely dead and was, thus, a lawful object for scholarly research. Even under the strictest of historical measures, it was already possible to work with him.

But the general was not simply dead. Unlike many historical figures, even when he was alive, he had considered death to be an unavoidable fact of life.

'Look at them,' he would say about those figures, 'they're acting as if they don't know that death awaits them.'

The general knew death awaited him. He was preparing for it as he marched in the foothills of the Carpathians and checked posts on the Perekop Isthmus. And afterwards, whenever someone knocked on his door late at night, the thought flashed through his mind, every time, that it was death knocking. And, yes, of course he was expecting death when he was an old man sitting on the jetty in his folding chair. He was surprised that it hadn't come sooner, though he never regretted that.

The general was once photographed in a coffin. He stopped by a funeral home, bringing a photographer with him, and requested permission to use a coffin for a short time. They could not refuse him. The general smoothed the fold lines on his creased uniform, lay down in the coffin, crossed his arms on his chest, and closed his eyes. A photographer took several shots amidst the undertakers' uneasy silence. The most successful shot is almost as renowned as the famous photo on the jetty. It accompanies the majority of publications about the general. Few people know the shot was taken during this prominent person's life. Without suspecting the level of their own astuteness, some researchers have noted the absence of signs of death in the shot. Moreover, employing a figurativeness traditional for these purposes, they expressed opinions to the effect that it looked as if the general was sleeping. In reality, the general was not sleeping. Looking out from under his squinting eyelids, he was observing the reaction of those gathered and imagining what they might have said about him in the event of his actual death.

It is possible he was sorry that he would not see his own funeral and had thus decided to arrange a sort of rehearsal. It cannot be ruled out that this sort of conduct was an attempt to either deceive death (I died long ago, why bother looking for me?) or to hide from it. The general did not hide from death in his younger years, but people do change in old age . . .

Another explanation—one originating from the general's long-standing and almost intimate relationship with death—appears more pertinent. Was what happened a way to flirt with death or—this is entirely possible, too—a manifestation of a particular elderly coquetry? It is impossible to answer these questions accurately now, just as it is impossible to reason in any reliable way about how life and death come together in someone's fate. All that can be ascertained is that in the end the general met with his death. It found him without any particular effort when the time came.

In pondering the topic of death in General Larionov's story, Solovyov sought to understand the psychology of a person for whom a preparedness to die is the first and primary requirement of their profession. Solovyov was attempting to get a feel for the state of a person on the eve of battle, when any action, thought, or recollection might be his last. Was it possible to grow accustomed to that? It is known that on the evenings before battle, the general gazed at himself for a long time in a pocket mirror as if he were attempting to memorize himself at the very end. He slowly turned his hand, as if he were imagining it lying in the next trench. The inseparability of the human body's limbs seemed overstated to him on those evenings.

Did a person have a right to attachments under those circumstances? War-time friendship is piercing, just as war-time love is piercing: everything is as if for the last time. This is grounds for experiencing those attachments with the utmost keenness or, conversely, for renouncing them completely. What did the general choose at the time?

He chose reminiscences. In the event of the possible absence of a future, he extended his life by experiencing his past multiple times. The general sensed, almost physically, a living room with silk wallpaper, along which his shoulder glided when he was escaping the attention of guests after— obviously at his parents' order—one of the servants had abruptly brought him here, into a kingdom of dozens of candles, clinking dishes, cigars, and huge ceiling-high windows that were recklessly thrown open in Petersburg's Christmas twilight. The general firmly remembered that the windows were open, against the usual winter rules; he remembered because for a long time he continued considering Christmas the day when warmth set in. Remembering that, he knew he had been mistaken.

But the general had a certain something else to recall on his evenings before battle: his first visit to the Yalta beach. It is described in detail in the portion of the general's memoirs published by Dupont, which permits stopping at key moments of that event while omitting a series of details. What affected the child more than anything else was the sea's calm force and the power of a frothy, ragged wave that knocked him from his feet and carried him away during his first approach to the water. Unlike the other members of his household, he was not afraid. As he leapt on shore, he was purposely falling on the very brim of the surf, allowing the elements to roll his small, rosy body. Overcome by all the sensations, he jumped, shouted, and even urinated slightly, observing as a trickle that nobody noticed disappeared into a descending wave, vintage 1887.

The beach occupied a special place in the child's life from that point on. Even in the 1890s, when circumstances did not always permit him to appear there naked, the joy of the future military commander's encounter with the beach was not diminished. As before, he encountered the waves with a victorious cry, though he still did not allow those excited behaviors that marked his first meeting with the watery element.

Despite the ceremoniousness of the nineteenth century, this period had its own obvious distractions. In those years, when dresses had just barely risen above the ankle and no one was even dreaming of uncovered knees, fully undressing was, in a certain sense, simpler than now. Nude swimming among peasant men and women and, what is more, the landed gentry, was not something out of the ordinary in the Russian village and was by no means seen as an orgy.

This simplicity of values concerned the beach at times, too. Prince Peter Ouroussoff's *Reminiscences of a Vanished Age* notes that visitors to private beaches in the early twentieth century could even bathe naked.

Even so, the beach had arrived as a Western European phenomenon, bringing its own series of rules. One needed to dress for the beach, albeit in a particular way: not in usual undergarments but in a special style of tricot that was striped and clung to the figure in an interesting way. The shortcoming of a beach outfit, however, was the same shortcoming of other clothes from that time: it left hardly any parts of the bather's body uncovered.

When fighting in continental Europe, the general invariably recalled the beach: the damp salinity of the wind, the barely discernible smell of cornel cherry bushes, and the rhythmic swaying of seaweed on oceanside rocks. With the ebb of a wave, the seaweed obediently replicated the stones' forms, just as a diver's hair settles on his head like a bathing cap that gleams with the water that flows from it. The general remembered the smell of blistering hot pebbles after the first drops of rain fell on them and heard the special beach sounds: muted and somehow distant, consisting of children's shouts, kicks at a ball, and the rustling roll of waves on the shore.

For the general, the beach was a place for life's triumph, perhaps in the same sense that the battlefield is a place for death's triumph. It is not out of the question that his many years sitting on the jetty were brought on by the possibility of surveying (albeit from afar) the beach, legs crossed, in his trusty folding chair under a quivering cream-colored umbrella. He only looked at the beach from time to time, his body half-turned, but that gave him indescribable pleasure. Only two circumstances clouded the general's joy.

The first of those was the presentiment of winter, when a beach drifted with snow transformed into the embodiment of orphandom, becoming something contrary to its initial intended designation. The second circumstance was that everyone he had ever happened to be with at the beach was long dead. Hypnotized by the beach's life-affirming aura at the time, the general had not allowed even the possibility that death would come for those alongside whom he was sitting on a chaise longue, opening a soft drink, or moving chess pieces. To the general's great disappointment, none of them remained among the living. No, they had not died at the beach (and that partially excused them) but still they had died. The general shook his head, distressed at the thought. Now, after the passage of time, it can be established that he has died, too.

4

Historian Solovyov appeared on the Yalta beach twenty years after General Larionov's death. Solovyov's first encounter with the sea did not proceed at all like the future military commander's. Solovyov came to the sea as an adult, so carefree rolling around in the waves seemed indecorous to him. The researcher had also had the chance to familiarize himself with the corresponding part of the general's memoirs before making his appearance at the beach and the very fact of that reading would not have permitted him to do—as if for the first time—everything the young Larionov had permitted himself. Undoubtedly, contrivance and even a certain derivativeness would have shone through any attempt of the sort. As Prof. Nikolsky's student, Solovyov essentially thought that no events whatsoever repeat themselves because the totality of conditions that led to them in the first instance never repeats. It should come as no surprise that attempts to mechanically copy some past action or other usually evoked protestation in the researcher and struck him as cheap simulations.

Solovyov's behavior differed strikingly from Larionov's. The young historian took a towel from his rucksack and spread it on the warm evening pebbles. After taking off his shorts and T-shirt, he laid them neatly on the towel, stood up straight, and was immediately acutely aware of his own undressedness. Each hair on Solovyov's skin—which was untanned and visible to all—sensed a caressing Yalta breeze. Solovyov knew this was exactly how people went around on the beach but he did not know what to do with himself. He pressed his arms instinctively to his torso, his shoulders slouched, and his feet sunk conspicuously into the pebbles. Solovyov had not just come to visit the sea for the first time: he had never in his life been on any sort of beach, either.

Making a concerted effort, he headed stiffly toward the water. The pebbles, which the waves had polished to shining, became surprisingly hard and sharp under the soles of Solovyov's bare feet. He tottered, shifting from one half-bent foot to another as he balanced his arms in the air and desperately bit his lower lip. This helped him reach the spot where the waves were already rolling in. This sparkling area only seldom remained dry, during the brief instant between ebbing and incoming waves. Even in that instant, though, he could see that it was covered with small, fine stones that were turning to sand, which the sea carried away. Standing here was thoroughly enjoyable.

Solovyov went still when he felt the water's milk-warm touch. This was comparable to his experience the first time Leeza Larionova's lips touched him. Standing in water up to his ankles, Solovyov no longer knew which of those touches made a greater impression on him. He felt dizzy when he looked at the two light swirls of water by his feet. Solovyov took several steps forward so he could stay on his feet. Now he was standing in water up to his knees. The waves around him were no longer seething, they were shifting instead with unfathomable motions akin, perhaps, to the play of muscles under skin. Here—a few steps from the surf where the sea was beating itself into froth and spray behind his back—there was not even a trace of that hysteria. The sea was greeting Solovyov with a powerful rhythm of rising and dropping, and with the calm inquisitiveness of its depths. Solovyov stopped when the water reached his chest. He did not know how to swim.

As has already been noted, there were no bodies of water at *Kilometer 715*. The adolescent's imagination was fed by books about nautical adventures and by radio shows (an old wall radio was the only form of mass media in the Solovyov home). Station *Kilometer 715*'s strictly continental location only stoked that imagination. Why did Solovyov not become a sailor? He himself could not have given a precise answer. Yes, his love for the sea and everything connected with the sea was infinite, but even so . . . We could approach the explanation from another angle. There exist people who possess the gift of contemplation. They are not inclined to interfere with the course life takes and do not create new events, because they believe there are already enough events in the world. They see their role as comprehending what has already taken place. Might that attitude toward the world be what begets genuine historians?

Oddly enough, contemplativeness was characteristic of General Larionov to a certain degree, too. This manifested itself, perhaps, in a special way, and not all at once, but let us ask ourselves the question: are there many generals who are known to be contemplative? Basically, no, there are not many. In essence, a general's task is contrary to contemplation. But seeing the commander's fogged-over eyes and seeing how, in the middle of a seething battle, his gaze hardens at the most distant point of the landscape—that place where you can no longer track down even the enemy's rear guard—well, anyone seeing a general like that would think that he was a contemplative person.

That is what those who accompanied General Larionov on the Crimean campaign in 1920 thought, too. The abrupt pensiveness that seized him, both during the breaks between battles and during the course of battles, was noticed not just by his brothers in arms: it often became a topic for discussion, too. Needless to say, these discussions carried the highest degree of confidentiality and were told only in the discussants' memoirs (the general was not the sort of person to permit himself to be discussed so unceremoniously), but they existed, which means there was a reason the conversations came about.

For many who had the opportunity to observe the general in 1920, Larionov made the impression of someone who was pensive and even slightly aloof. That impression was all the more unexpected since nothing of the sort had been noticed about him during his previous campaigns. To the contrary: he embodied action and decisiveness. In fact, those were the very qualities that had made him a general.

In fairness, it should be pointed out that not everyone noticed, to an equal degree, the change that took place with the general in 1920. Numerous memoirists thus seem to rely on later impressions and when they underscore the general's aloofness, they are obviously exaggerating the degree of his condition in 1920. Some agree, a bit uncertainly, with the descriptions, almost out of politeness, saying

that the facts could not be denied in 1920, either, in light
of the general's later mentality. By reconciling various testi-
mony, as Vladimir Blagoi does in his article 'Pensiveness:
His Special Friend,' all that can be established with veracity
is that General Larionov had revealed a certain contemplativeness by 1920. This quality developed as the years passed,
eventually leading to the general's utter engrossment with
the sea.

What ended General Larionov's activity became the
beginning of historian Solovyov's activity. A contemplative
relationship with the sea did not permit the latter to master
one single maritime profession. He was afraid that if his
relationship with the sea was too close, that could lead to
disappointment and force him to fall out of love with the
watery element. Standing up to his chest in water, the young
researcher experienced doubts (in view of his unstable position, this could also be called wavering) as to whether he
and the object of his love were engaged in relations that
were too intimate.

Apart from this wavering, which was completely new to
him, the Petersburg graduate student asked himself yet
again about the correctness of his chosen research topic;
though in some sense the topic had been chosen for him.
He had asked Prof. Nikolsky this same question at one time,
when Nikolsky first proposed he work on land-based topics.

'No matter what a person studies, above all he is studying
himself,' the professor said enigmatically. 'Keep in mind,
young man, that accidental topics do not exist.'

The words left the professor's lips in a shell of cigarette
smoke. The words' very tangible appearance, coupled with
his teacher's wisdom, played their role because Solovyov

decided not to insist on a nautical topic and threw all his passion into researching continental events. After the suggestion to conduct his graduate work on the fate of General Larionov, Solovyov went to see Prof. Nikolsky again and asked him the old question about the choice of topic. The old man no longer smoked because his doctor had forbidden it. Otherwise, though, his answer was the same as several years before.

Was Solovyov studying himself by studying General Larionov's fate? This was yet another difficult question the historian posed to himself. Sensing that he was beginning to freeze in the water, he knew he lacked the time to resolve the question now. Beyond that, the bather's motionless standing in the water had already attracted the attention of the few people remaining on the beach. Solovyov decided to leave the question open; he began slowly moving toward shore.

The researcher's body had taken on a cyanotic tinge and was covered with goosebumps because he had stayed in the water so long. His awkward inhibitedness before bathing had given way to something altogether mechanical that had no relation to walking. Not one of Solovyov's joints would bend, and only by force of will did the young man move his body in the direction of his towel. Solovyov felt much better after drying off. Neither the sea nor the air were cold that evening. Motionlessness (it occurred to Solovyov) is very unhealthy for a person.

The sun was no longer on the beach. Yalta's beaches are surrounded by mountains from the west, so the sun disappears fairly early. It sets beyond the mountain ranges, but for a long time its diffused light still streams over the quieting sea, the stalls for changing clothes, and seagulls pecking at watermelon rinds. The city beach after six in the evening is a peculiar beach. Its colors are dim, shot through with the yellowness of a vanishing sun, just as it shoots through black-and-white photographs of beaches in bygone years. Maybe, Solovyov asked himself, the Yalta beach in evening is actually a remnant of what the young Larionov saw? Or perhaps this was the beach the juvenile Larionov saw, only now, years later, through the depths, as it were, of decades?

Solovyov had forgotten to bring dry underwear with him so he had to put on his shorts right over his wet swimsuit. He was, after all, a person without the slightest bit of beach experience. After Solovyov sat down to buckle his sandals, the contour of his swimsuit developed on the back of his shorts, as if on wrinkled photographic paper. He, however, was unable to see that. He picked up his rucksack and pensively headed in the direction of the embankment.

As he walked along the waterline, Solovyov looked up and slowed his pace in surprise. Someone was sitting at the very end of the jetty in a chair that closely resembled the one he had seen in the photograph. That someone was a lady. And though the distance did not allow Solovyov to make out all the details, it was obvious that the lady was getting on in years. She was sitting motionless, like Larionov, with her legs crossed, and the breeze was lightly stirring the hem of her long dress. This woman undeniably knew the value of effective poses.

Solovyov was initially moved to approach the woman, but he did not make that move. He could not imagine what he could ask her or how to begin speaking with her. He did not even have a notion of how one should approach ladies like her. Should one immediately kiss her hand or was it enough to bow slightly? It was entirely possible that this case called for a smart clicking of the heels along with a simple tilt of the head. Solovyov might have decided to draw nearer to the unknown woman but when he wiped his sweaty hands on his shorts, he discovered that they, for their part, were wet, too. By now, the trace of the swimsuit had also managed to make its mark distinctly in the front. His clothing, frivolous in the first place and now dampened besides, excluded any possibility of introducing himself to her. After wavering for an instant, Solovyov dashed home to change his clothes.

The stairs were so surprised as he flew up that they managed not to produce a sound, whereas the key, slipping along the plate nailed around the keyhole, produced an inconceivable scrape. After managing to unlock the door, Solovyov flung his rucksack into the corner, tossed off his shorts and swimsuit, and left the house a second later wearing white, completely dry, pants.

He had hurried in vain. Even from the embankment, it was obvious that the jetty was deserted. Continuing to walk by force of inertia, Solovyov was puzzled that an older lady in such a long dress could have slipped away in such a short time. And with a chair, too. Now he was not even certain he had seen her. Solovyov stopped. Today was August 2, the day on which General Larionov had died. The date had arisen just as suddenly as the unknown woman on the jetty. Had she truly been sitting there? In a certain sense, it would have been simpler for Solovyov to regard her appearance as an optical illusion. At least that would have been less upsetting. Considering the date of the incident, Solovyov preferred in the end to give it a metaphysical explanation.

He resolved to consider what he had seen to be the general's spirit visiting the jetty.

Solovyov decided to stroll along the famous Yalta embankment before returning home. Twilight was falling and the first lights were burning on the embankment. These were old-fashioned streetlamps, in the spirit of the thirties through the fifties, with domed globes sprouting from sprawling cast-iron branches. Though not an admirer of the fanciful Soviet Empire style, Solovyov nevertheless had an interest in it, almost a fondness for it. Buildings in that style, which simultaneously resembled nothing but were reminiscent of everything on Earth, had outlived their empire. From time to time, guesthouses, camps for Young Pioneers, and centers for artists gazed out of the coastline's greenery, looking like elders who had lost their way. These were the last structures initiated into the secrets of labor union leisure, and they alone remembered steelmakers' placid benders, procedure nurses' hale and hearty voices, and party activists' laborious orgasms. The full complement of people who had filled those walls had departed for nonexistence, just as everyone who had made their way into the aging General Larionov's peripheral vision—policemen wearing white shirts secured with belts, medal-wearers in defiantly wide pants, sellers of hot spiced honey drinks, Pioneer-camp counselors, hip dressers, and ex-cons—had departed from the Yalta embankment, heading in the same direction.

When he looked at objects characteristic of the epoch, Solovyov often yearned for times he had not seen; this surprised even him. He did not aspire to live in those times and he did not consider them either gentle or even interesting, but still he felt a yearning. There was not, however, any reason for this feeling to surprise the young man; this was a yearning over *something other*, a burning desire to make it his own, because that *something other* was now forever deprived of those who had known it at one time as their own. Unaware of this, Solovyov experienced the paternal feeling of the historian who has adopted another time.

As he walked along the embankment, Solovyov observed its reflection in the meek sea. Neon signs, amusement rides, and streetlamps quivered in the evening's ripples, and were occasionally severed by boats, with the penetrating sounds of karaoke in the background. Awaiting him under fabric awnings were vendors of ice cream, popcorn, and glowing bracelets. Photographers with apathetic monkeys on leashes waved to him from beneath palm trees. Waitresses in black skirts and see-through snow-white blouses greeted him at every restaurant. Solovyov certainly liked the south but he was a reserved young man. He did not visit one single restaurant or purchase one single glowing bracelet.

Solovyov stopped at the Central Grocery and bought a stick of cured sausage. After some thought, he also bought bread, cheese, butter, olives, and two bottles of beer. Instead of walking home along the embankment, he took a quiet parallel street: Chekhov Street. Past the Lutheran church. Past an unusual building in the Mauritanian style. Past an adult store covered over in red paper. Being an adult, Solovyov wavered by the store but quickly pulled himself together and walked on by. Visiting that sort of establishment was a pursuit he considered unworthy of a historian.

Back at home, Solovyov first washed his hands. After the stuffy, hot street air, the water felt unexpectedly cold. It flowed from the tap with a pressure surprising for the south, as if it were the Uchan-su Waterfall, which was unknown to Solovyov, though while on the embankment he had received several invitations for excursions to see it. After drying his hands with a holey but clean towel, he got down to eating.

Solovyov's dip in the sea and walk had given him a healthy appetite. He ate up one little sandwich after another, washing them down with unrefrigerated local beer. The radio he'd switched on was broadcasting local advertisements. It hung on the wall like a black formless box and offered (*rototillers for sale, reasonable prices*) large non-resort objects rather like itself. It spoke in an aging female voice with a barely detectable southern Russian accent. The radio in Solovyov's house at the *Kilometer 715* station had spoken in roughly the same voice. Only occasionally (when leading morning exercises and reading the national news) did it shift to shameless Moscow tones. It even looked roughly the same: ebony and clumsy; sometimes speaking, sometimes singing. The main thing was that it was never silent.

Solovyov began the next morning with a visit to Yalta's Executive Committee. He set off for No. 1 Soviet Square with his graduate student identification. A calm, plump woman with a large bust met him at the Cultural Department. She sat in front of Solovyov, positioning her bust on her arms and her arms on the table. The firmness of her position, apparently reflecting the positions culture had conquered in Yalta, was pacifying. Solovyov forgot all his prepared phrases and stated the aim of his visit in an informal manner. The plump woman did not interrupt. After some thought, he told the story about his studies of the general and—surprising himself—even about graduate student Kalyuzhny, whose dreamy inaction had cleared the way to these studies for Solovyov.

The woman in charge of culture in Yalta knew how to listen. She took in all Solovyov's stories, remaining both kindly and impassive. A restrained smile never left her face. When her guest's eloquence finally ran dry, she responded with a full speech that, as became clear right away, had arrived too late.

From her explanations, it followed that Nina Fedorovna Akinfeeva—the woman who helped Larionov in the last years of his life—came to Yalta once a year, for the anniversary of the general's death. Nina Fedorovna came to the jetty (the functionary released one of her gelatinous arms and pointed toward the window) and sat there for a few hours in honor of the general. She then disappeared for points unknown and returned to Yalta again the next year.

'Yesterday was the day the general died,' said the woman.

Her breasts hung for a short moment, then froze in place again on her arm, as if in compensation for Akinfeeva's traveling nature. Solovyov was upset. He told his conversation partner that he had been a few dozen meters from Nina Fedorovna (how simple were the names of secrets!) but had not risked approaching her with wet splotches on his shorts and so had run off to change his clothes and then . . . The young man punched his knee in annoyance and apologized right then and there. The punch and the apology were both accepted with identical degrees of good will.

After allowing the Petersburger to vent his emotions completely, the representative of culture in Yalta announced the following important fact. Despite her unestablished place of residence, Nina Fedorovna Akinfeeva had not refused housing space (26.2 square meters) in Yalta but had registered her daughter there: Zoya Ivanovna Akinfeeva, born in 1976, unmarried, and a correspondence student at the Simferopol Pedagogical Institute.

'Ivanovna is an invented patronymic,' smiled the plump woman. 'Nobody has seen that Ivan.'

Judging from the girl's dark complexion, it might just happen that he was not an Ivan at all. Making up for her own long silence, the senior employee gave an account of the Akinfeev family's history.

In the early 1970s, a new resident, Nina F. Akinfeeva, moved into the communal apartment where General Larionov lived (how can that be? he lived in a communal apartment?!) Authorization for the room was issued from the city's housing stock and allotted through the Anton Chekhov Museum, where Akinfeeva, who needed housing, was employed. By the time the new resident moved in, the general had long been a widower. Here, the storyteller tactfully fell silent.

Solovyov knew from Dupont's book about the death of the general's wife in the mid-sixties. Lacking specific information about this woman, the French researcher had alluded to her rather briefly. The general's son was discussed even more briefly; the scholarly lady had not managed to trace his fate after he came of age. The Yalta civil servant had managed to trace his fate, though, if only partially. After resting her unblinking gaze on Solovyov, she announced that the general's only son had taken to drinking and left home. She just could not remember if the son had taken to drinking first and then left home or vice versa, meaning

taken to drinking after leaving home. Even in the absence
of chronological clarity, however, both facts were at hand
and both induced the storyteller's agitation. She stopped
smiling, leaned back in her chair, and mechanically adjusted
the straps of her brassiere under her blouse. Solovyov began
to think he was watching some sort of old movie, though
he could not remember how the movie ended.

In the early 1970s, Nina Fedorovna Akinfeeva was around
forty and she, like the general, was completely alone. After
moving into the communal apartment, Nina Fedorovna
unexpectedly acquired a reason to exist. The general became
the object of her reverence and care, occupying all her
thoughts, energies, and time. She took to reading books
about the anti-Communist White Movement. They power-
fully crowded out the Chekhov studies that had once
occupied an exceptional position in her consciousness. Little
by little, Nina Fedorovna's museum colleagues began to
notice, alarmed, that Anton P. Chekhov was no longer at
the center of her interests.

It is difficult to say what, exactly, served as the reason for
the museum employee's spiritual regeneration. Did her
vanity play a role here (residence in the same communal
apartment as a great person), or was it the opposite, meaning
pity (residence of a great person in a communal apartment)?
Was this the influence of the magnetic qualities of the
general himself, a person who at one time commanded
armies and was most likely capable of subordinating a lonely
museum worker to his will? And, finally, was there, behind
everything that happened, a banal communal apartment
dalliance, as some of the employees at the Chekhov Museum
were inclined to think (this opinion was reinforced by hints

of their colleague's unpredictable temperament)? This, however, should be qualified by saying that other museum workers categorically rejected the possibility of a dubious relationship with the elderly general. In the course of discussions that arose spontaneously, the supposition was expressed that Nina Fedorovna might just as successfully have developed a similar relationship with Anton Chekhov.

The following notable fact testifies, circumstantially, to the bond between these two lonely people being purely platonic. One fine morning (after numerous years of selfless service to the general), Nina Fedorovna embraced the object of her reverence and ran out of the house without saying a word. She returned about three weeks later in an unrecognizable condition. Her face was all scratched and her clothing was torn. The fugitive was breathing heavily. She brought with her the scent of the forest and cheap cigarettes, and a devastated bankbook. The general welcomed her without a single question. Several weeks later she burst into sobs and confessed to the general that she was pregnant. The general, sitting in his chair, lifted his head. Nina Fedorovna placed her trembling fingers into his extended hand, and he silently squeezed them.

Nobody, including the museum and the cultural department that administers it, ever learned what thickets had attracted Nina Fedorovna during her days of flight. Innate energy that had awakened within the museum worker drove her toward continuing the human race and threw her into the embrace of something age-old, savage, and natural. The museum's management saw this particular case as unprecedented as well as unworthy of imitation. Considering, however, that Nina Fedorovna had become pregnant on the very brink of the conclusion of her child-bearing years (it was emphasized in the trade union's character reference that this was the last chance for the member of the museum's collective) material assistance in the amount of seventy-five rubles was allocated to her. The fallen employee was also presented with *The Stone Foot*, a poetry collection by Grigory V. Ursulyak, the museum's director. The museum did not regret the assistance afterwards. Years later, when Akinfeeva left Yalta for points unknown, her daughter replaced her in that institution of enlightenment.

Life did not change a bit in the communal apartment after that. Nina Fedorovna returned to the responsibilities that she had previously chosen to take upon herself. Every day (in the early morning, and sometimes in the evening) she accompanied the general to the jetty, carrying his folding chair and awning behind him. The time after the onset of darkness was devoted to preparing his memoirs. The general had previously written them himself but was forced to set them aside after the age of eighty, when his hand took on a mind of its own. New opportunities opened up for the general when a helper appeared in his life. He began dictating his recollections.

Just before giving birth, Nina Fedorovna asked the general what she should name the child.

'Name her Zoya,' said the general.

It remained unknown whether he was emphasizing the life-affirming meaning of what had happened—in keeping with the name, Zoya—or was simply oriented to the church calendar, with its saints' days. The woman was only asking what to name the baby if it was a boy but the general replied that it would be a girl.

She was taken to the maternity hospital a few days later.

After ordering that a small icon of Saint Panteleimon be removed from the windowsill, the head doctor—in light of the arriving patient's age—made the decision to perform a caesarean section. During the entire nine months of her pregnancy Nina Fedorovna had feared childbirth complications and her anxieties, sadly, were warranted.

The complications were brought on by forceps that were forgotten in the birthing mother's belly during the operation. The doctors must, however, be given credit. When they heard complaints of sharp pain in the abdominal cavity, they flawlessly chose, from an abundance of possibilities, (the nurse who forgot the forceps made the diagnosis), the correct reason, which essentially ensured the success of the second operation, too.

Nina Fedorovna left the hospital about twenty days later. When she crossed the apartment threshold with Zoya, who was wearing a pink ribbon, the general was already gone. He had died.

Solovyov looked into the cultural worker's bottomless eyes. A deep knowledge of the city's cultural life and a willingness to share that knowledge were discernible there. Sympathy for the fate of General Larionov and those around him was also apparent. At the same time—Solovyov's conversation partner expressed this with a deep sigh—the Yalta City Executive Committee's influence on human fates had it limitations.

5

After lunch, Solovyov headed to the Chekhov Museum. He climbed up a long, winding lane, crossing from one sidewalk to the other, seeking out the shade. The ascent reminded him of scholarly work, which—as he had already managed to comprehend—never moves in a straight line. Its trajectory is unpredictable and describing the research requires inserting a hundred vignettes. Any research is like the motion of a dog following a scent. The motion is chaotic (outwardly) and sometimes reminiscent of spinning in place, but it is the only possible path to a result. It is essential for research to check its own rhythm against the rhythm of the material under study. If they resonate with one another and if their pulses beat in time, then research is ending and fate is beginning. Thus spoke Prof. Nikolsky.

Finally, Solovyov saw what he was looking for. Before him lay a small square that—amidst all Yalta's development—reminded him of a crater after an explosion. A group of hideous bronze figures was arranged along its perimeter, depicting, according to the sculptor, Chekhov's most famous characters. The sculptures, however, did not seem to insist on having any direct relationship with Chekhov. Seemingly too shy to walk right up to the writer's house, they huddled forlornly by the trees that framed the square.

The museum itself consisted of a concrete administrative building and an elegant cottage from the beginning of the century (this was Chekhov's house). Inside the concrete structure, Solovyov asked for Zoya Ivanovna. They looked at him with curiosity and made a telephone call. Solovyov stepped outside for some air while he waited for Zoya Ivanovna. A few minutes later, the Chekhov garden's little gate clanged and a young woman appeared. The honey-colored tone of her skin and dark hair left no doubt: this was Zoya Ivanovna. It was her patronymic that had been called into question at Yalta's city hall. There was something multi-ethnic about her, of the carnival in Rio—most definitely not Chekhovian. Her face was imperturbable.

She was wearing a gauzy, nearly immaterial dress, flustering the young researcher. Distracted, he began telling her about his study of General Larionov, for some reason alluding, again, to graduate student Kalyuzhny. Angry with himself, he switched abruptly to an analysis of mistakes in Dupont's book and unexpectedly finished with Prof. Nikolsky's response to the Latvian veterans.

'Would you like me to show you the museum?' Zoya asked sternly.

'I'd like that,' said Solovyov.

He followed Zoya ('just don't call me Ivanovna!'), mechanically copying her light, feline gait. How could her father have been an 'Ivan' . . .

It was cool inside the Chekhov house. Solovyov mentally thanked Russian literature as he went inside, out of the Yalta heat. It occurred to him that the coolness inside the house reflected something invigorating, some sort of well-spring source of the country's literature. He liked that phrase and so uttered it for Zoya.

'Unfortunately,' and here she touched the wall with her palm, 'it wasn't only cool here in the summer.'

Zoya told him the house was also impossible to heat properly in winter. It was put up by a Moscow architect who was unfamiliar with Yalta's climactic peculiarities and so was, consequently, incapable of building anything satisfactory here. Zoya's slender fingers slid prettily along the wallpaper's rhombuses. The portrayal of a boundless Russia systematically ruined by Moscow served as the backdrop to her story. She had a grateful listener in the Petersburger Solovyov.

The tour turned out to be very detailed. The museum guest visited all the rooms in the Chekhov house, even the ones not usually intended for visits. He was permitted to lift the telephone receiver in which Lev Tolstoy's voice was once heard, calling Chekhov from Gaspra. In the bedroom, he touched bed linens embroidered with the laundry's mark *ACh*. With the look of an illusionist pulling the final and most beautiful dove out of a hat, Zoya sat him down next to her on the writer's bed. Solovyov forgot about Chekhov entirely while sitting on the museum exhibit. His tour guide's dark body, which shone through the whiteness of her dress, commanded his attention.

Then they went out to the garden (out to the garden, Solovyov whispered). Walking past bamboo planted by Chekhov, Zoya led her visitor to two benches that formed a right angle in the very corner of the garden. At Zoya's suggestion (a restrained presidential gesture), they each sat on a bench, as if they were in negotiations. Solovyov explained again the aim of his stay in Yalta, this time more calmly and lucidly.

Zoya listened to him, almost leaning against the back of the bench but not quite resting against it. Solovyov recalled that in the cadet corps this was customarily done to improve one's posture. He reported on his trip to Yalta's City Hall, too, though he kept quiet about the details relating to Zoya personally. At the story about Nina Fedorovna's return from the maternity hospital, Zoya interrupted him, 'His room was completely ransacked when my mother and I came home. The new resident greeted us wearing the general's slippers.'

Zoya turned out to be very observant for a person who was wearing a newborn's pink ribbon when she arrived.

The Kozachenko family had moved into the general's room. They were not Yaltans. The Kozachenkos had landed themselves in the *Russian Riviera* from some remote place or other; they were from around either Ternopol or Lvov. On its own, life in the middle of nowhere was probably incapable of prying them from that spot: that life did not burden them. As it happened, Petr Terentyevich Kozachenko, a civil defense specialist, had taken ill with tuberculosis, an uncharacteristic illness for specialists like him; it was even a bit bohemian.

While undergoing treatment in Alupka, Petr Terentyevich managed to determine that the Magarach Wine Institute in Yalta had an urgent need for a specialist of his type. He was accepted quickly after offering his services and returned to his historical motherland as an employee of the wine institute. Petr Terentyevich's new employment turned out to be completely unexpected for his family. His wife, Galina Artemovna, was astounded at her husband's abuse of power and flat-out refused to move. In the family scene that followed, she inserted their son, Taras, between herself and Petr Terentyevich. Pointing at Taras, she accused Petr Terentyevich of irresponsibility. Ten-year-old Taras looked off to the side, plentiful soundless tears rolling down his cheeks.

It is possible that Petr Terentyevich might have backed down (meaning he very likely would have backed down) under different circumstances, but the struggle over the move seemed like an unexpected struggle for his very life. He exhibited an inflexibility that did not really typify his relationship with his wife. He had his name removed from government registries (for which his wife cursed him, daily), resigned from his previous job, and anxiously groped at the lymph nodes around his armpits.

Galina Artemovna, who had already mourned her husband mentally, even before his Crimean trip (she regarded his illness in all seriousness), was perplexed by Petr Terentyevich's obstinacy. The hope of maintaining the housing that was provided to him as a civil defense representative (and, according to rumors, an employee of certain other government agencies), reconciled her to her husband's possible death. Frightened by his feverishness to move, she stealthily clarified her right to their aforementioned living space and bitterly established that in the event of her husband's death or departure, the real estate would automatically return to the government. Galina Artemovna's stance softened as a result. She preferred departure to death.

The Kozachenko family initially received only a room in

a dormitory through the Magarach Wine Institute. Vexed, Petr Terentyevich began seeking out support from other government agencies and even offered to compile reports regarding intellectual ferment within the establishment that had hired him. Those government agencies reacted fairly listlessly. According to information from senior employees who had contact with Petr Terentyevich, all that was fermenting at the Magarach Institute was young Massandra wine. The intellects at the institute resided in a state of complete serenity. In and of itself, however, Petr Terentyevich's vigilance was acknowledged as laudable and so, as a form of incentive, he was assigned a room that had freed up in a communal apartment.

'And they moved in with us,' sighed Zoya.

She straightened her sheer dress and Solovyov's gaze settled unwittingly on her knees. The first evening breeze touched the crown of the Chekhov cypresses.

The Kozachenkos had packed light for their move. They sold their furniture in their native Ternopol before heading into the unknown. All they carried into the general's spacious room was three folding beds, several basins of various sizes, and a ficus purchased at a Yalta flea market. They hung a portrait of Ukrainian poet Taras G. Shevchenko (1814–1861) in the corner furthest from the window, underneath Ukrainian towels embroidered in traditional red and draped on the wall. A great deal of empty space remained.

The sense of expanse was enhanced because their neighbor Ivan Mikhailovich Kolpakov had removed all items from the general's room the day before the Kozachenko family moved in. This operation for seizing the deceased's property was conducted with military rapidity. One night,

Ivan Mikhailovich unglued from the general's door the strip of paper bearing an official seal and, with his wife, Yekaterina Ivanovna Kolpakov, aiding and abetting, transferred everything into their room, right down to the general's glasses and Grigory V. Ursulyak's book *The Stone Foot*. Back in the day, the general had agreed to browse through the book, at Nina Fedorovna's request.

An oak cabinet with carved two-headed eagles presented particular complications: the couple found themselves unable to lift it. After an hour and a half of fruitless efforts (a blow was inflicted upon Yekaterina Ivanovna's back, for her lowly lifting capacity), they managed to drag out the fairly mutilated cabinet after placing plastic lids under it. Yekaterina Ivanovna meticulously swept the floor in the general's room.

Needless to say, the actions undertaken by the couple ended up being too naïve not to be disclosed. However, they ended up being disclosed, at the very least, because of the cabinet's magnitude: the door to the Kolpakovs' small room would not close. The newly visible area contained stacked beds and bundles of books, which the Kolpakovs never read. Yekaterina Ivanovna's concluding attempt to cover their tracks certainly could not have deluded anyone.

The civil defense worker's inquisitive mind imagined what had happened in detail. After accusing the Kolpakovs of appropriating property that had been transferred to the state, he announced that he intended to inform the state of the loss inflicted. The undiplomatic Kolpakov immediately inflicted a blow upon Petr Terentyevich's face. The boy, Taras, who was standing in the doorway of the allocated room, began to cry. Infliction of serious bodily harm was added to appropriation of government property.

Ivan Kolpakov felt cornered and drank himself into a stupor. And, oh, was he amazed when Petr Terentyevich himself woke him up in the morning, a glass of beer in his hand. Kolpakov might possibly have considered his neighbor an *extraterrestrial* when he looked at the iridescent bruise around his eye. At first, Ivan Mikhailovich even deflected the hand holding the glass. Only after drinking the beer and coming to grips with his initial agitation did he prove capable of hearing out Kozachenko.

Petr Terentyevich let it be known too that there were potential options in the matter. The deceased's items that were crammed into the Kolpakovs' room—Kozachenko's hand soared over the alienated belongings—should be divided evenly among the conflicting parties. As a prominent item, the cabinet should be given to the state, to avoid a scandal. In addition (and here Kozachenko's voice took on a prosecutorial tone), the general's books were being transferred from the Kolpakovs' portion to the Kozachenko family, as compensation for the maiming that had been inflicted.

Kolpakov approved Petr Terentyevich's draft treaty unconditionally. The items were divided in half, the Kozachenkos took full possession of the books (with the exception of *The Stone Foot*, whose title had intrigued Kolpakov), and the cabinet was offered to the state.

The state initially displayed interest in the cabinet but was forced to refuse it in the end. The cabinet had been brought in before the apartment was renovated to accommodate more residents and now the cabinet simply was not fit for removal. It turned out that the entrance to the apartment had diminished during the elapsed decades of the Soviet regime. Kolpakov refused to keep an item that hindered closing the door, and it was reinstalled in its previous territory after Petr Terentyevich's lengthy doubts concerning the presence of the two-headed eagles.

The fate of the trophy literature proved more complex. After determining that there was not one single edition of Taras Shevchenko among the general's books, Petr Terentyevich lost interest in them and furtively brought them to a second-hand bookstore. He kept sulkily silent afterwards, when Nina Fedorovna returned and persistently questioned the neighbors about the general's books. When the truth came out later, Nina Fedorovna rushed off to the bookstore, to at least buy up what was left. Unfortunately, not very much remained.

As for *The Stone Foot*, Ivan Kolpakov attempted to begin reading it but was quickly disenchanted. Being unfamiliar with the basics of versification, he could not comprehend why the texts inside were arranged in columns. Ursulyak's imagery turned out to be equally unfamiliar to him: it was, as a matter of fact, pretty unadorned. Finally, he could not ascertain why the publication that had found its way to him had been given its name. Without making any arrangements with Petr Terentyevich, he brought the book to the second-hand bookstore where, it would seem, its story came to an end, but *habent sua fata libelli*.*

One fine day, Ursulyak stopped by the second-hand book-store, saw *The Stone Foot* on the shelf, and read the personalized inscription written in his own hand. Poet and director Ursulyak purchased his own book and gave it to Nina Fedorovna once again, pronouncing that every person should have something

---

* Books have their own destinies (Latin).

that cannot be sold. This was not, in fact, the first incident of the sort in his poetic practice: at second-hand bookstores, he sometimes bought up books he had once inscribed, returning them to their remiss owners with the notation *Reissued*. He developed a knack for determining the presence of *The Stone Foot* as soon as he stepped inside. Sales clerks knew that and readily took *The Stone Foot* on consignment.

'Zoya, we're closing,' came a shout from somewhere beyond the garden.

'We're closing,' Zoya corroborated sadly.

After opening the gate, she waited for her Petersburg guest to exit, then closed it with a clang already familiar to Solovyov. She entered the administrative building without saying a word. Solovyov huddled sheepishly by the gate. He had not been invited to enter the building, but nobody had said goodbye.

He did not want to be pushy. He did not want to ask if he could see Zoya home, though of course he wanted to see her home. On the other hand, it would have been strange and even disagreeable if Zoya herself had asked for that.

'You're still here?' Zoya asked, though she did not look at all surprised.

Solovyov nodded and they made their way out. Zoya was not headed toward the stairs, down which Solovyov had walked from the square to the museum. After going around the corner of the administrative building, they walked out toward another gate. From that gate, a path looped between the buildings of a sanatorium and led them out.

'And what happened to the memoirs the general dictated to Nina Fedorovna?' Solovyov asked. 'Were they in the general's room, too?'

The young woman shrugged absent-mindedly. 'Probably . . . it was such a mess then.'

They went down to the Uchan-su River, walked along it for about fifty meters, and ended up on a stone bridge. Leaning her elbows on the railing, Zoya observed the Uchan-su tirelessly fighting its way toward the sea, through cobblestones and chunks of wood. She looked calmly at Solovyov.

'Are those memoirs very important to you?'

'Yes.'

There was a small bazaar on the other shore. At Zoya's suggestion, they bought a watermelon and took it to a nearby park. After settling on a bench, Zoya took a Swiss pocket knife from her purse. This woman always carried the essential items.

After cutting the watermelon in half, Solovyov placed one half aside, on a plastic bag. From the second half, he cut thin, neat semicircles, divided them into smaller segments, and spread them out on the same bag. There was something primordially masculine in his handling of the knife, something that was undeniably expressed in Zoya's gaze, which was following his hands. Solovyov himself could see that he had been very deft; it surprised him a little. The watermelon was truly sweet.

'Your mother didn't lay claim to the general's property?'

'She didn't have any official rights.'

'But how did she keep living with the people who . . .'

'. . . Who robbed her? It was fine. That's life.'

Life dealt worse things, too. Nina Fedorovna found it challenging not only to lay claim to the property but even to express the offense she had felt. One could do that if seeing the offenders in court or perhaps only meeting them every now and then on the street. But having them alongside oneself every day, using a communal toilet with them, and leaving a pot of soup in a shared kitchen—that was utterly impossible. Most likely, the hurt that Nina Fedorovna felt did not so much pass as dull. The sight of the general's various small items (many of which she had given to him) popping up with one of the couples, reignited that feeling, though, overall, it was deemed to have faded.

Moreover, oddly enough, Petr Terentyevich began striking up conversations with her in his time away from his medical procedures. After half-sitting on a kitchen table that had been handed down to him, he told Nina Fedorovna about constructing a respirator under home conditions and applying splints to bone fractures, about antibacterial injections and the effect of chlorine vapors on the upper airways. Despite having never given a gift to anyone in his life, he suddenly gave her the evacuation map for a factory that manufactured reinforced concrete as well as a model of the ventilating opening of an emergency exit that he made himself. He even wanted to give his collection of toxic agents to Nina Fedorovna for her birthday, but Galina Artemovna opposed that adamantly when, by chance, she learned of her husband's intention. She quickly made a mental note of her husband's contact with their female neighbor. Galina Artemovna looked upon that ironically but did not speak up at all. Sometimes she even gave the impression that this state of things suited her.

In actuality, the work-related topics that so agitated Petr Terentyevich had always left Galina Artemovna indifferent. Neither highly detailed classifications of nerve agents, which he had mastered to perfection, nor his ability to determine the type and size of a gas mask with his eyes closed made any sort of impression on her. It is possible that he turned to Nina Fedorovna—who heard him out politely—to see out what the specialist lacked in his own family. Most likely, Petr Terentyevich's sympathy for Nina Fedorovna's late motherhood played a role, reminding him that he and Galina Artemovna, too, had been able to have a child when they were nearly forty.

There were some pronounced changes with respect to the Kozachenko pair. This might have been characterized as estrangement, if, of course, they had been close before. But they had not been close. Definitively caught up in his illness (which was not, by all indications, as scary as the couple initially thought), Petr Terentyevich made the rounds of Yalta's pharmacies after work. He compared medicine costs, attempting each time to ascertain their wholesale prices.

On one of those evenings, Ivan Kolpakov subjected Petr Terentyevich's wife to an unexpected sexual advance: in his state of drunkenness, he had thought she was his own wife. Galina Artemovna's lack of resistance confirmed his delusion and he did with his neighbor all that his modest fantasies directed. Kolpakov's mistakes began repeating regularly after that, with the only difference being that now it was Galina Artemovna herself who prompted him with regard to little novelties she had never seen from her civil defense specialist.

Petr Terentyevich, who suspected nothing, continued his platonic relations with Nina Fedorovna. At Petr Terentyevich's request, he was retold the play *The Cherry Orchard*, which vividly reminded him of his favorite Taras Shevchenko poem, 'The Cherry Orchard by the House.' Once he even asked Nina Fedorovna to show him the Chekhov Museum because he'd heard so much about him (Chekhov). His wife was copulating with Uncle Vanya (Kolpakov) as Petr Terentyevich stood in Chekhov's study with a group of museum visitors. Tears in his eyes, he hearkened to the story of Chekhov's deadly skirmish with the very same disease he had, feeling himself to be a bit like Chekhov at that moment. It is possible that in the depths of his soul, Petr Terentyevich also wanted to tell a German doctor, *'Doktor, ich sterbe,'** but there were no German doctors in his life and could not have been.

After thinking about death at the Chekhov Museum, he decided to order himself a funeral with music. This was the only thing from the realm of the beautiful that he could permit himself. In the will he had prepared, five hundred Soviet rubles from an unshared bank book was allocated specifically for that purpose. That sum seemed to him like more than enough for a performance of Chopin in the open air. And though he was not really planning to die, the instructions he had made brought a certain tragedy and loftiness into his life.

His life did not end in a Chekhovian manner. When he returned home one day at an inopportune hour, he found an *abominable love scene* in his very own bed. That was the description that escaped from Petr Terentyevich. Beside himself with rage, he rushed at Ivan Kolpakov and proceeded to pepper him with punches. Being under the influence of

---

* 'Doctor, I am dying.' (German)

alcohol, Kolpakov initially took the blows fairly meekly. In the end, he lost his temper and, cursing, flung Kozachenko away from him. As Petr Terentyevich fell, he hit the back of his head on one of the heads of the double-headed eagle carved on the cabinet and lost consciousness.

The ambulance doctor who arrived roughly an hour and a half after the call ascertained that the trauma to Petr Terentyevich was not consistent with enabling survival. Unable to figure out that wording, Ivan Kolpakov grabbed the doctor by the collar and demanded an answer to a simple question: is Kozachenko dead or alive?

'Dead,' the doctor answered curtly and left without saying goodbye.

Endeavoring to anticipate police questioning, Ivan Mikhailovich decisively enticed Galina Artemovna to his room. He persuaded her not to mention the true cause of her husband's death. Strictly speaking, there was no real need to persuade her anyway. She had already long been experiencing doubts about Petr Terentyevich's longevity so it was now only the mode of his death, rather than its fact, that could make much of an impression on her. The sobered-up Kolpakov displayed unexpected oratorical abilities. The first words he uttered ending up hitting the bull's eye: he promised to marry the widow.

She complied with his requests, without wavering or even displaying any particular coyness. When the police came, they were told that Petr Terentyevich had been weak from illness and grown dizzy. Waving her arms around, Galina Artemovna showed how unfortunately her spouse had fallen. They sat the inconsolable widow on the bed (it was already made up with three plumped pillows, one on top of the other) and ordered the neighbors to give her enough valerian so she'd feel better. Taras, who was fourteen at the time, stood in the corner of the room, holding the broken-off eagle head in his hands. Big, slow tears dropped from his eyes.

Petr Terentyevich was not buried as he had dreamed. Galina Artemovna was extremely indignant to discover her husband's unaccounted-for five hundred rubles; she buried him without music. In addition to Taras and Galina Artemovna, those walking behind the coffin were Ivan Mikhailovich, Nina Fedorovna and the little Zoya, and a representative of a certain organization (he mysteriously placed a finger to his lips at all questions) with which, it emerged, Petr Terentyevich's entire conscious life had been linked.

It was this very organization that took care that the event was fittingly solemn. Taking into account that the deceased had been housed in the room of a White Guard general, Petr Terentyevich's death from a two-headed eagle was assessed as almost heroic and, in the highest degree, anti-monarchical. The unknown person installed an aluminum tripod with a star and a pointed Red Army hat on Kozachenko's grave. For some reason, no representatives from the deceased's primary place of work were in attendance. Even so, the Magarach Institute allocated fifteen liters of wine for the wake, but, in light of Galina Artemovna's cancellation of the wake, Ivan Kolpakov, who was secretly engaged to her, drank all fifteen liters.

As for Kolpakov, he was in no hurry whatsoever for what had been secret to become evident. Either he thought the danger of unmasking had been overcome or the cost of the issue itself seemed too high to him, but he simply stopped mentioning the promise he had made to the widow. Moreover, even the small bed-based joys that had bonded him with Galina Artemovna ceased shortly thereafter. Their contact was reduced to Kolpakov's brief visits, for treating morning hangovers with Petr Terentyevich's leftover medicinal alcohol.

Another *abominable scene* took place one morning and, in many ways, hastened a denouement. As she waited for Ivan Mikhailovich to vacate the washbasin (he was washing at great length, gargling, grunting, and clearing out phlegm), the widow remarked, reproachful, that other people needed to wash, too. Exclaiming, 'Then wash!' Ivan Mikhailovich Kolpakov splashed her in the face with water from a large tin mug that was nearby. The water was cold but clean.

Galina Artemovna felt insulted and demanded an explanation. She pointed out to the boor that actions of this sort were inadmissible, reminding him at the same time of his promise to enter into marriage with her. With his characteristic harshness, Ivan Mikhailovich led the wetted woman to the mirror and suggested she remember how old she really was. The breaker of the marriage promise recommended she think not about a wedding but about a funeral. In response to the threat of telling the police the whole truth, Ivan Kolpakov burst into Homeric laughter.

He underestimated Galina Artemovna. She did not, in fact, go to the police; after all, what could she have said there after her own eloquent statements? Ivan Mikhailovich's line about a funeral sent her mind in an unexpected direction, though. After brief deliberations, she decided to die on the same day as her betrothed. Galina Artemovna waited for yet another visit aimed at hangover treatment (there was not much of a wait) and then dissolved her husband's collection of toxic agents into his alcohol and handed the solution to Ivan Kolpakov. Several minutes later, Ivan Mikhailovich passed away in the arms of Yekaterina Ivanovna, his lawful wife, whom he just managed to reach. Convinced of the preparation's efficacy, Galina Artemovna drank all that remained.

'They were buried in separate graves,' said Zoya, finishing her sorrowful story. 'And Taras was left all by himself. He's still living in our apartment.'

The watermelon rinds stretched into a short but even wedge on the bench. Solovyov neatly collected them and carried them to a nearby trash bin (a pack of tissues, so he could wipe his hands, immediately appeared out of Zoya's purse). Exactly half the watermelon, that which had been placed on the plastic bag, remained.

They left the park and headed toward the sea. In the evening's duskiness, signals from a lighthouse took on the ever-more distinct form of a broadening beam of light. The rhythm of its blinking attracted attention, forcing one to wait for another flash and involuntarily count out the seconds until it appeared. In the slight twilight breeze, it was finally obvious how very hot the day had been.

'I have the day off tomorrow,' said Zoya. 'Want to go to the beach?'

'I don't know how to swim.'

Solovyov uttered that almost as if he were doomed. Just as men announce their lack of experience when in bed with a lady who has seen everything.

'I'll teach you,' Zoya promised after a pause. 'It's not complicated at all.'

It was completely dark when they approached Zoya's building on Botkinskaya Street: it was a two-story building with high gothic windows. So, it occurred to Solovyov, this is where the general lived. A figure that had initially gone unnoticed moved away from the building's walls, which were overgrown with grapevines.

'Good evening, Zoya Ivanovna. I was walking by and saw there wasn't any light in the windows so decided to wait.'

Solovyov examined the unknown man in the light of the streetlamp. Before him stood a man of more than sixty, wearing a light-colored shirt in a quasi-military style. His appearance—from the carefully ironed trousers to the combed-back hair—was an example of a special old-fashioned luster as it appeared in the polished *Studebakers* and *Hispano-Suizas* that surfaced now and again in Yalta's flow of automobiles.

'Everything's fine,' said Zoya, unsurprised.

She took a few steps toward the front door and added, without looking at anyone, 'Good night.'

6

The beach was already packed with people when Solovyov and Zoya arrived at around ten in the morning. They stepped carefully over extended arms, glued-on paper nose protectors, and jelly-like rear ends glistening with lotion. It was body parts that drew the eye in this crowded festival of flesh. Forcing himself to regain his focus, Solovyov noticed an empty spot by a stand with a life ring. There was just enough space for two towels. Solovyov considered it an undeniable stroke of luck that this spot was located by a ring. The means of rescue was right at hand if he found himself in a critical situation.

The life ring turned out to be unnecessary. Solovyov was surprised to discover that Zoya was a born swimming instructor. As she walked into the water with him, she ordered him to lie, stomach-down, on the sea's surface. When Solovyov's body—which was unaccustomed to water—slowly began sinking, Zoya lightly but confidently supported him with both arms. He felt a bit shy about being in such a strange, baby-like position in a young woman's arms, though he could not help but admit that the training turned out to be a pleasant business.

They carefully made their way to their towels after coming out of the water. Zoya lay on her back, extending one arm along her body, and using the other to shade her eyes from the sun. Solovyov sat with his chin resting on his knees. This embryonic pose seemed ideal for an observer. The morning beach was something unprecedented for Solovyov and it evoked his curiosity.

Solovyov was very taken with the Tatar women peddling baklava and strings of nut candies on trays. They crouched next to buyers, pulling a plastic bag out from under a sash and putting a hand inside as if it were a glove, then taking their Eastern goods from a tray. Large beads of sweat glistened on their faces. The Tatar women settled up with baklava lovers, stood easily with no signs of tiredness, and continued their journey over the scorching pebbles. Their shouts, slightly muted by the tide, sounded along the entire expanse of the beach, mingling with the shouts of sellers of kvass, cola, beer, dried bream, and kebabs made of smoked whelks.

Solovyov examined the human bodies. Liberated from their clothing, almost nothing bound them and they felt no boundaries with anyone. He saw muscular types whose skin had been tanned by the sun, a result of a constant presence at the beach. Even tattoos that had been applied long, long ago, before they began to frequent the beach, were lost. These men moved toward the water with a special gait. This was the gait of the *kings of the beach*: torso swaying, holding their arms slightly away from their sides. When they came back onto dry land, their swimsuits clung to their bodies, clearly outlining their genitalia. Aware of this effect, the kings of the beach pulled at the waistbands of their swimsuits with two fingers, releasing them with a business-like snap. The swim trunks immediately lost their excessive anatomism. With their merits obvious to everyone, the kings of the beach needed no additional advertising.

Alongside them—and herein lay the great equality of the beach—there hovered the possessors of flabby breasts that had been bravely liberated from swimsuits, one-size-fits-all bellies, and old women's shapeless, ropy legs stitched with the violet threads of veins. Everything that would have given rise to protest in any other situation turned out to be permissible at the beach and, for the most part, evoked no indignation.

Solovyov leaned back and rested on his elbows. He began watching Zoya when he was certain her arm was firmly covering her eyes. His gaze slid from Zoya's shaved armpits to her thighs, above which ran the thin line of her bikini. Solovyov lost himself admiring the barely perceptible and somehow placid movement of her belly. When he raised his eyes, he met Zoya's gaze and smiled from the unexpectedness.

When they went back into the water, Zoya ordered Solovyov to turn on his stomach and try to make the froglike motions that she had demonstrated first. Zoya's strong hands supported Solovyov in his froglike motion and slid along the trainee's neck, chest, and belly, touching—anything is possible deep under water—his body's most sensitive points from time to time. When Solovyov's motion seemed insufficiently froglike to Zoya, she swam under him and synchronized the rhythm of their two bodies to show him how this actually looked. People standing on shore followed the lesson with undisguised interest.

Zoya's nontraditional and perhaps even somewhat eccentric methods could not help but yield fruit. The result of
their mutual efforts was that Solovyov swam several meters,
experiencing the fabulous sensation of *the first time*.

He had experienced this sensation only twice in his life.
The first incident occurred at about the age of seven, when
he suddenly rode away after an exhausting lesson in riding
a two-wheel bicycle: his grandmother let go of the seat by
accident when she grew tired of running after him. Solovyov
registered, forever, his abrupt acquisition of balance. The
smooth motion while coasting, akin to soaring; the crunch
of pine cones under the wheels.

He experienced the second sensation of this type at the
end of the second seven-year period in his life. It concerned
a realm unconnected with grandmotherly help, something
of a far more delicate nature and not at all bicycle-related.
Out of necessity, Nadezhda Nikiforovna's censorship
concerned only printed sources, but prohibited information
had verbal distribution channels, too. Classmates supplied
Solovyov with certain details about relations between the
sexes, though that was all presented in the crudest, most
mechanistic ways. Solovyov's education in that regard
progressed so one-dimensionally and chaotically that by the
time he had a notion of the essence of the sexual act, he
was somehow still unaware that children appeared as the
result of those same actions.

The connection between those two phenomena ended up
being thoroughly unexpected for him, even unpleasantly so.
Solovyov did not much want to connect a joyous and antic-
ipated event such as the appearance of a child with the
disgusting rhythmic motions that his classmates showed him

while laughing. It cannot be ruled out that, deep down in his soul, the boy platonically in love with Nadezhda Nikiforovna simply did not want to believe it. A sober look at things hinted to schoolboy Solovyov that he and Nadezhda Nikiforovna were not fated to have children in this fashion.

Solovyov was shaken by that revelation, and during a school gathering he imagined, in turn, all the parents in attendance during production of his classmates. Taking that further, he imagined the schoolteachers in the same mode, up to and including the principal (*Bigfoot* was her nickname), a bulky, unsmiling woman with braids folded on her head. Based on the existence of all their children, Solovyov came to the indisputable conclusion that each of them had done *that* at least once in their lives. Including the principal, difficult though it was to believe. Copulation scenes more or less emerged for the rest of the teaching staff, but Solovyov's fantasy turned out to be powerless when applied to the principal. In the end, the adolescent managed to imagine her, too, but the spectacle turned out to be ghastly. Peace of mind came only with the thought that the dreadful phenomenon had taken place one single time and would never be repeated.

After exhausting all available possibilities, Solovyov moved on to examining other people in his immediate surroundings. Now, the portraits that had been looking at him from the classroom walls for so many years captured his attention. Solovyov was a child of the late Soviet period, so there was not a broad selection at his disposal. The central, largest portrait in the classroom belonged to Vladimir Ilyich Ulyanov (Lenin). It was he who attracted the adolescent's attention most of all.

Solovyov had to turn his head constantly to unite Lenin with his wife, Nadezhda Krupskaya, who occupied a modest spot in the classroom pantheon between Anatoly Lunacharsky and Anton Makarenko. The concluding picture turned out to be far more imaginable than that of the principal: either Solovyov's fantasy had managed to get some rest or this was an optical effect from the convergence of distant images.

'Did Lenin have children?' Solovyov once asked during a biology lesson.

'He did not,' said the teacher. 'But is that really a question on the subject of *amphibians?*'

'Yes,' said Solovyov.

Krupskaya's Graves-disease profile, along with her part-ner's small, spiteful motions lent the pair a defiantly amphibious look. Well, then, needless to say, they did not have children; they just made each other nauseous.

Karl Marx turned out to be the concluding entity in this portrait-driven period. No matter how Solovyov struggled, in his imagination, Marx only ever united with Friedrich Engels. Not yet suspecting the possibilities of this kind of alliance, Solovyov left the founding fathers in peace.

Solovyov acquired his own first experience of this sort in the vicinity of the *Kilometer 715* station. Looking back on the circumstances of his life, that hardly seems very unex-pected. The majority of what happened during Solovyov's adolescence was tied to the station in some way or other, with the only exceptions being Solovyov's relationship with Nadezhda Nikiforovna and his study at school, both of which took place an hour and a half's walk from his place of residence. Needless to say, the tender experience under discussion could not have been acquired either at school or, even more so, at Nadezhda Nikiforovna's. It was acquired in Solovyov's home.

The house was a fairly dilapidated structure. It consisted of an entryway, a kitchen, and two small rooms adjoining the kitchen. The windows looked out on a railroad embankment that was not high but was overgrown with grass. After his mother's death, Solovyov, who had previously been housed in the same room as his grandmother, moved into his deceased's mother's room. He did that from an instinctive striving to fill the emptiness that had arisen after his mother's departure. When he entered that emptied room, he creaked the cracked floorboards and slept on his mother's bed, making her departure seem less irrevocable to him. In the end, the room's emptiness was partially filled because someone else, in addition to Solovyov and his grandmother, also began spending time there: Leeza Larionova.

Leeza had been at the Solovyovs' before. She was Solovyov's only peer in the whole area around *Kilometer 715*; in fact, she was the only child there besides him. When she came back from school with Solovyov she would go home to eat but would show up an hour later at the Solovyov home, where the two of them would sit down to do their homework. Leeza listened attentively to Solovyov's reasoning when solving math problems, hardly ever contradicting him. And when Solovyov struggled, she would prompt him, timidly and often in question form, about the correct way to solve them. Sometimes it seemed to Solovyov that even in cases when he was incorrect, she wrote the same things in her notebook so as not to offend him. There was no doubt that verity was not an end, in and of itself, for Leeza.

Leeza could have been what was defined, in previous

times, as the head of the class. She had a clear mind but lacked the key thing for a career as head of the class (or, admittedly, for any career): ambition.

Their shared walks to and from school were a manifestation of nothing more than ordinary neighborly relations. At least in the beginning. They had walked together since first grade. This sort of travel seemed safer to their household members. In families that lacked men (Leeza lived with her mother) the word 'safety' possessed special weight.

Little Solovyov was embarrassed about walking to school with Leeza. The most distressing thing about those circumstances was that he and Leeza were labeled *bride and groom*. This common taunt for cases like theirs was all the more hurtful for Solovyov because, of course, he secretly considered Nadezhda Nikiforovna to be his bride. The moment they neared the school, Solovyov demonstrated in every way possible that an immense distance stretched between these two people who were apparently arriving together. The future historian turned away, lagged behind, made faces behind Leeza's back and, in brief, reached extraordinarily, extraordinarily high levels of detachment that nevertheless still allowed their shared return home.

His treatment of Leeza was especially harsh in the presence of Nadezhda Nikiforovna. True, there was nothing there that might have been deemed as not *comme il faut*: Solovyov knew his chosen one tolerated no brattiness. At the library, Leeza's lot was to receive icy gazes and short answers in a scratchy voice. To Solovyov's annoyance, Nadezhda Nikiforovna did not understand that he was making these efforts, under the circumstances, for her sake. From time to time, she herself addressed Leeza when she was waiting for Solovyov. Oddly enough, the little girl was one of Nadezhda Nikiforovna's frequent visitors, too. Although the selection of books was not conducted as ceremoniously for Leeza as for Solovyov, Leeza read a lot. Perhaps even a little more than Solovyov himself.

By the time she was fourteen, Leeza had evolved into a nice-looking, slender young woman. She did not go to the head of the class and she had not become a beauty, either. The appearance that nature had given her—well-balanced, subtle facial features, wheat-colored hair, and gray eyes—presented vast opportunities for choosing a style. If Leeza had decided to become a beauty, a restrained drawing of her facial features would have imparted her appearance with a light impressionistic shading that striking faces lack. But that did not happen.

It would be incorrect to say that Leeza did not want to be a beauty. That would imply a certain purposeful will, a conscious position she had taken regarding the issue of beauty. Leeza conducted herself as if that realm did not exist for her. Knowing Leeza's poverty, others offered to let her use their cosmetics, but she politely declined. Unlike other girls, who shimmered with all the colors available in the Russian provinces, Leeza was not the object of her classmates' attention at school parties. The boys in her class preferred girls who had a look that was more mysterious and—considering the violet splotches around their eyes—slightly extraterrestrial. It was with these girls that they shared exhausting slow dances.

The thought of those dances flashed through Solovyov's mind one time after finishing some homework (perhaps not the most arousing thing to do), when he felt a burning-hot erection and unexpectedly found himself pressing his whole body against Leeza. The unexpectedness had come about not because Solovyov had never imagined this sort of possibility. He had, in fact, imagined it: whenever his grand-mother's snoring began resounding in the next room at night, his fantasy painted this event in full detail. He distinctly sensed the touch of his own hands as if they were Leeza's and fell still on the damp sheet after experiencing a blend of delight and shame as ancient as growing up. No, the unexpectedness was in the fact that his fantasy had never envisioned—as something real—everything he had just undertaken with Leeza. But now that had happened. Could Solovyov handle his arousal? Under certain circumstances, yes. For example, if his grandmother had been at home. But she was not there at that moment.

Sensing that he was shaking, Solovyov took Leeza's hand and pressed it to his bulging sweatpants. He nearly lost consciousness from the forbiddenness of what was happening and from the union of such contradictory inclinations (it seemed to him that the highest degree of contradiction also begat the highest degree of the forbidden). In the remnants of his consciousness that had not yet been lost, there pulsated the thought of Leeza touching the most secret thing on earth. Never afterward did the differences between genders excite him so much: this sort of union of contra-dictions turned out to be an ordinary matter in adult life and it was unavoidable, too, if approached dialectically. What had once seemed so hidden and inaccessible to him turned out, on closer inspection, to be almost the most sought-after object. In presenting it so insistently to Leeza, the future scholar did not yet know about its role in the history of culture or even history as a whole. He was acting without looking back at his predecessors.

Standing right up against Solovyov, Leeza looked at him with a calm and slightly surprised gaze. As was the case with homework, it seemed that only she knew the correct solution. She truly did know it. Leeza lightly touched her lips to his and lay her head on his shoulder. Emboldened, he thrust his hand under her blouse. He touched her back, her belly, and what was below.

He was unable to undo a single one of the hooks hidden under her blouse. Leeza did this herself. Leeza also took off the rest of her clothes and obediently lay on the bed, where Solovyov had led her by the hand. He did not utter a word for the rest of that scene. Solovyov quivered for real and from just his convulsive movements (all he had managed to finish doing completely was undress), Leeza was always able to guess what was expected of her. All in all, not very much guesswork was required here.

Accompanied by the wretched squeaking of springs (that squeaking communicated the condition of his body rather precisely), he somehow perched himself on Leeza and froze. Unable to unite their two bodies from the start, he no longer understood what, exactly, to do next. Here, Leeza took matters into her own hands again. He felt himself being directed and, with the indefatigability of an athlete, began making the same motions his classmates had so repulsively shown him. He experienced an orgasm several moments later. This was his *first time* with a woman. And it was far more intense than riding a bicycle.

The absence of blood surprised Solovyov. When he examined the spots on the sheet after Leeza left, he was unable

to find anything resembling blood. He could not even allow
the thought that Leeza had already become a woman before
their relationship. Solovyov knew, down to the minute, how
Leeza spent her time. Leeza's social circle was also well
known to him. Properly speaking, he was that circle.

Everyone at *Kilometer 715* knew there should be blood.
Even Nadezhda Nikiforovna—who excised any mentions of
a sex life—would leave, untouched, information about the
blood that resulted on a wedding night. Perhaps her stern
hand was stopped by the thought that the presence of blood
could serve as an important restraining factor for anyone
intending to enter into a sexual relationship. Under a worst-
case development of events, meaning entering into said
relationship, according to Nadezhda Nikiforovna's reckoning, the possible absence of blood would disillusion the
male entering into the relationship and deter him from
repeated attempts.

As comfort for the bloodthirsty Solovyov, the sheet turned
crimson during one of their subsequent lovemaking sessions,
the third or fourth of their encounters when his grandmother was not at home. The previous times—Solovyov
obviously did not understand this because of his lack of
experience—their contact had been too convulsive and
chaotic. When the unavoidable finally happened, there was
so much blood that the sheet had to be washed immediately.
Solovyov fetched icy water from the well and Leeza laun-
dered the sheet, periodically blowing on her numbed fingers;
there had been no time to heat the water. There was also
no opportunity to legitimately dry the sheet, so it had to
be put on the bed again after laundering. Only at night,
after his grandmother had begun to snore, did Solovyov

hang the sheet on two chairs and sleep on top of the blanket, covered by a jacket.

Their romps became regular. His grandmother's trips out were fairly rare, so every now and then they had to switch to Leeza's house when, needless to say, it was empty. The complication here was that Leeza's mother, a railroad track inspector, could show up at any time. The length of an inspection was surprisingly varied and depended on her degree of tiredness, her mood, and some higher industrial considerations, the essence of which were familiar only to those in the know regarding protocols for railroad track inspectors. Neither Leeza nor Solovyov, even more so, belonged to those ranks and so several times their undertakings nearly failed. More than once they were saved by the clang of an empty pail they had inconspicuously placed by the garden gate, but it was impossible to count on such an unreliable and, even more importantly, attention-attracting method. And so they returned to Solovyov's house.

As children of railroad workers, Solovyov and Leeza decided to make the fullest use of the railroad's possibilities, something that is, by the way, often underrated in contemporary life. With impeccable mastery of the schedules for passenger and freight trains, they effortlessly discovered that train traffic through *Kilometer 715* was nearly uninterrupted several times a day. In the most fortuitous cases, the unceasing running of trains in both directions took ten to twelve minutes. That was plenty for brief but torrid love. The din of the trains drowned out any sounds capable of arising under this sort of circumstance. First and foremost, the screeching of bedsprings. Solovyov's grandmother was not in the habit of entering his room during their endeavors, but in crucial situations, the participants briefly used the hook on the door.

Regarding the issue of noises. Solovyov's awareness of the female component of sex was not limited to *blood*. Prior to entering into sexual activity, he also already had a notion of *moaning*. As performed by his classmates, moaning turned out to be even less attractive than the motions they demonstrated. Be that as it may, under the sexual roles that Solovyov had adopted and delegated, Leeza was not responding to his masculine movement with feminine moaning. Having been convinced by his classmates at some point that one thing was guaranteed to evoke the other, Solovyov's unease was no joke. After sharing his doubts with Leeza, she faintly began moaning a little. Insecurely listening to her moans, Solovyov did not find them convincing, which distressed him even more. Sometimes it even seemed to him that Leeza was moaning out of a sense of duty rather than on account of a physiological necessity to moan.

Furthermore. At times it occurred to Solovyov that Leeza was experiencing far less need than he in these forbidden and, at the very least, premature relations they had entered into. This was not just because it was never she who initiated their little madnesses (that could be written off to female shyness) but that her attitude toward coitus was passionless in some sense. Leeza never had to be persuaded and she yielded right away but she *yielded*: calmly, benevolently, and without Solovyov's impatience and trembling. It seemed that in this realm, as in many others, she did not want to distress him. Generally speaking, Leeza's conformity seemed boundless. At times, when Solovyov was especially impatient and there was no opportunity for seclusion in the offing, they made love without preparation or undressing. Leeza agreed to that, too.

Later, when he remembered these hectic relations, which were for all intents and purposes childlike, despite their adult content, Solovyov never stopped feeling surprised that Leeza did not become pregnant. All they knew about the realm of precautions was that there were safe and unsafe days in terms of conception. Leeza had won math meets so she calculated the days. As far as birth control devices went, there was no opportunity at all for young people to buy them in a place where everyone knew them. Solovyov went several times to the regional capital, where he bought condoms, sweating profusely from embarrassment. The condoms were quickly gone and a trip to the city required an entire day. The only birth control device they always had in abundance was the ability to break their embraces at the right moment. This required no small force of will and malfunctioned several times. Solovyov regarded the absence of consequences as their exceptional luck since it would have been catastrophic for both of them at *Kilometer 715* if Leeza had become pregnant.

There is no doubt that the adolescents' luck truly was exceptional. They made love constantly, not just inside but also in the open air. Sometimes Solovyov and Leeza stepped into the woods on their way home from school to indulge themselves in love, on the mosses and lichens they had just finished studying in biology. The contours of those florae were imprinted on Leeza's pink bottom when she got up from the ground and brushed herself off. They did *that* more than once in the snow, too, spreading out Solovyov's skimpy coat and melting the snow's crust with their hot fingers. Even so, Solovyov's room was the primary spot for their intimate relations. The association of their encounters with the train schedule not only brought about a degree of order that was rare in cases like this but also lent them an unexpected Pavlovian nuance: trains passing through the station evoked an involuntary erection for Solovyov.

Now, he sensed an erection unassociated with any railroad effect. When Solovyov opened his eyes, he knew he had just woken up. The first thing he saw was Zoya's unblinking gaze directed at him. Solovyov turned over on his stomach. With a crocodile-like motion, he raked hot pebbles toward himself and squinted again. He realized that this time he had woken up as a person able to swim. He certainly did like Zoya.

7

Zoya invited Solovyov to her place that evening. He arrived with a bouquet of flowers but knew right away that what he had presumed would happen was not to be. There, in Zoya's room, in addition to Solovyov, was the old-fashioned gentleman he had seen the day before, as well as a thin old woman. She was wearing a black hat with the veil folded back and black mesh gloves. A few minutes later, the door-bell rang and a man with the look of a mighty warrior entered. He appeared to be over sixty. Despite his age, biceps of significant size revealed themselves under an untucked, cotton, pensioner's sort of shirt. Solovyov thought the group seemed worthy of a painting. At first, he just could not grasp what, exactly, had gathered such dissimilar people.

General Larionov had gathered them. This became clear when Zoya introduced the attendees to one another. At first, Solovyov thought he had misheard. The old woman turned out to be Princess Meshcherskaya, although—and here, a tinge of apology could be heard in Zoya's voice—she was not born until after the revolution.

'That never prevented me from being a princess,' the old woman said, before offering her hand to Solovyov.

He bent over her extended hand and felt the mesh texture of her glove on his lips. He was kissing a princess's hand (admittedly, *any* lady's hand) for the first time in his life. As was the case with the beach, no such opportunity had presented itself either in Petersburg or (even more so) near station *Kilometer 715*.

The two gentlemen in attendance were the children of White Guardsmen that the general had somehow saved from death. This circumstance permitted them, as they expressed it, to not only deeply revere the general but also to have been born in the first place. Based on several phrases these people uttered, Solovyov concluded that they had transferred their love for and devotion to the general on to Zoya, who was a sort of adopted daughter to the deceased, even though he had never seen her. This apparently comforting circumstance made Solovyov wary. He grew definitively upset upon remembering yesterday's encounter with Shulgin (that turned out to be his name). Given the terms of his guardianship, something obviously taken very seriously, the chances of developing a relationship with Zoya seemed slim.

Zoya asked Solovyov to help her as she was preparing to serve tea. They went to the kitchen, where there stood a balding man, five to seven years older than Solovyov. He could not be called a fat man in the strictest sense; he was more likely flabby. Slackened. Threatening to either collapse or deflate. Somehow, he was not completely standing, but slanted, resting against a firm support behind his back. Zoya nodded at him, barely noticeably, and turned on the gas under the teakettle. Solovyov greeted him to avoid awkwardness. Answering 'hi' (it was quiet and perhaps even shy), the unknown man disappeared into his own room. Though they had never met, Solovyov recognized him immediately: this was Taras Kozachenko.

As they waited for the teakettle to boil, the curious Solovyov examined the spacious kitchen where the legendary general had put in an appearance every day over the course of more than half a century.

'This was *his* table.'

Zoya pointed at the oilcloth-covered wooden structure that Taras had been leaning against. The oilcloth had been finely hacked up (vegetables were chopped there) and stained red from a dried sauce. Next to a glass containing wilted dill there lay a whetstone of implausible size, and behind it—as if to illustrate its capabilities—were two knives with unevenly sharpened blades. At the very corner of the table, wrapped in gauze, stood a jar of kombucha with the fungus. This was *his* table.

Solovyov cautiously bent back the sticky oilcloth and touched the surface of the table. He attempted to imagine the general wiping this table with a rag. And regulating the flame on a primus stove with fried eggs crackling.

'The general hardly ever cooked,' Zoya announced.

According to Zoya, Varvara Petrovna Nezhdanova, who was assigned housing in the general's apartment in 1922, helped him with all his household matters. She was a quiet, terse young woman who came to Yalta from Moscow and then stayed in Yalta. After finding a job at city hall as a typist, she was given a room in the general's building.

'I can cook for you,' Varvara Petrovna said one day.

'Then cook,' said the general.

They married two years later.

Over tea, Zoya told those in attendance about Solovyov. It turned out that Shulgin's friend, whose surname was Nesterenko, already knew of Solovyov. When in Petersburg on business, he had gone to a conference at the Institute of Russian History and heard Solovyov's paper that had made such a strong impression on everyone: 'Studying the Life and Activity of General Larionov: Conclusions and Outlooks.' Nesterenko himself had initially been upset that the young researcher's conclusions had turned out to be far fewer than the general's true venerators wanted. The abundance of outlooks envisioned in the paper, however, compensated for the disappointing situation in the realm of conclusions. In the final reckoning, this permitted Nesterenko to return home feeling almost uplifted.

In speaking about scholarly topics, they also recalled that the conference 'General Larionov as Text' was scheduled to begin a few days later, in Kerch. Neither Shulgin nor Nesterenko understood why the conference was being held in Kerch rather than Yalta. They listed, at length, grounds for why a conference devoted to the general could only be held in Yalta. Displaying unexpectedly practical thinking for a princess, Meshcherskaya suggested that hotel prices were significantly lower in Kerch. At the same time (and here the princess's erudition in the field of semiotics manifested itself), she was distressed to acknowledge that, unlike Yalta, Kerch was not a *signifying* (semiotically speaking) place in the general's life history. In the end, it was the princess who spoke in defense of the conference's title, parrying attacks from Shulgin and Nesterenko, who bluntly refused to imagine General Larionov in text form.

The conversation livened up even more when the

attendees learned that Solovyov planned to speak at the conference. Since not everyone (notably Zoya) was able to leave Yalta during the days of the conference, they asked Solovyov to read his paper in this house. Of course, Solovyov—who pushed his cup so abruptly that a bit of tea spilled on the tablecloth—did not mind. He considered it an honor to read a paper in this company and (here was the main thing), in *this* house. Since he did not have the text of the paper with him at that moment (and it would have been strange if he had, confirmed the attendees), they agreed the reading would take place within the next few days. It would be difficult to dream of a reading in a more *signifying* place.

As for Solovyov's potential listeners, they had things to tell, too. With the exception of Zoya, they had all known the general personally and well. The atmosphere Zoya was raised in, however, had furnished her with information about the general to such a degree that during their subsequent reminiscing about the general over tea, she permitted herself to supplement and even correct the guests' statements. The Chekhov Museum employee's wonderful memory made up for her absence of personal experience. Based on the stories told by the figures gathered in the general's home that August evening, his post-revolutionary fate unfolded in the following way.

The general greeted the Reds' arrival within the walls of his own Yalta dacha (Princess Meshcherskaya made a circular motion with her hand, indicating these very walls). This was where he lived when he did not need to stay on the armored train. The general not only avoided death in a surprising way but had not even been evicted from his home.

The general was subjected to *having additional residents moved into the premises.*

A local Komsomol cell was stationed on the first floor of his dacha. In previous times, nobody could have thought this space capable of housing such a number of figures wearing pointy, woolen Red Army hats. They straightened their uniform shirts and saluted each other when they met by the front stoop. On the second floor, one room was assigned to the aforementioned Varvara Petrovna, another was given to the revolutionary sailor Kuzma Seregin, and a third went to the general. Since the second floor had no kitchen, a large room there was modified for the purpose.

The Larionov family built this house with gothic windows in the nineteenth century, during the mid-nineties. Despite the family's deep army connections, the dacha was built using the labor of civilian workers who were paid, furthermore, out of the Larionovs' own money. Like the majority of Yalta dachas, it had only two stories but each was high. When the future general stepped over the threshold, he was already at an age when the magical words *art nouveau*, which his mother uttered in the foyer, were not empty sounds for him. Those two French words had resounded repeatedly in Petersburg, too. They accompanied the home's entire construction and his parents uttered them with a special sort of progressive facial expression. When showing the house to Yaltan neighbors, the general's parents comported themselves a little like Columbus and, strictly speaking, they had a right to do so: the style was still almost undiscovered, in Yalta as well as the capital.

The style was unfamiliar to Kuzma Seregin, too, when he moved into the general's house in 1921. Art nouveau turned out to make a dispiriting impression on this representative of the navy. For the first two days of Seregin's stay in the house he dropped everything (he was a member of the Red Navy's firing squad) and worked on modifying the room that had been handed down to him. After rejecting the intricate moldings on the ceiling as bourgeois excess, he chiseled them off the ceiling. He painted the oak paneling with gooey green paint and went over the oak parquet with it, too, after finding the color interesting. The general observed the clashing styles but kept calm, never once rebuking the master of firing squad matters. By comparison with changes across Russia, events in Larionov's own house could no longer genuinely disturb him.

Being rowdy by nature, though, Seregin was a bit afraid of the general. For him, the general was a phenomenon no less alien (and perhaps even more alien) in nature than art nouveau, but he could not proceed with the general as he had with the ceiling moldings. Despite his revolutionary consciousness and propensity for cocaine, the sailor saw his neighbor first and foremost as a general.

The Red Navyman's servile reflex was also reinforced one time after he initiated hand-to-hand combat with the general and was quickly knocked off his feet, dragged to the front steps, and dunked in a rain barrel. For some time, he tried to take it out on Varvara Petrovna, who had witnessed the event, but he dropped that, too, after seeing the general's benevolence toward her. He did not calm down for good until he quietly enquired at his place of employment as to the prospect of the general becoming an object for the firing squad. So as not to burden his comrades with extra work, he offered to do the work independently, as a house call, so to say. He was genuinely surprised when he received a categorical refusal; he then began respecting the general even more. It was Seregin, incidentally, who was the first to ask the key question of the general's biography: why was he not shot?

Seregin lived in the general's house for seven years. Once caught in the vortex of the revolution, he simply could not return to a tranquil life. His revolutionary consciousness and increased consumption of cocaine pushed him toward actions and words (and words are also actions, as Lev B. Umansky, a member of the Joint State Political Directorate troika, said) that were unacceptable to the young Soviet system of political power. Seregin's very own firing squad executed the troika's verdict for Seregin. According to his comrades' recollections, that was Seregin's only consolation.

Umansky, whom the general recognized as the person who commanded the Red Armymen during Seregin's arrest, moved into Seregin's room. As the Red Armymen tied up the resistant tenant, Umansky checked the condition of the window frames and doors, and confirmed the exact measurements of the vacated room with Varvara Petrovna. It later emerged that Umansky, who did not yet have housing in Yalta, did this whenever he conducted an arrest. Seregin was shot on very short notice, so there is no reason to doubt that the accommodations suited him.

Umansky differed, favorably, from Seregin because he did not engage in nighttime debauchery. If he brought ladies home now and then, he made them take off their shoes and handed out slippers he had readied specially. The women were initially from the Komsomol, spirited away from the cell on the first floor. Those who slept with him thought that (as an honest person) Umansky should marry them. Without involving himself in discussion of his own honesty, he rationally announced that he simply could not marry everyone at once, despite his desire to do so.

Regular scandalous scenes on the second floor caught the attention of the cell's leadership and they began investigating the issue of *amoral behavior*. Umansky, who had thoroughly chickened out, was forced to go to the cell and explain, in the presence of the Komsomol's core membership, why marriage should be considered an obsolete phenomenon. His speech made a fairly good impression on the core membership, which was largely composed of males. The female portion of the group regarded it with more restraint but could not resolve itself to object openly.

From that day forward, the Komsomol women did not set foot in Umansky's room. On the one hand, the young women in the cell were too offended to go up to the second floor again. On the other, upon reflection, Umansky himself decided to get by with ladies from the embankment: they may have been more distant ideologically, but they were preferable in terms of their mastery of sexual techniques. Unlike the Komsomol women, whose inflexibility thoroughly irritated Umansky, Marxist worldviews did not prevent them from kneeling when necessary.

In fact, out of everyone the general had occasion to see in a communal living situation, Umansky was not the worst neighbor. During the years Umansky was a flatmate, the potent smell of urine (which had appeared when Seregin settled into the apartment) disappeared from the bathroom. Umansky (usually in the person of one of the ladies who visited him) invariably took his turn washing the floors in the kitchen and other common areas. From the general's point of view, Umansky's striving for outer cleanliness and orderliness compensated, to some degree, for his inner impurity.

The general considered Umansky a scoundrel and did not particularly hide that. At the same time, there was also a sort of sentimental shading in his attitude toward Umansky. This manifested itself in full measure later, when the general expressed regret that the room next door had been freed up prematurely. As far as Umansky went, it was flattering for him to live in the same apartment as someone so famous. Although he was once tempted to expand his living space by arresting the general and his wife, to the Political Directorate employee's credit, his taste for good company prevailed in his soul over strictly mercenary interests.

It emerged years later, though, that before Umansky's best feelings triumphed over his worst feelings, he had, in fact, made a move to free up the apartment. A certain mysterious power, however, had hindered an arrest of the general that time, too. Moreover, during the course of his attempt, Umansky also determined that Larionov, whom he had thought to be unemployed, was on the books at the Museum of City History as a consultant and was even receiving a salary.

Knowing better than anyone that the general hardly left the apartment (his strolls along the jetty were the exception), Umansky made quick work of sending an inquiry to the Museum of City History regarding the former general's employment activities and the nature of his consultations. Unexpectedly, the answer came from Umansky's own department and, judging from the tone, it assumed no further questions. Umansky stopped there: he was a pragmatist and essentially it was not his calling to be a spiteful person. He decided that in the long run he could find another apartment elsewhere but would not be able to find another general.

Motivated by those considerations, he even attempted to gain the general's favor. It is interesting that the general, who had narrowed his social circle to an absolute minimum, also conversed with Umansky from time to time. Being people of polar opposite temperaments and convictions, there is no doubt they interested one another. They discussed tactics for close combat and the admissibility of the Brest peace, the expediency of women serving in the army and the work of field kitchens during the autumn-winter period, and, in moments when the general was in a philosophical mood, the moral problematics of *Dead Souls*, which Nikolai Gogol called a poem.

Life close to the general seemed so edifying for Umansky that it distracted him from the apartment question for a while. The Political Directorate employee even initially had doubts when the opportunity came up, by chance, to move into his own well-appointed apartment. After his superior, Grigory G. Piskun, announced to him that everyone housed on an entire floor had been shot to improve conditions for his subordinate, Umansky thought it awkward not to move into the vacated apartment. After receiving the housing assignment, he arranged a farewell banquet at his former place of residence and did not begrudge the Political Directorate's stupendous special supplies.

The banquet exceeded all expectations, both in terms of the quantity of refreshments and, so to say, its degree of farewell-ness. There was an unexpected ring at the door as the event

was coming to a close, and the apartment filled with opera-
tives in their leather jackets. Recognizing the arrivals as his
co-workers, the man of the hour felt touched, thinking this
was an ingenious form of congratulations that befitted the
department; he offered drinks to the arrivals. When he was
knocked to the floor and held face down, he remarked to
those in attendance that the joke had gone too far, but nobody
laughed in response. Contrary to Umansky's expectations, his
removal from the apartment was not accompanied by merri-
ment, nor was his shooting, which was carried out in a most
serious manner a week after his arrest.

It later became known that the direct reason for Umansky's
arrest turned out to be the ladies he brought home from
the embankment. The vigilant Komsomol women—who
had been rejected by the person under investigation—sent
signals regarding those visits. After the very first face-to-face
questioning with some of the ladies (as well as with the
Komsomol women), Umansky admitted that his sexual liaisons were indiscriminate and repented sincerely. His
statement that—despite an abundance of casual relations—
the Political Directorate was the only organ that he,
Umansky, was genuinely dedicated to, was also entered into
the record of his interrogation.

The problem, however, was not with the ladies from the
embankment. It lay in the fact that during a rare visit of
foreign vessels to Yalta, those ladies had managed to converse
with a crew that had come ashore and allegedly conveyed
information of state importance overseas. It was also established that the indiscriminate sexual liaisons were shams,
intended in the capacity of cover, and the female citizens
who visited Umansky were actually nothing more than

intermediaries between him and eleven foreign spies (investigators determined that eleven people had visited Umansky).

Umansky began by objecting that his liaisons were indiscriminate but not shams (this, by the way, was confirmed by all eleven females involved) and that the only thing that had reached him via an intermediary turned out to be gonorrhea (medical documentation was presented), but that was no help. Crushed by the gravity of the evidence, the suspect confessed in short order to everything he was being incriminated of and, to the pleasant surprise of the investigation, even added several hitherto unknown episodes.

In those days, General Larionov and Varvara Petrovna awaited arrest, too: in the eyes of the investigators, the fact that the general was Umansky's neighbor should, in and of itself, have become one of the most important proofs of Umansky's guilt. But that did not happen. This is all explained by the fact that Umansky's superior, Piskun—who had initially favored him and even vacated a large, well-appointed apartment for him—had been severely criticized by his own wife at one time. She had pointed out the fact that the living conditions of his subordinate, Umansky, now surpassed Piskun's own. Shaken by that fact, Piskun began seeking a way out of the situation that had arisen. Their establishment's code of honor did not assume the direct reallocation of living space, so Piskun decided to execute Umansky. Only after that—in light of the uselessness of so much living space for a man who had been shot—did Piskun consider it possible to move into the apartment given to Umansky. Under those conditions, neither the room belonging to the general nor the general himself was of interest to Piskun.

Umansky's mother came to Yalta not long after he was shot; oddly enough, she had come from the city of Uman. She packed her son's things into three canvas cases then piled everything that would not fit on a huge velvet table-cloth and knotted its corners together in pairs. The general helped her to the bus station. Carrying one case in his hand, he pushed the neighbors' pram, with the velvety bundle on top. Umansky's mother carried the other two (lighter) cases. Poplar leaves showered down on them as they walked along Moscow Street on that sunny October morning in 1934. Umansky's mother set the cases on the ground from time to time and caught her breath. During one of those rests, the woman said she had never approved of her son belonging to the Political Directorate and tenderly recalled the time when he had been a well-known card shark in Uman. That sort of activity seemed more lucrative and not as dangerous, despite regular beatings.

In the early 1970s, that autumn farewell merged in the general's memory with another, which was also autumnal, but occurred much later and became a typical case of déjà vu (which is, essentially, what permitted those events to blend). Surprisingly, the general could name 1958 as the year for this farewell but could not recollect the circum-stances attending it. He even cited the name of the lady he was seeing off: her name was Sofia Christoforovna Pospolitaki. The general was carrying a suitcase and pushing a pram then, too, but there was a child this time. Contrasting with the child's complete silence, the pram's springs produced a piercing, almost hysterical, screech. Sofia Christoforovna was embarrassed about this unpleasant sound, even though she was not producing it. She shrank

her head into her shoulders with a confused smile. Contrary
to the chronology, the general sometimes thought he was
accompanying Umansky's mother again on this second occasion, when she was taking her small son, who had not yet
been shot, away from Yalta and out of harm's way.

Whose child was this? According to the general's recollections, the child could not have belonged to Sofia
Christoforovna, due to her age. All the general could assert
with veracity was that the child was not his. Poplar leaves
fell on them on Moscow Street, too. A gust of wind blew
several leaves under the collar of Sofia Christoforovna's
between-season coat. The general stopped and extracted
the leaves out from under her collar and Sofia Christoforovna
thanked him, with unexpected duration and warmth. The
general found it difficult to say who this lady was and why,
exactly, he was seeing her off.

This circumstance prompted him to think that the
majority of events in his long life had managed to repeat
themselves. And not just once. In order that they not merge
completely, the general decided to return to the work he
had abandoned as a historian.

'That,' said Zoya, 'was precisely when he began dictating
a continuation of his memoirs to my mother.'

Umansky's room sat unoccupied after he was shot.
Piskun's actions with regard to his colleague had been so
rapid that there had just not been enough time to take the
latter off the housing registry. Responsible tenant Larionov's
payments had shielded the housing office workers from
seeing the bloody, truly Shakespearean drama that had
played out between the two Chekists. The housing office
simply had not learned about the death of the man from

the city of Uman. Now, by a strange confluence of circumstances, the executed Umansky, who had been a big fan of
Nikolai Gogol during his lifetime, had turned into a *dead
soul* himself, freeing the general from the threat of someone
else being moved in. Umansky's silent otherness in the
housing office's lists went on for an entire twelve years—
right up until the post-war housing audit in 1946, which is
when the person who later became Ivan Kolpakov's father
moved into the apartment.

The general's son was born in an apartment lacking
flatmates. It will evidently never be known now if it was
the fact of the apartment freeing up that inspired the general
to have a child or circumstances of a more personal character
(according to rumor, Varvara Petrovna was infertile until
she was thirty). Princess Meshcherskaya was of the opinion
that the general had simply not wanted to have a child
previously because of his uncertainty about remaining alive.
The thought of possible arrest sat so firmly in his head that
even after marrying Varvara Petrovna in 1924 (this was done
secretly) the general did not consider registering their relationship officially with the Soviet authorities, so as not to
subject her to danger. On the other hand—and here Shulgin
practically refuted the princess's point of view—why should
the general's perspective on his future have changed at that
particular time, in the mid-thirties? An unbiased analysis of
the sociopolitical situation did not give even the slightest
grounds for that.

Whatever the case, the child appeared. When the general
greeted Varvara Petrovna in the lobby at the maternity
hospital, he examined the dirty-yellow floor tiles with
disgust. Each little square of tile, along with the smell of

bleach, came laden with something unbearably Soviet and devoid of human qualities. The general attempted to remember the smells in the military hospitals he had seen— of course bleach had been used to clean there, too, what else did they have for cleaning?—but for some reason the smell was not as oppressive. Sisters of mercy, their hair gathered under white kerchiefs with a red cross in the middle, walked inaudibly from bed to bed.

Glass doors that had lost their transparency (from haphazard whitewash smudges) opened. The first to exit was a fat nurse with a parcel tied in blue ribbon. Varvara Petrovna looked bashfully out at her husband from behind the nurse's back. The general took the parcel from the nurse and peered at it. He looked long and hard, as if attempting to read the infant's future fate in his wrinkled and almost hideous face.

'He looks like you,' said the nurse, interpreting his gaze in her own way. 'Couldn't resemble you more.'

The general silently held out fifty rubles for her. He had been told the day before that medical personnel should be properly thanked: fifty rubles for a boy, thirty for a girl. Talk of equal rights was still out of the question back in 1936.

No, the boy did not resemble him. More specifically, his features—the form of his nose, line of his lips, and shape of his eyes—thoroughly reflected the general's, but this outward likeness only emphasized the full degree of their overall dissimilarity. This was how wax figures of the greats have nothing in common with their originals precisely because they do not convey what is most important: their enormous force field. The general showed no interest what-soever when his wax figure was put on display at Madame

Tussaud's museum years later. After absentmindedly glancing at the photograph they sent him, the general placed it in some book or other and forgot about it forever. The wax copy could not surprise him. He saw it in his own son for many years.

They named the boy Filipp. He was born during a time when, in the general's opinion, it would be better not to be born a man. In the grand scheme of things, it was better not to be born at all.

'A time of servitude,' the general defined it in brief, pushing Filipp's pram uphill, along Botkinskaya Street.

This was the very same pram, the neighbors', in which Umansky's things had been delivered to the bus station. The neighbors had handed over the pram to the general's family for good, in commemoration of the arrival of the general's firstborn. By the time of the handover, the pram had a thoroughly museum look but, then again, the general was already a museum consultant at the time. Given the state of things, the general found no reason to refuse the gift.

The general neatly cut four narrow strips from his military map case and used them to replace worn-out straps in the pram's inner workings. He sewed a new canopy from a duffel bag of the thinnest calfskin and attached its edges to the pram's metal frame.

'That's not a pram,' Tsilya Borisovna Prozument, an employee at the milk kitchen, would repeat. 'It's a masterpiece of applied art.'

They respected the general at the milk kitchen. They gave him the very best milk, called him *papochka* and Varvara Petrovna *mamochka*, and the general liked that. For their part, the employees at the milk kitchen liked that a genuine combat general was doing such civilian things. In that they saw the symbol of something they themselves were unable to express thoroughly, getting by (and what would you say about a general like that?) with only rhetorical questions and interjections.

Unlike his father, Filipp began talking at an early age. Even so, almost nothing that Filipp said when he was very small (admittedly, just like later) lingered in witnesses' memories. By contrast, the general's spirited silence was more eloquent. Out of fairness, it is worth noting that Filipp was also not very eager to use his ability to speak, despite having acquired it early. Filipp's speech primarily boiled down to naming objects he needed but since his require- ments were always surprisingly few, his sentences came out sounding correspondingly spare.

Filipp was not a stupid child. When necessary, he dealt with the complexest of tasks, in both school and nonschool contexts. The main difference between him and his father was that there were very few tasks on this Earth that he recognized as necessities. Everything the general did during his life was a necessity for him—he simply had no other reasons for his activeness. What (as Dupont asked in her day) transformed *can* into *must* in the general's life, what forged that life into a continuous chain of necessities? A sense of duty? Ambition? A thirst for activity? All those qualities taken together, defined as a life force? This (asserted Dupont) was in the general. And this was not (asserted Zoya) in Filipp.

After some consideration, Filipp's mother signed up the ten-year-old for a stamp collecting club. The little boy was

taught to pick up stamps with tweezers but no interest in
stamp collecting sprang up in him.

'It develops a child,' Varvara Petrovna loved to repeat.

'It envelops a child,' the general once said.

To the general, collecting stamps seemed like a wretched
matter. Filipp stopped going to the stamp collecting club.

At his mother's insistence, Filipp enrolled in the correspondence program at the Institute of Light Industry after
he graduated from high school. Light industry was not
Filipp's calling and had never been an area of interest for
him. (It remains unknown if there was ever an area of
interest for him.) At the same time, Filipp had never
displayed any particular dislike of light industry (he heard
an airiness in the very definition of light industry) and he
was not against taking courses at the institute.

Filipp worked as a laboratory technician at the Magarach
Institute when he was a correspondence student. After
finishing his higher education, he became a senior laboratory
technician. Although Filipp's career growth stopped there, he
had acquired a genuine passion for the first time in his life:
the degustation of wine. Those who explain this passion as
an elemental inclination toward alcoholism are not completely
correct. In a certain sense, this point of view is based on a
statement from the general himself, who once suggested that
alcoholism is the lot of low-energy people. This was said in
another regard, without specific explanations of what ought
to be understood as energy, but the phrase was used
concerning the general's son after some time had passed.

In actuality, Filipp's initial passion truly was degustation.
After several years working at Magarach, he could effortlessly not only determine, by taste, any brand of Crimean

wine and its harvest year, but also name the exact place where the vine was located on the mountain's incline. His degustation sessions were imprinted on the memory of Magarach Institute employees. As one memoir reported, he would swirl the wine with a light wrist motion and observe its slow, thick flow along the sides of the glass while telling of the variety's characteristics.

It was he who was invited to the most crucial Crimean degustations. Filipp's soft-spokenness and his long, melancholic fingers made an indelible impression on the Party elite. And though the high-placed guests also asked to have a bottle or two of Stolichnaya (out of foresight, these were kept in the refrigerator, along with brined cucumbers) set out for when they heard stories about the Golitsyn wine cellars, that did not diminish their respectful regard for the taster's knowledge.

Filipp truly did take to the bottle. Needless to say, that did not happen instantaneously, as some individual employees of the Magarach Institute were inclined to assert. These assertions are explainable because they were fundamentally an attempt to separate the concepts of degustation and alcoholism and, thus, defend the uniform's honor. By naming 1965 as the date of the senior laboratory technician's slide into alcoholism, they turn a blind eye to the fact that his consumption of alcohol had, wrote one insider, obviously gone beyond the boundaries of degustation even before 1965. It is another matter entirely that this particular year turned out to be a fateful year in the history of Filipp's fall: Varvara Petrovna died in 1965. She was the only person who had been restraining Filipp at the precipice that had long loomed.

His relationship toward his father was respectful but could not be called love. Meaning, perhaps, that it was love, but a love that preferred not to meet with its object, inasmuch as possible. Filipp avoided contact with his father from a very early age. The general had never been rough with his son and had not even raised his voice at him, but that fact had not made their relationship any warmer.

Freud played no part here. If Filipp was jealous of his father's attachment to anyone, it was most likely to fate, which distributes such unequal gifts to people close to one another. He felt like a shadow of his father, and that annoyed him. Abstracting oneself from Filipp's personal defining traits, it is appropriate to ask: was it possible at all to love a person like the general? Varvara Petrovna considered it possible.

In the end, things even worked out that the general spent his nights in one room and Varvara Petrovna and her son in another. From the perspective of housing permits, this division seemed impeccable. The Kolpakov family lived in one room, the general in another, and in the third were Varvara Petrovna and Filipp, whose father was never officially determined. Nevertheless, even an official determination of paternity would never have canceled out the striking dissimilarity between the general and his son.

Varvara Petrovna's death caused yet more estrangement between them. Now, they almost never communicated. Filipp locked himself in his room when he came home from work. One could gauge what happened in the room only by his departures for the bathroom during the night: there was paralytic shuffling of feet and spasmodic groping at the whitewashed walls in the hallway. Nothing was known, either, about what happened when he was at work, though his early returns home on cold days evoked constant and unvarying questions from the Kolpakov family. From time to time, acquaintances told the general that his son had been sitting for long periods on benches at the former Tsar's Garden. That he was standing on the little bridge over the Uchan-su River, leaning heavily on the railing, or simply dozing at the bus station snack bar. The general would nod silently in reply. When he ran into his son on the embankment during daytime hours, he realized Filipp was no longer working anywhere. Filipp refused the help (including money) that the general offered. Eventually, he disappeared.

What was later called a disappearance was most likely an unexpected departure. During the general's usual outing to the jetty (everyone knew very well what time that was), Filipp showed up at the apartment with a large suitcase. According to Kolpakov, who had recently finished his army service, it was a typical demob suitcase, with aluminum stars fastened to it, a decal of an unknown beauty (made in the GDR), and sweeping letters that indicated the air force. According to Kolpakov, Filipp was absolutely sober. He spent no more than a half-hour in the room then left with his own suitcase (purchased, in Kolpakov's opinion, at the Yalta flea market), locking the door of his room with a key and saying nothing. Nobody saw him after that.

'No, people saw him,' Zoya corrected herself after pausing. 'He came over soon after the general's death. They looked at him like he was from Mars.'

Filipp's room was vacant for several years, until his absence was officially determined. The general had no rights to the room: his marriage to Varvara Petrovna was not registered and Filipp had not even used his name. According to a decision at Yalta's city hall, the vacant room was given to Nina Fedorovna. The housing commission that came to assume the room used the word *emptied*. When they forced open the door Filipp had locked, the meaning of the word became apparent to its full extent. It turned out that behind the door there were no books, no furniture, not even any flower pots. There was nothing at all in the room.

8

Solovyov's doorbell rang at eight o'clock the next morning. It was Zoya.

'It's Saturday,' she said. 'I'm going to the beach. Want to come with me?'

Solovyov could not wake up at all. It seemed like he kept having a strange, perhaps not completely seemly, dream, in which either Zoya or Leeza Larionova was waking him up early in the morning . . .

'Yes, I do.'

Leeza Larionova really had woken him up when he was young, and he had liked that. She would appear soundlessly, like the first snow, which betrayed its own arrival by imparting a certain glow to a room and an improbable whiteness to the ceiling. She would close the door behind her and look at him silently. He would wake up from that gaze.

'Of course I do.'

He was planning to invite Zoya to have some breakfast and was about to put on the teakettle but Zoya said they could have breakfast at the beach. She even refused to sit down and half-smiled as she observed Solovyov hastily tucking his shirt into his shorts.

At the beach they bought a few hot savory pastries—
chebureki—and two bottles of cola. They settled on their
towels and began their breakfast. The *chebureki* turned out
to be so hot—and greasy, too—that Solovyov froze in a
position of bewildered expectation, his back straightened,
and making a helpless gesture. The fatty liquid oozed
through his fingers and disappeared into the pebbles,
steaming. Zoya took some tissues out of her bag and wiped
Solovyov's hands, one finger at a time, unhurried, then
showed him how to hold a *cheburek* properly. She was never
at a loss, this Chekhov Museum employee, even in the most
complex of situations.

But the cola was cold, very cold. And not fatty. Solovyov
placed the neck of the bottle to his mouth and observed the
cola's vortex-like motion inside the bottle. What seethed right
in front of Solovyov's own eyes blended with the surf, even
seeming larger and more significant than the surf, and it
entered his parched throat as if it were the Black Sea's most
festive wave. He drank the whole bottle without stopping.

After breakfast, there was swimming. As they approached
the water (Zoya took Solovyov by the hand), they took
several steps in the foam of a departing wave and walked
into the approaching wave. The feeling of *the first time* did
not leave Solovyov. Surprised at his own recklessness, he
followed Zoya into the deep water. His froggish flailing was
no match for the rhythmic smoothness of Zoya's motions,
but he was swimming even so, and he was swimming
without anyone's help.

Zoya's obvious superiority did not dishearten Solovyov;
on the contrary, it probably attracted him. It might even
have aroused him a little. In the end, superiority in the

watery element really indicates nothing; everything could take a completely different turn on solid ground anyway. But every bar set higher than his own gave rise to Solovyov's competitive interest, and that interest (as he pondered the matter in hindsight) had been lacking in his relationship with Leeza. Why had Leeza been embarrassed about her merits?

The sun was no longer a morning sun and it stood, unmoving, somewhere over the central part of the beach, burning full blast. Zoya took out some thin lotion that squeezed out on Solovyov's scorching back with a snorting sound. An instant later, he sensed it spreading concentrically along his neck, shoulder blades, and lower back. The lotion's cool freshness was becoming a quality of Zoya's fingers.

'You know, I keep thinking about what the general dictated to my mother. You must want to find that?'

She had switched to the informal *you*. And so naturally.

'Yes, I do.'

Zoya's fingers were massaging Solovyov's thighs. He felt his legs shuddering, involuntarily, in time with Zoya's motions. It felt to him as if the whole beach was enviously following along with his pleasure, not allowing him to receive that pleasure to its full extent.

'Those sheets of paper couldn't have just vanished without a trace. This doesn't hurt?' He sensed the rhythm of Zoya's hands somewhere a little below his knee. 'I think I even know where they could be.'

Zoya held her pause. Solovyov turned, grasping that a continuation would not follow in the same breath.

'Where?'

'At Kozachenko's. Those dung beetles were digging up

everything they could while my mother was busy having me at the maternity hospital.'

The Kozachenko couple rolling a ball of manure popped up in Solovyov's consciousness: sheets of the general's memoirs, stuck to the sides of the ball, flashed through his mind. Zoya thought the younger Kozachenko would not give up those sheets very easily. Not because he needed them (what, after all, could he have done with them?) but because of the unshakable inherited rule not to let out of one's hands anything that had ever fallen into them.

Now Zoya—they had left the beach and were walking slowly along Botkinskaya Street—had a plan. Solovyov looked from time to time at the museum employee's jet-black hair, which was tangled after swimming; he was discovering her for himself all over again. Absolutely nothing Chekhovian remained in what she was proposing. Zoya thought the only chance of obtaining the manuscript from Taras Kozachenko was to conduct a secret search of his, Taras's, room. Zoya leaned on Solovyov's shoulder as she shook beach pebbles out of her sandal.

'But maybe,' Solovyov was awkwardly supporting Zoya by the waist, '. . . maybe we should start by actually asking Taras?'

'No way. Then he'll bury that manuscript once and for all and we'll never see it again. Our strength is in him not knowing *what*, exactly, we're going to look for.'

Solovyov looked at Zoya with doubt; his gaze did not escape her.

'This was dreamt up for your sake, after all . . .'

Solovyov felt that in full. Lagging a half-step behind Zoya, his shoulders grazed against willow branches that drooped almost to the sidewalk and he thought about the unpredictability of a historian's work.

When they reached her house, she asked him to come inside. All the residents were present on Saturday. Besides Taras, Yekaterina Ivanovna Kolpakova was standing in the kitchen: Solovyov had only heard about her up until now. Despite Galina Artemovna (Taras's mother) poisoning Yekaterina Ivanovna's husband; despite his cheating on Yekaterina Ivanovna with that very same Kozachenko woman and his murder of Petr Terentyevich, Taras's father; and despite, finally, Galina Artemovna ending her life as a result of all those events . . . The relationships among those still alive were completely calm. Their relationships could even be called amicable, to that certain degree possible under communal apartment conditions.

Among Russian people, a vendetta ceases just as suddenly, and without motivation, as it begins. Hostility fades in a chain of uninteresting events, just as an echo fades in a sultry Crimean pine forest and just as graves fade in the tall weeds of Russian cemeteries. Yekaterina and Taras frequently went to Yalta's cemetery together, which was notable, even by Russian standards. This was not so much a triumph of reconciliation as a matter of something being convenient and perhaps even mutually beneficial for both of them. Yekaterina Ivanovna bought inexpensive begonias for the three graves and Taras brought a cart with a twenty-liter canister of water, something that was in catastrophically short supply at the cemetery. While visiting their relatives (*landsmen*, as Yekaterina Ivanovna sometimes jokingly called them), they divided the begonias and the water evenly amongst the graves.

Zoya and Solovyov stayed in the kitchen after greeting the neighbors. To Solovyov's surprise, his companion not only entered into conversation with the others but also asked him to tell them about the Hermitage—you know, what you were telling me today—after which she went to her room anyway, leaving Solovyov in the middle of the kitchen with his strange story. Taras and Yekaterina Ivanovna stood in the corner, leaning against the general's cabinet, and were, ludicrously enough, truly prepared to take in Solovyov's narrative. After stating that the Hermitage, along with the Louvre, is one of the leading museums in the world, Solovyov noted, unseen by his listeners, that Zoya had left her room with a finger to her lips. As Solovyov told of the number of exhibits at the Hermitage (to Yekaterina Ivanovna's restrained moan), Zoya flattened herself against the wall and sidestepped her way to Taras's door. Solovyov faltered from the unexpectedness. Zoya made a scary face and—making her hand into a sort of bird's beak—gestured to the storyteller that he should not stop speaking.

If one were to stand next to each exhibit for thirty seconds (Zoya disappeared into Taras's room) and be at the Hermitage every day from morning until evening, one would need eight years to see *all* the exhibits.

'Eight?' Yekaterina Ivanovna asked for clarification.

Zoya appeared in Taras's doorway, noiselessly tossed up her hands, and disappeared into the depths of the room once again.

'No fewer than eight,' Solovyov reiterated.

Taras took a bottle of kefir from the refrigerator, shook it, and poured some into a tea bowl with chipped edges. He chose an unscathed section and pressed his puffy lips to it.

Taras asked nothing about the Hermitage. He listened silently to Solovyov, licking away his broad white mustache from time to time. And Solovyov, who would never have agreed of his own free will to infiltrate Taras's room, felt like a genuine plotter, if only because he had to conspire a story with a plot for those standing before him. His descriptions grew more emotional, evoking in his listeners interest mixed with light surprise. The surprise increased when the story suddenly cut off (Zoya had silently closed the door behind her and slipped into her room) and Solovyov vanished to Zoya's room, saying goodbye along the way. Those who remained, standing, had the sense of something left unsaid.

'I didn't find the manuscript,' said Zoya after Solovyov closed the door behind him. 'But this turned up in a drawer.'

She twirled a ring of keys on her finger.

'I'm sure he has the manuscript. We'll have time to look at everything carefully on Monday, when he goes to work.'

'Zoya . . .'

This turned out to be the only objection Solovyov was allowed to utter. Zoya placed her finger with the keys to his lips and peered into the hallway. Once she was certain nobody was left in the kitchen, she stole toward the front door on tiptoe and beckoned to Solovyov. Involuntarily copying Zoya's motions, he took several steps toward the exit. He stopped between Zoya and the door. Her hand touched the massive hook hanging on an eye, attached to the side of the door that did not open. The hook readily began swinging as it slid along an indentation that had formed over the years.

'Foucault's pendulum,' she whispered right into his ear. 'I'll take Monday off.'

Solovyov spent Sunday morning in church. This was the Alexander Nevsky Cathedral, which was elegant, its five cupolas towering over Kirov Street (formerly Autskaya Street). As Solovyov ascended the stone staircase, he imagined the general entering the church.

The general came here often during his trips to Yalta. In the winter of 1920, he flew up this staircase like a large bird of prey; the flaps of his military overcoat extended over the steps, his entourage dispersed at his sides. He walked a little more slowly in the summer, as if he were watching a military formation on the platz, but he saw messy columns of paupers who had flowed there from all of boundless Russia, as they did in those days. A military orderly walking a half-step behind him tossed coins to them.

It was stuffy in the church during the summer. Neither an open side door nor a flung-open window lent any coolness. Through them poured Yalta's damp, sweltering heat, scented with acacias and the sea, and vaguely trembling over the candles' unmoving flame. Streaks of sunlight pierced the duskiness inside the church, illuminating the large drops of sweat that flew off the priest's nose and chin with his every movement. Even the general, who usually hardly perspired, kept wiping his forehead and neck with a silk handkerchief. In those services, which were anything but simple, Larionov saw a special southern charm that consisted of the fact that, for one thing, at the end of the liturgy he would take a hundred-meter walk along Morskaya Street and find himself on an embankment that glistened in the surf and he would breathe, full-chested, after unfastening the top buttons of his service jacket.

He came here as a very elderly man, too. With a cane,

and wearing a canvas jacket with a pocket stretched by a massive case for his glasses. People recognized him, as in days past. As in days past, they stepped aside, making way for him, and took deep bows for the coins he gave them. He walked with the special firmness of one striving to maintain his balance (occasionally he swayed anyway). At times he would stop, place both his hands on his cypress cane, and inspect the toes of his shoes. Sometimes he would sit on a bench in the yard and observe from the shadows, businesslike, as people carried infants into the church, straightening lacy bonnets along the way. Observe how, in the far corner of the church grounds, water from a hose moistened dust and the first drops that fell on the asphalt turned to steam. In those moments, his face lacked all expression and seemed to be falling away. It brought to mind a mask that had been removed, and came to life only with the old man's barely noticeable chewing.

Looking at the general, it was difficult to grasp whether he noticed everything happening around him or if, according to the words of a poet unfamiliar to him, his eyes were addressing other days. Those who observed the general in those moments (including in the line of duty), confirmed afterwards that they did not consider his gaze to have halted, despite the motionlessness of his face. That gaze might be categorized as unlifelike, unlit, or unearthly, but not at all halted.

Yes, General Larionov's eyes were addressing other days. Even so, nothing escaped their attention. Through the paramilitary guise of paupers, vintage 1920, wearing uniform tunics with holes instead of epaulets and through carts that delivered barrels of water to the church (they were rolled

from the carts onto the earth along twenty-inch boards),
the general's eyes undeniably saw trolleybuses that drove
noiselessly along the former Autskaya Street behind the
church fence, carrying 1970s female worshippers, and saw
women taking neatly folded headscarves from their bags in
front of the church and hurriedly tying them. They used
their thumbs to tuck in strands of hair that came out. Why
were there hardly any men there?

When Solovyov showed up at Zoya's on Monday morning,
none of the others were in the apartment. After closing the
front door behind him, Zoya lowered the huge hook with
a clang. 'That's just in case,' she said.

Solovyov remembered the pail he and Leeza used to set
out as a signal but did not mention this memory. He was
experiencing excitement of a completely different kind now.

With a calm motion that was somehow even expert, Zoya
turned the key in Kozachenko's door, opened it, and
gestured to Solovyov, inviting him inside. Solovyov initially
wanted to make the same gesture but then he crossed the
threshold after realizing that gallantry was out of place in
this situation.

The first thing he saw in the room was the oak cabinet
with the two-headed eagles. The elder Kozachenko had
knocked his head on one of those heads. The double bed
was the center of the drama that had played out. And so
Kozachenko the younger had not thrown away the furniture.
In the corner, displayed below a decorative Ukrainian towel,
was a cross-stitched portrait of poet Taras Shevchenko. To
the right of the portrait (and how about that—Solovyov did
not even grasp this at first) were two photographs of Zoya.
Zoya in the kitchen at the general's table with a vase of

chrysanthemums in the background. Zoya at the beach. The bottom of her bathing suit slightly slipping off a bone covered with taut skin. Solovyov thought the life of a bachelor in the company of photographs like that could not be easy. Even under Shevchenko's supervision.

'Is he in love with you?'

Zoya shrugged. Standing at the bureau desk, she pulled out drawer after drawer, looking through the contents. Zoya's calm in conducting this quiet search surprised Solovyov, who was, at the very least, extraordinarily agitated, even though he was not shaking. Her thumb inspected stacks of paper (blank, as a rule), sliding along the edge of the sheets. The sheets generated a light fan-like sound at the motion, reminiscent of the rustling of a deck of cards being shuffled before a deal. Sometimes there was jingling, sometimes there was clicking. Zoya would lay items on the desk then put them away after she had finished looking through yet another drawer.

Solovyov confined himself to examining Taras's scanty book selection. The majority of them were devoted to the city of Alupka and the Vorontsov Palace. It was emerging that Taras had a one-track mind. The only book unrelated to the palace was a publication describing various alarm systems.

'What does he do for work?'

'He's a guard at the Vorontsov Palace.'

Zoya looked through piles of linens, plunging her hand deep under each sheet. The linens were shabby. There were holes and frayed spots even on the folds. It inopportunely occurred to Solovyov that they could even be the result of Kolpakov's activeness. Objects frequently outlive those who have used them. Bed linens with Chekhov's embroidered initials had been preserved, too. The bed in the museum was still made with them. Although . . . Maybe these holes were the consequence of the love-struck Taras's insomnia? Solovyov cast another glance at the photographs.

'I found it.'

Zoya said that with the same calm that she had been searching, but Solovyov flinched. Was that really possible? Contrary to Solovyov's absolute lack of faith in success (and he himself did not understand why he had gotten mixed up in all this) there were yellowed sheets of paper, with fine writing, between two flowery duvet covers.

'It's my mother's handwriting.'

Solovyov lifted the top part of the linen pile and Zoya pulled the papers out of the cabinet with a magician's gesture. This was a victory. Despite the dubious method of achieving it, it remained a victory, and what a victory! In the end, Taras had no rights whatsoever to the manuscript. In the end, his parents had simply stolen this manuscript . . . Researcher Solovyov's brief history, which had unfolded primarily in libraries and archives, had made an obvious *salto mortale* and transformed into a detective story. Never before had the search for scholarly truth seemed so gripping to him. The dramatism of research, something unknown to the world, took on visible forms when it came out into the open. Solovyov stood by the window and held the sheets of paper on his outstretched hand. He was not reading them. He simply inspected Zoya's mother's minute handwriting, sensing Zoya's breathing at his temple. From time to time, little bird-like figures appeared over the handwriting, introducing additions and edits in another hand, one very familiar to Solovyov. Meaning the general had worked on the dictated manuscript later . . . From somewhere in the very depths of those lines—and Zoya's hand was squeezing his elbow—Yekaterina Ivanovna's sad eyes slowly surfaced. Yekaterina Ivanovna was standing on a little metal bridge that had been built to reach the terrace of the next house (a bed's headboard served as its railing); she held a grocery bag and was wordlessly watching Solovyov through the window glass.

They left Kozachenko's room. Zoya locked it with the key and hurried to unhook the front door. Pressing her back to the door of her own room, she listened to Yekaterina Ivanovna's heavy steps in the entryway, reminding Solovyov in some sense of Princess Tarakanova in her dungeon. Zoya quietly let Solovyov out of the apartment after Yekaterina Ivanovna entered her own room.

Walking downhill along Botkinskaya, the uneasy Solovyov wondered what would happen to Zoya now. His unease was momentary, though, and without it, Solovyov, a person with scruples, could not have surrendered himself to the joy of possessing the manuscript. The small packet of sheets, which were inscribed with a compact, precise script, belonged only to him. It fluttered with each swing of an arm that was beginning to tan, and (this was unbelievable) the packet evoked not the slightest interest among pedestrians.

Solovyov did not feel like going home. It was tough to be alone with his happiness, just as it is tough when someone's relationship is condemned, illegitimate, and, perhaps, even criminal. People put that out in the open. They rush out in public with it, visiting receptions, clubs, and shows

. . . Solovyov went to the embankment. As he stepped down from its upper sections, he saw a row of seats like those that line stadiums. These grandstands for spectators faced the best show on earth: the sea.

Solovyov delighted in the motion of the waves and himself felt a little like the general. Like the inveterate smoker who lingers before lighting a cigarette (a special type of voluptuousness), Solovyov was in no hurry to begin reading. Rejoicing in his spoils by feel, he stroked the slightly limp edge of the sheets and knocked the packet against his knees to give it an ideally correct appearance.

The general's memoirs began like this, 'At the age of ten, my parents sent me to the Second Cadet Corps.' Ten years old. The description of everything that happened before that had been published by Dupont, who, as we know, assumed that a continuation existed. And so the French researcher's scholarly intuition permitted her to predict this sweet moment Solovyov was experiencing on the embankment in Yalta. He read sheet after sheet, placing what he had read at the end of the packet. Distancing himself from the first sheet even as he inexorably neared it. Tearing himself away from Akinfeeva's close lines from time to time, he scanned the horizon and thought about how his reading process was akin to a round-the-world journey whose goal is to return to the starting point.

9

The general's parents sent him to the Second Cadet Corps at the age of ten. We will acknowledge the anachronism of the previous sentence and leave it at that. In some sense, he was already a general as a ten-year-old because strictly (although nonhistorically) speaking, he was always a general. Who could have dared imagine him as anything other than a general? Dupont had already posed that question in her day. And—in the article 'This Is Not Today's Tribe'—she answered in her characteristically uncompromising manner: nobody.

In dictating to Nina Fedorovna his recollections of the years of his life at the Second Corps, the general emphasized that the gold stitching on the black uniforms at that educational institution was somewhat thinner than in other corps (the First, the Nikolaevsky, and even the Alexandersky, for example), not to mention that the trousers for the Second Corps' cadets, unlike those for many other corps, were dark blue, not black. The general also pointed out that later, when weapons handling was introduced in the combatant companies, the Second Corps was given the right to carry dragoon sabers on sword belts as the guards did.

They rose early, at six in the morning. To a horn. That was fine in summer, during the white nights, but it was intolerable in winter. In summer, the future general rose a half hour before reveille so he could greet the horn fully conscious, in order not to let it horn in on his sweetest morning dreams. That did not work out in winter. He could not bear to leave a bed warmed during the night and plunge into the bedroom's penetrating cold. The temperature never rose above ten degrees there, that was the rule. In the late nineteenth century, it was not recommended that young men sleep in warm quarters.

They washed in cold water to the waist and that was a little worse than the horn. They went out on the platz in just woolen jackets. In any weather. It is possible that this Spartan training drew cadet Larionov's attention to King Leonidas's feat. The opposite, however, cannot be ruled out, either: that the Spartan king's feat reconciled Larionov to such a harsh routine. What does remain a fact is that both the Spartan training, and the cadet's extensive familiarity with the course of battle, came in very, very handy for him during his mature years.

When he walked outside for morning formations, Larionov would try not to notice the snowflakes melting underneath his collar. He thought about how the Spartans—who, generally speaking, were connoisseurs of difficulty—did not have a problem like the Russian cold. Larionov would lift his head from time to time and look at his classmates huddled in the darkness of the December platz. They were small, not awake, and covered in bits of ice. In the glint of the gaslights, only the insignias on their hats, polished to glimmering, and their red noses, were visible. Their eyes watered from the prickly morning wind and from sleep that had not passed. The difficulties did not break them. On the contrary, they nourished them, tempering body and spirit. They grew into strong fellows and genuine officers. 'They have all died,' the general wrote over one line.

Cadet Lanskoy had a special place in the general's life at that time. The general obviously singled out this handsome and, judging from the description, arrogant boy in his reminiscences. Cadets Larionov and Lanskoy stuck together for several years. Their relations were not friendship in the usual sense. Lanskoy did absolutely nothing to bring about or, later, strengthen those relations. His contribution to the friendship was that he permitted himself to be admired.

In some certain way, Lanskoy was worth admiring. He was possibly the best student of all, without making visible efforts. He pronounced his answers softly and even, somehow, condescendingly. This annoyed the teachers, but there was nothing to find fault in. His audacity was reckless. On a dare, he swam under the ice of the Zhdanovka River, from one hole in the ice to another. Despite very strict rules, he sometimes left the corps' billeting before bedtime and returned toward morning, through the window.

One time, cadet Larionov escaped with him. After changing into civilian clothes, they rambled around snow-covered Petersburg for half the night. Larionov felt absolutely wretched about it. Violating discipline felt like genuine betrayal to him. He himself would have been hard pressed to say *what*, exactly, he had betrayed, but he had no doubt that betrayal had come to pass. Around 2:30, the cadets dropped in at a tavern and ordered a half-glass of vodka each. They managed to return unnoticed that night but in the morning Larionov, who had never before been sick, got sick. His temperature rose. He was hit with the chills. Tears streamed from his eyes. They were tears of repentance but nobody knew that. Nobody but Lanskoy. He visited Larionov at the infirmary on the third day and said, 'Larionov, you're a decent person. You're sick from violating the routine. You shouldn't have escaped with me.'

Cadet Larionov expected his friend to visit him again but that did not happen. After Larionov's release from the infirmary, Lanskoy greeted him from afar. Larionov nodded and did not even approach him. They fell out of touch after graduating from the corps.

The majority of subjects (other than languages) were taught at the corps by military men. Cadets were supposed to have six lessons a day, followed by horseback riding and drill training. At first, riding devoured almost all Larionov's attention. It is likely that this is the age that should be considered the beginning of the general's long conversations with horses, something referred to in the literature (such as cavalry commander Semyon Budyonny's *A Good Attitude Toward Horses*) multiple times.

After familiarizing himself with the events at Thermopylae, tactics became another of the boy's favorite subjects. When he read those lines, Solovyov recalled a pencil sketch of a battle map that he had discovered in a Petersburg archive. By comparing the document with analogous sketches—at least eighteen battle maps of Thermopylae are attributed to cadet Larionov—it was possible to prove, without a doubt, that it belonged to the future general. The particular interest of that discovery consisted not only in the drawing being the earliest of those known but also that Leonidas himself was depicted in the upper right-hand corner of the sheet, in a general's epaulets and with a two-headed eagle on his chest.

Among non-military subjects, Larionov liked dance. Considering the child's overall mentality, this passion might appear somewhat unexpected, but that was only at first glance. Unlike their successors, in those days Russian officers loved to dance and did so capably. The Russian officers' corps was very refined. Their well-balanced development— this was exactly what the cadets of the Second Corps were striving for—supposed more than manliness. It supposed elegance, too.

On top of all that, the cadet's attitude toward dance was affected by a statement from the corps' charter that had been framed and placed in the dance hall. According to Gurkovsky's *The Cadet Corps of the Russian Empire*, the note held that the system for teaching dance was developed by a French dance school and took into consideration grace and beauty as well as the human body's possibilities for expressing itself, both when resting and when moving. This text was the first to direct Larionov's attention to the human figure's plentiful possibilities.

The child also had a weakness for extracurricular reading. A housefather conducted this, reading classic Russian litera-ture aloud to his charges. After noting Larionov's interest in reading—as well as the cadet's exemplary pronunciation—the housefather often instructed the boy to read aloud. The elderly soldier would sit in a corner of the classroom, cover his eyes with his hand, and listen to his pupil's reading. He would bob his head approvingly in time with the reading, which would have given the impression of absorbed attention had the bobbing not been implausibly rhythmic. Sometimes a faint whistle would sound from his inflated nostrils, through a brush of coarse hair. They read Pushkin's *Poltava*, Lermonotov's *Borodino*, and Gogol's *Taras Bulba*, but everyone especially liked *Singer in the Camp of Russian Warriors*.

The whistling would cease at the first lines of the Zhukovsky. Absolute silence, though, came with a later stanza: 'Our Figner, dressed as an old man, enters / The enemy camp in the dead of night; / Steals like a shadow among their tents, / Sees everything there with his sharp eyes . . .' Over all, just 'Our Figner, dressed as an old man' would have been enough, on its own, to attract attention, pronounced as it was almost as one word. And he was stealing in, too, among tents . . .

In 1894, Larionov allegedly read aloud the short story 'Surgery', which his father had brought for him. Accustomed to Russian classics, the housefather woke up but did not interrupt the cadet. The housefather liked the story, thanks to his own experience in dentistry. Upon learning that Chekhov was the author of the work, he wrote a letter to Lev Tolstoy, asking him if Anton Chekhov was a classic. Tolstoy did not answer. It should be concluded from this that in 1894 Chekhov was not yet a classic. Construction had not even begun on his Yalta home.

The reading repertoire for the wards of the Second Cadet Corps was not limited to the aforementioned works, however. Under their mattresses, hiding from their house-father's eyes, were novels by Madame Genlis, verses from

Mister Barkov, and Nikolai Chernyshevsky's *What Is to Be Done?*—all copied out in the cadets' distinct hands. When the elderly general recalled those years, he expressed admiration in the fact of copying Chernyshevsky's novel. It was not just the copying but also the very reading of that thing that seemed like some sort of feat to him. From the memoirist's point of view, Russian letters had never generated a more helpless text.

The old housefather discovered those books during an inspection of the cadets' bedroom. After lengthy convincing by his students, he left them Madame de Genlis. In the end, he even agreed to turn a blind eye to Barkov. But he simply could not reconcile himself with Nikolai Chernyshevsky's work: the very mention of that surname sent him into a fit of rage. He threatened to expel from the corps and court martial the boy who had copied the novel. His identity could not be established then (it is possible that nobody wanted to), but the general knew it well. He considered it possible to mention only eight decades later, when there was no longer any threat to the copyist. He was cadet Lanskoy.

The housefather's reaction was explainable. The Second Cadet Corps felt a share of responsibility in everything concerning Chernyshevsky. He had entered the corps as a tutor in 1853, while preparing his master's dissertation. It is unlikely that this particular circumstance served as the beginning of all his troubles, but speaking purely chronologically—there is no getting around this—that circumstance preceded his troubles. Temporal as well as spatial patterns were later established, too.

Colonel Pazukhin, the ballistics instructor, drew widespread attention to the fact that the key points in the city for this writer and democrat fell along a single straight line. The

Second Cadet Corps (place of work) ➜ No. 7, Zhdanovskaya Embankment (place of residence) ➜ Peter and Paul Fortress (place of imprisonment) ➜ Mytinskaya Square (place of mock civil execution). In becoming familiar with these patterns, cadet Larionov could not have known that, by virtue of the connectedness of everything on earth, historian Solovyov—a researcher studying General Larionov's battles with the consequences of Nikolai Chernyshevsky's work— would rent a room on that very same straight line (No. 11, Zhdanovskaya Embankment). This method for structuring thoughts, which was far from simple, forced Solovyov to tear himself away from the text and look at the sail of a distant yacht. A moment later he was reading again.

Entering the corps did not at all signify that the future general was isolated from the outside world. After passing an exam for his ability to salute and stand at attention, he was granted the right to go outside. Like cadets of other corps, the wards of the Second Corps had but one limitation: they were prohibited from walking on the sunny side of Nevsky Prospekt. It is possible that this prohibition was seen as a part of their Spartan education, as a necessary measure for acquainting the cadets with the shady side of life.

Sometimes the cadets were taken to the theater. These outings were a real holiday for them. Their time did not yet possess contemporary entertainment opportunities. Theater, which has now receded into the realm of the elite, was at the vanguard of the nineteenth century's *entertainment industry*. As a means for education, theater was considered a mixed blessing or—depending upon the type of show—even dangerous. The theater was closed for Great Lent.

At the cadet corps, the preferred theater was the Alexandrinsky and the preferred show was Alexander Ostrovsky's *The Storm*. According to the future general's calculations, the cadets went to see *The Storm* sixteen times during his years of schooling. Such an obvious preference for one play over all others was explained by the housefather's personal biases. His sympathy for Katerina manifested itself so visibly at the theater that those around him would begin to turn to look at him. From the very first line of the show, the aging soldier would sit, grasping at the armrests of his seat. Indignant at Boris's spinelessness, he would crumple his peaked army cap and hit himself on the knee with it. During Kabanikha's monologues, he would lift his own huge fist and, slowly, with a despairing grimace, sink it into the loge's raspberry-colored velvet. When Katerina said, 'Why is it that people can't fly!' the housemaster's facial features would collapse immediately and he would cover his face with his hands, then begin sobbing as loudly as if he were baying. The civilian audience, who had already long been looking into the hall rather than the stage, would fall silent in respect. They were shaken by the Russian Army's sentimentality.

Larionov returned home during school vacations. Oddly enough, his parents' attempts to spoil the child brought him no joy whatsoever. He visited sweet shops primarily out of filial obedience and, to the surprise of those around him, did not exhibit his previous enjoyment when washing down airy éclairs with orangeade. It seemed to him (and this was the whole point) that with conduct such as this, he was betraying the Spartan ideals he had adopted, that each outing to an establishment of this sort nullified his months of drill training, washing with ice-cold water, and wakeups before the morning horn. All that reconciled the cadet with visits to the sweet shop was that, generally speaking, the food at the corps was pretty good. According to those in command, food limitations were not part of a Spartan-style education. Future officers needed to eat well.

Larionov's parents' non-military conversations seemed strange to the boy. He heard vagary and something uncon-vincing in the tone of their conversations, though the topics under discussion agitated him very much at the time, despite (or perhaps because of?) their civilian nature. And so the cadet recalled discussions of the life philosophy of their distant relative Baroness von Kruger, who had entered into marriage four times. They had talked about the baroness in the family before, too, but this grew more frequent when she entered into new marriages. At the same time, the elder Larionovs, who held dear their repu-tation as liberals, allowed no direct condemnation of the baroness and when in public even remarked along the lines that what was happening with the baroness only empha-sized her exactitude and maximalism.

The fact that Baroness von Kruger gathered all four husbands together and had dinner with them at a restaurant called The Bear became a critical point in the Larionovs' relationship with their relative. Larionov's mother burst into tears upon learning that news and said she would not allow the baroness in their home. At the meek objections of Larionov's father, who held that such a meeting could not make their relative's quadruple-marriage situation any worse, Larionov's mother shouted, 'How can you not under-

stand that this is absolutely, simply shockingly unseemly?!'
The cadet, who had witnessed the scene, mentally swore
to himself not to do anything of the kind. For many years,
the notion of shocking actions was, for Larionov, linked to
that very incident.

'To that very inci—' is, if one is absolutely precise, the
end of the manuscript that reached Solovyov. The page to
which '. . . dent' was carried was missing and thus, in some
sense, the full word was reconstructed. Solovyov looked
through all the pages again. There was no doubt: the manuscript was incomplete. He thought about how it held a huge
value even though it was incomplete, since any publication
of new information about the general's childhood years . . .

Even so, his primary feeling was disappointment. During
the time he was reading the manuscript, Solovyov had
managed to get used to its completeness, rather he had not
allowed the possibility that it was incomplete. With its
sudden cut-off, it was as if Solovyov had slipped from the
height of happiness where he had initially found himself.
'There it is,' thought the historian as he stood, 'ingratitude.'
His legs had fallen asleep from sitting still and he had difficulty negotiating the several steps that led to the top of the
embankment.

Solovyov bought a plastic folder at a kiosk, placed the
manuscript inside, and set off aimlessly along the embankment. He skirted the Oreanda Hotel and ended up by the
monument to Maxim Gorky. He could not remember
anything the general had said about Gorky, though he
certainly had said something about him . . . Gorky was
standing in his peasant shirt and tar-blackened boots. The

road behind him divided in two: an upper road and a lower road. Not a word on the marble pedestal indicated what awaited the traveler. Along which road, one might ask, would Gorky himself have traveled? After choosing the lower, Solovyov remembered, word for word, the general's statement about the writer: 'He is walking along a downward path' (1930). This was truly a Yaltan image. Other than the embankment, all the city's paths led downward.

There was a café at the end of the lower, tree-lined path (interwoven acacia branches, a thick shadow). They served cold kvass soup as a first course and rice pilaf as the second. The pilaf was nothing special but the soup was wonderful. Solovyov ordered another serving of soup instead of dessert and ate it slowly. Very slowly, the way one eats something that cannot go cold. He was sitting on a covered veranda, watching the tablecloth and a mysterious potted plant flutter in a refreshing wind. Solovyov ate the soup; his free hand rested on a cool metal railing. Beyond the railing—with no transition whatsoever—there began the huge blue sea.

He did not return home until after dark. The doorbell rang about fifteen minutes after his arrival. Solovyov was not expecting anyone. Knowing that one should exercise caution in southern cities in the evenings, he asked, 'Who's there?'

'Zoya.'

Solovyov could not have confused that voice with any other. Zoya truly was standing outside the door. She had changed out of the gauzy, sheer dresses he had seen on her all these days and into blue jeans and a light-colored T-shirt. A gym bag hung on her shoulder. Solovyov stepped aside and Zoya came in, unhurried. There was something in her new guise that made her look like a camper, but there was no doubt that it became her. She even sat down as people sit at a train station, placing the bag on her knees and pulling her crossed feet under the chair.

'How's the manuscript?' Zoya asked. 'Were your hopes justified?'

'It turned out to be incomplete . . . it cuts off in the middle of a word, can you believe it?'

'Is that right?'

Zoya unzipped the bag with a slow, somehow even sleepy motion.

'That manuscript's still very important,' said Solovyov, checking himself. 'I couldn't have dreamt of a stroke of luck like that.'

'Well then, we'll look more,' said Zoya, extracting a huge bunch of grapes. 'We need to find it in its entirety.'

'Need to? But where?'

'We have to think.'

A two-liter plastic bottle appeared on the table right after the grapes. Contrary to the inscription on the label, it was certainly not Pepsi-Cola sloshing inside. The dense, wavy flow along the bottle's walls attested to the nobleness of the beverage. Just as a person's breeding can be sensed by a very first motion.

'It's Massandra wine, Nesterenko brought it,' said Zoya, nodding at the bottle. 'His sister works at the winery.'

There were no wine glasses to be found in the apartment so Solovyov brought two faceted glasses from the kitchen. He held the massive bottle with both hands as he poured the wine. The wine came out in irregular glugs, yielding from time to time to air that wanted to enter. The bottle seemed like a living being to Solovyov. It grunted, as if offended, when it inhaled. Its plastic sides trembled spasmodically under the young man's hands. He set the bottle on the floor after pouring half a glass each for himself and Zoya. The vessel turned out to be disproportionally large for the table where they were sitting, and even the faceted glasses lacked the power to ease that contrast.

'To the success of our searches,' said Zoya.

The wine's unusual properties stunned Solovyov. Its full body and bouquet reminded him of a liqueur, but still it remained wine. After drinking some, Solovyov imagined what the contents of amphorae had been like. He sensed the flavor of a nectar he had read about when studying ancient sources. The young historian had no doubt that the ancients had extolled this very liquid. It was this very liquid the Greek gods had tasted during their rare forays into the Northern Black Sea Region.

Zoya saw that he liked the wine. She herself was drinking it in small swallows, first as a lady, and, second, as a person spoiled by a divine beverage. Plucking off the grapes, Zoya brought them to her mouth without hurrying, then placed them between her front teeth. The grapes held that position for a few moments, offering a demonstration of both the elegant form of Zoya's teeth and their whiteness. Then the grapes disappeared in her mouth and rolled around behind her cheeks for a while. The Petersburg researcher found this transfer of grapes erotic but could not bring himself to say anything aloud. Solovyov's helper was, without a doubt, a connoisseur of the grape.

'Taras knows we were in his room today.' Zoya did not

change her pose or stop eating grapes as she announced this. 'Yekaterina Ivanovna told him everything.'

Solovyov leaned against the back of the chair. The old-fashioned lampshade was stratifying in their faceted glasses, blending its dark-pink light with the wine's burgundy color.

'How will you . . .' Solovyov took hold of his glass (the colors disconnected again). 'How will you go home now?'

Zoya shrugged. 'Who the hell knows what that Taras will do? You can never guess what to expect from someone timid like that.' Zoya plucked yet another grape. 'They told me he was beside himself.'

'You can't go home today. Stay with me.'

The grape in her teeth stayed there longer than usual and Solovyov knew Zoya was smiling.

'I think that would look strange. No. I'll crash at the train station today and tomorrow the whole thing will be forgotten. Everything gets forgotten in the end.'

'You're spending tonight at my place.'

Zoya fell silent. She took a sip of wine and used an easy football-like motion to roll a stray grape along the table. They could hear nocturnal cars driving past outside the window, on the former Autskaya Street. The shaven-headed Crimean elite was racing around at high speed in imported cars with blinding headlights. The baleful sighs of a trolleybus were occasionally audible when silence set in. The trolleybus would slow down, its crossbars clicking somewhere up among the junctions of the overhead wires, and then the vehicle would gather speed again. Cafeteria workers—tired and untalkative, with bulging shopping bags at their feet—were riding the dimly lighted trolleybus. Young

Yaltan ladies, their faces made up, were riding. Veterans of various wars, intoxicated by alcohol, were riding; they had put on their medals beforehand so the police would not beat them. The veterans swayed along when the trolleybus turned and their decorations produced a quiet, melodic jingle.

Zoya went to bed on the couch, Solovyov on a folding cot. The only sheets (the same ones Solovyov had been sleeping on) were given to her. Zoya herself expressed readiness to accept them. The guest also assigned sleeping spots. Solovyov was fairly happy that everything was resolving itself without his involvement. Even so, when Zoya flicked the light switch, it was not without sadness that he acknowledged he had assumed events might develop differently. But it turned out this assumption of his was unacceptable for the girl from the Chekhov Museum.

'Good night.' There was the sound of a T-shirt being pulled off.

'Good night.'

Lying in the dark, Solovyov listened, futilely, for Zoya's breathing. The silence in the room felt unnatural to him. He thought that perhaps Zoya was purposely not moving because she was listening for him. He was afraid even to inhale loudly: the fold-out bed let out a savage screech at the slightest motion. He did not know what time it was, though all he would have to do to find out was turn toward the lighted electronic clock. But Solovyov did not turn. He was afraid even to open his eyes.

When he opened them, the room turned out to be less dark. Meaning not absolutely dark. Whether it was the moon or the coming dawn, the outlines of objects could be seen fairly clearly. The bottle's silhouette on the table. An uneaten bunch of grapes resembling Mount Ayu-Dag. The glisten of Zoya's belt buckle on the chair. Solovyov caught his breath: that glisten intensified his feelings to their limit, just as the motion of a train had in another time. Perhaps even more strongly. He tried to figure out if Zoya was sleeping. Her head was dark on the white spot of a pillow; her arms were behind the back of her head. Nobody sleeps like that . . . The fold-out bed squeaked as Solovyov touched the bottom of his belly and sensed moisture. Whether Zoya was sleeping or not—for some reason, Solovyov did not doubt this—she was lying there completely naked.

Cool air was beginning to waft through the open window. That meant it really was dawn.

'I'm cold,' Zoya said, as calmly as if she were continuing a conversation.

'I can close the window,' said Solovyov, not moving.

'I'm cold.'

In that repetition there was no apparent point and there was no intonation—there was nothing there but rhythm. Solovyov recognized that rhythm flawlessly. With a feline motion, he leapt off the fold-out bed without a single squeak. He went over to Zoya's bed and pressed his legs into her. He felt Zoya's hair on his damp skin. A moment later he was lying next to her.

'Hold on . . .'

As if out of nowhere, she took a condom and placed it in Solovyov's hot hand. As he put on the condom, Solovyov had no time to be properly surprised that it had appeared. A second later, Zoya's legs had entwined behind his back with unexpected strength. This was no comparison for Leeza's bashful love. There had never before been such energy, flexibility, and passion in his life. Never before had Solovyov felt such powerlessness over his body. Never before had the image of a boat amid waves been so close for him. That image was the last thing that flashed through Solovyov's mind before his final plunge into the abyss. A hurricane had been hiding behind the museum employee's outward phlegmatism.

10

The next morning (which began late), they realized that this was the day Solovyov had promised to read his paper about General Larionov. The reading was to be held at Zoya's house. Despite recent events, Zoya thought the reading was appropriate; this puzzled even the lecturer himself. He was even more surprised that evening when he was coming into the entryway of the communal apartment and ran straight into Taras. Taras was absolutely calm, even courteous. He was the first to greet the guest, after which he backed away, toward the kitchen, and continued standing there, leaning against the general's cabinet. He was not invited to hear the paper.

The attendees were the same as the first time: the princess plus Shulgin and Nesterenko. It occurred to Solovyov that the fact of the powerful Nesterenko's presence might also be restraining Taras from repeating yesterday's hysterics. In any case (Taras's face expressed its usual shyness), Zoya's neighbor was fully able to calm down naturally. Solovyov himself gradually calmed down, too. Coming here was not nearly as simple for him as he had led Zoya to believe that morning.

Solovyov felt a sudden awkwardness as he took the text of his prepared paper from the folder; this time, the feeling was not related to Taras. What Solovyov wanted to report could not appear either important or even worthy of attention for the group that had gathered. All his findings and corrections regarding the Crimean operations seemed like utter pointlessness by comparison with what they knew about the general. But it was too late to retreat. So Solovyov began his reading.

Strictly speaking, this was not even a reading. When he sensed that method of delivering the material was out of place here, the young historian switched to telling a story; this was close to the text of his paper but did not lack for improvisation. This was happening for the first time in his scholarly life. It was not that he could not render his previous papers without reading aloud—every phrase of what he had written was just right and he knew the texts by heart. The academic honor code mandated speaking from a prepared text. The folder of papers lying on a lectern was the first, albeit most approximate, attestation of a report's scholarliness. It was as if all further qualities of what was pronounced did not exist without the written text. Solovyov knew of only one exception: a paper that Prof. Nikolsky had read at a conference lectern, in a monotone, sentence after sentence, from sheets containing nothing but caricatures sketched with a ballpoint pen. It was Prof. Nikolsky who had forbidden Solovyov from speaking without a written text.

Solovyov did not even glance down as he turned page after page of his paper. A feeling of flight had seized him, almost the same as that first ride on a bicycle. He recalled the dates of battles, the strength of subunits on both sides, and the military ranks of all the senior officers taking part in combat.

The topic of Solovyov's paper was 'General Larionov's Rout of Zhloba's Cavalry Corps.' It concerned a key operation in 1920 that allowed the Whites to hold on to Crimea until late autumn. Solovyov began by briefly touching on the composition of the troops positioned on the front line in Northern Taurida. Here he could not help but speak of General Kalinin's Second Cavalry Division (1,500 sabers + 1,000 bayonets) and about General Guselshchikov's Third Cavalry Division (3,500 sabers + 400 bayonets from general Abramov's Don Corps): these troops were positioned from the Azov Sea to the village of Chernigovka. Naturally, he did not forget about the Drozdov Division, either (it was located by the village of Mikhailovka) or about General Morozov's Second Cavalry Division. In speaking about the line of the front to the west of Mikhailovka, Solovyov mentioned General Babiev's Kuban Cavalry Division and the Native Division positioned to its left along the front. Finally, the Markov and Kornilov Divisions were located in the region of Kakhovka, while General Barbovich's division was positioned closest to the Dnieper Estuary.

Opposing those forces were divisions of the Reds' Thirteenth Army, including the First and Second Cavalry Divisions of Dmitry Zhloba's Combined Corps. The numbers for just that one corps—including the troops attached to it—reached 7,500. After some wavering, Solovyov decided not to dwell on the numerical data of other divisions that supported Zhloba (for example the Latvian and the 52nd Rifle Division, which were in the area of Beryslav).

After casting a glance at his listeners, the researcher felt that an overabundance of figures might dull their attention.

In speaking about the Reds' plans, Solovyov began by limiting himself to pointing out Zhloba's corps' intention of attacking the Don Corps and taking Melitopol. After grasping, however, that this picture would be incomplete, the speaker nevertheless elaborated that four divisions were mobilized from Fedko's group in the area from Zherebets to Pologi at the same time as the 52nd and Latvian Divisions were already moving out of the area from the region of Berislavl to Aleshki. Zhloba placed particular hopes on Fedko's group, something that raised no doubts among the attendees. Fedko, however, did not warrant those hopes.

Did General Larionov know about the Reds' plans? Sources available to researchers (Solovyov carefully evened out the file of papers lying in front of him) gave no answer to that question. The general acted as if he was familiar with the enemy's plans in full detail. He had always been a half-step ahead of the Reds before, but those half-steps invariably determined the outcome of the fighting. Zhloba's most cunning schemes broke down against the measures the White commander had taken, regardless of whether they were the result of reconnaissance activity or the general's ingenious foresight. Solovyov preferred to think the latter.

After the general had studied his opponent's way of thinking (this happened fairly quickly), he flawlessly guessed all the operations Zhloba had conceived. In Solovyov's opinion, the general's strength consisted of an absolutely precise assessment of Zhloba's strategic potential. It was not overly high (which was natural) but was not lower than average, either. As General Larionov himself once said, flight school is capable of raising anyone—Dmitry Zhloba among them—to an average level. Then again, it was the hand of fate that threw Zhloba into the cavalry before he had the chance to take wing as he should have. This merging of the earthly and the heavenly in his fate (along with unfavorable genetics, according to some data) significantly twisted the Red commander's brains. To General Larionov's credit, he was able to sort through those intricacies.

Early in the morning, he ordered that strong coffee be served; he would drink it in small sips, sitting on the steps of his armored train car. After the coffee, he smoked his first cigarette. When the weather was not windy, he blew smoke rings, observing their melancholy motion toward the sky. When there was wind, the general released the smoke in a thin stream, unconcerned about its further fate. It is usually thought that it was during those moments that he formed the plans that ended up ruining Red commander Dmitry Petrovich Zhloba's career.

The steppe's drowsy breathing, which moved in barely perceptible waves, and the scent of grass that was still fresh, instilled calm and joy in the general. The sun rose quickly over the horizon, as if it were in a speeded-up film, and the steppe changed its colors. The steppe appeared to the general in the form of a kaleidoscope that had been hurriedly deployed around the armored train. It was unlimited in its capabilities, boundless, and strewn with the ash of his cigarette.

Sometimes General Larionov would lie down in the grass and observe the life of its inhabitants. In his eyes, this life appeared just as petty as human life. Perhaps not as brutal.

The grass's businesslike residents ate each other but they did so out of necessity, conforming to biology's ancient laws. They did not experience mutual hatred. Encouraged by the general's motionlessness, these creatures ran along his splayed fingers, between which something was already sprouting, springing up, and maturing. One could maintain that more than a dozen or two ants, grasshoppers, aphids, beetles, and numerous other creations he would have had difficulty giving names to had passed through his hands. Located in a region of embittered battles between the Red and White Armies, they maintained strict neutrality. Their ability not to notice social cataclysms achieved an absolute, evoking the general's admiration.

There was something posthumous in the general's fingers when they were plunged into the grass. If this was connected with life, then it was in some sort of broad, age-old sense of converting human bodies into grasses and trees. Pressing his face to the crushed stalks, the general imagined himself dead on that field. Arms outstretched. Head sprinkled with earth. This is how he saw his soldiers again and again after battle.

The general remembered how one time, when he was still a cadet, he had gone to military summer camp. During field exercises, he had to dig trenches while being timed. There was a hot spell. He was digging a trench for the first time and became horribly tired. Nausea rose in his throat and his legs began to shake. He was soaked in sweat. After digging the trench, cadet Larionov lay down in it and closed his eyes. A fabulous coolness replaced the scorching sun. The shouts of officers, clanging of shovels, and clatter of horses on the road still carried to Larionov, muted, as if from hundreds of versts away, but none of that was with him any longer. Maybe it was in another world.

'A blissful coolness,' he whispered, imagining he was lying in a grave.

'It's not the time to rest up, cadet!'

An officer was looking at him from somewhere above, almost as if from the clouds that were sailing past, over the trench.

'I'm *deathly* tired,' said the boy.

The officer walked away without saying anything. The expanse he had vacated was immediately covered over by a celestial curtain speckled with white clouds.

'Thank you,' the cadet uttered soundlessly. He did not rule out that this had been an angel.

The general continued to lie there. He already sensed a powerful call from below. He was experiencing the soothing sense of growing into the earth that, as it seemed to him, was familiar to everyone killed in battle. The killed understood that everything was over for them and they could enjoy the repose that had arrived. The general's immobility was almost otherworldly. Only the cautious glance of the sentries—the general knew they were observing him, for security reasons—prevented him from giving himself over, completely, to merging with the earth.

In speaking about the essence of what happened during the summer of 1920, Solovyov could not help but quote from Mikhail A. Kritsky's famous characterization in *The Kornilov Shock Regiment*, which discusses how, over the course of multiple battles, the Russian Army surrounded Zhloba's cavalry, squeezing the troops into a dead-end situation and severely reducing their maneuverability.

Because of the natural crowding that came about, Zhloba's group lost a significant degree of the cavalry's most important qualities: movement and maneuverability.'

The natural crowding into which Zhloba cast the troops entrusted to him was the result of General Larionov's considered and protracted actions. Like an experienced chess player, the general offered a sacrifice to his adversary: a few pawns at the center of the board that Zhloba swallowed very readily. After winning a series of localized battles, the Higher Aviation School graduate did not notice that the places he was victorious were located on a defined axis and had a precisely delineated direction. The victories ceased when the general was of the opinion that Zhloba had moved far enough in that direction. Zhloba continued to attack out of inertia, but this time the adversary was not thinking of retreat. And although the general's army did not counterattack, all the Reds' attempts to move further were crushed on that very first line of trenches that, it turned out, had been dug more than a week earlier.

Only after familiarizing himself with how solidly the defense had been prepared in this spot did Zhloba begin to understand that his own victorious march had done nothing more than enable the Whites to occupy previously arranged positions. That understanding became complete for him the morning the Whites' first lines appeared at the rear of the troops he headed. General Larionov had personally led them into battle, leaving his habitable armored train for the occasion. The general was not one to take a risk for the sake of risk. He simply knew that sometimes one must lead the troops oneself. He sensed those moments flawlessly.

After warning his listeners that he was going to depart

from the Zhloba theme for a while, Solovyov reminded them of the famous breach in Kakhovka. He had in mind an episode of the war when part of General Larionov's army ended up surrounded. Discussions began about surrendering as prisoners.

The general formed his troops and lit a cigarette. He released several smoke rings and those who had gathered watched, entranced, as they soared.

'This is the sort of question I do not wish to decide for you,' said the general. 'Whoever wants to may go ahead and surrender.'

The general began heading toward his horse but stopped halfway. The smoke rings he'd released were still hanging in the air, like doleful zeroes. The general's horse was stamping its hoof. Several dozen people broke ranks and gloomily wandered toward the front line. The general did not utter a word. He looked at them without judgment, most likely surprised. He himself could not explain his certainty that death awaited them. He knew cases when the Reds had shot only officers and then mobilized the rest. Everyone watched, silent, as those who were leaving moved toward the grove: it was a red grove. With clouds gathering over it. They choked up when they saw those people moving under that leaden sky. And felt better after they had finally disappeared behind the trees.

This is how strange the war was—Russians against Russians—when soldiers taken prisoner could fight the very next day for the other side. They did so just as selflessly as before. There were quite a few people for whom shifts of this sort became a habit. For some, it was the only possible work under war conditions. For some, it was a way of life at a time when, by and large, people were indifferent about who they fought for. *L'existence* for civilians did not give them the thrill they needed. Or that intoxicating military brotherhood that is available only in the face of death. As a rule, it was a bullet that stopped those shifts. Or a saber. Essentially, there were not many choices.

Lightning flashed beyond the grove where the departed had disappeared. It was still very far away: the thunder only caught up a minute after. Another minute later, several bursts of machine gun fire sounded from the grove. Both the general and his soldiers remained silent. It is possible there were more bursts of fire but they were no longer audible through the drumming of the rain pounding at their tents, helmets, and field kitchens. It was the drumming before marching out. They began a prayer service under pouring rain.

The general did not lead them toward the grove. They moved along the steppe, southwesterly, to where the thunderstorm was slowly heading and where—according to the general's notions—the encirclement was less dense. They walked for a long time. Water flowed from their soaked clothing into their boots, squishing loudly. Larionov formed his soldiers into a hollow square a few hundred meters from the Red positions. The cavalry was placed up front, at the head, with the general. What alcohol remained was distributed to his personnel.

The general broke into a trot, as did his horse cavalry. The general drew his saber and the cavalrymen galloped off, their sabers drawn, too. He felt the cold drenching rain snaking down his back and it was pleasant. They rode into the adversary's position—this happened on its own—as lightning struck. The celestial electricity glinted threateningly on the general's saber. Along the way, he remembered 'Our Figner, dressed as an old man . . .' Our Figner . . . Lightning flashed three times in a row, illuminating listless shadows by the tents. Three brief flashes did not pinpoint any movement among the defenders, though they were not really defending anyway. Forlornly pressing into whatever was closest to them, these people first let in the general, then the cavalry and then, of course, the infantry, too. This all happened without a single shot.

In Solovyov's opinion, the history of the Kakhovka breach was the complete opposite of what happened near Melitopol. Since an oppositeness in substance implies a particular resemblance in form (Prof. Nikolsky called this 'historical circumstances'), the young historian did not consider it possible to examine these two cases of encirclement in isolation. After showing a map of the Kahkovka breach with bright red arrows, Solovyov took a map of Zhloba's encirclement from his folder, too. The sheets were held up briefly and then handed around. The princess held them longest of all. She drew her index finger along the arrows and looked pensively at the lecturer from time to time.

Zhloba began racing around after (as Kritsky so aptly put it) falling into the cul-de-sac. At first, Zhloba tried to get away from the general's cavalry that had overtaken him, but he ran into intense machine gun fire. This is where Zhloba finally grasped that he was surrounded. He again turned his troops to meet the cavalry but that could no longer improve matters. The appearance of the legendary general heading up the attackers made a stunning impression on the Reds. They began surrendering.

Zhloba successfully boarded his armored train and began

rolling north, fighting battles along the way. The armored train, accompanied by a detachment of about two hundred men, managed to leave the encirclement. This was all that remained of a cavalry corps of many thousands. Lacking troops, weapons, the armored train (which eventually had to be abandoned during the retreat), and, most importantly, horses, Zhloba fell into severe depression. All that remained at his disposal was an old airplane that he had never used in battle, for reasons of principle. Forgotten by everyone, the machine was collecting dust in a hangar outside the combat zone.

Zhloba remembered the plane. After reaching the sought-after hanger, he rolled it outside with the help of local peasants. The women hurriedly wiped down the fuselage. Someone applied strength to turn the propeller, and, to everyone's astonishment, the motor started. The propeller rotated fitfully at first, as if it were gathering strength for each new movement of its blades. Little by little, the rotation grew uniform and the two propeller blades transformed into a large, translucent circular area. The machine jounced and snorted for several minutes but would not budge.

'The motor's warming up,' the peasant men nodded knowingly.

They puffed on hand-rolled cigarettes to reconcile what was happening with their own agitated consciousness. And to attach an everyday quality to the nearness of flying technology. Using an expert motion, the aviator turned some sort of lever and the machine jerked sharply, then stopped as if it were rooted to the ground.

'Get away!' Zhloba yelled, almost flying out of his seat.

He placed in that shout all his hatred for his former flying classmates. All the pain of the insults he had suffered at various times. All the bitterness of the defeat that had come to him. The peasants, who were already on edge, scattered. The airplane began moving and rolled along the steppe, shuddering on the potholes. A minute later, it took off.

After circling over the disheartened witnesses to the takeoff, the plane set a southerly course, to where General Larionov's units were finishing disarming the Red Armymen they had taken prisoner. Everything was proceeding peacefully, even somehow routinely. The regimental clerk was compiling a list of the prisoners, also indicating the types of weapon confiscated and the names of the horses. The former Red Armymen stood in a long, joyless line, waiting for the clerk to record them. After registration, they were led off in groups for lunch.

Some who were standing there lifted their heads when they heard the airplane's motor. They all knew the general had eleven such machines in his equipment, so this must have been one of them. Nobody was concerned. The clerk dipped his pen into a spill-proof inkwell and stretched, satisfied, lacing his hands together in front of himself. Indifferently and near-sightedly, he observed the dot growing in the sky. The mere fact of flying technology no longer attracted attention in 1920.

There was something unusual in the airplane's movement. Observed from below, its flight lacked that grand tranquility that usually accompanies large flying objects (organisms) in the air—from balloons and dirigibles to eagles and seagulls. More and more heads turned toward it. The airplane turned somersaults in the air. It resembled a fly, an angered bumblebee, or perhaps even a hummingbird.

This was not the height of aerobatics: Zhloba was extraordinarily far from even the thought of executing Nesterov's 'dead loop.' This was not even a manifestation of the aviator himself being so extremely wound up, either, though the abruptness of his motions, needless to say, could not have been conducive to fluidity in flight. The reason for what occurred lay in the cables for the steering rod: they were not in working order because the machine had been in the damp hanger for so long. Need it be said that Zhloba's affective state had not allowed him to verify their tension?

Whether it was that a wind rose or the energy of desperation that had carried Zhloba toward his flight destination, well, at some point he actually ended up over the Whites' positions. When he saw below him the scene of his disgrace, he threw his arms on the fuselage and hung down. The airplane finally stopped jerking after losing its steering and began flying over the steppe at low altitude. Hanging over his adversary's positions—as if he were leaning on a window-sill and conversing with someone on the street—Zhloba floated over the field kitchens, lines of prisoners, and the herds of horses they had lost. His fluttering hair and pale, unshaven face were very visible from below. Tears from the head wind glistened in his eyes. He was an ideal target. Each person standing below understood that the aeronaut was seeking death. And nobody shot at him.

On Prof. Nikolsky's advice, Solovyov saved one of his important findings for the conclusion of his paper. During his work on the topic 'General Larionov's Rout of Zhloba's Cavalry Corps,' the young historian had decided to compile a maximally precise, inasmuch as was possible, hourly account of the activity of both commanders during the month of June 1920.

Many of Solovyov's colleagues regarded that work as deliberately unachievable so suggested that for starters he write down his own hourly life in June (during the previous year, for example) and then later set his sights on events seventy-six years in the past. The hidden irony in that advice touched on not only the possibility of searches of this sort but also their practicability. To his colleagues, these searches seemed, to some extent, like scholarly pedantry or (this sounded more offensive) scholarly poseury. It turned out that Prof. Nikolsky was the only person who approved of the graduate student's plans, without reservations. And that was enough.

Solovyov disagreed with his colleagues' irony and actually did compile his own life story for June of the previous year. This proved to be completely straightforward. He spent the entire time of his final examination period—that was what fell in June—sitting in the Public Library. All his remaining actions were associated with exams. Their times were calculated easily, according to the schedule of exams and other tests he had kept. From his course on source study, the young man had internalized the idea that any piece of paper, even one of little significance, could later become an important historical source. He knew the value of documents and never threw them away.

As far as June 1920 went, that task did turn out to be more complex, though it was not at all unachievable. Solovyov first pieced together the texts from all the memoirs regarding that stretch of time. After ascertaining the basic character of General Larionov and Zhloba's actions, the scholar moved on to highly focused archival searches. He looked through thousands of written orders, telegrams, and telephonograms from that time (frequently they specified not only the date but also the hour and minute of sending) and compiled—in spite of his colleagues' doubts—a fairly detailed listing of what happened during the month of June. The result turned out to be stupendous.

It emerged that on the night of June 13 into 14, e.g. before the start of active military operations, General Larionov and Zhloba's armored trains stood facing one another. This occurred on territory that was neutral at the time, namely near Gnadenfeld, a settlement of German colonists. Aided by telegrams sent by both sides, the historian managed to establish that Zhloba's armored train arrived at 23:30 on the first track, stood there until 04:45, then headed north. The sources Solovyov used allowed him to calculate the arrival time of the general's armored train as 23:55. It departed at 03:35, in a southerly direction. And though the number of the track where the second armored train stood is not indicated in the documents, the process of elimination managed to determine that, too: it was track No. 2. There were only two tracks at the Gnadenfeld station.

Prof. Nikolsky was very satisfied with his former student (and are any students 'former'?). More than anything, he approved of the result from the point of view that Solovyov had been on the right track with his methods. Despite all his love for brave deductions, the professor considered empirical research the only possible basis for any scholarly work. On top of that, he emphasized that any work, even if it looks pointless at first glance, will certainly bear fruit if the work has a source. In this regard, by the way, he did not rate the future Crimean conference very highly. He called the majority of its participants 'inspired blowhards' but did not talk Solovyov out of going.

'You need to see that, too,' he told the graduate student in parting. 'Once, at any rate.'

The second circumstance that evoked the professor's interest in Solovyov's finding was its significance for the history of the war itself. Until now, no documents had existed that directly or circumstantially confirmed a personal meeting of the two adversaries. Even so, conjecture about the possibility of such a meeting had been expressed in the émigré press back in 1930. Lacking any factual confirmation for his conjecture, in *Ten Years Later*, author Yuri Krivich permitted himself to go even further. He posed the question of whether the hypothetical meeting was the general's attempt to arrange a secret connection with the Reds. Since the question was posed in an accusatory tone, the essence of the general's betrayal remained unclear. How did it come about that he prevailed over the Reds in one of his most convincing victories as a result of a deal with them? And, consequently, why did the Reds need that sort of deal? The only thing the author could produce to support the theory was the unchanging question: why did the general remain alive at the end of the war?

It is interesting that the Red side later also expressed a supposition regarding the general's meeting with Zhloba. Moreover, this mention of a deal—this time, naturally, in favor of the Whites—no longer sounded like a hint. The deal was announced as if it were a verified, albeit uncon- firmed, fact. Since Zhloba had already been shot by that time—under a decision of the 'troika' of the People's

Commissariat for Internal Affairs—in his article 'At the Last
Boundary', Sergei Drel expressed restrained satisfaction that
justice had triumphed after all with regard to the traitor,
albeit slightly in advance of the determination of his guilt.
Solovyov concluded his talk with this sarcastic phrase, which
he thought was not lacking for effect.

Princess Meshcherskaya nodded silently but genially. Zoya
watched as Shulgin finished constructing some sort of
complex, albeit two-dimensional, figure out of matches.
Since the table shook constantly, he had thought it pointless
to create a figure with volume. Nesterenko was sleeping.

11

Zoya spent the night at Solovyov's again. This time there was none of the uncertainty that had tormented them both, and so they made love without hesitation after a light dinner with wine. There was no tension at all. Unhurried and even with a certain flirtatiousness, Solovyov undressed and waited for Zoya under the sheet. She took off her clothes, standing half-facing him. Solovyov delighted in how she moved: Zoya knew how to undress.

She removed her attire calmly and elegantly, with a subtle portion of the resignation any Russian woman simply felt obliged to display for her possessor. After taking off her jeans, she glanced at them in her hand and tossed them onto a chair, with a quick jingle of the belt buckle. She extracted a pair of panties out from under a long shirt with a man's cut and carefully, using her index finger and thumb, placed them on her jeans. She touched her shirt collar with both hands, slowing down. She undid the long row of buttons as if she were in doubt. The shirt slid from her shoulders but its edge remained in Zoya's small fist. Set against the background of her dark skin, the bright linen of her shirt fell to the floor casually, folding into an unusual flower scented with deodorant. A bikini tan line flashed on Zoya's supple bottom.

She was different that night. After revealing her spirited-ness the night before, today Zoya demonstrated technique that was no less outstanding. To Solovyov's surprise, the museum employee's knowledge of this non-Chekhovian realm was boundless. The image of a boat amongst waves that had entered the researcher's thoughts yesterday had faded. There was now something else that did not lend itself to instantaneous definition. Solovyov had no time at all for deliberation, though.

The morning was fabulous. Relaxed, quiet, and contented. There was complete calm, like after a visit to the bathhouse. The body's absolute lack of inhibition, delight emanating from each of its cells. Or even the feeling a day after playing football. A pleasant ache in the leg and pelvic muscles, an unwillingness to get up. Combined with a feeling of deep satisfaction: Solovyov thought he was genuinely experien-cing this phrase for the first time.

Zoya sat on top of him and began giving him a massage. She started with his hair. She gathered it in waves, clasping her hands together on top of his head. She kneaded his neck and back. At first she touched him, just barely, with the very tips of her fingers, as if she were injecting through them a mysterious electricity that made goosebumps cover Solovyov. Then her palms made powerful grasping movements. They turned Solovyov's back to gelatin, to clay, removing the crystalline current it had received and instead pouring in a muscle-stretching energy. From time to time, when Zoya's movements were particularly vigorous, Solovyov felt the touch of her intimate hair in the small of his back. Then—

after Zoya resettled on his legs—she massaged the lower back itself, then his behind (what an apt name that is, anyway). That turned out to be especially pleasant; its softness was made for massages. Zoya sank her palms into the stillness of his strongest muscles. The pulsing of her palms repeated the rhythm of those very same muscles, imitating their ancient movement. She moved on to his legs. She achieved their full relaxation by rubbing them on both sides. This was how footballers going in as substitutes were handled, too. Soles of the feet. Heels, with a rubbing, circular motion. Each toe thoroughly. The apotheosis of the corporeal. A fresh morning breeze with a juniper aroma rushed through the open window and blended with the smell of their bodies.

After breakfast, they headed for the embankment. Solovyov took the opportunity to check his height and weight along the way. He thought medical scales were something one would no longer run into on Petersburg's streets: splotchy white after having been repainted, the quiet clanging of the hanging weights. Where had they disappeared to? Where had the machines selling carbonated water gone? What about the barrels of kvass and beer? It occurred to Solovyov that not one history book had noted their departure, just as not one history book had said anything about their arrival. But they truly had existed. They had defined a way of life, making it more bearable, if only, needless to say, to the limited degree they could.

An elderly man wearing glasses weighed Solovyov. The lenses of his glasses were large and bulging. His eyes seemed to be, too, as he monitored the markings on the scale. Strictly speaking, he was not monitoring the markings. He could determine anyone's weight from a distance. There was a rubber band instead of a right temple on his glasses.

'Sixty-eight and a half kilos. Would you like your height, too?'

'I would,' said Solovyov.

He stood at the height measurer and the moving part of the apparatus lowered onto his head with an unexpected knock.

'One meter seventy-nine. You need another half kilo for full harmony.'

Solovyov tossed up his hands and paid. He felt Zoya's cool palm under his T-shirt.

'I'll feed you,' Zoya promised in a whisper. Her lips touched Solovyov's ear. 'For full harmony.'

Despite the bright sun, it was refreshing on the embankment. A strong wind was blowing off the sea. Splashes rose over the concrete ledge by the water and settled somewhere far away, on the second tier of the embankment. A small, neat rainbow accompanied their flight. The splashes evaporated with improbable speed after shining one final time under the pedestrians' feet.

Zoya took off her sandals, picked them up, and began walking barefoot. Based on her glowing face, Solovyov knew she expected the same of him. Hiding his inner unwillingness, he took off his sandals and carried them in his hands, too. The asphalt turned out to be incredibly hot, so walking on it was almost torture. The squeamish Solovyov experienced no less suffering from the assumption that he was most likely walking over someone else's gobs of spit, dried though they might be. He understood Zoya's line of thinking, though. This was an essential shot for a romantic movie. Except that shoeless walks in the movies usually included rain. Nobody burned the soles of their feet in those situations, and besides, everything generally looked more hygienic.

It was hot for Zoya, too. She bounded all the way to the steps leading to the lower embankment, then turned. Everything was different on the lower embankment. The water had not had a chance to flow back into the sea and it quivered on the concrete in huge warm puddles. The surf sloshed over, splashing them from time to time, but that was pleasant.

Near the pier, they went back to the upper level; this was a remnant of the former embankment. The one Chekhov knew, with two-story brick houses, curlicue railings on little balconies, and palms in huge pots. From afar, a cupola of the St. John Chrysostom Church shone golden, rising over Yalta's greenery. Zoya's hand directed Solovyov into a gap between buildings and they found themselves by a chairlift. Seats for two swung around with a metallic growl, returning from somewhere up high. They approached the platform with jerky, paralytic motions and received passengers without stopping. After letting Zoya go first, Solovyov managed to sit at the last moment. He plopped down hard on the seat, and the whole structure began to rock. Of course Zoya noticed his agitation, but she didn't acknowledge it.

The surface slowly slid out from under their feet. The wooden platform ended, and next came bushes and a tree with a rubber sandal on top. Roofs and yards. Flying over the yards was most interesting of all: people were hanging out laundry, playing dominos, and punishing children. They were repairing a car, a tiny Zaporozhets that stood on wooden trestles. Carefully, finger by finger, wiping their hands with rags, walking off to the side, and pensively looking at the car. Life was showing itself in all its diversity.

Solovyov took Zoya's hand and experienced a persistent sense of déjà vu. At one time he had loved recognizing the past in the present. He saw that almost as a historian's destiny. Later, influenced by Prof. Nikolsky, he rid himself of that unidirectional view of things after learning to recognize the present in the past, too. 'Contrary to popular notions,' wrote Prof. Nikolsky, 'time is a two-way street. It is also possible that there is no traffic at all. One should not think tha . . .' Solovyov looked again at the roofs below. Chagall, well, of course. His painting reflected them.

As they floated over what was formerly Autskaya Street, Zoya swung her feet (this, it belatedly struck Solovyov, was how sandals ended up in trees). There was something child-like in the smoothness of the skin on her legs. But they were adult, purely feminine, and arousing at the same time. Trolleybus rods slid along wires right under their seat. The trolleybus roof proved to be unexpectedly large and peeling. Not resembling something intended to be streamlined. Some things are not usually seen from above.

Solovyov felt some inner nervousness when he jumped down, but he did not lose face. A view of a strange structure with columns unfolded at the spot where they touched down. It might have been considered a cult building if not for its particular resort-area monumentalism, something that is an integral part of southern Soviet cities. It is possible this was a Soviet cult: Solovyov imagined himself and his traveling companion as Komsomol members. Elder comrades were bringing two young creatures to mysterious communist spirits in sacrifice. Against the backdrop of the sea. The hair of those in attendance flopped dramatically in the wind. Solovyov wanted to have Zoya amid these columns, but made no signal. It was enough for him to acknowledge that she would have agreed, without a second thought.

The peak where they now found themselves was no longer truly Yalta. Solovyov walked along a path in the woods, lagging a little behind Zoya. He liked watching her. Zoya knew this and made no attempt to slow her pace. He repeated to himself for the hundredth time that this lithe young woman was his, and for the hundredth time this gave him a feeling of delight.

The forest grew thicker, but they were not alone there. Branches cracked here and there, multicolored T-shirts flashed, and people called out to one another. Not being alone gave Solovyov particular pleasure, too. Those accompanying them (they had gathered from throughout the area, purposely) saw Zoya's litheness. Perhaps they sensed her spiritedness. But only he (only he!) truly knew her liana-like qualities that drove one insane. Even the first sensations he had experienced with Leeza (Solovyov compared everything that happened afterwards with those sensations) now seemed adolescent and silly to him. It felt awkward to even recall Leeza now. Awkward not because of Leeza (her chances were minimal by comparison with Zoya) but because of himself, who had drawn her into such an unfavorable comparison. He tried to push Leeza out of his consciousness, as one might gently push away a grandmother who had wandered into a party raging in the living room. A minute later, he truly had forgotten about her.

They crossed a paved road during their walk downhill. They walked past small yards overgrown with grape vines. These yards were even smaller than the one where Solovyov was housed. They were enclosed by headboards, steam heat radiators, prams, and even the doors of a microbus—a Playboy bunny blushed saucily on one of those doors. Judging from the inscription below it, the car had some connection to St. Pauli, Hamburg's entertainment quarter. Solovyov thought about how objects' fates are sometimes more interesting than humans'. What had that bunny seen in its previous life? A light Hamburg rain? Street musicians, asphalt glistening with lights from strip bars, pushy barkers, prostitutes in uniform orange overalls (that arouses), paupers with dogs, and English sailors waddling along the whole breadth of the street? Who had the bunny driven around St. Pauli? That, in essence, was not important. The bunny's innocence had been returned to it here, in the quarter where the door now resided. Children were playing in a sandbox. It was just a bunny to the new family. Nobody was interested in its past.

The enclosure, which was entwined with vines, acquired an artistic unity. And the aesthetic of a poor but honest seaside existence that gratefully accepted everything, saved everything, and did not permit itself to squander head-boards. Solovyov peered into one of the little yards. He saw a family lunching under an awning. A woman dishing boiled potatoes onto plates. A man with a lucid face who had already dispensed the 150 grams of vodka he was ready to swallow. A child on a tricycle. A southern bird unknown to Solovyov that was swinging on a cypress branch and singing, non-stop.

Zoya stood at a distance and waited patiently. Her friend was absorbed by the same romanticism that had become the essence of her everyday life, even as a child, something for which she had another word: poverty. Zoya was thinking she knew a seamy side of that romanticism but Solovyov did not. That was not the case. Solovyov pictured life in these small worlds very well. He himself had grown up in one of them. He was not seeking unfamiliar sensations. He saw in those small yards a reflection of his childhood.

They came home (to Solovyov's) toward evening. At Zoya's insistence, they stopped at the market on the way back and bought some meat and vegetables. Now Zoya was sautéing meat. Solovyov inhaled its aroma and thought about how long it had been since he had eaten home-cooked food. Pressing against Zoya from behind and resting his chin on her shoulder, he watched as neat pieces of pork browned all over, sizzling and spattering grease. Zoya had intended to fix something else after cutting vegetables for salad, but Solovyov took the tireless young woman in his arms and carried her into the other room. The young man feared he would not survive yet another of her merits.

They washed down the meat with wine diluted with cold mineral water. It tasted delicious. The wine had ceased being nectar and its thick crimson color turned a bright pink, but the wine's flavor now felt more refined. Then Zoya made coffee. She said that they needed to be in excellent form tonight.

'Why?' asked Solovyov.

'Because today we're going to search for the end of the general's memoirs. I know where it might be.'

Solovyov looked closely at Zoya. She knew. A wasp flew in the window and flew right back out after uncertainly circling over the table. Solovyov did not break the extended silence and did not ask where they were going. That would only have consolidated the strange hegemony that Zoya had begun to establish over him. Let her say it herself if she wanted.

Zoya washed the dishes and then began getting ready. She opened the bag she had brought over the day before; something inside clanged like it meant business.

'Here, you carry this.'

Performing the search in the evening did not trouble her in any obvious way. Though (Solovyov cast a glance at the mysterious bag) what time could be considered 'natural' for this sort of search?

They left the house at around eight. They took a trolleybus to the bus station then transferred to a small shuttle van. It scrambled up a winding mountain road with a roar that was unexpected for a small vehicle, then ended up on a highway running parallel to the sea. An evening coolness was already apparent here. One of the passengers slammed shut a roof hatch. The only open window was next to Solovyov but he had no intention of closing it. He stuck his elbow out, enjoying the cooling Crimean breeze.

The vehicle stopped at settlements and guest houses. The passengers lowered their heads exaggeratedly as they got out so as not to hit them on the door frame. Nobody boarded. When the vehicle stopped in the forest, there was nobody left but Zoya and Solovyov.

'Alupka Park,' said the driver. 'Last stop.' As he watched the couple make their way along the little road and stretch their numbed legs, he added, 'Last van's at 10:30.'

'Thanks,' Zoya said, turning. 'We'll be leaving on the other side.'

The vehicle turned around right there, on the park's tree-lined alley. A minute later its engine fell silent behind the trees. In the engine's slow, dying sound there rang something of farewell and additionally, perhaps, something alarming. What Solovyov was experiencing was not fear in the usual sense. It was the uneasy feeling of one who turns out to have bought a one-way ticket. To a huge, drowsy park. With an eccentric traveling companion. With a heavy bag holding unknown contents.

'Count Vorontsov's Hungarian lover lived with him.'

A pause. Solovyov was already starting to get used to Zoya's habit of omitting all manner of prefatory discussion. Zoya thought it was up to her conversation partner to connect the links of the chain that led her to make some statement or other. More accurately put, she did not think about this. She had not even contemplated it.

'Vorontsov was old and she acquired yet another lover. A young cornet . . . This Lebanese cedar.' Zoya walked over to a sprawling tree and stroked its unembraceable trunk. 'Everything here was planted at Vorontsov's order.'

The Lebanese cedar tree's bark consisted of what looked like large tiles that had just recently been glued on. Ants that were just as large ran along them. A squirrel sat about two meters from Zoya's hand. Its reddish-brown coat blended with the tree trunk, making the squirrel almost undetectable. Its arched tail quivered now and then. The squirrel did not run away, staying in place by force of will.

'One time Vorontsov caught them in bed together,' said Zoya, now addressing only the squirrel. 'When the cornet ran out of the bedroom, covered in a sheet . . .'

Zoya ripped her hand from the tree trunk and the squirrel jumped right off, onto the grass. It sat there for an instant, as if deliberating on what it had heard. Solovyov beckoned to it, motioning with his fingers.

'Have you noticed that squirrels are twitchy?'

He drew a little closer but the animal hid behind the nearest cedar, following the cornet's example.

'The Hungarian woman thought Vorontsov would shoot her right then,' said Zoya, her gaze taking on a rigidity. 'She knew his temperament. But he rang the bell and told the servant, "Wash madam and change the linens."'

Zoya walked right up to Solovyov and hissed into his lips, 'She de-tes-ted him from that day on.'

Zoya stood so close that it was impossible not to kiss her. It was a long, exhausting kiss, filled with gratitude for the information about Vorontsov.

Walking past a pond with swans, they ended up at *Big Chaos*, a majestic heap of stones brought here at Vorontsov's order. Zoya began jumping from boulder to boulder, climbing higher and higher. Solovyov reluctantly followed her. He painstakingly assessed each jump but his foot slipped several times. Stubborn, he did not ask Zoya about today's plans. Her silence and this ridiculous moving around on the rocks was beginning to irritate him. Zoya stopped when the gently sloping ascent ended. Continuing to climb up would have been insanity. It even seemed so to Zoya.

They sat down on one of the rocks. The sun had disappeared behind the trees long ago but the rock was warm, almost hot. There was not a soul around. Sitting on the rock in such a strange place, set against the thickening dusk, Solovyov felt like he had gone astray. Having a girlfriend had not made things easier. More likely the opposite.

It was almost dark when they began climbing down. Zoya took a flashlight from the bag she had handed to Solovyov and directed its light at the closest boulders. Solovyov, whose eyes had already begun to grow accustomed to the dark, finally lost his orientation. The flashlight distorted the form of the rocks. The angle of the light made barely noticeable indentations seem to be huge hollows, but Zoya's beam completely ignored real crevices between the rocks. Fantastical shadow play intensified all that: Zoya waved the flashlight from time to time as she showed Solovyov the way. Solovyov held on to the bag, which was swinging on his shoulder; he did not much believe they could descend safely. He was completely wet when they finally made it down.

The flashlight proved far more useful below. It revealed trees that had sprouted up suddenly (they had not been there an hour ago), roots snaking along the paths, as well as boulders the tireless Vorontsov had scattered here and there. Zoya's flashlight accentuated a bronze plaque on one of the boulders, drawing it out of the dark. The boulder was a memorial stone for Vorontsov's dog. A minute later they saw its ghost. An indeterminate four-legged creature stood about ten meters away, where the flashlight just barely reached. Its infernal gaze reflected the remnants of Zoya's light. Judging from its height, the animal might even have been a cat.

Solovyov had figured out long ago where they were going. Maybe he had already figured it out when Zoya first mentioned continuing the search. In reality, there was not much need for imagination here since they had examined everything thoroughly in Taras's room. If there was anything more to search for, to add to what they had found (where, other than at home, might this kind of person store something?), then only his workplace remained. Lighted by the moon that had risen, Taras's workplace revealed itself in all its oriental majesty. It was the Vorontsov Palace, seen from below.

The seekers of the manuscript climbed over a fence and ascended toward the centaur-like palace. They turned a corner and found themselves in the English part of the grounds, which Solovyov particularly liked. He had never been here, ever, but even at night he found his bearings with ease on this small street leading toward the main entrance. A good half of Soviet historical films had been shot on this narrow expanse. Solovyov felt a little like d'Artagnan. As a person with a European way of thinking, he would have preferred to come into the palace from this side.

Zoya saw matters differently. After showing Solovyov the palace from all sides (as the museum employee saw things, there should be a tour even if there would be a break-in), she led him to a Moorish façade that looked out on the sea. A wire stretched along a wall to the left of a mosaic arch that gleamed in the moonlight. Zoya took a penknife from her pocket and cut it.

'Alarm system?' Solovyov whispered.

Zoya nodded silently. They walked several meters along the western wing and stopped by a glass door, where Zoya asked Solovyov to take off the bag. Solovyov suddenly felt completely calm; his initial fear had subsided. These goings-on had obviously stepped outside the bounds of reality. Using the flashlight, Zoya took out two objects, only one of which Solovyov recognized: a glass cutter. Zoya did not begin with that, though. She took the second object (three rubber circles, arranged in a triangle), placed it against the glass, pulled some sort of lever, and the contraption remained, hanging on the window. It had suction cups.

Then came the glass cutter's turn. Zoya used it to trace an oval around the suction cups stuck to the glass. As Solovyov observed the Chekhov specialist's dexterousness in wielding the glass cutter, it occurred to him that in the event of their capture, the clause about break-ins with previous concert would not apply to them: there was no previous concert between him and Zoya. She had not uttered a word about her plans. And he had not asked her anything.

Zoya used the handle of the glass cutter to knock lightly on the glass a few times. Then, grabbing the suction cups, she noiselessly removed the oval traced on the glass and handed it to Solovyov. Thrusting her hand into the opening that had formed, she flicked a latch from inside. The door opened.

Zoya took the suction cup device from Solovyov's hands, placed it on the ground, and unstuck it from the glass oval. The suction cups were returned to the bag with a clang. Of everything that had happened, what struck Solovyov most was probably Zoya's composure. She was first to enter Vorontsov's kingdom.

Zoya found her bearings flawlessly in the deceased count's

palace, even with the flashlight switched off. She took Solovyov's hand and led him through several rooms where all he could see (this was a strange tour) were several gleaming vases and the fire alarm system's lifeless flashing. Darkness intensified the sound: the creak of a floor, the squeak of door hinges, and even—this was right by Solovyov's ear—the bag chafing on his shoulder.

They ended up in the staff area. Solovyov figured that out from the size of the rooms and, most importantly, the windows. They stopped in one of the rooms. Zoya squeezed Solovyov's hand and froze. The light came on suddenly. After his eyes adjusted to the light, Solovyov saw they were standing by a wall. Zoya's free hand was lying on the switch. She was smiling.

'This is Taras's room.'

The space was tiny. A window covered in metal shutters. Shelf hanging on the wall, heaped with some sort of electronic odds and ends. Chair. Desk. Zoya's photograph on the desk.

'I'm sure he's in love with you.'

A steamship's whistle sounded from somewhere far away, as if from another world.

'He loves me.' Zoya turned the photograph upside down. 'Is it really possible not to love me?'

She turned the chair and sat, straddling it, then pulled out the desk's side drawers, one after another. They were all empty. They were all noisily sent back. The desk's middle drawer turned out to be filled with papers. Zoya pulled out an armload, carelessly dumping them on the floor. Taras's papers slid into a formless mass, surrounding a chair leg. Solovyov crouched beside it. Zoya plucked a plastic folder out of the papers before he'd managed to examine what was lying there.

'That's it!'

Zoya's mother's hand, familiar to Solovyov, was visible through the transparent folder. Zoya offered her cheek and tapped it with her finger.

'Clever girl,' said Solovyov, kissing Zoya.

They crammed the other papers into the drawer. At first it would not close, so Solovyov had to pull the papers back out and stack them in a compact bundle on the table. Zoya seemed to ponder something before turning out the light.

'Want to make love in Vorontsov's bedroom?'

The light went out. Depth and resonance had been restored to the silence. Solovyov felt Zoya's hand on his belt.

'Are you sure you want that?'

The hand pulled lightly at his belt. It was a gesture of disappointment. The selfless female accomplice's terse *oh, you*. And Solovyov understood that. But he truly *did not feel like it*. A sense of danger suppressed other instincts in him. Unlike in Zoya. She was constructed the exact opposite way.

They walked through several rooms without turning on the flashlight (Solovyov thought they were not walking the same way as when they arrived), then stopped in one of the rooms. Solovyov's knee bumped into something soft. A bed. A canopy hung over it like a formless blot.

'Are you planning to screw me here or not?'

The echo of Zoya's question resounded through all the palace's chambers and returned to the bedroom, where it flung Solovyov on the bed with a quick push to the shoulder. He froze as he sank into Vorontsov's feather bed. Zoya descended upon him the next second. Despite his light shock, Solovyov noted that she had managed to undress. She was so worked up that she had not managed to pull off his clothes (come on, why are you acting like a corpse!?) All that remained for Solovyov was to give in. His jeans were lowered. Zoya was convinced that the corpse comparison was unjustified.

Solovyov had never experienced anything like this before. Even yesterday night, which had seemed so absolutely stupendous, faded. He felt the silk of the palace bedspread with his buttocks as he saw Zoya's profile dancing against the background of the enormous canopy. Maybe it was actually the canopy, not Zoya, that lent his senses a keenness he had not known before. Such intimate relations with the past aroused him as a researcher. At that instant, he did not feel like history's guest. He was a small but integral part of it. His merging with Zoya seemed to him like a merging with the past. Which had become accessible and discernible and had undressed before him. This was the orgasm of a true historian.

Zoya was lying on Vorontsov's vast bed with her arms spread wide. Her breathing was almost back to normal but her heart (Solovyov laid his head on her chest) was still pounding rapidly and resonantly. Creaking floorboards sounded in the doorway.

'Did you hear that?' whispered Solovyov.

She did not stir. The creak repeated and Solovyov squeezed Zoya's hand.

'I think it's Vorontsov's ghost,' Zoya said without lowering her voice. 'No big deal. Anyway, we did his favorite thing.'

She lurched and sat up on the bed.

'It's time.'

Solovyov heard the slapping of bare feet and the rustle of clothing being donned. He fastened his belt and stood, too. He was experiencing a pleasant weakness and a lack of desire to move. The task of leaving unnoticed, which is important for any burglar in his right mind, now seemed of little significance to him.

'It's too early to relax,' said Zoya.

She noticed his apathy. Zoya handed him the bag and again led him through the dark rooms. How did she know this palace so well? They ended up in the same place they had entered. From here they could see the sea and the moon's path on the water. Little lights of different colors were blinking in the corner of the room.

'That's strange,' Zoya muttered, 'I shut off the alarm system. Why is it lit here?'

'The door's open anyway. We can leave.'

'We can, of course . . .'

Without saying a word, Zoya approached the blinking panel and tugged a long switch.

In the first seconds, Solovyov did not even realize it was a siren. The noise was deafening. It came out of nowhere, out of utter quiet. In terms of strength, this noise could only be compared with silence. This noise was the converse of quiet: like all opposites, they possessed common characteristics. Crimea's entire southern coast was being notified of the trespassers at the palace.

Zoya grabbed him by the hand and they set off running. Solovyov turned by one of the famous Vorontsov lions. Inside the palace, lights went on one after another, almost like in the movies. There was nothing Solovyov wanted more at that moment than to turn into a stone lion and greet, calmly dignified (his paw on a sphere), the police, dogs, and volunteers who would come running. To greet everyone who would set off to defend the deceased count's property. Following Zoya, he leaped lightly onto a metal fence. His foot caught on something as he was jumping down and he rolled below, along the incline. Stones dug at him, roots caught at him. Zoya's bag with the break-in tools and the general's manuscript hit his face and chest. He stopped in some kind of bushes. Which, to top things off, scratched him very painfully.

'Still in one piece?' asked Zoya.

Zoya's silhouette was still spinning but the alarm was no longer sounding. Why had she turned it on? Why had they run below where there was nothing but the sea, where they would be much easier to catch? It would have been better to make their way upward, to the highway. At least they could have hailed a car there. Solovyov was jogtrotting obediently behind Zoya. She was in high spirits despite the circumstances. Pointing out, in a chipper voice, where to turn. She jumped off the parapets with a happy whoop. Why was she so elated?

They made their way to an open patch of ground over the sea. There was a strong wind blowing here that had not been noticeable in the park. Waves were rolling over huge boulders that formed something like a bay. Tatters of foam looked rather sinister in the moonlight.

'It's Vorontsov's bathing area,' Zoya said, gesturing below. 'There should be a boat somewhere among those rocks.'

They went down some steps and began walking to the left, along the rocks. There really was a boat between two boulders. Ten meters from the boat, waves slapped heavily at the rocks from the outside of the barrier, slipping off them with an offended grunt. Back in his adolescence, Solovyov had learned from books that landing is the most dangerous thing for shipwreck survivors. Or casting off, like now. A wave tosses a lifeboat against the crags and smashes it to bits. The end.

Solovyov left the bag on shore and jumped onto the boulder nearest the boat. He still vaguely hoped there would be no oars in the boat. No, they lay on the bottom. Solovyov caught the mooring clamp and leaned over the water.

'The boat's on a chain,' he said, almost festively, 'with a lock.'

Zoya took a hammer and chisel out of the bag and silently extended them to Solovyov. His companion's power of foresight astounded Solovyov almost more than the surf. He dragged part of the chain onto the rock, chose one of the links, and struck it with all the power of his desperation. He wound up and struck again. His strikes at the chain brought sparks from the rock but moved him no closer to his goal. The goods were solid. One time, Solovyov missed the chisel with the hammer and struck himself very painfully on the knuckle. He bit his lip and tolerated the pain in silence, but Zoya, who was sitting alongside him, apparently saw it all. It even looked to him like she was smiling. A piece of the chain finally fell from the rock with a jingle. They could (could!) set sail.

After sitting at the oars, Solovyov held out his hand to Zoya but she jumped into the boat herself. The boat swayed and floated away from the rock it had been chained to. Zoya sat at the stern. Solovyov meekly rowed toward a supposed exit from the bathing area.

'Not there!'

Zoya showed him two small crags. There was no longer any water between them, only foam. But this was where the boat passed through. The water had no set direction in that spot. There were no dangers hiding underwater here. Solovyov was able to row out of the bathing area and get a safe distance away. Only then did he dare raise his head. The shore they had left was calm and no visible signs of pursuit could be observed. The open ground that loomed over the bathing area was empty. The Vorontsov palace stood out on the mountain like a gleaming rectangle.

Solovyov relaxed too early. He realized when he saw the boat's stern in the air that they were on the crest of a wave.

'Head into the wave!' Zoya commanded 'Row right! Right again!'

The boat handled poorly. It seemed cumbersome and unwieldy to Solovyov, and too big for one rower (why had Zoya not once offered to row with him?). On the other hand, he sensed all the boat's fragility and insignificance in comparison with the night waves. After adapting to this, he began rowing more evenly. Solovyov's motions were no longer spasmodic, and the oars rowed ever less frequently at the air. They went along the shore, roughly one hundred meters away. They met the waves head-first. They aligned the boat on its primary course.

About an hour and a half later, Solovyov felt like he had rowed his hands raw. Zoya gave him her handkerchief and he wrapped one hand with it. He used his own T-shirt for the other hand. Solovyov was tired, too. He had used a lot of unnecessary motion in the beginning but now that his rowing might be considered exemplary, he had very little strength left. He tried to alternate, rowing two different ways. Moving the oars with only his arms allowed him to rest his back. And, conversely, he could leave his arms motionless and push the boat forward by moving his back. This helped, but not significantly.

Solovyov rested during the intervals between large waves. He had started to feel nauseous from exhaustion and rocking. He felt like lying down in the bottom of the boat— just as cadet Larionov had once felt like lying down in the bottom of a trench—and enjoying the repose. He was so worn out that the sea's choppiness no longer evoked his fear. Zoya's presence was all that prevented him from lying down.

'I have no more strength,' Solovyov finally said.

They landed on some sort of beach. Even after the front of the boat had knocked into the pebbles, Solovyov still could not believe this was the end of their sail. He sat, bent, with his hands on the oars, and could not find the strength within to go ashore. With Zoya's help—he was no longer shy of his condition—he jumped heavily over the side and took a few strides through the surf.

Zoya attempted to push the boat away from the shore but it came right back. She took the boat by the remnants of the chain and led it to the breakwater. The current was different there. Rocking forlornly by the concrete wall, the boat began slowly drifting toward the open sea.

There were lounge chairs visible under a beach awning. Without saying a word, Solovyov wandered to the closest chair. He was out like a light before he had a chance to collapse onto it.

The beach caretaker woke them up in the morning. He

shook Solovyov by the shoulder and told someone (Zoya?) that vacationers would be coming here after breakfast at the guesthouse.

'What guesthouse?' Solovyov asked in a silent whisper.

He pulled his T-shirt, with brown spots from his bloody palms, out from under his head.

'Blue Wave,' said the caretaker.

Zoya was sitting on the next lounge chair, hugging her knees. Solovyov went to the water and rinsed off.

About fifteen minutes later, they were already on the highway, where they boarded a shuttle van to Yalta. Solovyov fell asleep right away when he got home and slept until evening. When he woke up, he could not believe what had happened during the night. On his first attempt to get out of bed, he realized it was all true. He got up on the second attempt.

His primary thought was about the text. Which had been procured with such difficulty and which he had never even glanced at. From the bag with the break-in tools he extracted a crumpled plastic folder, pierced in ten places. The papers inside were in a lamentable state.

That was not his primary source of distress, though. There were only three sheets of paper. They contained a detailed explanation of what comprised the unseemly behavior of Baroness von Kruger, who had dinner at The Bear restaurant with her four former husbands. All the baroness's husbands turned out to be officers. The general's relative was uncommonly consistent in her passions. Detailed descriptions were made of the husbands, down to their military ranks and places of service. In the general's final edits to the text, there were notes in the margin with the years of death and places of interment (they were buried in various locations) for each of the participants at the infamous luncheon. In touching briefly on the menu, the general highlighted in particular that there were oysters and—naturally—oyster knives on the table. 'Do officers of today's army,' the general asked rhetorically, 'know what an oyster knife is?' The general offered no answer in the initial text, but gave one in the margins of the final version: 'No.'

The text they had discovered said nothing about other events. There was no need to assume a possible continuation of the memoirs. The text ended in the middle of the page, under which there was a date (13/07/74) and the laconic 'Dictated by me. Gen. Larionov.' What had compelled Taras to keep these three particular sheets of paper at work? Perhaps that was the most enigmatic aspect of the whole matter.

12

Solovyov headed to the conference the next morning. Zoya saw him off at the bus station. She went to the museum after putting Solovyov on the Simferopol trolleybus. They had called Zoya the night before and insistently requested she show up at work. They had few employees and some were on vacation, so there was nobody to tell visitors about Chekhov.

The trip to Kerch was not short. Crimea, which had formerly seemed small to Solovyov, was revealing previously unaccounted for expanses that required time to cross. Discoveries of this sort, thought the drowsy Solovyov, were what distinguished field research from office work. He fell asleep somewhere near the Nikitsky Botanical Garden. The trolleybus was already driving through Simferopol when he opened his eyes.

Solovyov had a snack in Simferopol. He bought a smoked chicken leg at the station and ate it without bread, washing it down with cold beer. It was delicious, if unrefined. He wiped his hands and mouth with a napkin. He tossed the bone to a dog that came to him; there are lots of stray dogs in southern cities. He took his unfinished beer bottle and headed for the platform. There was about an hour until the next local train to Kerch.

There were already people on the platform. Two women with children. Wearing cotton dresses that had wilted in the heat. One wearing a bucket hat, the other a straw hat that had slid back. Both with suitcases. Solovyov sat down on a bench, took a swig from the bottle, and set it alongside his foot. A peasant man with a sack on his shoulder. It was immediately obvious he was a peasant. A woman collecting bottles. A plastic bag in one hand, a stick in the other, to check the rubbish bins. Dark blue eyelids. Crimson lips. The tanned skin of a person who spent all her time outside.

'May I have the bottle?'

Solovyov nodded. The lady swished what was left at the bottom of the bottle and pressed it to her mouth. She sat down on Solovyov's bench (the bottle was sent into the bag with a clink). Leaned against the back. Pulled a cigarette butt out of the bin and lit it with delight.

A piglet hopped out of the peasant's sack, squealed, and began running around the platform. It was afraid to jump down. The peasant (they are capable of this) caught the piglet without losing his dignity. Put it in the sack and tied it. Lit a cigarette.

'And that's the end of democracy,' said the bottle collector. She was not addressing anyone in particular.

The local train somehow pulled up almost unnoticed. It was old, its paint had peeled in the sun, and there was plywood where the glass had been smashed. Everybody boarded except the bottle collector. She continued sitting on the bench; this platform was her workplace. Maybe her home, too. The carriage began to move and she disappeared. Forever, thought Solovyov, as he fell sleep. Forever . . .

He woke up about an hour later and fell back to sleep. He

thought he would never catch up on his sleep after the night in Alupka. That night, he had borrowed his own strength from the coming month and was now slowly paying it back. The palms of his hands (Zoya had smeared them with sea buckthorn oil the night before) hurt as before. And Zoya could not come with him. He caught himself thinking he was glad about that.

The owner of the piglet was sitting across from Solovyov. Solovyov observed as the sack squirmed despondently on the floor; he sympathized with the piglet. The peasant was looking out the window, lost in thought (or not thinking about anything?) There was something wood-like, cracked, in the peasant's face. It radiated motionlessness. The age-old motionlessness of the Russian peasantry, decided the young historian. That was what made the gaze so sustained, intent, and absent.

Solovyov was housed in the Hotel Crimea. The hotel's gray granite exterior presented a restrained solemnity from the late 1950s. This was apparently the city's main hotel. And the first hotel in Solovyov's life. He received his key from a sleepy woman at the reception desk ('a porter,' Solovyov whispered, since this was how he wanted to picture things).

'Close the window at night,' said the woman. 'Cats jump into the rooms.'

'Cats?'

After crossing the lobby, he turned and said, 'I love cats.'

But the woman was no longer there.

Solovyov went up to the second floor. The keyring was weighted down by a vaguely pear-shaped wooden fob, making it difficult to turn the key in the lock. Within the lock, Solovyov overcame (pressing firmly into the door) some sort of impediments invisible to the world. Dull scraping and the pear thudding against the door accompanied whatever happened inside the lock.

The door opened anyway. Solovyov looked around after entering the small rectangular room. The window faced what was not quite a garden: it was an ambiguous green environment where all the objects (bed frames, bar counters, tires) served as plant stands. There really were cats strolling along a wall overgrown with ivy.

Solovyov left his things in the room and went out into the city. He enjoyed taking a deep breath of Kerch's evening air. The sea in Kerch was not Yalta's resort sea. The sea was regarded completely differently here. It even smelled different. It had an ancient port aroma that included a light tinge of decay: seaweed on the breakwaters, fish in crates, and fruit crushed during shipment.

Solovyov walked along Kerch's main street and liked it. 'Le . . . Street,' he read on a half-faded sign. Some sort of French continuation might have followed that, and the street itself did seem a bit French to him. The crowns of old acacias had intertwined over the street's three-story houses, giving it the look of an endless gazebo. It was cool in the thick shadow that was turning to darkness. Le . . . Street. Solovyov could guess the street's full name.

He bought himself some yellow bird cherries. When he saw a pump in a courtyard, he stopped there to wash them. To do so, he had to make several motions with the pump handle (it was cast iron with a lion on the grip) and then quickly run over to the spout and put the plastic bag of cherries underneath. Solovyov filled the bag with water, turned it upside-down, and released the water. The water disappeared through a blackened metal grate. Several cherries rolled down there, too.

The cherries turned out to be delicious: ripe, but firm. Solovyov took them in pairs, by their fused stalks, and gently—one after another—removed them from their stalks with his lips. He rolled the cherries in his mouth. Delighted in their form. Carefully bit into them, sensing the cherries' special (yellow) sweetness. The flesh came away from the pits easily and the pits moved toward his lips, as if on their own, casually jumping down into Solovyov's palm.

It was already dark when he returned to the hotel. Solovyov noticed some sort of motion even before turning on the light in his room. When he flicked the switch, he saw a cat on the windowsill. The cat neither hid nor ran. He walked away calmly, even seeming to hesitate. If Solovyov had addressed him, he would have stayed. His smoke-colored tail quivered. A clump of fur, also smoke-colored, hung on the zipper of Solovyov's bag.

'So you were digging around in my bag?' Solovyov asked and then remembered, with shame, how he himself had dug around in Taras's things.

The cat looked out the window with affected indifference. He was observing Solovyov with his peripheral vision and attempting to understand what might follow this sort of tone. Anything at all could follow. When Solovyov took a step toward the window, the cat jumped down from the windowsill to the ledge.

Feeling tired after his day of travel, Solovyov decided to go to bed. He fell asleep immediately and slept dreamlessly. A heavy slapping on the floor woke him up at dawn. He opened one eye halfway and saw two cats next to his bed.

Solovyov waved his arm drowsily and the cats left, in a dignified manner. Solovyov thought that he ought to close the window after all, but fell straight back to sleep.

Participant registration for the 'General Larionov as Text' conference began at nine that morning. It took place at the Pushkin Theater, a stately building with a hint of classicism, on Kerch's central square. The city was offering the best it had for studying General Larionov as text.

Solovyov saw the registration table when he entered the theater's cool lobby. A young woman with red hair was sitting on a swiveling barstool beside the table. Her nose ring sparkled dimly.

'Solovyov, Petersburg,' said Solovyov. He thought the woman was no younger than thirty.

'Wow!' She made a full turn on the swiveling stool and was once again face-to-face with Solovyov. 'Dunya, Moscow. I'll register you, Solovyov.'

Dunya jumped down from the stool (Solovyov noticed the same kind of stools at the bar at the other end of the lobby), marked something in her papers, and held out a conference folder with the program. Solovyov opened the program and walked slowly toward the auditorium.

'Your badge,' Dunya bleated after him.

Solovyov turned. Dunya was sitting on her stool again and holding a nametag with his surname.

'Mizter, you forgot your badge,' she said, beckoning to him. 'I'll pin it on for you.'

Without getting up from her stool, Dunya pinned the nametag to Solovyov's shirt, breathed on its plastic glossiness, and wiped it with her skirt hem. Solovyov examined Dunya's untanned legs for several seconds.

'Thank you.'

He started walking away but Dunya politely took him by the elbow.

'What about your folder?'

He really had left it on the table.

'Another absent-minded professor,' said Dunya, shaking her head. 'Your type needs looking after.'

Several people were already standing behind Solovyov and he rushed to get out of their way. He glanced at the program as he walked. His paper was set for the conference's second—and final—day.

About forty minutes remained until the beginning of the morning session, so Solovyov decided to go for a walk. During that time, he managed to have a look at the Lenin monument, the post office, and the Chaika department store. When he returned to the theater, he saw Dunya by the columns. She was smoking.

'Is it time?' Solovyov politely asked.

'It's time to get out of here. The opening's the most insipid part. That's right, young man.' Dunya put out her cigarette on the column's rough surface. 'You'd be better off treating a lady to coffee. I know a place nearby.'

A Volga sedan pulled up to the theater. A fat man in a light-brown suit got out and headed toward the entrance, tucking his shirt into his pants as he walked.

'Local boss,' said Dunya. 'With a story about the cannery that's sponsoring us. You interested?'

Solovyov shrugged. Dunya made such a face at the word 'cannery' that it would have been awkward to take an interest.

As Solovyov followed the energetic Dunya, he was angry with himself for his indecisiveness. In the first place, he did want to see the conference opening. In the second place (Solovyov suddenly realized this in all its clarity), more than anything, he felt tired of Zoya. This was the start of the second reel of some strange film he did not even seem to have agreed to be involved in.

They walked half a block and ended up in a dark vaulted basement. A chandelier shaped like a steering wheel hung from an enormous hook where the basement's vaulted ceiling came together.

'This little joint reminds me of "Gambrinus",' said Dunya. 'I discovered it yesterday.'

Solovyov ordered two coffees with Chartreuse. The liqueur was served in faceted vodka glasses. Dunya poured half her shot into her coffee and drank the other half in one swallow.

'When will academician Grunsky speak?' asked Solovyov.

'I think it's actually right now. Alas, neither academician Likhachev nor academician Sakharov will be here today. So you can relax.' Dunya lit a cigarette and the smoke began rising prettily toward the steering wheel. 'I'd advise you not to get caught up in the academicians, the title has depreciated a lot. And Grunsky's just plain stupid.'

'Then how'd he get to be an academician?'

'He had enough maneuverability. Connections.' She blew out smoke in a thin stream. 'Well, and he was brownnosing everybody in charge at the Academy.'

Dunya's attitude seemed too categorical to Solovyov but he kept quiet. He refused to imagine a stupid academician.

The break was ending when they returned. The theater was crowded and the attendees' muted buzz reminded him of an intermission at an operetta. Scenery of a medieval castle in the mountains intensified that impression. The

gothic scene swaying in a draft might not have fit the conference theme but the organizers thought it created a pacifying,
romantic backdrop.

Solovyov could see a small fat man on the stage, to the
left of the castle wall. The man stood at the chairman's
table, half-facing the auditorium, with one hand thrust in
his pocket (not a flattering pose for the short-legged). Using
his free hand, he carefully piled hair on his bald spot. The
name card on the table said, 'Acad. P.P. Grunsky.' Nothing
that Dunya had reported was mentioned on the card.

There was something unnatural—in the sense of theat-
rical—about even the conference attendees' appearances.
Despite the hot spell, they were strolling around in suits
and running their hands along the lapels of their outmoded
jackets again and again. This wasn't even because of the
hot spell; the suits were blatantly out of character for their
owners. And for their faces, which were rough and devoid
of expression. These people pressed their arms to their
torsos as they walked timidly around the theater. Looked
at themselves in the mirror in the foyer. Dampened their
combs in the little fountain outside the theater and fixed
their hair. These were cannery employees, sent by their
bosses to lend the event a more mass scale. According to
the conference organizers, very broad swaths of the population should hear papers about the general.

Two cannery employees approached Grunsky and asked
for his autograph. This was audible thanks to the numerous
microphones that equipped the stage. They were all over
the place, dangling from somewhere above, like motionless
black lianas. Grunsky led the requestors to the table and
wearily, but with visible pleasure, signed the two programs

they held out to him. This was the first time in his life he had been asked for his autograph.

Solovyov and Dunya took seats in the parterre. Solovyov removed the program from his folder. Leaning toward his shoulder, Dunya ran her fingernail along the second surname listed after the break.

'Tarabukin's a terrible pain but he gets a lot done. One of the few who'll say anything relevant here. He's sitting to my right.'

Solovyov slowly turned his head. The left-handed Tarabukin was nervously noting something in a folder of papers lying on his knees. His gnarled fingers and their countless knuckles might have made an even bigger impression than his left-handedness. Tarabukin was chewing the fingernails on his right hand and kept examining them pensively.

'Before lunch . . .' Grunsky tapped his fingernail on the microphone and the hall shook with a deep, drumming sound. '. . . we have one more paper before lunch, so I ask you to focus. The floor goes to Professor Tarakubin with the paper "Larionov and Zhloba: a Textological Collision".'

'Tarabukin, if you will,' protested Tarabukin, but his voice was drowned out by the general noise.

Dunya shook with silent laughter. Meanwhile, Tarabukin was already energetically making his way to the stage. He gestured as he walked and his entire appearance expressed indignation, either from the incorrect pronunciation of his surname or the impossibility of making his way to where he was to speak.

'Quiet, please,' Grunsky tapped at the microphone again. 'One more paper before lunch. The speaker prepared *hand-outs*, they'll be distributed now.'

Tarabukin clambered up the little stairs onto the stage, continuing to gesture, and walked under the hanging microphones.

'. . . ucking smarty pants, what are you talking about, *handouts*? In Russian . . .'

Tarabukin stopped short when he heard he was on the air. Now he silently crossed the stage—small and rumpled—without a shadow of regret about what he had said. After Tarabukin had taken his place behind the lectern (at his height, he truly proved to be *behind* it), a heavyset woman with braids arranged on her head started making her way toward the stage. She moved slowly, placing her feet heavily on the steps, and reminding Solovyov of his high school principal, a woman nicknamed Bigfoot. Judging from the hand she extended in Grunsky's direction, she was saying something to him, but her words were inaudible.

'Who's the co-chair?' Grunsky asked again, into the microphone. 'You're the co-chair? Where were you before?'

The women answered him again after conquering the final stairs. The academician shrugged and glanced at the program.

'Nobody said anything to me about co-chairing.'

The woman who had come up on stage turned to the audience and pointed out someone on the parterre for Grunsky. Despite her gait, she certainly was not Solovyov's high school principal.

'So, may I begin?' Tarabukin asked sarcastically, but nobody was paying attention to him.

'She's corresponding member Baikalova,' said Dunya. Her face expressed delight. 'Fiesta with a bullfight.'

'There's not even a second chair here,' said Grunsky,

slightly lifting his chair by its back to illustrate. 'I don't know where you'll sit.'

'One of us should prove to be chivalrous, Petr Petrovich,' said Baikalova.

She was already within range of the microphones. Grunsky threw up his hands, 'Well, that's a fine how-do-you-do!'

Baikalova bowed low, from the waist, to Grunsky and turned to face the audience. Tarabukin, suffering, rolled his eyes. The cannery workers smiled shyly.

Grunsky approached the edge of the stage and signaled to someone to bring a second chair. A man in a pensioner's shirt with patch pockets jumped out of his seat and shook it, demonstrating to Grunsky that they were fastened not only to the neighboring seats (everyone sitting in that row shook) but also to the floor. Grunsky gestured his under-standing and returned to the table.

Two men in overalls hurried up the steps to the stage. They disappeared behind the curtains but reappeared a minute later, dragging a massive throne with a scraping sound. They pulled it up to the table and explained some-thing to Grunsky, who was grasping the back of his own chair as a precaution. Grunsky nodded and showed Baikalova the throne with a gallant gesture. She sized up Grunsky with a malicious gaze and moved heavily across the stage.

Baikalova had to ascend to the throne—which did not look out of place by the castle—in a literal sense. She first climbed onto a step attached to its base and then, holding the lion heads on the armrests, clambered up to the seat, which required some effort. Since the throne was not an item envisaged for use by someone sitting at a table, it turned out to be rather high. Baikalova's legs did not reach the floor, swinging slightly instead, like shapeless sausages, under the thin tabletop. Further beneath the tabletop—this was visible to the audience, too—the academician's feet were moving chop-chop, as if he were in the homestretch. There was no question he had won this little competition.

'Please, go ahead, colleague,' said Grunsky, turning to Tarabukin.

'Yes, do,' said Baikalova, looking down on Grunsky.

'Thank you very much,' Tarabukin responded. After thinking, he uttered it in pieces. 'Thank you. Very much.'

Leaning against the armrest furthest from Grunsky, Baikalova rested her cheek on her hand. Her lips stretched apart, forming a raspberry-colored diagonal line along her face.

Tarabukin huffily began his paper. He uttered the introductory phrases—which in and of themselves contained nothing nasty, offering a listing of sources he had used—with a bitter, almost denouncing, intonation. It was they, his sources, who took the blame for the scholar's disrespectful treatment of the scholar. It was they who answered for his mangled surname, for his ridiculous waiting on the stage, for everything that had thrown the scholar utterly off balance. Even in this difficult frame of mind, though, the presenter spoke in particular about two sources he had studied.

The first of them was General Larionov's *Notes for an Autobiography*, in Dupont's edition. Only when turning to that did Tarabukin forget the offenses committed against him. In characterizing Dupont's publication (and speaking of it with the highest praise) the speaker switched to an unusual tone, as if he were anticipating an important statement. Which is how things turned out. What Tarabukin was thinking about was the second source he had used: a heretofore unknown report by Dmitry Zhloba about his troops' entry into Yalta in November 1920. Tarabukin himself had found this source in the Archive of the Ministry of Defense.

But the researcher's revelations did not just consist of that happy finding; there was more. Propelled by a sixth sense (without which, as we know, no discoveries are made), he revealed unbelievable things by juxtaposing Zhloba's report with General Larionov's childhood remembrances.

A first glance at Tarabukin's materials for distribution made it obvious that the two texts were very closely connected. The texts had been created by utterly dissimilar people and they described completely different times. That is what made their resemblance so striking. An astonished buzz ran through the slightly hushed hall.

The most vivid coinciding occurrences in Zhloba's report and the general's recollections were in the printouts (not wishing to utter the borrowed English, *handouts*, he called them *handgrips*) that the speaker offered. Enjoying the impression he had made, Tarabukin slowly read off the first of the coinciding spots:

Fragment No. 1

Gen. Larionov	**D.P. Zhloba**
Notes for an	*Report Regarding Entry*
Autobiography	*into the City of Yalta*
A group of young Tatars greeted us as we entered the city. They were all on horseback, all dressed up.	. . . when we reached the city limits, a brigade on horseback greeted us. Tatars everywhere, attire:

Upon seeing our carriages, they shot into the air and shouted something in Tatar. *Maman* and my governess, *Dolly*, were very frightened but *Papa* explained to them that the Tatars were just welcoming us. *Maman* waved her hand to them. One of them rode over to the ladies' carriage, unfastened something from his saddle, and handed it to the stunned *Dolly*. 'It's kumys,' smiled the Tatar. 'Drink to your health.' *Maman* wanted to pay for it but the Tatar only flapped his arms. They shot a little more and galloped off into the mountains, going about their Tatar business. '*Charming*,' said *Dolly*.

national. They began firing into the air upon seeing our armored vehicle. They didn't understand Russian. I felt uneasy but our commissar, comrade Rozaliya S. Zemlyachka, explained that this was their way of greeting. Meaning, firing weapons. I saluted them. One of them rode over to comrade Zemlyachka and handed her a canister. 'It's kumys,' said the Tatar. 'Drink to your health.' Comrade Zemlyachka signaled to him that we would receive the kumys free of charge. The Tatar flapped his arms. They turned around and galloped into the mountains. 'Very nice comrades,' said comrade Zemlyachka.

Corresponding member Baikalova, who had not received one of Tarabukin's *handgrips*, was leaning heavily on the armrest closest to Grunsky and ostentatiously squinting to peer at the papers on the table. With exaggerated amiability, the academician pushed them in Baikalova's direction but they remained in place. Glancing at the audience, Baikalova threw up her hands.

'You're sitting up too high,' Grunsky said, also to the audience. 'And therein lies your misfortune.'

There was absolute silence in the hall when Tarabukin moved on to read the second excerpt.

Fragment No. 2

Gen. Larionov *Notes for an* *Autobiography*	D.P. Zhloba *Report Regarding Entry into* *the City of Yalta*
Many paupers gathered at the corner of Autskaya and Morskaya Streets, by the Alexander Nevsky Cathedral. This was a strange and varied public. Alongside old women wrapped in black there sat young women with children, tradesmen who had succumbed to drink, and *the barefoot tramps* whom Gorky would describe later. I would not be surprised if Gorky himself had been sitting there . . . They all crossed themselves devoutly. When leaving the service, *Maman* gave something to all of them, without	We found a lumpen element by the church at the corners of Autskaya and Morskaya Streets. Predominantly of male gender. Everyone who sat there was engaged in panhandling. The appearance of one of the aforementioned persons reminded me of the proletarian writer A.M. Gorky. I will not allow the thought that this was comrade Gorky, given his location on the isle of Capri. Everyone crossed themselves. Comrade Bela Kun warned them strictly with regard to crossing themselves and seized change from their hats

exception. Her favorite was a tall, one-legged old man. He would sit, displaying his peg leg for all to view. When we walked down the stairs, out of the cathedral, he waved welcomingly with his crutch. Sometimes he bowed. Smiled at us toothlessly. And one-leggedly.

One time *Maman* forgot money and was very upset. When the old man realized that, he approached her unnoticed and gave her everything he had: a ruble and a half in change. He didn't want her to leave distressed. 'Well, isn't that just lovely?' *Maman* said, giving the money out to the paupers.

as unearned income. A one-legged old man particularly attracted comrade Kun's attention. He smiled at our comrades and waved to them with his crutch. Comrade Kun suspected him of being two-legged and ordered him to stand and produce his missing leg for inspection. When the one-legged man began to refuse, Kun kicked him in the face and forced him to empty his pockets, where there happened to be more change, beyond what had been taken away earlier. 'What was I telling you?' comrade Kun asked those present and everyone agreed with him.

Snoring became audible in the hall when Tarabukin paused. The sounds were muted, like distant thunder, but that did not make them less apparent. Academician Grunsky put his hand to his forehead and peered out from under it at his neighbor sitting at the table. Sometimes he covered his eyes with his hand and shook his head as if lamenting the co-chair he had received. It truly was Baikalova snoring. The corresponding member had fallen asleep quickly and easily while squinting at the texts that had been distributed, and now the microphone that hung over her head was broadcasting her snoring for the audience. This was first-class snoring, with a rumble on the inhale and a whistle on the exhale. With rolling and modulation, complaints and threats, sincere sighs and mockery. Unfortunately for Baikalova, Tarabukin could not find the example he needed and was feverishly flipping sheet after sheet. The ruthless academician took the table microphone, walked around the table on tiptoe, and brought it right to his co-chair's nose. The hall shook with a thundering peal. The snorer awoke and looked, crazed, at the microphone the academician was extending.

'We have a schedule to keep,' said Baikalova in a husky voice.

With an emcee's gesture, Grunsky pointed at Baikalova and returned to his place.

'What a jerk,' said Dunya, beginning to laugh.

'I won't . . .' Tarabukin was still shifting his papers around. 'I won't, because of the lack of time, read all the examples, I have twenty-three of them . . . But excerpt No. 19 . . . uh-huh, there it is . . . I'll still cite this one.'

<u>Fragment No. 19</u>

Gen. Larionov *Notes for an* *Autobiography*	**D.P. Zhloba** *Report Regarding Entry into* *the City of Yalta*
One time I *vanished*. I was around six years old. I left our house without saying anything to anybody and	They'd already reported to me that the general hadn't evacuated. We'd searched the whole city for him. I rode to

wandered aimlessly. Why did I do that? I don't know. I didn't have any set goals, I remember that. I walked downhill, along Botkinskaya, examining my surroundings. Laborers were placing a huge carved cabinet on a cart and the carthorse was pawing at the ground, its flanks trembling. Both the cart and even the horse seemed small compared to the cabinet. The cart began moving heavily up the hill and the laborers supported the cabinet from both sides. This contraption moved jerkily, in time with the horse's steps. With a sad creaking. I stared after them, until they disappeared around the corner. And even then they continued creaking, unseen, for a time.

Later, I ended up on the embankment. I stood, leaning against the fence at the Tsar's Garden, and watched street musicians. Cello, two violins, and a

the general's house at the head of the advance party but he wasn't there. 'Vanished, did he?' shouted comrade B. Kun. 'Vanished,' confirmed the maid. 'He went out an hour ago. Didn't say anything.' Comrade Zemlyachka jabbed her in the thigh with a pen knife and we galloped downhill, along Botkinskaya Street. A group of laborers was loading a cabinet with a two-headed eagle onto a cart. 'Have you seen the general?' I asked the laborers. 'We saw him,' said the laborers. 'He walked by here in 1888. And it's 1920 now.'

'Ah, so that's it!' I shouted. 'That's your idea of a joke? Well, here's mine.' I lashed their mare with my whip and she dashed off. The cabinet fell on the roadway but didn't break. A sturdy item. The laborers silently went after the cart. I ordered that the cabinet be brought into the general's house.

flute. They played there for many more years, I saw them on each of our trips to Yalta. My back could feel the cool rhombuses of the fence. I admired their ancient Jewish faces, nubby fingers with fine hair on the phalanges, and dusty black clothing. Their leader was an old violinist. The wind brought his long gray hair to his lips, flattening it there. He would blow the hair away or toss it by nodding his head. He made horrible grimaces as he played, and I watched him, unable to tear myself away. Everybody knew this was an expression of devotion to the music. Nobody laughed. The musicians played music by request or for no particular reason. Copper coins scattered into the open violin case. There was nothing they couldn't play. To this day, I think most of them when I hear the word *music*. I listened to those

We saw some musicians by the Tsar's Garden. I halted the squad and listened, spellbound. They were playing on two little violins and one big one. Plus a wind instrument flute. 'The soldiers' hearts have coarsened from war,' I told the musicians. 'Play something touching for them.'

A violinist stepped forward and said, 'Soldiers, have a listen to Oginsky's *Polonaise*.' He swung his bow and the musicians simultaneously began playing. The first violinist's face changed as he played.

'He's full of emotion,' comrade Kun told those present, a large tear flowing down his own cheek. As I listened to the heartfelt music of the *Polonaise*, I thought we'd missed the general after all. He couldn't, in his right mind, stay in the city of Yalta.

We stayed there a fairly long time. Several privates dismounted and sat on the ground, listening to the musicians for a long time— the entire time they played there. I didn't budge, even when they were taking their ceremonial bows. Only when their instruments ended up in their cases was the magic gone. I knew then that not another sound would be heard.

I continued my journey along the embankment. The embankment was narrow then, not like it is now. I walked right next to the cast-iron railings; the sea's edge was just on the other side. My hand slid over the lower crosspiece of the railing: it was black with silvery, hanging drops. I collected those drops in my hand and they ran along my arm, flowing up my sleeve. That was nice.

I turned on Morskaya Street and ended up by a pharmacy I knew. It was cool inside the pharmacy. It smelled of oak cabinets and music. I didn't prevent them. And didn't say anything. And comrade Kun didn't say anything, either, though he wanted to in the beginning. That's how it seemed to me. And the horses stood still and didn't stomp their feet because an animal understands everything, even music. It's a medical fact. Horses have never failed me, that's a fact, too. But people have failed me more than once. I place little hope in them.

Then we went to ride along the embankment. It's narrow so we re-formed into columns of two as we rode. A horse loves that formation. I rode silently. Generally I'm quiet when I'm on the move, so I don't get distracted from my thoughts. And I look at the horse's mane if I'm not in battle. I finger the mane with my hand. Now and then you burrow your face in the mane, too. The mane has a special smell.

medicines. 'What can I do for you?' the pharmacist asked and patted me on the head. The tip of his nose was bulbous. I was proud to have come here by myself. I was quiet because I didn't need anything at that time. After showing me a chair, the pharmacist disappeared into the next room. The chair was huge, with leathery folds. It reminded me of an old bulldog. I have not seen such a good chair since. The pharmacist brought me a cough drop. I popped it in my mouth and went outside.

Finally, I ended up at the jetty. I stepped onto it because that, it seemed, was where my road lay. When I reached the end of the jetty, I saw that the sea surrounded me on three sides. I didn't grasp that when I was walking. But I saw it after stopping. Wet green stones rocked from

From the embankment, we turned on Morskaya Street and went to the pharmacy. Comrade Gusin and I. He needed a new bandage because the old one was soaked with blood. Comrade Zemlyachka had licked away the blood that soaked through. 'What can I do for you?' asked the pharmacist. It seemed I'd seen this person with the weather-beaten face somewhere.

'Change his dressings,' I told the pharmacist and pointed at Gusin. While the pharmacist bandaged Gusin, I sat in a soft chair. It was cool and calm. I could have stayed there forever.

'Try not to lose blood, comrade,' the pharmacist told Gusin in parting. 'A person only has six liters.'

'Two three-liter jars,' joked comrade Zemlyachka.

We set off along the embankment again. Where comrade Kun touched me on the waves, the wind droned somewhere at the top of the lighthouse but—and this was most important—there was no more road. I stood, pressing my back against the lighthouse, and I was scared. I thought the jetty had pulled away and started moving out from under my feet. I froze with horror when I sensed the pitching. I got down on all fours, pressed into the warm, rough wall, and crawled to the opposite side of the lighthouse. Only there did I dare rise to my feet and slowly, step by step, head toward the other end of the jetty. When I raised my head, I saw my father: his anxious face, his arms open wide for an embrace. I knew that those arms would not allow me to perish now. I ran the rest of the distance. I ran to my father and cried. I threw myself into his arms.

the leg—there!—with the crop. Lightly. And pointed at the jetty with that same crop. I looked around and couldn't believe my eyes: the general. In the flesh. Just standing, at the edge, arms on his chest. The general!

Our sailors were already keeping watch at the jetty. That's why we were in no hurry. The general already had nowhere to go but into the water. Comrade Kun proposed tying up the general along with two critically wounded Whites and tossing them into the sea, but comrade Zemlyachka condemned that method as ultra-liberal and bloodless. Comrade Kun was offended and later drowned all the critically wounded without consulting comrade Zemlyachka. They galloped on to the jetty and I stayed on the embankment. The general walked slowly toward them.

Tarabukin poured himself some water from a pitcher as he finished excerpt No. 19. He drank thirstily and with a light moan, like a person who still has a lot left to say. Grunsky sensed the speaker's frame of mind and stood up from his chair: this was an eloquent appeal to finish up. These gestures were inaccessible for Baikalova, who was lodged in her throne and limited to ostentatious glances at her watch. Tarabukin had been standing half-facing the co-chairs but now quickly turned in the opposite direction, toward the second-tier loge (left side), and began expounding on the results of his intertextual analysis.

And those results—paradoxical to the highest degree!— consisted of the following.

First. The events described by the general (1888) preceded, chronologically, what Zhloba (1920) recounted. That said, however, the time when Zhloba prepared his report preceded the time when the general created his memoirs (presumably the late 1950s to the early 1960s).

Second. Notwithstanding the obvious resemblance of the chosen compositions, textual borrowing from either author could not be ascertained. Further. From the scholar's point of view, there was not even a hint of one author being familiar with the other's text.

Third. Both texts were also impossible to trace back to a common source because, despite their closeness, they recount (and here the speaker pounded his fist on the lectern) different events.

Tarabukin poured from the pitcher again. Standing as before, with his back to the co-chairs and his side to the audience, he proceeded with the second glass. The noise of Tarabukin's deep swallows rang from the hall's loudspeakers, sounding like a gigantic metronome. Grunsky, who had just sat down, stood again and tapped at the microphone.

'We have a schedule to keep,' said Baikalova, in order not to yield the initiative to the academician.

Powerless to ignore what was happening, Tarabukin turned sharply toward the co-chairs and grazed the pitcher with his elbow. After a slow-motion, almost infinite moment of flight, the pitcher shattered to smithereens on the stage.

'I understand,' said Tarabukin, quietly but tragically, 'that standing between a person and his lunch is a thankless matter but I still have a fourth point. And I ask that it be heard out.'

Grunsky and Baikalova stared wordlessly at the same point in the distance, as if they were in the finale of some sort of play. The falling pitcher had drawn them together a little. Both they and the audience members understood it was best to hear everything the speaker had to say. Grunsky sat down, in a clear expression of submissiveness.

Tarabukin's fourth point turned out to be his longest. By developing the ideas of Alexander Veselovsky on historical poetics and Vladimir Propp on the morphology of the folk-tale—while polemicizing with them at the same time—the researcher transferred conversation about the resemblance of the general's and Zhloba's texts into the realm of the correlation of motifs. To Tarabukin's misfortune (and, admittedly, the attendees', too), he got bogged down in clarifying the reasons he agreed and disagreed with his predecessors. Tarabukin understood well that these details were unnecessary but drifted further and further away from the topic of common motifs, even as he strove with all his might to return to it.

The speaker's—and the audience's—anxiety increased with every minute. With bated breath, the whole audience followed his tragic floundering in the maelstrom of scholarly thought, but there was no life ring. They did not want to throw it from the presidium; it could not be thrown from the audience. The cannery workers (the portion of the audience sympathizing most with Tarabukin) were ready to applaud, but the speaker needed to stop or at least pause for them to do so. He did not stop. Shrinking his head into his shoulders, he spoke ever faster and less distinctly, as if he hoped to find in his flow of speech some magic word that would crush his opponents for good.

When Tarabukin looked up from the lectern, he saw Grunsky's all-forgiving eyes. Baikalova was pensively examining her fingernails. This was the final blow for the speaker and he burst into tears. Thunderous applause rang out in the hall. Everyone headed off for lunch.

13

The cannery director headed up the column of people exiting the theater. After chasing off the factory employees who had begun attaching themselves to the column, he led the researchers to Cafeteria No. 8 on Lenin Street, where lunch had been set for the conference's participants and guests. Grunsky walked to the director's right, Baikalova to his left. The director's arms were flung half-open, as if welcoming a speedy oncoming wind; this kept making the edges of his jacket flap against the co-chairs, who were trying not to fall behind him. The column's leading edge was moving through the middle of Lenin Street, a pedestrian area, splitting the oncoming walkers into two even groups that flowed around the column. Everyone in the city knew the cannery director. Even from afar, pedestrians yielded the road to him and his scholars, regardless of their attitude toward his wares, which spawned controversy.

Inside the cafeteria, there was a smell of bleach and unappetizing food that had been eating into the establishment's walls for decades. Spray cans of air freshener that were used at the factory director's request (the cafeteria workers pointed them at the artificial flowers on the table) only worsened the situation. They added a sickening, sweetish undertone without removing the old smell.

The positioning of the rectangular tables reminded Solovyov of his old school cafeteria. A paper tablecloth covered each table, which seated four. Solovyov had already started sitting down at one but then, at the last minute, he noticed Dunya waving to him from the other end of the room. She was standing by a big oak table that was unlike the others. Solovyov hesitated for a moment then walked toward her. As a member of the conference's organizing committee, Dunya had been seated at the same table as the cannery director, Grunsky, Grunsky's secretary, Baikalova, and a man with crossed eyes. Dunya had decided to invite her new acquaintance.

Tarabukin was the last to enter the cafeteria. After finishing his presentation, he had initially entertained no thoughts of food. Tarabukin had categorically refused to go to the cafeteria with everyone. He walked down to the parterre, collapsed in a fourth-row seat, and sat there motionless for a few minutes. But he began to feel hungry after calming down a little so, after some hesitation, decided to go to the cafeteria anyway.

Right from the start, it looked to him as if there were no empty places; Tarabukin felt like nobody was expecting him. His tortuous decision to come to lunch had suddenly turned out to have unwelcome results for everyone, effectively rendering it ridiculous. His tragic figure in the doorway made everyone fall silent.

'As might have been expected, there aren't any places,' Tarabukin said quietly.

It turned out, however, there were still empty places at

three tables. As Tarabukin (who was a little flustered) was choosing where to sit, the cannery director rose a little and—pressing his necktie to his stomach—loudly invited the latecomer to his table. The invitation was accepted. Tarabukin proudly straightened his shoulders and began shuffling over to the director's table.

Women from the cannery helped the cafeteria workers carry lunches to the tables. They built pyramids of dishes on flowered plastic trays, lifted them in one sharp motion, and, weighted down, transported them through the dining hall. They placed them on the corner of a table and neatly unloaded them with help from those sitting at the table. The soup and main course were served in identical dishes inscribed *SocNutr*. The dessert was in cups with the same inscription; the handles were broken to stave off theft. The handles of the aluminum spoons had been twisted into spirals for the same reason. The fork handles had no spirals since they had been brought from the cannery for the conference (forks were not used in Cafeteria No. 8). As it happened, there were no knives, even at the cannery.

Despite the uniform crockery, the meal service was not identical for all attendees. Solovyov noticed that at his table (unlike at the others), some olives stuffed with shrimp had appeared and there was black caviar gleaming bashfully from a *SocNutr* salad dish with chipped edges. Dunya caught Solovyov's gaze and, barely perceptibly, mimed a sigh. As someone clued-in, she knew there was no equality in the world.

'I'd like to introduce you to Valery Leonidovich,' said Grunsky, turning to the cannery director. 'He's one of the managers at the Solovyov Foundation.'

The director stopped spreading caviar on his bread and looked at Valery Leonidovich.

'And I'd like to introduce Solovyov himself,' said Dunya, with a smile.

'At such a young age . . .' began the director, but then he suddenly went silent and finished spreading his bread with caviar.

'Why was the conference moved from Yalta to Kerch, anyway?' Baikalova asked Valery Leonidovich. 'After all, Yalta is the general's city.'

Grunsky rolled his eyes, unnoticed by Baikalova. The same expression flashed across his secretary's face; he was a young man with dark hair parted down the middle.

'What, don't you like it here?' asked the director, making a showy gesture at the table.

'I'll answer your question about why it was moved,' said Tarabukin. 'The Fund simply didn't have enough money for Yalta.'

Valery Leonidovich rubbed the end of his nose. He seemed to think it unnecessary to comment on Tarabukin's statement. One of his eyes was directed at Baikalova, the other at the cannery director. It felt to Tarabukin as if they were not even looking at him. The reality of things was rather different.

'Really, where, as a matter of fact, can that money come from?' Tarabukin went on, his fury growing. 'Where, I ask you, can it come from, if the Foundation's renting half a palace in the center of Petersburg? If the salaries for people who *help scholarship* are the sort even a Nobel laureate wouldn't dream of? Mind you, I'm only speaking right now about the legal side of their activities . . .'

Tarabukin had switched to an impassioned whisper and everyone sitting at the table stopped eating at once.

'Forgive me, what's your name?' Valery Leonidovich asked Tarabukin. Baikalova and the cannery director simultaneously introduced themselves by name and patronymic.

Grunsky's secretary giggled.

'Valery Leonidovich asked for Nikandr Petrovich's name and patronymic,' said Dunya, unperturbed.

'Nikandr Petrovich,' said Valery Leonidovich, 'do me a favor: never count someone else's money. Never. That can end badly.'

'Are you threatening me?' Tarabukin asked slowly.

Those sitting at the neighboring tables began turning around. Valery Leonidovich's eyes diverged to opposite ends of the room. Grunsky's secretary sighed and served himself more shrimp-stuffed olives.

'A young person's body needs shrimp,' said Grunsky.

'Are you really Solovyov?' asked the cannery director.

'I really am,' said Solovyov.

He felt Dunya step on his foot under the table. The director pulled a business card out of his pocket and handed it to Solovyov.

'You don't regret that the conference is taking place in Kerch?'

'No,' said Solovyov, 'I don't regret it.'

There was still an hour and a half of free time remaining after lunch. Dunya suggested to Solovyov that they go to Mount Mithridat. Dunya thought it should be interesting for him, as a historian. Solovyov nodded pensively.

They walked up the mountain along dusty little streets that had a slummy look. A foot could slip easily on the roadway's loose cobblestones, and Dunya nearly fell once. She linked her arm through Solovyov's after that. The trees ended with the last buildings, the cobblestones underfoot changed to crushed limestone, and, gradually, the road turned into a path. Solovyov thought they were wading in a sea of wormwood that hung over the road. A petrified, motionless sea. There was something biblical in that image that did not correspond to post-lunch strolls, and he tried to free himself from Dunya's arm without being noticed. Dunya, however, noticed, but didn't let on to Solovyov.

Dunya was talking about the city of Pantikapaion and King Mithridates. She was unexpectedly fervent in describing Pantikapaion's vexed relationship with the superpower of his time. They approached the ruins of Mithridates's palace. A large lizard was sitting on a chunk of a column.

'After his own son betrayed him, Mithridates ordered a slave to stab him with a sword.'

Dunya made a dramatic stabbing lunge and the displeased lizard crawled down onto the ground. It did not like the sharp motions.

Solovyov sat down on one of the chunks of the ruins. It was hot. Warmed air was rising, visibly, over other chunks. It seemed to Solovyov that those hazy-transparent streams were ancient history that had lingered in some inconceivable way until his arrival but were now evaporating from the remnants of rock, under the heat of the sun. Might Mithridates have placed his palm on this column? In the evening, when the sea was already blowing cool air and the column was still warm? After ordering everyone to leave— concubines, bathhouse attendants, and bodyguards—did it really matter who? And then he himself would place his palm on this column and stand there? And sense its porous surface? And admire the fading strait? Looking out at where the sun turns into the sea, not tearing himself away until his eyes began to smart? Of course he might have. How, then, does his history differ from the general's history? Both fought in Crimea. Neither could hold on to Crimea. Everyone falls into exactly the same traps.

The evening session bore a very promising title: 'The Other General.' Grunsky and Baikalova co-chaired again, this time sitting side-by-side in identical chairs. The throne and the previous scenery were gone from the stage. Instead of a medieval castle, a tavern on the Lithuanian border now swayed slightly behind the co-chairs' backs. The cannery director thought this backdrop acclimated the audience to the session's informal character.

As he announced the first paper, academician Grunsky expressed the hope that the post-lunch presentations would offer a fresh view of the question and that *generaliana* might possibly become a new word. The academician likened blind following of a source to splitting hairs and pledged his support to everyone unafraid of breaking with tradition. In passing, he recalled Prof. Nikolsky's (Solovyov winced) proposed classification of researchers—offered in his *Archivists and Orators*—and declared Nikolsky's approach methodologically unsound. After condemning tradition-alism as a phenomenon, the chair turned over the floor to a presenter with the surname Kvasha. As Kvasha was coming on stage, Baikalova said she endorsed her colleague's remarks and expressed certainty that the vener-able scholar's nontraditional orientation might be a good stimulus for many young people dedicating themselves to science. The audience looked spontaneously at Grunsky's secretary.

'That's in revenge for the throne,' Dunya whispered to Solovyov.

Kvasha was already standing at the lectern. He had dark skin and closely cut hair; he was fairly gloomy. After asking to be forgiven for playing with words, he began by saying that his innovation—the paper was called 'General Larionov as Holy Fool'—had its own tradition. Needless to say, he was referring to Alexander Ya. Petrov-Pokhabnik's article, 'The General's Holy Foolishness', published back in 1932 in *The Phenomenology of Holy Foolishness*.

This article listed some of the general's traits and actions that did not fit with the usual accepted notions of army life overall, or with the officer corps' upper echelon, in particular. Among other things, there were references to the general's recurrent conversations with horses, his pathological (in the author's opinion) passion for railroad transport, and also the four birds (crane, raven, swallow, and starling) that lived in the general's train car, something witnesses had confirmed; some were cited in Alexei Ravenov's article 'The Blue Train Carriage.' Beyond those facts, there were also veiled allusions regarding certain allegedly strange orders from the general immediately before the Reds captured Yalta. Nothing concrete was said about these orders except that Larionov's subordinates were extraordinarily surprised to hear them. It was apparently at this time that the term 'holy fool' was first applied to the general.

Kvasha began his criticism of Petrov-Pokhabnik's work by offering details from the author's biography. Kvasha had

managed to ascertain that before Petrov-Pokhabnik evacuated from Crimea, he had been registered as holding the
position of stableman (Kvasha was of the opinion that this
may explain Petrov-Pokhabnik's jealousy toward the general's conversations with horses, as well as his obvious distaste
for railroad transport) in the army entrusted to the general,
after which, following his move from Constantinople to
Prague, he made a living writing out clean copies of works
by the Prague Linguistic Circle. Having grown accustomed
to the process of making copies, Petrov-Pokhabnik himself
did not even realize he was writing his first paper on the
informational structure of sentences, evoking Roman
Jakobson's unfeigned amazement. Petrov-Pokhabnik was
forced to leave the circle in the early 1930s as a result of his
openly Saussurean understanding of the problems of
synchrony and diachrony. Members of the circle were
prepared to forgive him anything at all, just not following
Ferdinand de Saussure.

It was during that same period—while making a clean
copy of a collection of articles, *The Phenomenology of Holy
Foolishness*—that the former stableman would prepare and
submit his piece about the general for the collection. As a
person who gave his all to his material, Petrov-Pokhabnik
himself began holyfooling it a bit, too. He would walk
Prague's streets barefoot in any season—something people
there still recall—and shock passers-by with announcements
about how there had simply not been any truly scientific
studies of holy foolishness until his. Sometimes he tossed
stones at the windows of the Prague Linguistic Circle.

Oddly enough, Kvasha's primary grievance with his predecessor was that he did not understand *the phenomenology of*

holy foolishness. His predecessor's infatuation with holy fools' external attributes (this infatuation manifested itself, among other things, in the curses Petrov-Pokhabnik addressed to his opponents) meant he could not gain genuine insight into holy foolishness as an occurrence. From Kvasha's point of view, by focusing on the eccentric side of the matter, Petrov-Pokhabnik did not discern the foremost aspect of holy foolishness: the spiritual sense.

Alongside this was the Prague researcher's misunderstanding of several Church Slavonic texts. After all, noted the unrelenting Kvasha, Petrov-Pokhabnik's previous line of work did not assume his familiarity with Church Slavonic. Kvasha himself knew the language perfectly, which allowed him to not only quote Church Slavonic texts with ease but also to fully understand them. After briefly touching upon the history of the study of holy foolishness as a whole, referencing myriad articles from around the world, Kvasha appealed for the most important points to be stressed, and then moved on to examine an issue related to the general.

Kvasha did not deny elements of holy foolishness in the general's behavior. Beyond that, he showed—basing his discussion on research into the hagiography of holy fools—that the general's contemporaries' recollections about him were often rooted in ancient Russian examples. For the presenter, one of the key points of this juxtaposition was the description of holy foolishness as being *dead for the world*. '"The hagiographical hero",' Kvasha read, bringing his glasses to his eyes to read from Tatyana Rudi's 'On the Topic of the Hagiography of Holy Fools', 'withdraws from the everyday situation, from life in his "native" society, and shifts into another society or—from the point of view of that previous society—into an "alien" one, as if he has ceased to exist for it (the previous society) and has thus shifted within it to the status of "dead".' After finishing the quotation from Rudi's article, the researcher offered eloquent examples of how the general left his society.

First and foremost, he addressed statements about the birds staying in the train car with the general and mentioned, as a parallel, a story (from the Kiev Caves Patericon) about Isaac of the Kiev Caves, in which an incident with a raven served to push Isaac into becoming a holy fool. The presenter, however, answered in the negative regarding whether the general's holy foolishness began with the appearance of the aforementioned birds in the train car.

Continuing the avian theme, Kvasha also recalled parallels that were closer to the general, both in terms of time and line of work. He had in mind facts from the biography of Russian Field Marshal Alexander Suvorov, who did not consider it disgraceful to crow like a rooster in cases of objective necessity. And so, after announcing for all to hear that he would attack the Poles under Kościuszko's command at the first rooster's crowing, he misled them (the Poles). In fact, the field marshal himself cock-a-doodle-doo'd that evening, without waiting for the morning roosters. He also flapped his arms against his sides, striving for an external resemblance to a bird. His troops marched out at twilight and thoroughly routed the enemy. Under more tranquil circumstances, the great commander was known to wake his soldiers with a cock-a-doodle-doo.

Beyond that—and this was the closest parallel to the general's behavior—at Great Lent, Suvorov ordered that one room in his house be strewn with sand, then he arranged potted firs and pines there and let in birds. The birds were released into the wild after Easter, upon the arrival of warm weather.

Needless to say, the presenter mentioned the general's infamous conversations with horses, something Petrov-Pokhabnik had examined in his day, too. Kvasha considered his predecessor's coverage of this topic detailed but tendentious.

Kvasha also acknowledged that the general's ride on a cart with a load of sand along the frozen Sivash was not exactly traditional for the upper echelons of the officer corps. Despite the ride being explainable—to verify the ice's strength—the method itself could not but provoke questions.

In working with materials from the Crimean Agricultural Archive, Kvasha was also able to discover a statement about how the general ordered soldiers and officers to help peasants plow the land in their free time away from battle. As grounds for this order, he cited the expropriation of the peasants' horses for the cavalry, which obliged the army to at least help them (the peasants), if only in this way. Irritated by having to fulfill functions not appropriate for them, according to the discovered document, the officers 'indulged in grumbling.' All that reconciled them with the strange order was that the general personally harnessed himself up and pulled a plow, accompanied by a tiller of the land who smiled, bewildered. In analyzing the fact that he had cited, the presenter cautioned attendees against considering this a complex form of Tolstoyism. Despite the special places in Lev Tolstoy's writings for both the horse theme (*Strider, The Story of a Horse*) and the railroad theme (*Anna Karenina*), the writer's position on religious issues was not close to the general's. It is well known, too, that Lev Tolstoy's tilling of the land did not mean he foresaw the human being replacing the horse.

Amidst the extensive material that drew Kvasha's scrutiny, there was a special place for the famous instance when the general was being photographed in a coffin. Going against long-standing research traditions, the presenter was not inclined to explain that action simply with the general's eccentricity. From Kvasha's point of view, in this instance, the general's striving for the *dead world* received one of its most visible expressions. The presenter also reminded his listeners that some saints chose a coffin as their permanent residence.

In Kvasha's opinion, this intense attention to the theme of death was a distinguishing feature for the general. As a component of his profession, death, it seemed, needed to become a customary thing for him ('Although can one grow accustomed to death?' Kvasha asked, taking his gaze away from the lectern for a moment) and, in some sense, work-aday. That is likely how things were during the general's service in the active army. His—if it could be expressed this way—liveliest interest in death began manifesting itself after the Civil War, and only grew over the years.

The general gathered information about the lives but, even more meticulously, the deaths of his fellow pupils, brothers-in-arms, and even enemies, at least those who did not leave him indifferent. He even created two folders, accordingly labeling them *Living* and *Dead*. One of the folders—the choice depended on the state of the person of interest to the general—held a sheet with basic information about each person's life or death. The *Living* folder was initially unbelievably plump, while the *Dead* folder seemed nearly weightless. The situation changed over time. The general was forced, ever more frequently, to transfer sheets from one folder to the other. This continued until only one lone sheet remained in the *Living* folder. That was the sheet titled *General Larionov*.

And then the general began to doubt the accuracy of the records he had kept. He lost faith that he was the only one alive and all the others had died. This appeared illogical. 'Why,' noted the general on the sole remaining sheet, 'am I, who should have been shot back in 1920, alive, but those whom nobody had planned to shoot are dead?' The situation seemed so provocative to him that he transferred all the sheets from the *Dead* folder into the *Living* folder. After a pause, he put his own sheet in the *Dead* folder. Only that way—Kvasha raised his gaze to the audience again—was it possible not to allow the living and the dead to mix.

The researcher also examined, apart from the other proceedings, two oral stories about the general taken down by a folklore expedition in the Crimean village of *Izobil'noe*. The first told how, allegedly, the general took Perekop without the permission of Anton Denikin, Commander-in-Chief of the White Army, and sent Denikin a telegram with the following content: 'Glory to God, glory to us, Perekop's captured, it's here with us.' The second story described a Christmas dinner that took place in the commander-in-chief's Sevastopol headquarters. In answer to Denikin's question about why General Larionov, who was sitting at the table, was not eating, the general replied, 'It's Lent, dear father, one mustn't eat before the first star.' Purportedly, Denikin ordered right then and there that the general be awarded a star.

Kvasha's paper subjected the stories to criticism, both from a factological perspective and for the handling of information sources. In brief, that boiled down to the following:

1) the commander-in-chief during the period under examination was no longer Anton Denikin but Baron Petr Wrangel;

2) General Larionov had not taken Perekop but had, rather, defended it; and

3) stories about Alexander Suvorov were precursor texts for both accounts.

In the initial story about the dispatch in verse form, it was not Perekop under discussion but the Turkish fortress Turtukai; additionally, the letter was addressed to none other than Field Marshal Petr Rumyantsev. In the story about the star being awarded, Suvorov was addressing not Petr Wrangel (and certainly not Anton Denikin) but Catherine the Great, accordingly calling her 'dear mother'. For Kvasha, the most interesting aspect in both folkloric pieces seemed to be that folk art made no distinctions whatsoever between Generalissimo Suvorov and General Larionov. The researcher called that circumstance 'symptomatic'.

In concluding his paper, Kvasha lamented that, other than Petrov-Pokhabnik's vague allusions, there was nothing known about the general's strange actions during the time Yalta was surrendered. The presenter called on his colleagues to make every effort to ascertain what actions might have been under discussion. From his point of view, clarifying those circumstances would not only add color to the portrait of the general, but might also shed light on the question that still remained unanswered: how, as a matter of fact, had the general remained alive?

Kvasha appeared to want to add something but Grunsky was tapping on the microphone. Kvasha tossed up his hands, put his papers in a folder, and calmly (by comparison with Tarabukin, at any rate) descended from the stage. Kvasha's conflict-free departure heartened Grunsky, who announced the next paper and called on the presenter to stick to the schedule. Everyone understood that the moderator's stern tone referred to the previous presenter.

Solovyov listened inattentively to this paper and the next. His head had begun to ache. Likely from an abundance of impressions that day, he thought. Or was it from the outing to the scorching Mount Mithridates (sun stroke)? Striving to grasp what exactly the presenter wanted to say increased the ache, extended it, and forced him to feel every brain cell.

'The operation's name was *signifying*,' said the presenter, Kholin.

The presenter's exceedingly soft voice and inability to speak directly into the microphone did not encourage focus. The discussion concerned operation *Foxhole*, something Solovyov himself had studied a little. Kholin quoted the operation's English-language name, the one Larionov used with western envoys. Before the Reds' decisive storm of Perekop, the general had ordered two additional rows of trenches be dug, as if the quantity might still change something.

'So these trenches replace the fighting spirit that I need, but my army has lost!' the general shouted to the shovelers.

He was walking along the defensive lines and earth was

scattering out from under his boots into the freshly dug trenches.

'I want to lie down in your trench, so everyone will leave me in peace!' the general shouted in another place.

The shovelers did not know that was the general's old dream. They silently went about their work, puzzled as to why he needed such a big trench in this case.

'The name of the operation was *signifying*,' Kholin repeated. 'If you divide the word *Foxhole* in two, you'll understand what the general wanted to say.'

Kholin observed, not without pleasure, as the whispers of everyone reading at once ran through the audience.

'It was as if,' said the presenter, waving his hands but still speaking quietly, away from the microphone, 'the general was saying goodbye with that word, that he would survive.'

The audience absorbed this for an inadmissibly long time.

'The key word is *whole*,' said a smiling Kholin. 'He was saying that he was a sly fox and would escape *whole*.'

The whispering gradually transformed into a buzz. With a bob of his head, the presenter returned some unruly hair to its place. Baikalova wrote something on a piece of paper and showed it to Grunsky. Grunsky read what she had written, moving his index finger from one word to another. Twice. He shrugged.

'But the second part of the word,' the concerned Baikalova said into the microphone, 'I mean, in "foxhole", it would be "hole", with just an "h", which means a pit. So it's not "whole" with the "w" for entire . . . I did study English . . .'

Kholin leaned on the lectern and his head twitched toward

his shoulder. His face expressed nothing but fatigue. He smoothed his hair and slowly began shifting his papers on the lectern. Baikalova rose from her place and looked questioningly at the presenter.

After a silence, Kholin said, almost as silently, 'I will verify your information.'

Solovyov felt like getting some fresh air. To do that, he would have to give an excuse to Dunya but did not know what to say. In any case, he had missed the transition to a new presenter and now it would be awkward to leave. Solovyov was annoyed at his own indecision. Alex Schwartz, a gender studies specialist from Boston, was speaking. She spoke Russian in a pleasant masculine baritone. She selected her words carefully, preferring infinitive verb forms and nouns in the nominative case. Solovyov's headache kept worsening.

Schwartz began her report on the general with a detailed story about famous 'cavalry maiden', Nadezhda Andreevna Durova (1783–1866). The American researcher reminded attendees that it was not easy for women to make their way into the Russian Army at the turn of the nineteenth century. A woman's lot was considered to be needlework (Schwartz demonstrated several motions for embroidery). The kitchen (cutting imaginary vegetables). Bed (motions of horseback riding).

But. Young Nadezhda had trouble with needlework. Lace. To tear (miming). To ruin (miming). To tangle (miming). Schwartz read a quotation from Durova's book *The Cavalry Maiden*: "'These two so very contradictory feelings,'" Schwartz quoted Durova, "'love for one's father and repugnance for one's sex—perturbed my soul with identical force and so,

with a firmness and constancy very uncommon for someone
my age, I devoted myself to contemplating a plan for leaving
the realm to which nature and customs assigned the female
sex."''

For her upbringing, the girl was sent to flank hussar
Astakhov. He taught her to wield a saber (miming). To shoot
(miming, with onomatopoeia). To ride horses (miming,
same as bed). Noticing that Baikalova had stood up, the
presenter addressed her with a calming gesture: 'Are you
interested in how this all ties in with the general?'

'I am,' said Baikalova.

Schwartz came out from behind the lectern, approached
Baikalova, and half-embraced her. 'It's just the general was
a woman. Like Nadezhda Andreevna. Like you and me. You
not know?'

Baikalova preferred to keep silent. She was, after all, still
in Schwartz's embrace.

'Why Zhloba not shoot him?'

'Why?' Grunsky asked, cautious.

'He knew general's secret. Loved him.'

Solovyov got up and began making his way to the exit,
not looking at anyone. Only when he was out in the fresh
evening breeze did he sense that his shirt was wet with
sweat. He undid two or three buttons and unstuck his shirt
from his chest. Dunya came up behind him and placed her
chin on his shoulder, 'Shall we go?'

Solovyov moved his shoulder, barely noticeably, 'I have a
headache.'

'I have aspirin in my room,' she rubbed her nose against
his neck.

Solovyov was looking at the Chaika department store, staring. 'My head aches because of you.'

Dunya did not say a word. She turned and vanished behind the theater's columns. Solovyov headed slowly toward his hotel.

14

The next morning did not portend scandal. The surface of the sea looked polished, without ripples. The wind that had been blowing in the evening had been replaced by conciliatory airy waves. Those waves blended a morning coolness with a barely discernible smell of fish, and Solovyov liked that mix very much. But scandal did come to pass.

Kvasha and Schwartz led the morning session. More precisely, Schwartz led it and Kvasha sat next to her. She took the microphone at the very beginning and then did not let it out of her hands. Kvasha did not protest. Initially, he contemplated the crystal chandeliers in the hall, but then he began quickly writing something on the papers lying in front of him.

Just before the first presenter came on, a rather short man wearing a tracksuit appeared on the stage. Swaying slightly, he walked to the moderators' table and leaned his hand on it. He stood motionless for a while, gazing at the floor.

'Who are you?' the good-natured Schwartz asked him in her choppy, accented Russian.

'Me?' The man paused. 'Well, let's say I'm the lighting technician.'

He crouched and placed his elbows on the table.

'You look very tired,' said Schwartz.

The man calling himself the lighting technician nodded. He reached for the pitcher, poured himself some water, and drank.

'I'm just a little tired.'

He rose to his feet and slowly walked away. Moscow researcher Papitsa was already standing below, by the stairs, waiting for the stage to free up. The small Papitsa cast a contemptuous glance at the lighting technician then flew up the stairs. He was wearing a tuxedo and his bow tie peered out only occasionally from underneath a long beard that seemed to be the wrong size. His icicle-like mustache scattered threateningly in various directions. This made him look simultaneously like Don Quixote, Salvador Dali, and Felix Dzerzhinsky. Taken individually, those figures had nothing in common with Papitsa. The presenter's beard, tuxedo, and abrupt motions reminded Solovyov of the puppet show that came to his school before each New Year holiday.

He'd loved those performances for the puppets' spiffy costumes, the spangles on the curtains, the aroma of a holiday tree that had already been placed in the corner of the assembly room but was not yet decorated, and the thought of an upcoming vacation. He loved those performances even in high school, when completely different things interested him, when he stealthily squeezed Leeza's hand while they were in the assembly room and thought about how they were sitting at a children's show but were connected by a relationship that was not childlike; that made him unbelievably turned on.

Solovyov cautiously turned his head and scanned the room for Dunya. She was sitting two rows away from him. She was sitting very straight, and not taking her eyes off the stage. That, thought Solovyov, must be how an outcast woman sits. For the first time, he felt something like sympathy for her.

The audience awaited Papitsa's paper with impatience. This was not related to the researcher having some sort of high standing in historical science. Papitsa did not have high standing. This was not even connected with Papitsa's beard, which made his oral presentations far more attractive than the written ones. The reason for the interest lay in general-iana's fundamental question, which was expressed in his paper's title: 'Why Did the General Remain Alive?'

There was movement in the lighting balcony, just as Papitsa began his paper. The face of the man who had gone onstage came into sight behind the balcony's steel structure; a moment later, spotlights began shining, one after another. Backlighting was coming only from the right balcony, causing sinister black shadows to form onstage. Two colored beams—green and dark blue—were directed at the co-chairs.

Papitsa read with an energetic delivery, gesturing and stamping his feet as he stood. He was reading in the literal sense, without taking his eyes from the text. His gnarled fingers slid along the edge of the lectern, sometimes coming away from it, sometimes falling still. Papitsa leaned on the microphone from time to time, deafening the audience with the crackling of his beard. Then he would push himself sharply away from the lectern so his body would stretch up perfectly straight, inclining and then freezing at that unnatural angle.

Papitsa painstakingly enumerated the reasons why the general should have been shot. There were, in the researcher's assessment, twenty-seven reasons. At the same time, there were only two alternatives for avoiding execution. The general did not use either; implied were escape to Constantinople or going underground. From this, there followed the existence of a third alternative, hitherto unknown. This alternative for escaping the firing squad was—and here the presenter straightened up and looked into the audience—collaboration with the Reds.

The researcher's argumentation was not new. Papitsa repeated conjecture about the general meeting with Dmitry Zhloba, things that had been stated back in the day, both in the émigré and the Soviet press, in Krivich's *Ten Years Later* as well as Drel's *At the Front Line*, but he did not draw in any additional evidence. Papitsa did not know the results of Solovyov's work, showing that on the night of June 13–14, 1920, from 23:55 until 03:35, Zhloba's and General Larionov's armored trains stood facing each other at the station in Gnadenfeld. Going further than his predecessors, Papitsa also surmised that Dzerzhinsky (at this moment, the presenter looked, extraordinarily, like Dali) had recruited Larionov back in 1918 and that Larionov fulfilled all the Cheka's assignments to the letter from then on. The researcher explained the general's resounding victories as tactical considerations. He surmised that they were launched with the goal of deflecting attention from the decisive battle in the autumn of 1920 at Perekop, which the general alleg-edly lost under an agreement. Papitsa called all the battles waged before that 'staged' and appealed for them not to be taken seriously.

'General Larionov was a Cheka agent for the entire Civil War, from beginning to end,' concluded the presenter. 'And there's your answer to the question of why he was not executed.'

'He's lying,' rang out a female voice in the auditorium.

A lady was moving toward the stage along the center aisle of the parterre. A click sounded in the lighting balcony and Papitsa found himself in the center of a red beam.

'If I may,' said Kvasha, moderating, 'The general had better alternatives for helping the Reds, though. Why, then, one might ask, would he wait around until November 1920 . . .?'

The lady walking through the hall went up on the stage and approached the presenter. Solovyov recognized her when she turned toward the audience. She was Nina Fedorovna Akinfeeva.

'He's lying,' Nina Fedorovna repeated into the microphone.

She was exactly a head taller than the speaker. Papitsa ran a hand along his red beard, 'I'm open to counterarguments. Prove to me that I'm wrong.'

Without saying a word, Nina Fedorovna took him by the beard and led him out from behind the lectern. Papitsa did not resist. As they walked through the parterre, another spotlight came on and followed them right to the exit. Nina Fedorovna's face expressed rage. Papitsa's face (it was turned upward) was devoid of expression. Once the two of them had disappeared behind the velvet drape at the exit, Alex Schwartz announced Solovyov's paper. The emancipation of Russian women had exceeded all her expectations.

Solovyov felt close to desperation. This was the second

time he had seen Nina Fedorovna Akinfeeva and the second time she had eluded him. Even as he began his paper, he kept glancing at the velvet drape, hoping Nina Fedorovna would return after all. But she did not come back.

Solovyov handled himself calmly behind the lectern. He had read this paper for the small Yalta circle so felt no anxiety now. He did not even glance at the text. As he was presenting, he noticed everything taking place in the audience and on the stage. The cannery director nodded sympathetically from the first row of the parterre as Solovyov spoke. Schwartz occasionally said something to Kvasha, who shrugged in reply. The lighting technician's face flashed again somewhere among the spotlights and then, drawn by some outside force, disappeared from the balcony forever. Papitsa, who had returned to the room unnoticed, was sitting in the back row. Only Nina Fedorovna was missing.

Solovyov looked around again after finishing his paper. He had always been interested in how actors feel onstage. Do they hear chairs creaking? A cough? Whispering in the parterre? Now he knew: they hear it. They see when someone is leaving the hall, half bent over. That is annoying. At Kvasha's nod, Solovyov left the podium. Deliberately and with dignity, as a person not in a hurry.

Solovyov heard the next presenter begin as he walked past the first half of the rows of the parterre. He thought he should stay in the auditorium a few more minutes, if only as a courtesy. He thought that but did not stop. He felt fatigue. Without slowing his pace, Solovyov walked to the end of the parterre and exited the hall. Nina Fedorovna was smoking nervously by one of the columns. She was watching the door intently, obviously believing Papitsa had gotten out of this too easily. Deliberating whether or not to repeat her impressive performance with the researcher.

Solovyov felt unrestrained by gravity. It seemed as if he would be carried away by the very first gust of a sea breeze and his meeting with Nina Fedorovna would, again, not take place. But he was not carried off. After sensing solid ground under his feet, Solovyov took a step toward the elderly woman. He touched her arm with the gesture of someone capturing the Firebird. He knew she would not escape now.

'That was great . . . how you got him.' Solovyov smiled, lost. He had waited a long time for this conversation but had not imagined it would begin like this.

'Uh-huh.'

Surprise replaced indignation. Nina Fedorovna took a deep drag on the cigarette.

'I'm writing my dissertation about the general . . . I need your help.'

Solovyov began speaking quickly and muddledly, as if he were afraid Nina Fedorovna would refuse. He told her about what he had already accomplished in Petersburg and even named most of the corrections he had made to Dupont's data. Nina Fedorovna listened to him sympathetically, though a bit absently, too. Clearly, she could not keep up with the abundance of figures Solovyov cited. Nina Fedorovna went to the waste bin (Solovyov went with her), put out her cigarette butt on its concrete edge, and shot it into the urn's maw like a catapult, with two fingers. Nina Fedorovna lit another cigarette when Solovyov began telling her about his Yalta investigations. She livened up noticeably during the story about his searches with

Zoya. After some hesitation, Solovyov decided to describe it all.

After hearing him out to the very end, Nina Fedorovna said, 'But the general's memoirs about his childhood were with us, at home. Why did you have to get into Kozachenko's?'

Solovyov looked closely at Nina Fedorovna. She was not joking.

'It's just that Zoya said . . .'

'Zoya's a difficult girl.' Nina Fedorovna smiled. 'I was the same. You don't believe me?'

Solovyov did not answer. After a pause, he said, 'So that means none of the general's memoirs are lost?'

'What the general dictated to *me* was kept . . .' Nina Fedorovna went silent. Her tone assumed further questioning.

'So then what has been lost?'

'Not long after the general's death, his son came to visit. He asked what of his father's was left. I gave him a notebook the general himself wrote.' Nina Fedorovna leaned against the column and closed her eyes. The corners of her lips turned up.

'And where's his son now?'

'I don't know.'

Solovyov leaned against the column opposite her. Atlantis and a caryatid. His fatigue had returned.

'I remember. He went to some little settlement. He left an address.' As before, Nina Fedorovna kept her eyes closed. 'Not even a settlement, a railroad station. A platform.'

Solovyov felt the column begin wobbling behind his back.

'And what . . .' he was already listening to himself from a distance, 'what was the station called?'

'I don't remember. Some woman there took pity on him so he stayed.' Nina Fedorovna opened her eyes and her face grew serious. 'She simply took pity on him.'

'Maybe it was *Kilometer 715*?'

A street-cleaning truck emerged out from behind a bed of nasturtiums. A rainbow began developing in the droplets that hung over the flowers.

'Maybe . . . May well be. That's where he went.'

Solovyov went back into the hall. He listened inattentively to the other papers. The presenters and the conference and Crimea itself had suddenly lost his interest. He was thinking about the only spot on earth where everything that had been significant to him at varying times in his life had come together: the general's manuscript, Leeza Larionova (Leeza *Larionova*!) and, finally, his own home. He was thinking about *Kilometer 715*.

Solovyov understood that this coincidence was not accidental. It was no longer a coincidence but a coalescence. The more unbelievable the joining seemed, the more non-accidental it became. This non-accident proved the correctness of the direction that had opened up for the searching, but its importance—the sudden realization of Leeza's importance in his life made him shudder—was the main proof. On top of everything else (Solovyov remembered this in the final moment and felt drops of sweat on his brow) Leeza's patronymic was *Filippovna*. This final proof was already unnecessary—it was superfluous—but Solovyov accepted it gratefully, too. He did not understand why he had not written to Leeza once in all those years. That was inexplicable.

No matter what a person studies, he is studying himself. Thus spoke Prof. Nikolsky. It fascinated Solovyov that the direction of his search was approaching, closer and closer, the line of his own life. He was stunned by the interweaving of material from his research and his own fate, and by their indivisibility and harmony. If he had ever genuinely loved Leeza, then that was what was happening at this very moment.

Stroking the armrest of his seat on the bus every now and then, Solovyov imagined her hand. He remembered the freshness of her lips as his temple sensed the coolness of the window glass. He thought only of Leeza the whole way to Yalta. He wanted her as never before. Wanted her as the general's granddaughter. As the one to transform him into a relative of her important grandfather. And, of course, as Leeza, his first woman. The scholar's coalescence with his material had reached its apogee.

What did he know about Leeza's parents? Her mother was a railroad track inspector. A weary woman with hair as coarse as wire that was always coming out from under her headscarf. Melting snowflakes glistened on it when Leeza's mother came in from the cold. Leeza had different hair. Very soft. Smelling of sweet smoke because she dried it over the woodstove. Leeza's mother smelled of fuel oil. She did her rounds of the tracks depending on her mood. She could be out for the whole day. Or an hour. It was impossible to guess in advance how long she would be absent. It was he who had thought to place the pail by the garden gate as a signal. It could not be used all the time; it would have raised suspicion.

Her father . . . Solovyov remembered him vaguely.

Remembered he was tall. Unshaven. He began all his sentences with *well*. Well, hello. Well, a blizzard. Not an especially distinguishing feature; nobody would have noticed it, if not for Solovyov's grandmother. You don't have to say 'well' all the time (she would say). He would smile. Ask for three rubles until payday. Don't worry, everything will turn out well anyway (said Solovyov's grandmother). She would give him three rubles. Moistening her fingers with saliva as she counted out each ruble. Rarely did she give just one bill, a three-note. Banknotes over one ruble made her leery. Sometimes change popped out of her fingers and he would gather it off the floor. Occasionally, he would ask permission to sit for a while on the bench. Well, I'll rest a bit, okay? He smelled of alcohol. Solovyov did not yet know it was alcohol. It was the smell of Leeza's father. Leeza's father would not go home. He would sit down on the bench, not taking off his coat. His rabbit-fur hat would slide down his face. He would sleep and be calm. Finally, he disappeared somewhere. Completely disappeared.

Solovyov arrived in Yalta late that evening. It began to rain as he was standing at the trolleybus stop. It was raining even though there did not seem to be clouds in the star-strewn sky. Solovyov decided against waiting for the trolleybus and headed home on foot. The rain was nice after the afternoon heat. It was not a heavy rain; its fine drops reminded him of a thickly condensed fog. By the city market, Solovyov turned on Kirov Street, formerly Autskaya Street. Music carried from the embankment and every so often a spotlight beam appeared somewhere overhead. The beam slid along the tops of the cypress trees and the wet cupolas of the Alexander Nevsky Cathedral.

Everything on Palmiro Togliatti Street was just as it had been two days ago. The creaky staircase, the dim bulb under the canopy over the door. It occurred to Solovyov that this resembled a homecoming. After many years. Coming home as another person. He lingered as he was turning on the light in the room, as if he feared seeing something unexpected there. No, everything was the same. Everything.

Solovyov took the bag off his shoulder. It was heavy. The cannery director had handed him some examples of their products when they said their goodbyes. He had called Solovyov 'the very same Solovyov' again and said he was proud to know him. Neither the director nor Solovyov clarified the meaning of 'the very same.' Solovyov was, for himself, always 'the very same.' He had taken the cans so as not to offend the director. Now he decided to sample them.

Solovyov pulled out one of the cans at random and opened it. The right-angled can with the lid flying up over it reminded him of a grand piano. It was goby fish in tomato sauce.

Someone rang the doorbell.

It rang again. Solovyov continued looking, focused, at the fish. Their understated tomatoed existence seemed like the height of orderliness. It did not allow even the thought of having chaos in one's life. But chaos existed. It had raced into Solovyov's life and carried him away, into its vortex. Flinging him into the Kozachenko apartment, into the Vorontsov Museum, and into the insane nighttime rowing amidst raging waves. That chaos was Zoya. Solovyov had no doubt it was Zoya ringing. He stood and looked at his reflection in the china cabinet. Went to the door. After one more ring, he moved the bolt aside. Taras stood in the doorway, 'I knew you were home. I've been watching the windows.'

Solovyov silently invited him in. Taras moved toward the center of the room fitfully, as if he were sidestepping. He set his hands on the back of a chair. He stood crookedly, his head bent toward his shoulder.

'I have a favor to ask you,' said Taras. 'Leave.'

Solovyov remained silent. Somewhere outside, a door opened, spilling out the sounds of clattering dishes, music, and guests' cries. A moment later, everything went quiet.

'Leave. She's impossible to handle. You'll be done for with her.'

'What about you?'

Taras kept silent.

'Did you know about the searches in your room?' asked Solovyov.

'I put the papers there myself, where she said to.'

Taras lowered himself slowly onto the chair. For a moment, Solovyov was afraid Taras was losing consciousness, but he was not.

'Did you know we'd go to the Vorontsov Palace, too?'

'Of course. I was there that night.'

Taras looked Solovyov in the eye for the first time. There was nothing in that gaze but sadness. Solovyov turned away, 'So why did you agree to it?'

'That's what she wanted.' Taras's fingers touched the fish can. They slid along the rim of the lid, as if symbolizing Taras's own rather difficult journey. Solovyov felt like he had become a witness to some sort of drama that he did not quite understand but that was undoubtedly a drama, and he started to feel sorry for the man sitting before him.

'Do you want some tea?'

'I got you a ticket for tomorrow, to Petersburg.'

Taras said this without taking his gaze from the fish in tomato sauce—Taras himself (it occurred to Solovyov) was essentially one of those fish. Why was he suffering like this with Zoya? Why was he enduring all these passions? Taras hesitated, then took the ticket from his breast pocket and placed it in front of Solovyov. It was curled. Not wanting to flatten out.

'I'm not going to Petersburg,' said Solovyov, sticking the ticket back in Taras's pocket. 'But I am leaving. Tomorrow. And I'll try not to see Zoya.'

Taras silently offered his hand. It was limp and damp. Of course, with hands like those Taras could not count on Zoya's love.

Solovyov left the house early in the morning. He truly was going. He did not feel that he owed anything since he had paid for more days than he had stayed. He left the key to the room with the neighbors.

Solovyov turned onto Chekhov Street instead of going to the trolleybus. Despite the weight of his bag, he felt like walking part of his route to the bus station. He was saying goodbye to Yalta. Without knowing it himself, Solovyov was walking along the same route as General Larionov walked one evening in August, around the 24th, in 1938. He was walking around in military-style trousers, albeit without stripes. And a tunic. The general did not stand out in the crowd wearing that clothing. Many people dressed like soldiers during the thirties. The military style was fashionable in that epoch.

The general was walking around without stripes on his

trousers, but of course it was obvious to everyone that this was a general. His army bearing could be sensed in how he held his head, the way his shoulders turned, and the confidence with which he treaded, from his heel to his toes. A military man through and through. Upper echelon of the officer corps. His arms moved in time with his gait: lightly, confidently, but not swinging. The general displayed restraint in his every action.

At the corner of Botkinskaya and Chekhova Streets, he stopped at a kiosk selling carbonated water. Water cost ten kopecks without syrup, thirty with syrup. The general asked for water with syrup. He took the glass, which sweated instantly, and observed the swirling bubbles for a few seconds. The foam on the surface was exploding with thousands of the very finest droplets; they could just barely be felt when the glass came close to the cheek. The general delighted in how little bubbles rose behind the thick glass, after springing up within each of the glass's facets. Oleander blossoms pinkened through the bubbles as if they were in a magic lantern. Pedestrians slipped past. A bicyclist rode past. A cart with milk canisters. The sharp smell of a horse.

It was hot in Yalta despite the evening hour. The general delighted in drinking his carbonated water. His Adam's apple moved in time with his swallows. He took a handkerchief from his tunic pocket and wiped his sweaty brow. Noiselessly placed the glass on the wooden counter. Elongated contours of growth rings retained remnants of paint. Wasps crawled along round syrupy spots. The general lifted his glass again, slowly turned it over, and covered one of the wasps. Both he and the water saleswoman observed the insect's behavior. The wasp slowly took flight, made several circles under the glass, and touched the top with a buzz. Fell. Clambered up again, climbing along the side, and went still. The general turned the glass over (the gesture of someone releasing doves), allowing the wasp to fly out. The wasp was in no hurry. Moving in a spiral, it reached the edge of the glass. Flew off, dignified. The drinking glasses jingled finely when a truck drove by. The water saleswoman wiped her hands on her apron.

'Another glass?'

The general looked pensively at the saleswoman. The carelessly styled hair, the starched headpiece. He was looking through the saleswoman.

'No,' the general said. Focus returned to his gaze. 'There's no need.'

Yes, this was August 24. There was no doubt. 1938. Judging from the stuffiness of the evening, there would be a thunderstorm during the night. The first clouds were gathering over the Oreanda Hotel. The sun was shedding its final rays on the St. John Chrysostom Church. The general was walking along Chekhov Street. He watched holidaymakers with beach bags, parasols, and towels on their shoulders. Some were wearing pajamas.

The tango. So light, as if from afar. Swelling. A high male voice soared over an orchestra. A band stage revealed itself behind wrinkled acacia trunks. Woodwinds glinted. And a banjo glinted. Musicians in white suits and Latin American hats just as white. A trumpeter soloed. He gave all his air to the trumpet, barely able to inhale on time. The embodiment of exhalation. His cheeks were like a caricature but his lips were refined and sensual.

People were dancing by the band stage. Little by little,

they made way, yielding the space to one couple. He. A predator with hair the color of a raven's wing. A belligerently straight part. A roomy, pleated shirt that hung over narrow trousers. A wet stripe on the back. She. A dove in a white dress. When he spun her, her head tilted back slightly. Weak-willed to some extent. All of her in his arms. His leg sank into the froth of her dress. She still managed to elude him.

From Chekhov Street, the general went to Morskaya Street. To his left, a two-wheeled cart turned with a clatter. Its wheels skidded slightly on the polished cobblestones. Grass was breaking its way through a stone drain gutter. The street led to the sea and the general's heart filled with joy. Even as a child he had loved streets leading to the sea. He saw grounds for hope with the sudden appearance of blueness between two rows of houses.

The general walked up to a pharmacy. It occupied the first level of a squat two-story building. Oak door, copper doorknob, little bell. Art nouveau style. A spring pulled the heavy door back with a creak. The pharmacy seemed cool after the street. And quiet. The general appreciated coolness and quiet. He waited until the pharmacist, Kologrivov, came out after hearing the bell. There were small test tubes, little boxes, and vials behind the cabinets' thick glass. The smell of liquid medicines and *Extra* tooth powder. The general wanted to have a talk with the pharmacist about causes of death. About death overall.

Kologrivov welcomed the general. He was a quiet, gray-haired man with a fleshy nose—the end of his nose looked bulbous. Blue eyes. The general came here to relax because he found Kologrivov's calm pleasant. The general usually sat in the chair behind the dressing screen and listened as

Kologrivov sold medicines. Those who came to the pharmacy required iodine, Vishnevsky ointment, diarrhea remedies, cotton wool, bandages, dried chamomile, condoms, and Condy's crystals. Rarer: castor oil and fish oil. They required advice. Pharmacist Kologrivov gave it in a soft voice (he never raised his voice). This gave General Larionov a sense of coziness. He felt as he had in childhood when he would hide among the coats and furs in the entryway, listening to the servants' leisurely discussions. Sometimes he would fall asleep. Sometimes the general fell asleep and Kologrivov would speak with clients in a half-whisper, so as not to wake Larionov.

It was nine in the evening. Kologrivov locked the pharmacy and invited the general into the adjoining room. There were educational posters hanging there, depicting the human body at various ages. Michelangelo's David divided the ages up to thirty and the ages after thirty. Separate visual aids there highlighted the circulatory system, digestive system, nervous system, and male skeleton (front view). With pointer in hand, pharmacist Kologrivov intended to talk about each of the systems but began his story with the skeleton.

The skeleton, which supports everything, is composed of 206 bones. The skull—which had always seemed, to the general, to be something seamless—has 29 (for a total of 235, the general mechanically noted). As Larionov attempted to imagine himself as a skeleton, he groped at his eye socket with a finger. This was far from the first time he had acted this way, something the pharmacist was aware of.

The general interrupted Kologrivov, 'People say the skull's contours show through on a person's face before his death.'

'That happens when death sets in by natural means.'

The general nodded and looked pensively at the skeleton. 'And what if death sets in by unnatural means?'

'Then the skull's contours show through only after death.'

It was darkening outside. Kologrivov spoke of blood circulation. In front of him was a yellowed diagram of lesser and greater blood circulation. Arteries were denoted in red, veins in blue. The general liked this combination of colors. He unbuttoned one of his tunic sleeves and examined his blue veins. This did not escape the pharmacist's gaze. He continued his story about blood: a person has an average of five or six liters. It is pumped by the heart, (weight: around 300 grams), which consists of two halves, left and right. Each half has an atrium and a ventricle. Kologrivov circled them with the pointer. The atrium received blood, the ventricle pushed it out.

'Cold metal pierces my living heart . . .' the general softly declaimed.

'The most perfect pump in the world.'

'Piercing something so well thought-out,' said the general, choosing his words, 'a creation so refined and vital, is that not a crime?'

'Instant unnatural death.'

'What could be more unnatural . . .'

The general fell silent. He discovered there was a double 'n' in the last word he had uttered.

Pharmacist Kologrivov explained briefly about the digestive system and the nervous system. At the general's request, he moved on to examine natural death. Now there were posters in the foreground depicting the body at various ages. After hesitating slightly, Kologrivov took out a depiction of a person's development in the womb and hung that along-side the others. He scratched the back of his head.

'I don't see the one about conception,' said Kologrivov.

'You want to say that conception is the beginning of natural death?'

'Perhaps. I suspect our delivery boy took that one.'

Kologrivov talked about conception without the poster. Addressing the time in the womb, he showed the embryo's position. This pose was familiar to the general. His soldiers sat this way in Perekop during autumn 1920. The general ordered them to use their last supplies of kindling wood to light fires. He forced the soldiers to jump over them. He raced around that icy desert like a madman, saving the remnants of his army. He attempted to rouse his soldiers, prodded them under the ribs, pounded their cheeks . . .

Could an embryo be roused? As he listened to pharmacist Kologrivov, the general felt an understanding coming to him in hindsight. His soldiers had no longer thirsted for victory. They were not dreaming of women. Or money. They were not even dreaming of warmth. Their exhaustion was deeper than wishes like those. More than anything on earth, his soldiers wanted to return to their mothers' wombs.

The transformation of a pink, wrinkled creature into a child. Adolescent age. Pubic hair growing in, enlargement of the member (for men), change of voice. Awakening of sexual instincts.

'That was the age I suddenly realized I would die, too,' said the general. 'This was the time of first nocturnal emissions.'

'Immortality leaves along with innocence,' said the pharmacist. He moved the pointer again from the *Adolescent* poster to the *Child* poster. 'Children don't believe they'll die.'

Complete rebuilding of the body. Intense growth of the skeleton and muscle mass. Changes in the hormonal realm, the metabolism, etcetera. The body begins having a smell, especially the soles of the feet. Socks have to be changed as frequently as possible. Pimples. Under no circumstances should they be squeezed with dirty hands. A child's soft features sharpen, cheekbones become prominent. A beard and mustache begin growing (primarily for men). The human body develops—Kologrivov approached the image of David—until around the age of thirty.

'And then?' asked the general, admiring.

'It develops then, too, but in the opposite direction.'

Kologrivov sighed and pointed to the poster *Person at age 40–50 years (Male. Frontal View)*. The fat layer under the skin thickens. The skin stretches. The face becomes flabby and bloated. The body accumulates stores of fat, particularly in the stomach and hips. The torso seems disproportionally large, even caricature-like, compared to the legs. Round fatty lumps begin forming on the legs and arms. On other parts of the body, too. They distort the former rigor of its lines and speak of metabolic troubles. Increased growth of hair on the back, chest, brow ridge, and in/on the ears and nose.

It goes from bad to worse. Hair grays. The smell of an old person's bitter sweat appears. The skin withers and bunches up in wrinkles. The body's aging is accompanied by sclerotic thickening of the arteries. They become tight and fragile, and threaten to rupture. The teeth gradually fall out. This can be partially rectified with false teeth (if made carelessly, they make pronunciation whistle slightly) but even a measure such as this is not capable of breaking the general negative tendency. Discs flatten between vertebrae, the spine loses its elasticity and settles. The person shrinks in height. The organs become impossibly worn out. The brain starts to contain excess amounts of water, making its work more difficult. In the end, it becomes hard for the person to live. He dies.

The horns of the evening's last boats sounded outside the window.

'Does that mean,' asked the general, 'that life is the fundamental reason for a person's death?'

Pharmacist Kologrivov sat on a chair and looked calmly at the general. 'One might, Your Excellency, say just that.'

15

Solovyov arrived in the regional capital early in the morning.
They told him he would be unable to reach the *Kilometer
715* station by rail. Even local trains no longer stopped there.
Solovyov took a bus.

The bus was old, just like in his childhood. Solovyov had
not even seen vehicles like this in Petersburg. When the bus
went over potholes, it shook for a long time, convulsively,
as if it had an asthmatic cough. When the doors opened at
the stops, the bus made a sound like glass being pressed.
Solovyov got out at the village where his school was. He
would need to go the rest of the way on foot.

Solovyov began heading along the familiar road but then
he stopped, turned, and walked briskly toward the school.
A padlock hung on the front door. Summer vacation,
Solovyov remembered. It was vacation. He walked up to
one of the windows and pressed his forehead to the glass.
The Russian literature room developed, hazily, behind
poplars reflected in the glass. The seats were flipped up.
Any answer began with those seats clattering; it ended with
clattering, too.

'Why is the military trilogy titled *The Living and the Dead?*

So . . .' and the teacher's finger would search the list in the grade book, 'Solovyov!'

Solovyov's seat flipped up. In actuality, the general had only two folders. When he learned that everyone he had attended school with had died, he transferred them from the *Dead* folder to the *Living* folder. And that was that. Would Solovyov himself have done the same? That was another question entirely. But his classmates' absence behind the desks gaped. It was like death. Worse than death because in their distinct absence, his classmates were simulating their existence somewhere (most likely not far away). Their shadows were visiting the glass factory. Or a cowshed penetrated by drafts. Maybe the tractor-repair station that served local collective farms.

'Whose side is the author of *And Quiet Flows the Don* on? Does anyone have any thoughts in that regard?'

Nobody did. They did not know for certain whose side the author was on. Or who, basically, the author was. The grade books and textbooks were on the teacher's desk. There were fat folders on the *Materials for Distribution* shelf. Were there any *Living* and *Dead* folders there? Did the school maintain records like that?

Without even realizing it himself, Solovyov had walked to the library. He stood on the front steps for a few minutes. What could he even begin talking about with Nadezhda Nikiforovna? He could tell her about what happened yesterday. Or maybe a week ago. It was impossible to tell a life. Several years in Petersburg had changed him a lot but to her he was his previous self. *Previous*. Solovyov felt awkward remembering his childhood dreams. He decided not to go in.

He went in anyway. A young woman was sitting in Nadezhda Nikiforovna's place. Solovyov did not know her.

'Would you like to register?' she asked.

'I'm already registered.'

The woman nodded, unsure, and Solovyov realized she had not been here long. There was no cameo ring on her hand. There was a small ring with an emerald. It would not make a good sound when touching a shelf. Just a quiet plasticky sound.

'What are you interested in?'

Solovyov was interested in where Nadezhda Nikiforovna was, but he did not say that.

'Do you have *Captain Blood: His Odyssey?*'

Solovyov waited for her to vanish behind the cabinets before he left the library on tiptoe. He was afraid the new employee would announce Nadezhda Nikiforovna's death to him as she handed him the book.

He walked toward the forest; the *Kilometer 715* station lay beyond it. In the woods, he was surprised that the formerly two-lane road was in disrepair and had narrowed, transforming into a path. The ferns beside the road, which always used to be trampled and stunted, had grown tall. They swayed in a warm breeze that carried the smell of the collective farm. Solovyov and Leeza had walked to school along this road. Very few people walked along it now, that was obvious.

Solovyov could walk here with his eyes closed. He could easily repeat all the words he and Leeza had said in this forest. He remembered precisely, down to every fir tree he saw, what had been said where. Or rather he had forgotten, but he remembered when he saw the trees. It seemed to him that at one time he had left those words to hang here, and now he was simply gathering them from the fluffy boughs as he walked along.

Solovyov was thinking about what Leeza would say when they met. He sensed his own guilt for his silence but his feeling for her was so complete that he was experiencing no fear at all before their meeting. The ardor that was rising in waves within Solovyov's chest was capable of—he had no doubt of this—melting away both his guilt and her possible feeling of offense. Possible. Deep down, Solovyov did not even think that Leeza might be offended at him.

The forest became sparser and Solovyov saw the first houses: his and Leeza's houses. The road led to them. In another minute or two, four more houses came into view on the right, and the station platform was on the left. Solovyov noticed there was no longer a *Kilometer 715* sign on the platform. None of the passengers on long-distance trains could now learn exactly what station they were riding through.

Solovyov began walking more slowly as he left the woods. The path disappeared completely right at his house. Tall grass wound around his legs and caught in the buckles on his sandals. It was attempting to hold him there. To prevent his unexpected return. What awaited him beyond the tightly drawn, sun-faded curtains? He stopped and looked at his house. He had not been here for six years.

The little gate would not open; Solovyov had to climb over it. When he found himself on the other side of the gate, he began pulling up the grass and thistle that had grown between the bricks in the path. Solovyov stomped on the thistle then took the broken stalks with two fingers and carefully tossed them aside.

Once he was able to open the gate, Solovyov dragged his
bag into the yard. The yard had turned into a jungle. The
plants stood as motionlessly as if they were in a photograph,
and even the freight train passing by (his feet sensed the
earth's trembling) did not disturb their peace. Solovyov
remembered a children's book, *The Land of the Dense Grasses*.
He had read it on the recommendation of Nadezhda
Nikiforovna, who might also have turned to grass. Solovyov
trampled tall, fragile August stems as he made his way to
the front steps. The dandelions' white parachutes flew out
from under his feet.

Wild cherry was growing on the front steps. It had fought
its way through separated boards and had already spread
its branches to the railing. Solovyov touched the sapling's
trunk, drawing his index finger along it. The trunk was soft
and smooth, as if it had been polished. Quiet set in after
the train left. This was full, absolute quiet; anything further
would be non-existence. Solovyov sensed himself growing
into nature. His house and yard had already become nature.
His turn was coming now. Solovyov pulled out the sapling
with one tug and felt like a killer. He understood he had
no other option.

Solovyov fumbled behind the door jamb and took out a
key. He did this before he remembered this was where the
key lay. His hand remembered this motion. The key worked.
At first it spun emptily, unable to handle the lock's rusted
mechanism, but then a familiar click sounded on the second
rotation and the door creaked open.

He entered a chilly dimness. Everything remained the
same as on the day he left. Everything but this: the ideal
cleanliness found only in abandoned houses. Solovyov had

left hastily six years ago. He was going to take his entrance exams and packed up a suitcase, just tossing aside unnecessary things. Leeza stopped him when he began stuffing everything into cabinets. She said she would tidy it all up. She looked at him, half-sitting on the windowsill. Solovyov remembered the motion of her fingers, touching the boards on the windowsill one by one, as if they were playing a piece nobody could hear.

He walked into the room and drew open the drapes. There were neither spiders nor cobwebs in the corners of the ceiling (they had been swept away by a twig broom wrapped in gauze). Because there were no flies. Solovyov realized that when a fly flew in from outside, buzzing. It was the only living being he had encountered thus far at *Kilometer 715*. The fly flitted uncertainly around spots on the tablecloth that had not come out in the laundry and then flew over to the doorknob.

A sturdy rag looped around the knobs on both sides of the door: Solovyov's grandmother had tied rags on the doors so they closed firmly and would not blow open in a draft. She had placed cardboard under wobbling table legs. Glued strips of newspaper to cracks in the glass. This was the inventiveness of old age. The resourcefulness of debility. Of an overall debility, of an inability to change anything in life. When Solovyov left the house after his grandmother's death, he was leaving that inescapability, too. He was afraid he would inherit it, too, along with the house.

There was a sound of shuffling shoes on the front steps. They were purposely loud, striving to attract attention. That was superfluous in the ongoing quiet. Solovyov turned slowly, 'Yegorovna!'

'You came back, my dear one . . .'

Taking tiny steps, Yegorovna walked into the room and pressed herself against Solovyov. Awkwardly, without bending, he caught her with his arm and felt an old person's cool tears running down his neck.

'How's life treating you, Yegorovna?'

'Life?' she pulled away, puzzled and almost offended. 'We're living it out! Yevdokia Firsova and I. Remember Yevdokia?' Her chin, fuzzy with little gray hairs, began trembling. 'We're the two waiting for death. Just two at the whole station.'

'Yegorovna, but where's Leeza'?

'Leeza . . .' Yegorovna stopped crying, and that was even more frightening for Solovyov. 'So, Leeza left. Her mother died and then she left. What, you didn't know?'

'Where'd she go?'

'God only knows, probably went to college, like you. A year ago. Maybe more than a year.'

Yegorovna took a rag out of her pocket and blew her nose, 'Leeza's mother was very sick so she took care of her. Then when her mother died, I wanted to bathe the deceased for her but Leeza did it herself. Bathed her herself. Buried her here with us. And then Leeza packed up and left . . .'

Yegorovna was making her way out. She went down the front steps, moving her hands along the railings, but her monotone still sounded. From somewhere far away, tailing off, Yegorovna continued telling Solovyov about Leeza, whom he seemed to have lost forever. Solovyov lowered himself onto his grandmother's bed and his head sank into a huge feather pillow. It was too much.

The room went dark abruptly after the sky darkened. A

vine on the window frame began fluttering and a weightless flower that had been lying by an icon floated down, right onto Solovyov. A lightning bolt struck somewhere far away, beyond the forest. Thunder merged with the sound of a passing train. After the train was gone, he could hear heavy raindrops drumming on the canopy over the front steps.

Solovyov no longer understood if he was watching a thunderstorm as he had done in his childhood or if he was dreaming a thunderstorm while lying on his grandmother's bed. Or if he was actually in his childhood, lying on his grandmother's bed and watching a thunderstorm. Bolts of lightning flashed outside the window, in the gap between the half-closed drapes. An oil lamp's jittery flame was reflected on the ceiling. His grandmother was bowing in prayer, touching the floor. Leeza was standing in the doorway and smiling. She placed a finger to her lips. Water streamed down her hair. This was not a dream. Leeza truly had come. She had drawn closer to Solovyov and was holding his hand.

Solovyov opened his eyes. Yegorovna was sitting on the edge of the bed.

'It's potatoes and mushrooms. Eat it while it's hot.'

She held out a tin dish for him.

'Thank you.'

He sat up on the bed, looking senselessly at Yegorovna's back. Leeza was not here. He had woken up with that sense and now could not get used to it. Leeza was not here.

'It'll get cold,' said Yegorovna. She was already at the door.

Solovyov nodded and took the spoon Yegorovna had brought. He had not eaten potatoes with a spoon for a long

time so it initially seemed as though the dream was continuing. But the dream had gone.

After his nap, he felt like washing. He went to the well,
lowered a pail on the well sweep, and attempted to collect
some water. The bottom fell out of the pail when Solovyov
raised it, disappearing into the depths with a matte gleam.
He found another pail in the shed and fastened it to the
well sweep with wire. He collected some water, washed,
and tasted the water. The water was just as fresh as when
he was a child.

The sun peeked out again and Solovyov was surprised at
the length of this day. Its length and variety. It was a quiet
summer evening, the kind when he and Leeza would often
sit on the front steps. Sometimes go for walks. They could
walk on the only street, on the platform, in the forest, or
in the cemetery. There were no other places for walks at
Kilometer 715. Solovyov put on a fresh T-shirt. He went over
to the cabinet with the mirror and combed his hair. He was
ready to leave the house.

The street greeted him with absolute quiet. Even these
six houses comprising the street had lived their own lives at
one time. Their life had not been turbulent, it had simply
been life, with shouting over fences, dogs barking, roosters
crowing, and the sounds of transistor radios. Now, though,
there was nothing but the sound of leaves. The rustle of
grass. This was life after a nuclear explosion.

Solovyov stopped next to the platform. In the tall grass,
the steps leading to the platform could be divined by their
railing. A young rowan tree was growing in the controller's
booth, where his mother had once stood. Groping for the
steps with his foot, Solovyov clambered onto the platform.

The grass was a little lower there, growing in intricate patterns that stretched along cracks in the asphalt. Solovyov walked over to a bench. In the strictest sense of the word, this was only a halfbench. One of its three cast-iron sections was lying on its side, covered with broken slats. He sat down cautiously on the part that remained standing. Leaned against the back. Closed his eyes.

If he imagined it was his mother in the controller's booth instead of the rowan tree (the rails had quietly begun humming) and if he imagined the bench was whole and Leeza was sitting on it (he was still not opening his eyes), then what was happening might be declared a quiet summer evening from his childhood. The rumbling of the rails was inaccessible to the untrained ear. This was not yet a rumbling, it was the soundless tension of metal prepared to carry a train that was still far away. But Solovyov heard it. He even knew which train it was. The 20:32. Moscow–Sochi.

Oddly enough, it truly was the Moscow–Sochi train. Despite all the changes in schedules and in the country in general, it passed through the station at exactly 20:32. In actuality, Solovyov was not surprised. Even if attempts had been made to tinker with the schedule, there would have been an obvious need to revert to 20:32. There was no better time to transit through the *Kilometer 715* station.

Freshness blew from the woods surrounding the station. Mowed grass on the railroad bed gave off a refined, slightly sharp aroma. That blended with the smell of railroad ties warmed by the sun. With the whisper of a weeping willow over the platform. This tree had grown as if out of nowhere; nobody saw where it began. Its roots were lost below, in the tall grass. Maybe it had no roots at all. It did not even have a trunk: there was only a crown over the platform.

Leeza announced the trains that passed through. She announced them by placing her palms together like a little boat and pressing them against the sides of her nose: it came out like a microphone, only quieter. They had heard announcements like this in the regional capital; nothing was announced at the *Kilometer 715* station. Solovyov gave permission for the trains to proceed through the station. Copying his mother's motion, he lifted the baton with his right hand. He looked through the train just as tiredly. After some time, he achieved the same kind of look from Leeza. Everybody passing through should know this work was just a routine for them.

Solovyov was still sitting with his eyes closed at 20:32. As the train approached, he thought that Leeza had managed to announce it after all. He was sure she was sitting next to him on the bench at 20:32. That his mother was standing in the controller's booth. She could not help but be there at that time.

They all needed to pull themselves together. To exhale and not move. This instant would remain if they did not frighten it away. Just as there was a moment when it is important for someone wounded in battle not to die. After prevailing over those critical seconds, the body accustoms itself to life once again. That was what the person who turned out to be Leeza's grandfather had said. If Solovyov behaved himself properly here, on the platform, life would again find its past. Catch hold of it. What had seemed dead would suddenly discover its own pulse and the three of them would return home together: Solovyov, his mother, and Leeza. Everything happening later—the deaths of his mother and grandmother, his departure, studying at the university—would turn out to be a misunderstanding, an impetuous departure from this evening's coziness.

They would return home. His mother (the clang of the valve on the gas tank) would put on the teakettle. Pour water into a basin and make him rinse off his feet. On the bottom there would be a triangular spot where the enamel was chipped. He would put a cork sailboat in the basin. His grandmother would read aloud from *Robinson Crusoe*. Leeza would take her cup in both hands. He would slowly move the water around the basin with his feet. The sailboat would begin rocking on the waves. A diesel locomotive whistle would sound somewhere in the distance. No, of course they would not return. Not Leeza. Solovyov raised his eyes toward the controller's booth. And especially not his mother. The wind from a passing locomotive engulfed him. The 21:47, St. Petersburg–Kislovodsk. The train had gone through unannounced.

Only after turning on the light in the entryway did Solovyov realize it was already dark. He boiled the vermicelli he had brought with him and opened yet another can of food. It was goby fish in tomato sauce again. It seemed almost absurd that they were here. The gobies looked at Solovyov with sadness, making him feel even more unhappy. Moths were beating against the kitchen window. Their wings never stopped working as they clutched convulsively at the frame, rose along the glass, and slid down again.

Solovyov went into his own room, the one he had occupied after his mother's death. Compared with the overall order in the house, his room constituted an exception. It was not exactly untidy, it was closer to 'untouched'. something that immediately caught the eye. A Russian language textbook lay open by a bed leg. The cover faced upwards, just as he had left it on the morning of his departure. Solovyov crouched and picked up the book. Tried to close it. It would not close; it could only be pressed shut. With difficulty. With the unyield-ingness of a stiffened body. He laid the book on the desk and it opened to the previous page again. The use of 'not' with verbs was what had interested him that morning. Always written as two words. What an idiot, thought Solovyov; he slowly stretched out on the bed. The bed squeaked, as usual. He pulled off his T-shirt and jeans, and threw them on the floor. He clasped the pillow with both arms and buried his face in it. Ceasing to exist.

Solovyov awoke from the jingling of bed knobs at the head of the bed. An endless freight train was passing through outside his window. It went slowly, waiting for the far signal to change. Wearily sat for a bit on the railroad tracks. Solovyov's whole body sensed its vibration. His arms were still embracing the pillow. He was curled around a balled-up blanket. One freight train replaced the other, heading in the opposite direction; this one went noticeably faster. It continued accelerating, drawing the rhythm of its wheels to the boundaries of the possible. A long time ago, Solovyov and Leeza had listened to that rhythm together. The rumble broke off at its upper limit. The sound of the departing train seemed like an echo in the sudden quiet. Solovyov settled in on his back. He felt a sticky dampness when he pulled the blanket out from under himself.

Solovyov headed for the cemetery early the next morning. On his shoulder he carried a small hoe that he had found

in the shed. In his hand was an inexplicably persistent gladiolus that had sprouted in what used to be the flowerbed.
The cemetery was in the forest, about twenty minutes from
home. It was difficult to divine the road that led there.

Solovyov remembered the first funeral he had seen. He
was surprised that people scattered flowers in front of
the coffin the whole way. He had seen the men from the
station who were carrying the coffin step on crimson aster
heads; he thought he could hear them crunch. He had
stopped and watched as the procession moved further
away. Leeza stayed and stood alongside him. Once
everyone had disappeared into the forest, he and Leeza
began picking up the flowers. Many of the flowers turned
out to be intact. Some did not even have road dust on
them. Solovyov's grandmother would not allow them to
keep the flowers in the house; that bouquet upset her
very much then.

Solovyov and Leeza went to the cemetery often, especially
in summer. They would sit on narrow memorial benches
and on stone pedestals warmed by the diffused forest sun.
Sometimes (balancing) on metal fences painted to look like
silver. Leeza's white legs would be crisscrossed with pink
streaks after sitting on the metal fences.

Crosses stood on the graves; sometimes there were iron
obelisks with stars. Monuments were a rarity at the cemetery. They were trucked in from other places, carefully
carried around the graves, and set in mortar, with a trowel
tapping from all sides. This installation method evoked
respect. There was something real and kindred in the name
of that action itself, in the trowel tapping or in driving a
cigarette butt into crumbly clay. And they were not installed

immediately after the funeral but later on, after a year or two, once the ground had settled.

One time a monument with a poetry inscription was installed at the cemetery. It was on the grave of a station chief who had fallen under the Moscow–Sevastopol express train. Solovyov liked the text very much:

> *Don't tell me he has died, for he still lives!*
> *Although the altar's smashed, its flame still leaps,*
> *Although the rose is plucked, it's still in bloom,*
> *Although the harp is cracked, its strings still weep.*
>
> *We mourn.*
> *The management of the N railroad hub.*

Because of the collective signature under the text, Solovyov thought for a long time that the management of the railroad hub had written the beautiful poetry. As was clarified later, however, out of everything that was carved into that slab, the only words belonging to the railroad workers (other than the signature) were 'We mourn'. While studying in Petersburg, Solovyov learned that poet Semyon Nadson (1862–1887) was the author of those lines that had remained in his memory. Be that as it may, the day the monument was installed, Solovyov told Leeza that in the event of death he would want to have the same kind of monument, with poetry carved into it, installed at his grave. Solovyov said: *in the event of death*. In the depths of his childish soul, he did not allow such an event.

Solovyov did not like the obelisks. They quickly became ramshackle: the paint peeled off and the iron rusted. Little by little, their fastening pins were exposed and the obelisks began listing, expressing their hollow essence. They produced an unattractive tinny sound when touched.

Wooden crosses were another matter. Solovyov regarded those differently. Crosses were not set in mortar. They were dug into neat round pits and the earth around them was stamped on for a long time; there was no waiting for it to settle. Little Solovyov saw in that motion—which was un-cemetery-like and even similar to a dance—a lightness that partially reconciled him with life beyond the grave. Finally, he even told Leeza that he would like to lie beneath a cross rather than beneath a heavy monument. Leeza agreed. She did add, though, that a person feels nothing in the grave. But she agreed.

Solovyov remembered how his mother had been buried. How she had been lowered into a frozen wintery grave. How they could not pull out the ropes, which got caught under the coffin, and how people looked at them, with regret, from a clay heap. Nobody wanted to crawl into a grave at *Kilometer 715* for the ropes. They simply tossed in the ends, which hit the coffin like sonorous gray icicles.

When they returned from the cemetery, Solovyov told Leeza that while they were warm his mother was in an icy grave. Leeza responded again that dead people feel nothing in graves, but that did not reassure Solovyov. He could not fall asleep. Leeza sat at the head of his bed all night while he thought about how his mother must be cold in the grave. Especially considering her high temperature during her last days.

That was the day he grasped the true essence of the cemetery. He began fearing that his grandmother might be carried off there on a morning just as cold and that the cemetery would accept her with the very same hospitality. He was frightened because his world was unraveling. Slipping away, like sand through his fingers, and nothing could be done about it. Even so, he still did not consider himself mortal at that time.

The realization that he would die came to him one summer day. After making love in the forest, he and Leeza went to the cemetery. Their feet stepped lightly on moss, where pine cones crunched from time to time. They sat on one of the metal fences and Solovyov asked, 'Do you understand that we'll die in the end, too?'

Leeza looked at him in surprise. She nodded.

'Well, I just figured it out now.'

'After we did . . . *that*?'

'I don't know . . . we do *that* all the time but it occurred to me now.'

Why had they gone to the cemetery after *that*?

Solovyov stood at the graves of his mother and grandmother. They were essentially one grave, inside the same metal fence, under the same cross. The two small mounds had even merged into one during the years that had passed. Solovyov placed the gladiolus right by the cross and made a few cautious motions with the hoe. The grass at the cemetery pulled out more easily than the grass in the yard at his house. This grass had grown in the shade and did not have resilience or an abundance of sun. Clump after clump fell under Solovyov's hoe with a short, rich sound. The graves were revealed little by little: their joining turned out to be imagined. The mound on his mother's grave was slightly higher because soil had been added at various times.

Solovyov often went to his mother's grave during the first year after her death. Whispering, he would tell her about everything that had happened that day and ask for advice. He had done that during her life, too, after his mother had stopped speaking with him, as punishment for bad behavior. She would keep silent until the moment he asked her advice. Agonized, Solovyov thought up questions and asked them with a serious look. Not sensing a ploy (or perhaps sensing a ploy), his mother would answer. But only while she was alive. She did not answer a single one of his questions after her death.

Although Solovyov continued telling her about everything, over time it worked out that he went to see her ever less frequently, and there were ever more events in his life. He gasped for breath, both from the abundance of events and because they remained unspoken. Feeling indebted to his mother, he attempted to at least tell her the essential things, but here, too, his debt grew with unbelievable speed. He realized he was hopelessly behind.

'You can't tell a life, Mama,' he whispered to her once and burst into tears.

He told her nothing after that. He consoled himself with the thought that she knew everything anyway.

The year his mother died, Solovyov attempted to imagine her in the grave. When spring came, he thought ground water had permeated her coffin and his mother was lying in a cold bath. In the summer, he was already certain her skin had turned black and her eyes had fallen in. He tried—but failed—not to think about the short white worms he had seen on animal corpses. A year and a half later, after the earth on the grave mound had abruptly settled, he guessed that the coffin's lid had rotted and fallen in. Several years later, Solovyov began to feel better when, according to his notions, only a skeleton remained in the grave.

The Solovyov who was tossing weeded grass over the fence did not yet know that it lay ahead for him to find General Larionov's notebook, in which all the stages of the human body's decomposition were listed in detail—from cyanotic spots to a fully bared skeleton. Some of the listings came about as a result of the general's note-taking on specialized literature regarding exhumation and postmortems. Most of the notes were based on his personal experience and reflected what he saw on his rounds of the battlefield. Since the battles did not cease for days, sometimes not even for weeks, the corpses turned out to have decomposed to varying degrees before the burial team's arrival. This significantly increased the general's research base.

Solovyov recited a prayer for the repose of the soul. In his memory, he always heard the prayer as recited by his grandmother, so it was strange for him to hear his own voice now. The wind stirred in the crowns of the pine trees. The grave by which Solovyov was standing was the only one in the cemetery that was cared for.

When he came home, he put the hoe in the shed but then he stopped in the doorway. He went back, took the hoe, and left the yard. He walked along the fence and stopped by the neighboring gate. This was Leeza's yard. It was difficult to open the gate: Leeza's yard was just as overgrown as Solovyov's, though she had left only a little over a year ago. Solovyov fought his way to her front steps with no less frenzy than he had come to his own on the first day, though this time he was armed with a tool.

The key to Leeza's house was hidden in the same place as the key to his house, behind the door jamb. Solovyov sensed an unlived-in smell in the house as soon as he entered. More accurately, the absence of a smell. That had never happened in this house. It always smelled of something here, most often of food. Leeza's mother had loved to cook. She made beef stroganoff, turkey in cream sauce and French-style meat, things that nobody else made around here. People at *Kilometer 715* ate filling meals but they lacked delicacies.

There was always a special smell in Leeza's house at Easter. It was the smell of sacredness and celebration, joy and gifts. It joined the aromas of farmer's cheese, fresh dough, and—for some reason—incense. There was no church near the station so to Solovyov, Leeza's house seemed like a place of worship at Easter. Remembering the smell, Solovyov thought that the general's son might just have shown up at the station at Easter. That would definitely explain why he had stayed here.

Solovyov went into Leeza's room. He extended his hand to the shelf over the desk and pulled out a book at random. It was the previous year's directory for college applicants. Solovyov sat on the bed and leafed through it carefully. There were no indications in the directory about which institution Leeza planned to attend. There was not one dog-eared page or one checkmark in the margins to be found. To Solovyov's chagrin, Leeza was very neat.

He found a packet of small notebooks in one of the desk drawers. These were his own school notebooks from various years, from the very first, with large handwriting that still lacked a slant, to his sloppy ones just before graduating.

Solovyov lowered himself onto the chair and began examining Leeza's collection sheet by sheet. After suddenly going still over a fifth-grade essay, he observed a wet drop spread on the rough paper and absorb the blueness of the ink.

Solovyov himself did not know why he was continuing these searches. He had already been sitting in Leeza's house for more than three hours but had not run across anything that might give him an idea about where to find her. Solovyov had realized long ago that he would learn nothing new here about either Leeza or her father. He was simply going through Leeza's papers and touching her books, and that calmed him.

He discovered a folder of paper airplanes in the bookcase. They were airplane notes he had sent to her over the fence. In a past life. Early in the mornings: the lines were blurry in places from dew. Of course he could have said everything over the fence but he preferred airmail. He liked to write and liked to watch his words soar up into the air. And she had saved all that. Where should he look for her now?

Solovyov caught himself thinking that Filipp Larionov interested him less as the general's son than as Leeza's father. He would have liked to see him again, place him alongside Leeza, delight in their kinship, and be amazed at how Leeza, who was infinitely loved and essential to him, had come out of the ancient Larionov line.

Leeza had not come out of the Larionov line. More accurately, she was from the Larionov line, but from a different one. Larionov's line had no connection to her. That realization came about with no transition whatsoever, all at once, like distant lightning. Filipp, the general's son, was not Larionov. The information written down in Zoya's apartment resurfaced in Solovyov's memory in all its obviousness. General Larionov and Varvara Petrovna Nezhdanova had not officially registered their marriage. Filipp, their son together, was Nezhdanov.

Solovyov left for Petersburg the next day. As he closed up his house, he thought that he was closing it forever. He tried not to look back. He took the rest of the Kerch canned goods to Yegorovna. She cried again. Solovyov cried, too, because this parting with Yegorovna was also forever. As he went outside, without the canned goods, he recognized the burden he had been carrying in his bag. And he smiled.

What had dawned on him belatedly in Leeza's house did not drive him to despondency. Oddly enough, it was even a relief. Leeza's ties to the general's line—and Solovyov felt this ever more distinctly with each minute—had carried a heavy weight. That connection had been lending Leeza a certain excess worth that she did not need. She was his love, his forgotten and rediscovered joy. He knew he had to search for her.

16

When Solovyov arrived in Petersburg, he realized autumn had set in. Autumn was reflected in the windows at the Tsarskoye Selo train station, it called out here and there in the porters' voices, and drifted along a platform in the form of a forgotten newspaper. The coming of autumn would not have been so obvious if there had been rain. But a feeble and irrevocably autumnal sun was shining. No doubt remained that summer was already over here.

The joy of return enveloped Solovyov. He inhaled the biting Petersburg air and sensed it was exactly what he had been lacking. He walked along Gorokhovaya Street to the Fontanka River and turned right. Cold air wafted off the dark water. Ripples coated the river. Solovyov noticed he was the only person wearing a short-sleeved shirt.

Solovyov lived on the city's Petrograd Side. As already stated, he rented a room on Zhdanovskaya Embankment that Prof. Nikolsky had found for him through acquaintances. The professor had explained that the embankment had nothing to do with Soviet politician Andrei Zhdanov. It received its name from the Zhdanovka River, which immortalized clerks by the name of Zhdanov, former owners of these lands. For its part, the surname Zhdanov dates back to the word *zhdan*, denoting a long-awaited child. With the addition of the negative particle *ne*, the word *nezhdan* denoted (correspondingly) an unawaited child. By all indications, a distant ancestor of Filipp Nezhdanov was such a child. Solovyov was thinking about that as he entered the archway of house No. 11 on Zhdanovskaya Embankment.

House No. 11 was special. This was manifested not only in the grandiose Stalin-era Empire style of its architecture: the workshop for engineer Mstislav Sergeyevich Los, a character in Alexei Tolstoy's (1882–1945) novel *Aelita*, was located in the building's courtyard. Los, who planned to fly to Mars, was seeking a travel companion. Tolstoy had lived right here, too, on Zhdanovskaya Embankment, in house No. 3. He had taken up residence near author Fyodor Sologub (1863–1927) and was not planning to fly anywhere, having recently returned from abroad.

House No. 11 was constructed in 1954. It stood on the same spot as the building and courtyard that Tolstoy described. Thus (Solovyov reasoned as he walked up the stairs) the fantasy writer's work took into consideration the actual particularities of the previous building No. 11. Given Alexei Tolstoy's death in 1945, the book did not take into consideration the peculiarities of the current No. 11. In that sense, the fictional make-believe in *Aelita* corresponded to actual life in the 1920s more than to the objective reality of the 1990s. Solovyov's next conclusion: the border between make-believe and reality disappears when time is taken out of the equation. He wiped his feet on the mat and shut the door behind him.

Solovyov lived in a two-room apartment. This was a happy version of a communal apartment: given its small population, it had not been reduced to a complete wreck. Additional happiness lay in the fact that Solovyov's flatmate hardly lived here. Once every two or three months he would arrive suddenly from somewhere like Murmansk or Syktyvkar and then leave just as suddenly a few days later. His girlfriends came to see him on those days, though Solovyov saw them only in passing, too, when they ran from the next room to the shower late at night, wrapped in towels.

The apartment had windows on both sides of the building: they looked out over the courtyard (including part of Ofitsersky Lane) and the embankment. The windows in the kitchen and his flatmate's room looked into the courtyard. Solovyov's room (and this was its amazing quality) had a view of the Zhdanovka River, a small chunk of Petrovsky Island with the Petrovsky Stadium, and, further, beyond the trees on the island, the Malaya Neva River. In Solovyov's opinion, the stadium spoiled the picture a lot, but nothing could be done about that.

The stadium did not just ruin the view. It complicated life. Existence near the stadium had its own shadowy and (in many of the courtyard's secluded corners) damp sides, because fans of the Zenith football team urinated with reckless abandon. They urinated under the archway, in the entryways, and by the fences; they urinated during matches, whether the main team or the reserves were playing; and before and after matches. They urinated as if Zenith were the champion although the team was not even in the top three at the time.

Fans left behind heaps of rubbish: beer cans, chip bags, dried fish heads, corn cobs, and newspaper cones, flattened on the asphalt. All this was thickly strewn with sunflower seed hulls. The hulls swirled in light little tornados that blew off the river and rose over the roofs of building No. 11, Zhdanovskaya Embankment, Ofitsersky Lane, and the entire Petrograd side.

Solovyov had arrived on a match day. He was not a fan and he regarded football matches with irritation. At the same time, there was something about how they took place that appealed to him. The roar of many thousands of fans at the stadium excited him: that roar was sometimes indistinct, like a distant waterfall, and sometimes explosive (after a goal). But it was always powerful.

Solovyov sat on the windowsill and watched spectators disperse after the match. They flowed across the wide bridge over the Zhdanovka River like a viscous mass that could not come apart: that bridge was directly under Solovyov's window. To Solovyov, the slow procession that was devoid of anything personal and the continuous, indistinct rumble seemed to be the embodiment of history's gait. Majestic and pointless, like any concerted movement.

Looking out the window at the motley crowd, he remembered the black-and-white crowds in revolutionary newsreels. The spasmodic motions of people walking. The comical rocking of those standing; in modern filming, you did not notice that those standing are also moving. Little clouds of steam. They came up suddenly, as if they had been added in. Disappeared suddenly. The same with cigarette smoke. People were now walking that same way past the Second

Cadet Corps (now the Military Space Academy), where the general once studied.

Football fans wearing Zenith caps were walking past the Second Cadet Corps. Thousands of dark blue caps. Thousands of dark blue scarves. They irritated Solovyov tremendously. And they did not know that a general had studied here. Solovyov began to feel lonely because of the abundance of people.

This feeling was new for him. He had never yet felt lonely in Petersburg. Even in the absence of friends, this city—with its strange aura and a people unlike in the rest of Russia—had sated him. He had not felt abandoned before when he was all by himself. He felt that now, though. It crossed his mind that Leeza had abandoned him, though in actuality it was the opposite. Solovyov picked up Tolstoy's *Aelita* and peered out the window.

Beyond the gate, a wasteland reached to the embankment of the Zhdanovka River. Beyond the river there stood the vague contours of trees on Petrovsky Island. Beyond them, there faded a doleful sunset that could not fade away. Its light touched at the edges of long clouds that seemed like islands reaching into the sky's green waters. Above them was green sky where a few stars had begun shining. It was quiet on the old Earth. That was the only spot in the book that Solovyov genuinely liked even though it twice referred to the sky's green color, for no reason. Sometimes it even seemed to him that there was no need to continue.

Solovyov went outside after the sunset had faded. Interesting, where had the wasteland been, anyway? Or was it a fantasy of Tolstoy's, who wrote his novel while still in Germany? Solovyov's foot grazed a beer can and it rolled off the sidewalk with a clink. Had Nikolai Chernyshevsky seen that wasteland? If he had seen it, that would affirm that cadet Larionov must have seen it, too.

Solovyov went to the institute the next day. Even as he was approaching the famous building with its columns, he caught a glimpse of academician Temriukovich. Temriukovich was walking along, dressed in a Mackintosh raincoat with a fifties cut: it had roomy sleeves (one of them was smudged with whitewash) and its shoulders, which had once been angular, were now sagging and rumpled. The end of its untied belt dragged along the ground. Solovyov did not want to catch up to Temriukovich. Elementary courtesy would have demanded pointing out the smudged sleeve and dragging belt to the academician, but something hinted to the graduate student that there was no point in doing so. Solovyov slowed his pace and followed the academician.

Solovyov regarded Temriukovich with respect and there was a special reason for that. It was through Temriukovich's efforts that the complete collected works of Sergei M. Solovyov were published during the Soviet era. Despite not being a relative of Sergei Solovyov, graduate student Solovyov believed in their spiritual kinship and felt favorable toward everyone who was somehow connected to the great man with whom he shared a surname.

As a scholar, Temriukovich was not one to reach for the stars, but there was no need in his case anyway. The necessities for the edition he had conceived were painstakingness and diligence in the task, and, to some extent, fortitude. An edition of Sergei Solovyov was not something that was taken for granted in the Soviet Union. As a reward for successful completion of the work, Temriukovich was nominated to become an academician. Nobody counted on his being elected. Above all, candidate Temriukovich.

'Neither Bakhtin nor Lotman were academicians,' he had consoled himself, 'they weren't even corresponding members.'

But Temriukovich's situation turned out differently from Mikhail Bakhtin's and Yuri Lotman's. Destiny was favorable to Temriukovich, unlike Bakhtin and Lotman. This manifested itself on one occasion, when the members of the Academy of Sciences had not come to any agreement about a candidacy. The generally foolproof mechanism—which had made academicians out of institute directors, members of the government, oligarchs, and people who were simply respected—went haywire. By not agreeing amongst themselves, the academicians intuitively voted for someone who, to their thinking, had no chance whatsoever of making it. They voted almost unanimously for Temriukovich.

There was widespread surprise at the moderate joy displayed by the newly elected academician. A much more enthusiastic reaction was shown by those who had worked toward this goal, spending years cultivating Academy members and trotting from floor to floor of the Academy's tall Presidium building with its strange-looking golden top stories that inspired the popular nickname *The Cologne Bottle*. Yes, Temriukovich accepted congratulations politely and expressed satisfaction with the academicians' vote but—as noted by corresponding member Pogosyan, who was in attendance when the results were announced—Temriukovich's thoughts were far away.

And that was the simple truth. The new academician's colleagues suddenly recalled the *overt aloofness* that had accompanied Temriukovich for the last few years. If his condition might initially have been described as *deep pensiveness*, nothing but *overt aloofness* could describe the current state of affairs. That, however, was still not the worst of it. Temriukovich's coworkers began noticing that he was talking to himself. The first to take notice was Igor Murat, a candidate of historical sciences.

'Let's have a look, see what kind of book this is,' Temriukovich said one day, as he approached a bookcase, 'probably rubbish.'

The publication that interested the academician was Igor Murat's book, *The Revolutionary-Democratic Movement in Left-Bank Ukraine During 1861–1891*. The author was standing on the other side of the bookcase, unnoticed by Temriukovich. Murat had just plunged an immersion heater into a glass of water and was preparing to have tea. Murat froze when he peered through the shelves and watched the academician pick up *The Revolutionary-Democratic Movement in Left-Bank Ukraine During 1861–1891*. Murat turned his gaze to the heater. It was now impossible to turn it off soundlessly. Murat listened, speechless, as the academician moistened his index finger and paged through the book.

'Shit,' said Temriukovich with a sigh as he put the book back. 'Premium quality shit.'

The water had begun boiling noisily in the glass and Temriukovich peered around the bookcase. He saw the pale Murat there.

'I heard what you were saying about my book,' whispered Murat.

'I didn't say anything,' said the unruffled Temriukovich, 'all I did was think about it.'

That calmed Murat slightly.

The academician's oddities continued, though. At first, he still showed consideration for his coworkers and only ventured to make sharp remarks when he believed he was alone. Later, he did not exactly stop noticing those around him but, as Pavel Grebeshkov, the institute's deputy director of scholarly affairs expressed it, he had crossed the line between internal and external speech. When addressing listeners, Temriukovich spoke expressively and intelligibly. He addressed himself in soft, rapid speech, just as theater actors utter texts with the stage direction 'aside.'

That was the format in which he accused administrative manager Vladlen Maslo of dishonesty in carrying out multi-year renovations on the institute's building. When he tripped over some scaffolding one day, the academician assumed, in an undertone, that Maslo was a thief, which was allegedly why the renovations were so grueling and unsuccessful. This occurred in the presence of witnesses. Unlike Murat, Maslo appealed to the director immediately, demanding that Temriukovich be fired from the institute due to his, Temriukovich's, mental incompetence. The thought that Maslo could appropriate government funds seemed insane to the director, too. To the latter's credit, he did not fire Temriukovich.

'Temriukovich is a full member of the Russian Academy of Sciences,' said the director, 'and under formal reasoning, I have no grounds for doubting his mental competence.'

And so membership in the Academy of Sciences helped Temriukovich avoid being fired. He continued coming to the institute only on required days, as he had been doing for the last forty years.

After entering the building, Temriukovich headed for the

coat check. The man at the coat check bent across the counter to take the academician's raincoat.

'Where'd you lean against something, Mikhail Sergeevich?' the attendant asked.

Temriukovich looked at the smudged sleeve and did not answer. Addressing himself on the stairs, he said, 'Can't a person ever hear anything nice?'

After Temriukovich had disappeared around a corner, Solovyov went up to the second floor. He went to the director to inform him that he was back from his trip. Strictly speaking, there was no real necessity to do so; a written report would have sufficed. But the fact that the trip had taken place in August and in Yalta gave Solovyov no peace. He remembered the director's look in parting and he thought the gaze was ironic. Solovyov wanted to tell the director personally about his findings, and, first and foremost, the text he had found. The plastic folder with the general's memoirs was melting in his hands and growing slippery; it had nearly fallen on the floor twice. Solovyov wanted rehabilitation. Maybe even encouragement.

The director's office door was ajar. The director himself was not visible but his voice was audible. He was telling someone off: 'Of all possible feelings, the only thing you have is a grasping reflex.'

After thinking, the director repeated it, syllable by syllable, 'A gras-ping re-flex.'

A listless objection was heard in response. The words were indiscernible (what could they be in a case like this?) and all that remained was intonation. Simultaneously ingratiating and tedious. A woman was speaking. She calmed the director a little.

'You can't live on reflexes alone,' he said conciliatorily. 'Forgive me, but you can't be such a reptile.'

This turned out to be an inopportune moment to visit. Solovyov had wearied instantaneously. He realized he was not even interested in finding out who, exactly, the director was addressing. Solovyov walked slowly toward the Twentieth-Century History Department, his department. Who could be called a reptile? At the end of the corridor, he turned to look back anyway. Tina Zhuk, a graduate student, was coming out of the director's office. She had a very loud voice and Solovyov was surprised she had just been speaking so softly. It turned out that Tina could do so when she tried. Temriukovich was her research advisor. The academician did not like his graduate student and everyone at the institute knew it. Nobody liked her.

In the Twentieth-Century History Department, Solovyov donated one hundred rubles for a gift for a coworker, Baksheeva. Baksheeva, a candidate of historical sciences, had just had a baby and they were giving her an electric teakettle. The trade union committee chair decided to show Solovyov the electric teakettle after she'd accepted his money. She placed a finger to her lips, opened the cardboard box, and took out the gift. She, Novoseltseva, had invested her own personal money, at least temporarily, until she had recovered the sum for the teakettle. She showed Solovyov the list of donors: it was always a big risk to collect money for an item that had already been purchased. Solovyov flicked the teakettle with his fingernail. The sound turned out to be unexpectedly low and muted. The department office was empty. Lots of people were still on vacation.

Solovyov saw Temriukovich again on the second floor:

he was headed toward the administrative offices. Tina Zhuk
was walking slightly behind him. When she saw Solovyov,
she pointed at Temriukovich and touched her temple with
her finger.

'He called me a snake in the grass,' she whispered to
Solovyov. 'Can you imagine? He's already completely lost
it.'

Solovyov observed as Zhuk's nose began moving in time
with her lips. He had not noticed this before. It was possible
this could be explained by her anxiety. Administrative
manager Maslo popped out of the closest door.

'Solovyov,' he said, without a hello. 'We're going to start
taking down the scaffolding in an hour. We'll need your
help.'

Solovyov nodded to Tina. Temriukovich turned around
as if he had remembered something and began walking in
the opposite direction. Maslo disappeared behind the door
as soon as he saw that.

'Stole a pile and now hides,' Temriukovich mumbled,
looking at the floor. 'Vacations on Majorca. And I, a full
member of the Academy of Sciences, vacation in the city
of Zelenogorsk. One might ask why!'

'Because he's greedy,' Tina Zhuk answered after the academician had moved further away. 'He's just a glutton. And
senile.'

Solovyov went outside and headed off toward the
University, the famous Twelve Colleges, a long red building
that stood perpendicular to the Neva River. Solovyov hoped
to find out something about Leeza in that building. Based
on what Yegorovna had said, Leeza had left more than a
year ago. If Leeza left to go to college, she should be in her

second year now. Solovyov realized he did not know what department Leeza might have entered. Furthermore, there was no evidence she had entered a university in Petersburg. Strictly speaking, there was not even any certainty that Leeza had entered a university anywhere at all.

He was greeted with surprise at the administrative office. They had no obligation to provide student information to him.

'This is very important to me,' said Solovyov.

When all was said and done, Solovyov was a recent student himself, so they accommodated him. There turned out to be three Larionovas at the university. Not one of them was Yelizaveta. One was studying in the geography department, the second was in Solovyov's very own history department, and the third was in journalism. Solovyov decided to meet all three just in case there was an error in the rolls.

He did not have to leave the Twelve Colleges building to go to the geography department. By checking the schedule, he learned where the second-year students had classes and went into the classroom during the break. A map of mineral resources in Siberia, speckled with red spots, hung on the wall. There were many resources. A great many.

Solovyov approached the first table and asked where he might find Larionova. They showed him. Even from afar, he knew it was not Leeza and thought about leaving without going up to her. He began taking a step but for some reason looked again at Larionova; her face was dotted with acne. It recalled the map of Siberia. This was probably what prevented him from making a fast exit. If he acted that way, reasoned the young historian, Larionova's classmates would decide her appearance had driven him away. He did not want to cause Larionova—even if she was not Leeza—additional distress.

He walked over to her and wanted to explain what, exactly, had happened but Larionova did not let him say a word. She took him by the elbow and walked out of the classroom with him. Larionova continued holding Solovyov by the elbow in the hallway but did not look up. She had a sweet face, despite the acne.

'I'm looking for a young woman whose surname is Larionova,' said Solovyov, 'but it turns out it's not you.'

Larionova nodded. That was how things always worked out in her life.

Solovyov searched out the second Larionova the next day. She was writing a term paper on ancient battle tactics but knew nothing about the prominent general who shared her surname. That surprised Solovyov. In the first instant, the thought even flashed through his mind to tell her about the general and his Thermopylae passions. The history department's Larionova was tall and broad-shouldered. Of all the Larionovas Solovyov had seen, basically, she deserved to be the general's granddaughter more than the rest. Despite that circumstance (or perhaps precisely because of it), Larionova the second did not inspire Solovyov. He did not even consider telling her about anything and kept the conversation to a bare minimum.

There turned out to be the most hassle with Larionova number three. They told Solovyov at the journalism department that Larionova was sick, so he went to see her at the dormitory. There was no immediate answer when he knocked at Larionova's room. Judging from the noise beyond the door, they were celebrating something in the room. Solovyov had lived in a dormitory for several years so he knew dorm sounds and smells so well that, based on the specifics of how they were combined, he could determine to a high degree of accuracy the reason behind the festivities. Most frequently, people celebrated birthdays, weddings, and passing exams in dorms. Sometimes they just drank vodka but there were no good smells for that. In those cases, they made do with bread, sausage, and marinated cucumbers.

It was not exam time. They were not celebrating a wedding (Solovyov cracked the door open). Birthday was left.

'Come in,' several guests shouted at once.

Solovyov went in. About ten people were sitting at two desks that had been pushed together. Two of them were on chairs, one was on a nightstand, and the rest were on two beds. One of the beds had needed to be pulled a little toward the table. A portrait of Fidel Castro hung on the entire wall over the bed that had not been moved.

Solovyov had not expected to recognize the television news host Makhalov as one of those sitting (as it happened) on the bed under Fidel. Makhalov, who was slightly drunk, rocked pensively and placed his head on a dark-haired young woman's shoulder. When Solovyov stated the reason he had put in an appearance, it emerged that she was Larionova. Her name was Yekaterina.

Yekaterina was celebrating her birthday. There was a glass bowl of Olivier salad in the middle of the table. A dish of olives right next to the salad. For beverages there was predominantly vodka, which they were drinking out of little plastic cups. Solovyov wanted to leave but they convinced him to stay and drink to Yekaterina. They convinced him loudly and spiritedly. Then they forgot about him.

Every now and then Makhalov kissed Yekaterina on the lips and each time there was a sound like quiet chewing. That—as well as the salad on their lips—gave their kisses a piquant gastronomical flavor. Makhalov called her by her full name—Yekaterina—and the others followed suit, calling her that, too, even those who, by all appearances, had long known her well.

Solovyov was sitting on the bed next to Makhalov. Oddly enough, he did not feel like leaving. Not because he liked it here (it is not very likely he could have said that) but because he did not know where he should go now. He felt enervated after determining that not one of these Larionovas had anything to do with Leeza. He realized that his searches could be endless. Why, really, was he looking for Leeza only at the University? And why only in Petersburg?

One of the guests was describing how he and his girlfriend had made love on a beach one night in Gurzuf. After a while, it felt to them as if a whole group of people was watching. They stopped what they were doing and approached the observers. Much to their surprise, they discovered it was rocks. Then they made love on those rocks. The girlfriend turned out to be Yekaterina.

Makhalov said that, as a rule, television news was a lie. Moreover, the problem was not the content itself (he drank, and inhaled through his nostrils, pursing his lips) but how it was presented: how much, the order, vocabulary choices, etcetera.

They poured vodka for Solovyov yet again. His little

plastic cup ended up filled to the brim. To his own surprise, Solovyov drank it all in one gulp and chased it with olives. Applause rang out. When Solovyov glanced at his little cup, he saw it was full again. Solovyov was no longer sure he had actually drunk the previous one.

'Sad though it is, you have to sleep with someone to get on television,' said Makhalov.

'I don't believe it,' shouted Yekaterina.

'Imagine,' Makhalov sighed, and Solovyov felt Malakhov's hand on his knee.

Then a person arrived with a bottle of Metaxa brandy. Solovyov no longer felt like drinking but they all began persuading him that he definitely had to try the Metaxa. Solovyov tried the Metaxa.

Unexpectedly, Makhalov farted loudly and several people began giggling.

'We'll make it through the winter,' said Makhalov.

Yekaterina nodded with an expression of calm certainty. The guests drank again. Their motions were growing ever more chaotic and at some point they themselves disintegrated into their component parts: eyes, arms, mouths, and little plastic cups. Solovyov unintentionally leaned back and hit his head on the wall. Fidel was the last person he saw before his head struck.

Solovyov came to late at night. He guessed that it was late at night from the darkness in the room and the absence of guests. Once his eyes had grown accustomed to the murkiness, he realized there were at least two people in the room other than him. There was a light disturbance on the next bed.

Solovyov discerned two silhouettes there: one lying, the

other sitting. The sitting one was unsuccessfully attempting to revive the lying one by shaking the person's head and whispering something in the person's ear, but the lying person only defended himself limply. The lying person spoke in a constricted, unintelligible whisper, but from the general tone of the answers, it followed that the person wanted to sleep. Based on a series of indirect indicators, Solovyov guessed that the attacking side was the birthday girl. This was confirmed when Yekaterina lost her patience and suddenly said loudly, in a bitter voice, 'If you don't want to love me, others will.'

Solovyov tensed up, anticipating something unpleasant. He hoped the lying person would not allow things to develop under that scenario. In answer, though, the voice resounded just as loudly, 'Good luck.'

It was Makhalov's voice. There was not a speck of jealousy in it.

The aspiring journalist jumped noisily over to Solovyov's bed. Solovyov squeezed his eyes shut with all his might. Yekaterina shook him by the shoulder but he did not wake up. An instant later, he felt her fingers on the zipper of his jeans. Solovyov could pretend not to wake up but he had no prerogative to resist if he was asleep.

'Objectively speaking,' said Yekaterina, 'he's already prepared to make love to me and that's despite being sound asleep. Unlike you, who's awake.'

There were sounds of someone flushing in a bathroom and, flipflops tapping, returning to their room.

'Don't flatter yourself,' Makhalov muttered. 'That has nothing to do with you. He's dreaming of another Larionova.'

17

Solovyov worked intensively in the archives throughout September and October. After finishing a section about events during the first half of 1920, he turned to the second half of that same year. On October 1, the young historian reached the October period of the Civil War; that seemed like a good sign to him. He and his material were beginning to resonate with one another.

October (one of Russia's most unfortunate months) turned out to be unlucky for the White Movement in Crimea, too. The White Army was retreating. After suffering defeat near Kakhovka, the army left Northern Taurida, fighting. The army's path lay toward Perekop, for which General Larionov had specific plans.

Solovyov estimated the White Army's numbers taking part in defensive battles at approximately 25–27,000 (by comparison, Dupont's *The Enigma of the Russian General* raises them for no reason, speaking of 33–35,000). In Solovyov's opinion, the Reds' forces totaled around 130,000 (Dupont writes of 135–140,000). These figures, however, did not fully take into account the losses the Whites incurred in defending Northern Taurida, something Solovyov particularly noted. He emphasized that only statistics for certain army units could be vouched for with any degree of certainty:

Consolidated Guard Regiment	400 bayonets and sabers, 3 heavy weapons
13th Infantry Division	1,530 bayonets and sabers, 20 heavy weapons
34th Infantry Division	750 bayonets and sabers, 25 heavy weapons
Kornilov Division	1,860 bayonets and sabers, 23 heavy weapons
Drozdov Division	3,260 bayonets and sabers, 36 heavy weapons
Markov Division	100 bayonets and sabers, 21 heavy weapons

Solovyov explained the Reds' four- or five-fold superiority over the Whites by the separate peace treaty that the Reds and Poles had concluded behind the general's back. The agreement untied the Reds' hands: after withdrawing their large forces from the western front, they moved them south, against the White Army. The Whites' position was becoming critical.

All that remained for the White Army of the entire, huge country was a patch of land surrounded by sea. It was connected to the mainland by the narrow isthmus for which the retreating army was striving. The White Army's fate depended on who reached the isthmus first: if cut off from Crimea, the White Army would not have the slightest chance of being saved. This did not just affect the army, though. The downfall of the White troops would subject to mortal danger thousands of others who had retreated to Crimea with those troops. They would not have time to evacuate.

The general was in a hurry. He had a slight time advantage that he was afraid of losing. After the battles near Kakhovka, he moved his troops southeast through Northern Taurida without giving them respite. He was still not giving up. As he reviewed episodes of the Kakhovka combat in his mind, he was still relying on the power of his soldiers' desperation and the special courage of the doomed. After that strange forced march began, however, the general sensed the beginning of the end for the first time.

This was not an army advancing toward Perekop, it was an unorganized column of sleepwalkers traveling along the ice-bound expanse of Northern Taurida. Leaning from his saddle, the general peered into his soldiers' faces and saw an expression of *mortal exhaustion* on those faces. He knew this expression. He had seen it on the faces of those who froze in snow banks. Of those who stood up straight and walked into machine gun fire. But never before had he seen this expression on every face. The general was beginning to understand that he had lost more than just an individual, if very important, battle. It was becoming clearer to him with every minute that the war, as a whole, had been lost.

His army could no longer fight. The reason was not the poor uniforms (though they truly were poor) and not the lack of ammunition (which was, indeed, lacking). This was not even about the army's demoralization: the general had managed to restore his soldiers' fighting spirit even after worse defeats. The reason was that the army had *depleted its entire reservoir*. It was this very expression that the general used in the telegram he sent to foreign envoys when he was halfway to Perekop. In their response, the envoys requested an urgent meeting. They needed the general's explanations. But what was the point of a meeting like that? What, in actuality, could he explain to them?

After dropping the reins, the general took a sheet of paper and a pencil from his map case. His horse slowed to a walk. He thought a bit and wrote to the envoys that there was no more rage in his soldiers' eyes. There was no joy. There was no fear. There was not even suffering. There was nothing there but an endless wish for repose. How does it happen, the general asked, that an object suddenly loses its qualities? Why does a magnet demagnetize? Why does salt stop being saline? After reading what he had written, the general folded the sheet in neat quarters and ripped it to pieces. They fell behind his back like large snowflakes.

The soldiers could not warm up. They stuffed straw under the thin broadcloth of their military overcoats but it did not help. Sometimes the soldiers burned tumbleweeds so they could at least hold their numbed fingers over them for a minute. Gusts of wind carried off the tumbleweeds; small fiery balls scattered along the steppe when dusk was falling. That wind flung prickly bits of ice into the marchers' faces and the wind got under their overcoats, removing the last bit of warmth radiated from the soldiers' fatigued bodies.

The soldiers wanted to sleep. After two days of uninter-rupted battle, some fell asleep on their feet. Lulled by the column's even pace, they closed their eyes involuntarily and continued walking in their sleep. The artillerymen began sitting on the gun carriages but the general forbade that. As they drifted into sleep, they fell from the gun carriages and under the wheels.

The general did not allow them to lie down on the carts. He pulled from the carts those wounded but still capable of traveling and forced them to walk. Cursing the general and his orders, they walked. They held the sides of the carts and left a bloody trail in the snow, but they walked. Their bandages trailed behind them. And they remained alive. The gravely wounded, unable to move, could not warm up. They shouted that they were freezing. Someone covered them with coats, mattresses, and rags, but still they could not warm up. The majority of them had frozen by the end of the march.

As the general straightened an overcoat that dangled from one of the carts, he touched the firm, oblong object that was holding the overcoat. It was a frozen soldier's arm. It held the overcoat in a death grip. The general rode off abruptly and observed the overcoat trailing behind the cart for a while.

The field kitchens had no provisions. The general ordered that what little still remained be given to the wounded. But only thin soup remained. This soup could not satiate the wounded; it could not even warm them. They looked upward incessantly as they lay on the carts, feeling nothing but the cold. This was a cosmic cold, emanating from distant, indifferent stars.

It was the kind of cold that made the soldiers think they would never warm up now. Not warm up and not get a good sleep. Many wanted to die and the general knew that. He forbade his soldiers to daydream about death.

'Whoever of you dies,' said the general, 'will end up in the grave unwarmed.'

There was no answer.

'He will freeze eternally,' said the general.

The soldiers walked in complete silence. They were afraid that their last remnants of warmth would leave, along with the words they uttered. All that sounded were the even clatter of horse hoofs, the creak of carts, and the crunch of frost under the gun carriages' wheels. And the groans of the wounded. A while later (their sense of time was dulled, too) a quiet glass-like sound blended in with those other noises. The general rode off to the side and saw ice chafing against rocks by the water. They had retreated to the Sivash. The salt-water lake was covered with a thin icy crust.

An explosion rang out somewhere in the distance. And then closer. Again in the distance. This was the Reds' artillery shelling. It created the impression that the Reds were shooting at random. The retreating troops did not slow their pace. Sometimes the shells landed a few dozen meters from the column. They raised pillars of water in the sea that flashed briefly and gloomily in the moonlight. At times they exploded with a deafening dry bang; the general understood then that the Sivash had frozen solid in places. This discovery made him feel uneasy.

'General Winter,' whispered General Larionov. 'He's made his appearance a month earlier than usual.'

They saw distant campfires at around two in the morning. This did not bode well at all for those retreating and the general knew it. Those campfires meant that isolated Red units had managed to go around his army from the east and enter the isthmus first. It was also possible that the

Sivash had frozen so much in places that the Reds could cross from the side of the village of Stroganovka. Now they awaited the general's troops along their retreat route. Movement continued, though those campfires meant death.

The general did not dismiss the idea that events could develop that way, though he considered it improbable. He surmised that the Reds would want to intercept him, but here he was counting on the Sivash, which did not usually freeze. His calculation did not hold true. He was left hoping that only the Reds' vanguard had managed to cross.

The general could not imagine that the cavalry—particularly the artillery weapons—could have crossed the first thin ice. He could not imagine that much of any significant enemy force could have made its way here during the time the Whites were on their inhuman forced march. Even so—regardless of how many of them there were—the Reds had arrived on the isthmus first. Despite the cold. And the barely frozen Sivash. The general's army was like a worn-out horse. He had worn it out in hopes of saving it. It was the first time in his life that the general had subjected soldiers to an ordeal like this. It was the first time in his life that he felt the inevitability of defeat.

He scrutinized the soldiers' faces yet again, as if searching for clues. The cold had smoothed the features of those faces, depriving them of expression. Frost lay on their mustaches and eyebrows. There was nothing in his soldiers' eyes but the campfires burning up ahead. Did they surmise what those campfires meant? Even if they did, the pull of that flame was so strong that it was already impossible to stop their motion toward it.

And the general did not even try. Stopping here would

have been tantamount to death. On this bare and completely unprotected plain, his troops would be swept away by the Reds' superior forces. Occupying positions on the well-fortified Perekop remained their only chance of salvation. For that, they now needed the impossible: an attack.

'Prepare for battle,' said the general, his words drowning in the beginnings of a blizzard.

The general said it loudly and nobody heard him. He knew it was useless to repeat. He spurred his horse and galloped off to the leading column.

Why had the Reds lit the campfires? Why did they not continue moving toward Perekop? Were they unable to? Had they made a quick stop to warm up? This will remain one of the war's enigmas. In Solovyov's opinion, the Reds also did not suppose the enemy was capable of ending up in this sector so early. According to all their mental calculations, the general and his army could not have turned up here until at least the next morning. It is possible the Reds did not expect the general to accomplish the unthinkable, so had calmly lit their campfires. Even if they had not lit them calmly, though, they simply could not have survived on a night like that without fires.

Solovyov attributed the Reds' mind-boggling carelessness to their being completely frozen. To the narrowing of blood vessels in the brain as a result of hypothermia. This was how the historian explained the fact that the Reds did not even have an outpost. They glimpsed the White Army only when the figure of a horseman emerged in front of them, out of the blizzard, which was finally running wild.

'Who goes there?' they asked by a campfire.

'Friend,' answered the general.

He slowly rode up to the nearest campfire, where those sitting recognized him. It was impossible not to recognize him. Even in 1920, in the absence of television and glossy magazines, the general was one of several faces everyone knew. When seen from below, he seemed huge. He looked like a monument.

Nobody stirred by the fire. People hold their breath like this when lightning balls appear: they feign nonexistence, hoping it will disappear. But the general was not disappearing. He and his horse grew each time the fire blazed. The Red commander emerged from the darkness. Stood still. His hand extended on its own to salute.

'Your Excellency . . .'

'At ease,' said the general.

The general's army was passing by behind his back but he was watching those seated at the campfires. For their part, they were still sitting motionlessly, watching the general. How his horse stamped its feet, how its flanks occasionally trembled. The bay horse was turning white before their eyes. The general was turning white: his military overcoat, his hood, and the reins in his hands. His face was also white. Never before had they seen such a white general. The cavalry was slowly floating past their very eyes in the drifting snow, as if it were surmounting sediment at the bottom of the sea. The infantry passed by. The heavy weaponry rode by. This went on for a long time, but nobody could grasp how long. Time had stopped. When the last infantryman had passed, the general nodded silently and vanished in the darkness.

They approached Perekop at dawn. The general ordered they demolish all remaining structures there and build campfires with them. A train with foodstuffs and firewood was already on its way from Dzhankoy. The general checked the condition of the fortifications and ordered they stretch barbed wire where there were breaks. At first he wanted to set up camp with tents but he knew that was already impossible. He commanded only that nobody lie in the snow. An instant later, everyone was sleeping but the posted sentinels. The sentinels needed to be relieved every hour. People simply had no strength for more.

The foreign envoys awaited the general in Dzhankoy. The general felt nothing but contempt for the envoys. He placed no great hopes in his meeting with them but decided to go anyway. The thought of evacuating the army had made his decision. He headed for Dzhankoy after leaving General Shatalov in his place.

The general rode his armored train car along the tracks he had laid. The warmth in the car and the clacking of the wheels made his head spin. The general felt something he had felt only in childhood. This was a feeling of joy and immortality.

'Joy and immortality,' he uttered.

This feeling had come to him several times recently, so the general thought he would most likely die soon. That was the last thing he had time to think before falling asleep.

A locomotive's drawn-out whistle awakened the general. It came from a passing train. They had stopped at a station.

'Dzhankoy?' the general asked the valet.

'Dzhankoy,' replied the valet.

He was holding a soap dish in one hand, a towel in the other.

The general went over to the washstand. For some reason,

the water was cold even in the warm train car, and the general remembered how he had doused himself with water every morning in the cadet corps. How his body and his comrades' bodies had been covered in goosebumps. He had a different body then. He took the towel from the valet and used it to rub his face until it was red. It was completely different.

The foreign diplomatic mission employees had gathered in a small chamber at the city council. They were sitting on bentwood chairs along both sides of a threadbare runner rug. The rug began at the doorway and led to a long oak table. Everyone rose when the general appeared, accompanied by an escort. The escort remained by the doorway and the general walked through the chamber, without glancing at anyone. He unbuttoned his military overcoat and half-sat on a chair.

'We are leaving Crimea,' the general said, in a silent whisper. 'We will hold Perekop as long as required to evacuate everyone.'

The diplomatic mission employees looked at the general, expressionless.

'I need to save my army,' the general went on. 'I need your help.'

'How splendid that you take your decisions without consulting your allies,' said the British envoy.

The general took a cigarette case from his pocket and opened it with a melodic sound.

'I appealed to your king, asking how many people he would accept in the event of our evacuation.'

Seeing the general had taken out the cigarette, an orderly brought him a match.

'He did not even respond to me,' the general's words blended with the cigarette smoke, sounding indistinct.

The British envoy wanted to object but the general raised his hand as if to save him the trouble.

'I'm appealing to all of you: accept my soldiers. *The comrades* will not spare anyone's life,' the general crushed the cigarette in a massive marble ashtray. 'Not anyone's. I shall take my leave.'

He walked slowly along the runner rug but stopped just short of the door.

'Half a year ago, England prevented me from planting minefields in Odessa's water zone. Why?'

He was standing, with his head lowered. He did not turn.

'I do not know,' said the British envoy.

'Well, I do know. British transports are now exporting grain from there, purchased for nothing from the Bolsheviks. That grain is soaked in Russian peasants' blood.'

The general returned to Perekop late that evening. The reconnaissance chief reported to him that the enemy had managed to move significant forces toward Perekop during the day. The general nodded. He already felt the Reds' pace and expected their offensive in the morning.

The general gave the wake-up signal an hour before dawn. He did not announce formation after they played reveille. He ordered only that the fires be stoked to blazing.

'Jump over the fires!' the general shouted and his voice came back to him in the regiment commanders' shouts, like a weak echo.

'Jump over the fires!' he shouted again in the quiet that had set in.

Several people hinted at slight movement then immediately dissolved into the overall motionlessness. The army
had fallen into lethargy in an obvious way. The general
rushed to the closest fire and began shaking those who were
sitting there. One after the other they stood and looked at
him with vacant, weepy eyes. Never before had he seen his
army *like this*. The general was genuinely frightened for the
first time in his life.

He tore around among the campfires, attempting to bring
his army back to life. Pounded soldiers on the face and
in the gut. Shouted that they would be slaughtered like
pigs.

Larionov distributed a half-glass of vodka to each but it
had only a sedative effect. He ordered that a march be played,
but the musicians' fingers would not move in the cold. He
buried his face in his hands and disappeared into the
commander-in-chief's tent.

When the other generals approached him in the tent, he
said, 'This army has died. And will never rise from the dead.'

A distant thundering sounded as he spoke. The Red artillery was beginning to shell. The Reds shelled often but
poorly. Their shells fell either in front of the fortifications
or far behind them. The lack of clustering in their shelling
showed the Red grenadiers' complete failure. If there was
anything the general needed to watch out for, it was only
a rogue shell.

The general calmed down once the battle had begun. It
was as if he had forgotten his momentary outburst: he led
using calculations from the artillerymen, who had determined the direction for a counterstrike. Their only reliable
reference point was the Reds' heavy weaponry. Using that

reference point to the fullest, the Red artillery was suppressed twenty minutes later.

In the quiet that set in, the general again walked along the fortifications and made certain that his order to repair them had been carried out. In some spots, they had dug out broken stakes. In their places they had installed intact ones that had just been brought from Armyansk. They had not bothered to remove the cut barbed wire: they just unwound new wire alongside it.

'Everything is ready for hosting *the comrades*,' said the general.

The comrades did not make them wait. Their first wave arose in the distance as if it had coagulated out of drifting snow; it began nearing the line of defense. The Whites did not shoot. Nor did the Reds. They walked, stooped, like someone still incapable of straightening up early in the morning. On a cold, early morning by a putrid gulf. This is how they would have walked to the factory in their previous life. Their ashen sleep-deprived faces were already visible. (As before, nobody was shooting.) Some had pliers in their belts for cutting barbed wire; this gave the approaching men even more resemblance to a crowd of workmen. But they were not workmen.

Behind the first wave was a second and a third and a fourth after that . . . The general lost count. It seemed those waves were moving from the horizon itself. They were creeping in with the indifference of volcanic lava. With the indivisibility of a locust swarm. This was a solid, unified force. The revolutionary masses in their highest manifestation. They were being created somewhere in the depths of a large country and had been pressed forward, to this narrow isthmus. The general knew these masses were enough for ten White Armies and, in the end, would engulf both his barbed wire and his machine guns.

He felt the defenders' gazes and their expectation of his command. He even seemed to think his troops had perked up a little, in light of the mortal danger. The machine gunners had already sat down by their Maxim guns. They were straightening the ammunition belts and stroking the barrels. There was no tension in their movements: on the contrary, there was something proprietary, and that irritated the general. He looked at his watch but could not figure out what time it was. That was not actually important anyway.

The machine guns could hit from two thousand paces and the Reds were already much closer. They were walking with an uncoordinated, hobbled gait, staring at the frozen grass. The soldiers were trying to deceive death, which had already taken up its position beyond the barriers. So as not to attract its attention, they were not looking it in the eye, just as one does not look into the eyes of the possessed. Death awaited the young and, thus, seemed insane to those soldiers. They saw it and deflected their gazes. The barrels of their rifles were half-lowered. They were not fighting, they were here for something else. They simply walked, bobbing on the hillocks. From north to south.

The general knew this wave was doomed. He wanted to give these soldiers an extra minute. Wanted to see them alive one last time. Could not look at them enough. Or enjoy, enough, observing their awkward forward motion. Their motion was a sign of life. Even their wooden strides and even the spasmodic waving of their arms differentiated life from death. That would be taken away from them in a minute. Replaced with the full repose that differentiates death from life.

Everything would happen upon his order. Several dozen waves destined for the passage from life to death were following behind the first. The speed of their passage depended on the speed of the shooting from his Maxim guns. Which were stilled in readiness. Everything would happen even without his order. These armies could no longer exist without one another.

The general feverishly tried to remember which side he was fighting on. He knew this was a useless trick of the consciousness and a withdrawal from another question—the most important one—but he just could not remember. Those around him watched with surprise crossing into alarm. The cavalry and infantry were watching. The artillerymen were watching. Only the wind could be heard.

'Fire,' whispered the general.

His command was just a cloud of steam. It contained no voice. The next second, though, machine guns hit the Reds' forward waves. The artillery began working on the rear guard. It seemed strange to the general that these consequences could be reached with one brief word. That they had not even heard. That they had uttered to themselves. He saw how deftly the machine gunners handled the ammunition belts. How the servicemen brought crates of ammunition with a calm, almost ant-like, focus. Volley followed volley. It was not uplifting for him. There was no more joy of battle in him. He knew (volley) that he already had another army now. Or maybe (volley) it was he who was different. Maybe his own (volley) sense of devastation had spread to the army and the army had ceased to exist. Died.

Everyone in the first wave fell in his own way. Some flapped their arms. Others grasped their bellies. Writhed on the ground with inhuman shouts. Some stopped moving then fell to the ground silently after standing in an already unearthly calm. Other people entered the gaping chasms that had formed. It had been a long time since this first wave had been the first. The machine guns became ever more precise as another wave approached, mowing down an entire wave at once. A new, live wave arrived where the first had perished; to the general's mind this was a very strange celebration of life.

Some broke ranks and ran over to the barbed wire. They attempted to get their pliers so they could at least sever one strand of barbed wire before dying. They did not manage to do so. They were killed by shots aimed from several rifles at once. Those who shot nodded approvingly to one another. They understood these dead were heroes.

The machine gunners' faces were sweaty and stern. Angels of death must have faces like that, thought the general. The machine gunners played first violin in this dreadful orchestra. They poured water into the cooling tanks of their Maxim guns, dipper after dipper, but the water was not fast enough to cool the metal. They could sense its temperature even through their gloves.

The Reds had many men—they did not need to count their losses. Never before had the general seen commanders sacrifice their own soldiers with such calm. The Reds had been carrying out a frontal attack for several hours already. From a military science perspective, the attack was pointless. What could they accomplish? Take all the bullets themselves? Cover all the barbed wire with their bodies? From

the perspective of dreadful reality, this attack was indisputable. An attack like this could not be countered forever.

The Reds, who had set out for unprecedented sacrifices,
knew this. The general, who would never allow himself to
have victims of that sort, knew this. He saw that a new
reality constructed on other fundamentals was arriving,
along with the Reds. He already had trouble understanding
it and thus rejected it with ever greater passion. And
continued resisting it.

The Reds' attack ceased with the early autumn twilight.
It dissolved in the semi-darkness. It subsided like water
during ebb tide. Unnoticed. Soundlessly. Revealing everything
preserved on the ocean floor. Bodies lay everywhere the
Red waves had been, as far as one could see in the
approaching darkness. Each lay alone. They lay on top of
one other. They hung on wires. Some were stirring. The
general sent a medical team to gather the living. He left
burying the dead to the Reds. The general was preparing
to hand over Perekop.

Solovyov made a very detailed description of the general's preparation for his final military operation. The
operation consisted of securing the troops' retreat to the
port. In this case, the issue no longer concerned organizing
a brilliant victory, as before. The general was working to
save his soldiers' lives. According to historian Solovyov, this
was about organizing a defeat with the fewest losses: a defeat
no less brilliant, in its own way, than the previous victories.

The general first dictated a special instruction turning
over to the White Army the entire fleet of ships assigned
to Crimean ports. He also designated five ports from which
the evacuation would be implemented. They were Sevastopol,

Yalta, Yevpatoria, Feodosia, and Kerch. But the main order, which stunned everyone, concerned the White Infantry's southerly march.

They had to act rapidly, without making too much noise, without extinguishing the fires, and taking a minimum of uniforms. The main and less maneuverable part of the army headed toward the ports in secret and began loading onto transports. The cavalry, machine gun detachments, and some artillery remained. They covered the departure of the White Army's infantry regiments. Perekop's defenders would need to abandon their positions and rush off, at a trot, to the ports at the very moment the last regiment reached the port. That was the general's plan. He set it out for those close to him and nobody objected. They never objected to what he said.

The general walked slowly along the line of defense and peered into the faces of those left hanging on the wires. Suffering was still present on those faces. The general knew this expression would leave them in a few days. Any expression would leave them. Especially if the weather warmed.

This was a strange inspection and a strange formation. The formation had been disrupted at each step. Those being inspected stood, their knees bent back, heels not aligned, and arms cast on the wire. They stood however they could and there was no reason to demand more from them. To the general, these people did not seem quite dead yet. Decomposition had not yet touched them. He still hoped to detect in their facial features at least a shadow of what separates life from death.

The general stopped next to a cadet who had been killed, a boy of around sixteen. The collar of his military overcoat had caught on the wire's barb, not allowing him to fall. The general straightened the cadet's collar as if this were a real inspection. The collar looked almost natural now: it was raised all around. The cadet's cheek and chin had been torn off: he had fallen on the wire face-first before being suspended by his collar. He continued pressing the pliers in his right hand.

The general immediately recognized the person standing beside the cadet. He could not help but recognize him, despite not having seen him in decades. He remembered his voice as deliberately quiet and remembered his gaze as condescending. That gaze was now more likely one of surprise. It was a one-eyed gaze because this man had no second eye. A bloody hollow gaped in its place. The general remembered the winter Petersburg night, the vodka in the tavern. The sense of weightlessness, the coziness of people who had escaped everyone. The intense unity of co-conspirators. The unbearable shame of one who had neglected his duty. Before him stood Lanskoy.

Lanskoy stood, his head pressed to a post. Both his arms were cast upon the wire. The general thought they hung with genuine lifelessness. There was something reminiscent of a puppet theater. Of a puppet conversing with a spectator. The comparison appeared to the general to be improper but precise.

What could Lanskoy tell the public? That he was a hero? That he despised death and threw himself on the wire? But that would be an untruth . . . Lanskoy despised life and threw himself on the wire. That was probably the reason he had gone to the Reds. The general walked right up to Lanskoy and attempted to close his only eye. His eyelashes fell with a barely audible crunch but the eye would not close. The general embraced Lanskoy. He pressed himself to his intact cheek. A tear ran down Lanskoy's cheek and froze in place. It was the general's tear.

'Bury him,' ordered the general.

His troops left almost soundlessly. The squeak of boots, muffled by gusts of wind. A farewell symphony, it occurred to the general. The only difference being, he thought, that his people were not extinguishing the fires: the number of campfires needed to remain the same, unlike in Joseph Haydn's version. A reduction in the number of performers should not be revealed to the viewer too early. That was the essence of the general's composition.

He approached one of the fires. Kologrivov, a captain in the medical services, was maintaining the fire. The captain was one of those who was staying on Perekop until the end.

'Good day, Your Excellency,' said Kologrivov, standing at attention before the general.

'At ease, Captain.'

He sat across from Kologrivov. He pushed a log that had burned through on one side closer to the center of the fire.

'The transition from life to death interests me,' said the general.

'It is, Your Excellency, inevitable.'

Patches of light from the fire changed the color and contours of Kologrivov's face.

'I do know that. How does it happen?'

'There are two ways: natural and unnatural. Natural . . .'

'Natural isn't a threat to us now,' the general interrupted. 'Tell me about the second way. Let's go.'

He took Kologrivov by the elbow and led him to the wire. As they walked past the staff tent, the general took the kerosene lantern that hung there. A broad but dim circle now preceded their motion.

The attackers had managed to upend one of the supports at the part of the barrier they had reached. It hung on the wire, almost touching the ground. Three bodies hung along-side it. They belonged to Red cadets (no longer belonged, thought the general). The bodies of several more cadets lay on the ground. Things had come to single combat in this defense sector.

The general cast light on one of the bodies on the wire. Somehow, this body was hanging particularly inconsolably: arms spread, head nearly touching the ground. Kologrivov took the dead man's shoulder and turned him on his back. With a squeak, the two other bodies began swaying.

'Aorta chopped in two,' Kologrivov said, showing it on the corpse. 'More than one liter of blood flowed out.'

'More than one? How much is that?' asked the general. 'Three? Five? Ten?'

'A person has only five or six liters of blood. At least two and a half flowed out of him.'

The general directed the lantern at the ground under-neath the wire. It was crimson. The blood had frozen as it flowed out. In concentric circles. Like lava. It was still warm in the body but had frozen on the ground.

'Blood is a special liquid tissue,' said Kologrivov. 'It moves through the circulatory vessels of the living body.'

'What does this body lack for being alive?' asked the general.

'Blood, I suppose. Approximately two and a half liters.

I'll use this opportunity to point out that one-thirteenth of the weight of the human body is blood.'

'One can come to understand the combined action of the organs, but for me that still doesn't add up to life,' said the general. He outlined a circle with the lantern. 'Life as such.'

'And one hundred grams of blood contains approximately seventeen grams of hemoglobin.'

'But even if you gave that cadet two and a half liters of blood, he still wouldn't come back to life.'

'He wouldn't come back to life,' said Kologrivov. He crouched in front of one of those lying on the ground. 'And this person was struck on the skull by a saber. Shine the light, Your Excellency . . . As I thought, the right temporal lobe is cut in two.'

'You've explained the causes of their deaths but I still have no clarity,' agonized the general, seeking the right words. 'Maybe the whole trouble is that you haven't explained the causes of their life to me.'

'A person's life is inexplicable. Only death is explicable,' said Kologrivov. He stroked the dead man's hair, which stood like wire. 'The saber entered about five centimeters into the temporal lobe. In my view, he had no chance. It's interesting that the right temporal lobe is responsible for libido, sense of humor, and memory of events, sounds, and images.'

'Does that mean that when the soldier was dying he no longer remembered events, sounds, or images?'

'He did not even have a sense of humor. And his libido was missing. This death belongs in the "unnatural" category.'

A cannon struck somewhere in the distance; indistinctly, as if groggy. Its echo rolled through the sky and went quiet.

'Come to think of it,' said the general, 'who among us knows what's natural and what's not?'

'I'll note, à propos, that the human brain weighs an average of 1,470 grams.'

'Maybe death is natural if it comes to a person in the prime of his life?'

'And has a volume of 1,456 cubic centimeters.'

'Maybe there's a certain logic to death at that highest point?'

'And it consists of eighty percent water. That's just for your information.'

'Then why bother to wait for the point when the body's becoming decrepit and almost disintegrated?'

The captain stood up.

'Because, Your Excellency, by then nobody begrudges the loss of the body, when it's like that.'

The general looked closely at Kologrivov. He walked over to him and embraced his shoulders.

'Well, of course: death comes only to a person's body. I'd simply forgotten the most important part.'

18

Solovyov continued searching for Leeza. The unexpected complications he ran into at the university had not stopped him, although they had made him more cautious. The scholar realized that direct contact with women possessing a surname dear to him harbored its own dangers. He had already made paper-based correspondence a top priority in his appeals to other educational institutions because he was able to analyze the responses carefully and keep personal communications with the Larionovas to a minimum.

Since Solovyov did not know which university city Leeza might have gone to, he decided to try his luck in Moscow, too. To some extent, using postal communication methods also disposed him favorably toward Moscow. Considering his challenging experience with the search, the postal method struck the young historian as the safest way to go.

Solovyov wrote a long letter to the rector of Moscow State University, asking that his request be treated sympathetically. He composed the letter with an informal air, even telling of his childhood friendship with a person he had (regretably, largely due to his own fault!) lost. To sound more convincing, Solovyov also referred to the readers' triangle consisting of himself, Nadezhda Nikiforovna, and Yelizaveta, the person being sought. Not wishing to create the impression he was a simpleminded person, Solovyov did not let slip a single word about his designs on Nadezhda Nikiforovna.

For some reason, Solovyov was counting a great deal on his appeal to MSU so waited impatiently for a response. He did not know exactly how long it took for letters to travel from Petersburg to Moscow but figured they should not take very long. He still remembered, from a university course on Russian literature, that Dostoevsky's letters from Germany took four or five days. Considering that fact—as well as the technological revolution that had taken place— Solovyov allocated about two days for letters to travel from Petersburg to Moscow. He assumed the same for the return journey. Solovyov allotted about three or four days for the Moscow rector to check into his question.

To his surprise, no answer had arrived ten days later. Nor did one arrive twenty days or even a month later. Solovyov wanted to send another letter to Moscow but feared being pushy. So as not to lose time, he decided to look for Leeza in other Petersburg educational institutions. Solovyov was flabbergasted when he opened a directory for college applicants. The number of educational institutions was beyond the bounds of reason.

Solovyov appealed first to the Herzen State Pedagogical University, which had still been called an institute not long before. This establishment—where opportunities had broadened after the renaming—not only found a Yelizaveta Larionova among its ranks but also allowed Solovyov to take a look at her personal records.

Solovyov heard his heart beating as he entered the dean's office at the philology department. It reverberated out from under the ceiling, where two workers nailing up a cable seemed to be echoing his heart. Solovyov was asked to wait a little. In case they checked biographical data, he had the years Leeza had started and graduated from high school. They were the same as his years. What else could be in the document? He crossed his arms over his chest to muffle his heartbeats. The sad-faced workers slowed their pace, too, as they drew a green cable along a pink wall. A woman from the dean's office brought a thin folder and extended it to Solovyov.

'Is this her?'

There was a photograph glued to a left-hand corner of the form so Solovyov did not need the biographical data. The photo was not very large, but nothing larger was required for full clarity.

'No.'

Solovyov did not give up. He appealed to all institutions, even the very unlikeliest. Sometimes they gave him information over the telephone, sometimes they required a visit. They hung up rather frequently, suggesting he not pester them. In those cases, Solovyov beseeched. Insisted. Several times he bought candy for female employees in rectors' offices. One of them jokingly asked Solovyov how much she might be able to replace Leeza for him. It felt as if the list of educational institutions would never end.

Another two weeks later, a student named Yelizaveta Larionova turned up at the Lesgaft Institute of Physical Education. When Solovyov learned of this by telephone, he caught a taxi and went to the institute. He simply had no time to consider Leeza's association with sports.

An older, broad-shouldered woman, obviously a former athlete, greeted him in the administrative offices. She sized up Solovyov and asked his height.

'One meter, seventy-nine,' said Solovyov.

During his time searching for Leeza, he had grown out of the habit of being surprised.

'Our Yelizaveta is two meters, four,' said the woman. After a silence, she added, 'So you're not an athlete?'

Solovyov could tell from her face that she was not making fun of him.

'I'm a historian,' he said. 'Peter the Great was two meters, four. Yelizaveta has a promising future.'

'She's a nice girl. She's on the city basketball team.'

She straightened a lamp on the desk. Her face was serious, as before.

Notification of a registered letter from Moscow arrived at the very end of October. Solovyov discovered it in his mailbox when he returned from the library. He was invited to bring his passport to the post office to receive the letter. As he closed the box, Solovyov thought this kind of solemnity must mean something in and of itself; there would be no point in sending a negative answer by registered mail.

He was at the post office ten minutes before it opened. Addressee Solovyov's heart was beating as never before. After signing for the letter, he tore open the envelope right there at the window and proceeded to read it. It was signed by the vice rector for general affairs (the surname was feminine) and reported that a Yelizaveta Filippovna Larionova truly was studying at MSU. Following that, however, was the supposition—and here the letter's tone became less formal—that this was not the same Yelizaveta the Petersburg historian was seeking. This Moscow Yelizaveta was 39 years old and working toward her second degree. At the end of the letter, the vice rector wished Solovyov success in his search and expressed the hope that he would certainly find his Yelizaveta. Judging from the date on the letter, she had expressed that wish exactly a month ago.

Solovyov started to leave but then returned and demanded to see the post office manager. When that person appeared, Solovyov silently showed him the postmark. The manager took his glasses out of his uniform smock and carefully studied the postmark.

'A month,' he said. 'Sometimes it's longer. Sometimes they don't arrive at all.'

Solovyov looked over the manager's head. He felt his hatred boiling. Hatred and despair: the hand on the wall clock was leading them around in a circle.

'Dostoevsky's letters from Germany took five days,' Solovyov informed the man.

'Dostoevsky was a genius,' retorted the manager.

A few days later, Solovyov resorted to yet another option. He published brief appeals to Leeza in Moscow and Petersburg newspapers, with a request to telephone (a number was given). There were quite a few calls in the days following the publication. Four Leezas telephoned, two of them were Larionovas. A Taisia Larionova telephoned, saying she was prepared to answer to *Leeza* if necessary. A woman who did not give her name telephoned. She offered a discounted portion of Herbalife. The calls ceased roughly a week later.

Solovyov directed all the force of his striving for Leeza and all the resentment that had accumulated during his fruitless searches into his dissertation research about the general. Never before had he worked so much or so passionately. He found document after document but they brought him no closer to Leeza. After catching himself in that thought, Solovyov realized he subconsciously hoped they would help him close in. Why?

One day he ran into Temriukovich in the corridor at the institute.

'You're studying General Larionov, if I'm not mistaken?' said Temriukovich.

'I am,' said Solovyov.

He took a few steps toward Temriukovich.

'I read a folkloric text way back when,' said Temriukovich, 'and a strange thought occurred to me: might it be connected with the general?'

Temriukovich fell silent. Solovyov could neither confirm nor even deny the academician's thought. He could only nod respectfully. Temriukovich approached him, right up close, and Solovyov smelled his rotten breath.

'How do you regard strange thoughts?' asked Temriukovich.

'Well . . .' Solovyov backed away slightly. 'Do you happen to remember where you saw that text?'

'Where I saw it?' Temriukovich suddenly burst out laughing. 'Do I remember? Well, of course I remember: *Full Russian Folklore Collection. Entries for 1982.* Part two of that year's volume. Starting on approximately page 95.'

Temriukovich's face fell. He turned slowly and walked off down the hall.

Solovyov heard him say, 'Maybe my suggestion will help that young man.'

Despite the academician's hunch, the young man doubted the utility of the information he had acquired. He remembered it, though, when he happened to be at the public library, so decided to have a look at the *Full Russian Folklore Collection*. Much to his surprise, he really did discover the text Temriukovich had referred to, in the second of two volumes of entries from 1982. It began, in complete accordance with the citation, on page 95 and ended on page 104. It had been recorded by participants of a folklore expedition, from the words of 89-year-old Timofei Zhzhenka, a resident of the village of Berezovaya Gat in the Chernigov Oblast's Novgorod-Seversky region.

Timofei Zhzhenka told the folklore expedition's participants about events of some long-ago war. Commentaries to the text spoke of the impossibility (as commonly happens in folklore) of clarifying what war was actually involved. The publishers were inclined to regard its time of action as the epic period, though they also pointed out, in all honesty, that there was a definite obstacle to that sort of conclusion.

They had in mind the mention of the railroad, something that, as a rule, was not in epic texts. Futhermore, the narrative opened by referencing a railroad station—Gnadenfeld, where the events described unfold—something uncharacteristic of folklore. Just that name made Solovyov grab hold of the embossed cover of *Full Russian Folklore Collection* with both hands.

Timofei Zhzhenka used ornate dialectical expressions to describe a summer night when two armored trains stopped, almost simultaneously, at the aforementioned station. Two generals emerged from the two armored trains; this looked fully folkloric. Each of them presumed the station was in his troops' hands and pensively (*they had things to think about,* explained Timofei Zhzhenka) took a walk next to his armored train. Suddenly, one general (*the general that was ours,* according to Timofei's scant definition) recognized the other in the light of a station streetlamp. Without emerging from the darkness, he signaled to his valet, who was with him, and they crossed under the carriage to the second armored train.

Meanwhile, the second general put out his cigarette with the toe of his boot and began going up into his own train carriage. When he was standing on the carriage's platform, he gave the guards permission to go to bed. They did not need to be told twice; they disappeared into the next carriage. The guarded man went to his quarters. A minute later, there was knocking at the second general's door.

'What do you want?' He opened the door abruptly and was pushed inside.

'So we meet after all,' said the one who entered.

He placed the barrel of a Nagan revolver to the forehead of the carriage's master and commanded the valet take the other's weapon.

'I'm not afraid of you,' uttered the man who had been disarmed.

'Sit,' said the one who had entered, nodding at a chair that stood by a small round table. Several sheets of paper lay on it, under a spill-proof inkwell. For some reason, there was no pen. The carriage's master awkwardly (*uncomfortably,* Timofei characterized it) slid down the back of the chair to its seat. Perched on the edge, he laid his hands on the sheets.

'You won't dare shoot.'

'Why?'

'Because my guards will come running if there's a shot.'

Beads of sweat covered his forehead.

'I don't think so,' said the one who had entered. He took a watch from his breast pocket and opened it with a barely audible clink. 'A train with our wounded will pass through this station very soon. It's a very long train . . .'

'I don't give a shit about you.'

'Nobody will hear a thing.'

The watch returned to the pocket with a click. A light tremor could already be sensed under their feet.

'You feel that? That's our wounded coming. Of course many are deceased, too.'

The sound swelled. The eyes of the one at the table froze on the inkwell. The medical train reached the station and the station was drowning in its rumbling. The inkwell began coming into resonance with the train and set off on an unhurried journey across the table. It began trembling hard. It turned on its axis and advanced inexorably toward the edge. The man at the table grabbed the inkwell and hurled it at the wall with all his strength when it was about to fall off.

'Damn it, why the hell aren't you shooting?'

Shards scattered in all directions. The inkwell shattered to the floor in thousands of little glass pieces. It had cracked through the unbearable noise. The last carriage of the medical train rumbled past outside. In the absolute silence that followed, the general answered the question that had been posed, 'Because death is incapable of teaching anything.'

He let his valet go ahead and followed him. He closed the door behind himself without a sound.

When Solovyov went outside, he felt like he was over-flowing with new knowledge. He was afraid of spilling it. He thought he seemed too fragile for this knowledge and could easily smash, like the inkwell.

When recording folklore, a text like this truly could be taken as folkloric: everything depended on the force of expectation. The narration was conducted in a good vernacular language. It took on a rhythm through its multiple repetitions. And what could have been recorded in the village of Berezovaya Gat but folklore, anyway?

That was the reasoning of those who published the text. In a commentary to the publication, they called upon the reader not to worry about certain details from modern history that were undoubtedly present in the story. The researchers determined its plot to be ancient to the highest degree. In elaborating on their point, they indicated that in this case they regarded the narration of the judge Ehud's murder of Moab king Eglon as a precursor.

Despite the bloodless finish to Zhzhenka's narration, the commentary's authors took notice of its high degree of resemblance to the biblical narration in the Book of Judges. As examples, they offered the high status of the characters, intrusion into their apartments, and the complete nonparticipation of their guards. It would have been naïve to suppose, pointed out the commentary's authors, that such an ancient text would not undergo any changes when reproduced.

A line of reasoning like that was legitimate. It could, seemingly, satisfy the most demanding researchers, not to mention numerous specialists in the field of textual deconstruction. It did not satisfy Solovyov. The historian knew something the folklorists who wrote the commentaries did not know: Timofei Zhzhenka was General Larionov's valet in 1920.

Solovyov decided to walk home. He was deliberating over whether a folkloric text could be considered a historical document. And, strictly speaking, was that text folkloric? Posing the question that way automatically ranked folklore in the realm of make-believe. After stopping on Palace Square, Solovyov asked himself to what degree history itself was make-believe. That question seemed completely natural on the main square of an empire.

It was a warm evening for the beginning of November. Warm and damp, in Petersburg's way. An angel's lowered head was looking at the gleaming cobblestones. Solovyov looked at the angel. A silvery haze shimmered in the beams of spotlights directed at the column. That Timofei Zhzhenka did not, prudently, give his characters names still did not render his story make-believe. Maybe he was not so simple, this Timofei. Who in Soviet Russia would have published the general's valet's memoirs? (Did the valet write his memoirs? Did he write at all?) Timofei Zhzhenka had seemingly found a witty way to tell future generations about what he had seen. Having no doubt that the general's life would be studied one day. Solovyov smiled at his thoughts as he opened his umbrella. *Sapienti sat.** That was about what Timofei might have thought.

The rain intensified as Solovyov approached his building. It was draining from somewhere above in long, cold streams, drumming on the tin of the ledges and bursting with a roar from rainspouts plastered in adverts. His umbrella saved

---

*   Enough for the wise (Lat.).

him only partially. It did not shelter him from the water-saturated wind. The wind swooped down out of nowhere and the gusts stung Solovyov as if he had been hit by a wet rag. The wind twisted the arm holding the umbrella, bending its spokes and exposing the fabric's inner and defiantly dry side. Solovyov had to close the umbrella when it nearly flew away at the corner of Zhdanovskaya Embankment and Bolshoy Avenue. He felt cold rivulets under his shirt and could hear a repulsive squishing in his shoes, even through the sound of the downpour. The only thing left for him to do was run.

At home, Solovyov undressed and got into the shower. Water manifested itself completely differently now: its flows were hot and friendly here, its embraces ticklish and tender. There was something of Leeza's touch in that, which made him feel her absence even more acutely. Leeza did not know of the discovery he had made today. And it was so important to him to tell someone about it.

When Solovyov came out of the bathroom, he threw on his robe and dialed Prof. Nikolsky's number. Nobody came to the phone at the other end of the line. Solovyov dialed the number again and waited a little longer. He almost heard the crackling old apparatus in the professor's hallway. The professor would hurry for the second call after being too late for the first. That happened with old people. Old people asked that callers wait as long as possible before hanging up. The professor was making his way through a cluttered hallway. Losing his slippers as he went. Holding glasses that were slipping from his nose. (Solovyov felt uncomfortable but did not put the phone down.) The professor's sleeve caught on a door knob. On a nail sticking out of a bookshelf.

His foot grazed a pile of journals on the floor. The pile scattered into a fan that would refresh nobody.

In the end, the professor did not answer. Solovyov wanted to call someone else but there was nobody else to call. He realized that when the tones inside the phone changed, as if they had tired. He kept listening to them, not wanting to put the receiver down; they sounded like signals from Mars might sound. That sort of connection was, essentially, organic at house No. 11 on Zhdanovskaya Embankment. Contact with Planet Earth was ruled out for that evening.

Prof. Nikolsky's absence troubled Solovyov. He headed to the university in the morning and learned there that the professor was in the hospital. The dean's office employee was reluctant to answer his question about what had happened to the professor. It was not customary to give out this sort of information.

'Something about his lungs . . . They're doing tests.'

The hospital where Prof. Nikolsky was undergoing tests was in the northern part of the city. Solovyov bought some oranges along the way. Upon reflection, he also bought some German cookies. His thought was that these foodstuffs were incapable of harming the professor's lungs.

Solovyov had no trouble finding the pulmonary department. There was no sense of the usual stench of Russian hospitals there. Perhaps lung disease did not assume a smell. The nurse on duty was sitting in the corner of the hallway. She was noting down something in a journal, slowly tracing out letter after letter. Solovyov asked which room the professor was in. The nurse answered without raising her head. Her knitting lay next to the journal. Based on her reverie, it was clear she had only just set it aside.

'What happened to Professor Nikolsky?' Solovyov asked.

Her pen was moving with the placidity of a knitting needle.

'Nothing good.'

Prof. Nikolsky had a small but private room. Nobody answered when Solovyov knocked. He pressed the door handle and cautiously opened the door a little. Prof. Nikolsky was half-lying on the bed. This was the same unusual pose the professor himself had talked about at one time, during lectures about the Petrine period. At the time, this—half-sitting (half-lying?)—was considered healthful for sleeping, so blood would not rush to the head. Prof. Nikolsky was half-lying (half-sitting?) like that in his room. His eyes were closed.

Solovyov's purposeful gaze proved more efficacious than his knock. The professor opened his eyes. It is possible he was not even sleeping. Most likely (Solovyov grasped this from the professor's tranquility) he had heard the knock. Solovyov greeted him before crossing the threshold.

'Come in, my friend.'

The professor gestured, barely noticeably, pointing to a chair beside the bed. There was a whiff of his usual good-will in that gesture, but there was something more now, too. What Solovyov initially took for tranquility was undoubtedly something else that customary words did not fit.

'So, I brought . . . here.'

Solovyov took the oranges out of the bag. When he was on his way here, he had intended to ask the professor about his health but now he could not do so. He remembered the cookies and pulled those out.

'And these . . .'

Disheartened by his own eloquence, Solovyov held out the packages for the professor.

'Thank you.'

He put the packages on the blanket. Now the packages and the blanket moved, barely noticeably, in time with Nikolsky's breathing. His breathing—so it seemed to Solovyov, anyway—was rapid and irregular. The professor's pale, hairless chest was visible behind baggy pajamas; a small aluminum cross shone on his chest. Solovyov thought that he had never seen the professor's body: he did not remember seeing him without a necktie. Nikolsky took Solovyov's hand.

'How's the dissertation?'

'I'm almost finished.'

'Good work. Bring it to me, all right?'

Solovyov's dissertation lay in his bag. He nodded.

'How are you feeling?'

'Not so great . . . But even so, better than your general.' The professor was trying to sit up more and the oranges slid down to the edge of the bed. 'Did you manage to find the end of his memoirs?'

'Not yet. But I found something else.'

And Solovyov told of yesterday's discovery. Nikolsky heard him out without interrupting.

'The truth is more wonderful than make-believe.'

A nurse came in and held out a plastic lid with several pills for the professor. He tossed all the pills into his mouth at once with a familiar motion that even had a devil-may-care feel, then drank them down with water. This made no impression whatsoever on the nurse.

'You know,' said Solovyov after waiting for the door to close behind the nurse, 'with everything almost done, right now a sort of unusual feeling has come up. Maybe it's dissatisfaction. It's hard for me to express . . .'

'Dissatisfaction is a *usual* feeling. Especially when finishing work.'

Nikolsky said that somewhat sluggishly and Solovyov wondered if there had been a sedative among the tablets.

'I had something else in mind. Dissatisfaction . . . with the general's life. Maybe with life overall. Anyway, that's pretty heavy material . . .'

'No, go on.'

The professor's hands were folded on the blanket.

'So, imagine: there's this general. Clever. Hero. Living legend. Then, it's as if his fate short circuits. Darkness after a bright light. A squalid Soviet pension. A communal toilet. Somehow, it's even silly.'

'Why?'

Solovyov shrugged.

'It's a strange thought: maybe for him it would have been better to be shot?'

The nurse came in again, this time with a syringe on a tray.

'Turn around.'

The professor slowly turned on his side and lowered his pajama bottoms a little. Solovyov went over to the window. The street was barely visible in the November dusk. The poorly washed glass reflected only the nurse and the professor. But the professor did not know that.

'Relax. Don't squeeze your buttocks.'

Nikolsky began coughing uncontrollably. Something

glassy clinked on the tray and the nurse left the room. Nikolsky wiped the tears that had formed in his eyes from coughing.

'I could say that I should have died a little earlier, in some more pleasant kind of place. And not be living out my last days here . . .'

Solovyov wanted to object, but the professor threatened him with an index finger.

'But I'm not going to say that. Not because I like what's happening. It's just that the meaning of life is not in reaching a peak. Life's meaning is most likely in its entirety.' He pressed his palms into the mattress and returned to a half-sitting position. 'What does your general write about most?'

'I don't know. Probably about his childhood.'

'So there you go. That's very distant from all his victories but it's the most important thing for him. After all, he gauged everything later based on his childhood . . .' Nikolsky looked up at to Solovyov. 'Does that seem far-fetched to you?'

Solovyov abruptly walked over to the window and sat on the window sill.

'No, damn it . . . Pardon me. I suddenly realized why the two descriptions coincide . . . The general's childhood reminiscences and Zhloba's report about entering Yalta; imagine, they coincide right down to the details! I heard this during the summer, at the conference . . . I'll need to check it all, but it seems like I understand . . .'

Nikolsky was sitting with his head tilted toward his shoulder. It seemed to Solovyov that the professor's attention was dissipating. That impression went away when Nikolsky raised his head.

'I was just thinking about the peak in the general's life. Of course that's what you found yesterday.' (The professor had begun muttering.) 'It works out that he lived more than half a century after that. After or as a result of that? It's a good question. It's probably both things . . .'

Solovyov saw the nurse through the door, which was ajar. She was looking sternly at him, even shaking her head. Solovyov nodded that he understood everything. He turned toward the professor to say goodbye but the professor was asleep. He was dreaming of the article, 'Regarding a Christian Understanding of History', that he had begun writing before ending up in the hospital. Despite the fact that the article opened with a minutely detailed examination of the category of progress, the scholar did not perceive substantial signs of progress in history. The majority of nations had periods of ascent but as a rule achieved those a) at the expense of other peoples and b) for an extremely limited time. The interaction of those rises and falls was the sum of the vectors that absorbed one another and constituted the essence of world history. It had no common vector. With this state of things, it remained unclear what historical progress, which is now taken as an axiom, was composed of. Was it in the ability—the professor dreamt of a rhetorical question—to destroy ever larger numbers of people with each century? He did not consider it necessary to answer that question, but even in his sleep he did not forget to cite studies, such as Nikolai Berdyaev's *The Meaning of History*, on similar problematic issues. With this state of affairs, Prof. Nikolsky refused to assess events in world history according to their degree of progressiveness. He allowed only one single criterion for their assessment: the moral criterion. Declaring the notion of progress a fiction, the sleeping historian noted that the structure of a nation's life is very much reminiscent of the life of an individual and that it ends in the exact same nonprogressive way: in death. This gave him grounds to move on to the problem of the correlation of history and the individual. Prof. Nikolsky preferred the question of how history allows the individual to play a role over the traditional exploration of the role the individual plays in history. In the scholar's treatment, history, when compared with the individual, appeared as something derivative and, in a certain sense, ancillary. To him, history looked like a frame—sometimes meager, sometimes sumptuous—where the individual placed his portrait. The scholar did not propose another intended goal for history. His fingers slid, barely noticeably, along the blanket's creases as if he were attempting to fumble for that frame. As he moved on to the next point in his article, the professor dreamt that he would very likely never finish writing it.

19

A quiet whistling began sounding at dawn. Solovyov opened his eyes a little, just the tiniest bit, so as not to let his dream slip away. He did not exclude the possibility that the whistling had been in his dream. The dream was pleasant. The dream attempted to hold on to Solovyov's flickering eyelashes even as it receded. Solovyov could not have retold the dream; he could not remember, even roughly, what the dream had been about, though he continued to feel its mood. The mood was all that remained of the dream and Solovyov realized he had woken up. Despite the early morning hour, it was not dark in the room. Solovyov knew this light. It was the light of the first snow. The freshness of the first snow was drifting through a small open window in the kitchen.

The whistle was sounding in his waking life. It was a quiet, cautious whistling, more of an intermittent whistle. Solovyov raised himself up on his elbow and looked around. The whistling disappeared. There was nothing unusual in the room. Solovyov lay down again and the whistling resumed. He slid his feet into his slippers and went to the kitchen. He stopped in the kitchen doorway. A great titmouse was sitting on the cupboard door.

The bird was obviously watching him, though for some reason it was not facing Solovyov. Only one of its eyes was visible, lending the bird an inappropriately coquettish appearance. The bird had flown in through the high ventilation window, which had been opened for the night. Why had it not flown out through the window? Unable to find it? Or did it not want to? Solovyov thought that they might live together. He took a step toward the bird, who fluttered to the ceiling light fixture. The sound of wings was unexpectedly loud in the quiet of the kitchen. The thought even flashed through his mind that the word *fluttered* was onomatopoeic. This was exactly how bird wings sounded.

Solovyov shrugged and walked over to the window. A drum beat was streaming through the little window along with the frosty air. Initially it was pure rhythm, barely discernible and almost lacking sound. This rhythm was resounding from Ofitsersky Lane, just in front of the Military Space Academy. It was located in the buildings of the former Second Cadet Corps.

Solovyov stood with his forehead pressed to the glass, surprised at the unusualness of his current place of residence. Its markedly military-space orientation. He watched as a column of cadets moved, implausibly slowly, toward the archway of his building. They probably wanted to salute the spot where engineer Los's workshop had stood. After all, they must want very much to go to Mars if they had entered the Military Space Academy.

Despite their outward unhurriedness (and in this lies the monumentalness of how the masses move), the forward column had managed to cover a significant distance in the murky snow. Solovyov had already discerned several drummers leading the column. A man with a banner was marching ahead of the drummers. His legs rose to waist-level and with each step that imprinted itself in the snow, a tassel on the banner's peak flew up recklessly. Perhaps he wanted to go to Mars more than the rest.

A whistling sounded behind Solovyov's back. The bird was sitting on the cabinet again. This time the bird was not looking at him sideways. His bright yellow breast faced Solovyov. Solovyov stood on tiptoe and opened the window wider. Out of uncertainty, he spoke to the bird at full volume, 'If you don't want to stay, then fly.'

He walked away from the window for effect and pointed at the small ventilation window with his hand. Both the gesture and his intonation felt utterly false. The bird preferred not to move and if Solovyov were the bird, he would not have flown away, either. When Solovyov attempted to come closer to the cabinet, approaching from the other side, the bird flew up toward the lower window and hit the glass several times with a ringing thud. The bird fell to the floor, flew up, and struck the glass again. Solovyov rushed to the window and the bird flew off into the other room, tracing a semi-circle around the kitchen.

Solovyov followed the bird slowly into the other room. The bird was sitting on a bookshelf, prepared for a further encounter with the glass. Its eyes shone with the determination of a kamikaze. Solovyov stopped at the threshold, leaning against the doorjamb. He pitied the bird. He pitied the glass that might not withstand it. But the sound of the bird striking the window was genuinely unbearable for him. A prolonged, throbbing sound. The sound of live clashing with unlive.

'Now listen, bird . . .'

Solovyov thought this was a voice for addressing someone standing on a ledge. Someone who had strapped on explosives. It was an unnaturally calm voice. A voice for difficult situations.

'The big window's taped up for winter. But I'll open it so you can fly away . . .'

The bird was listening. Solovyov slowly moved along the opposite wall. After reaching the window, he forcefully slid the latch and pulled the window handle. The frame gave way with a dry crackling. Shreds of loosened cotton wool began fluttering in the wind. Holding his breath, Solovyov stole back to the doorway. Steam came out of his mouth when he finally exhaled. The surprised bird observed snowflakes melting on the parquet floor. The first column of cadets had managed to come through the archway and was now drumming from the side of the house with the open window.

'Are you going to fly?'

The bird hesitated a little and flew over to the windowsill. Solovyov took several cautious strides toward the window. The bird could not stride. After starting to jump around the windowsill, it moved closer to the open window. Sat on the window frame as if it were a picture frame. Froze like a tiny yellow paintbrush stroke. In the mix of air currents behind the bird, there quivered towers of light and, under them, the stadium's pseudo-classical columns. Down below, right by the window frame, the cadets were flowing like jelly over the bridge that led to the stadium. Ignoring the laws of physics—and the danger threatening them—they continued their drumming and collective marching on the bridge. The surprised bird turned its head several times. It flew away, without waiting for the bridge to collapse from the force of all those marching feet coming down at once.

When Solovyov arrived at the Institute, they told him that some woman or other from Moscow had been asking for him. She was now sitting in the institute library. Solovyov started off for the library but ran into Temriukovich along the way.

'Listen, Solovyov . . .' said Temriukovich, but then Tina Zhuk came up behind him and interrupted.

'Not bothering you, am I? I just wanted to say . . .'

Temriukovich's hand unexpectedly landed on Tina Zhuk's lips.

'Just for your information: you have a very loud voice. Intolerably loud for an academic establishment.'

Temriukovich turned and began shuffling down the corridor. Zhuk made a ghastly grimace and dashed off after Temriukovich.

'Loud and unpleasant,' Temriukovich sighed to himself. 'With a voice like that, it's better to keep quiet.'

'I wanted to say that the academic secretary was looking for you,' Zhuk uttered defiantly.

But the academic secretary himself was already approaching Temriukovich. He took the academician by the elbow and whispered something fiercely in his ear. Temriukovich continued moving, ferociously looking over the academic secretary's head every now and then. They stopped by the library door.

'Did you hear about how our senile one caused a stir at Cinema House?' Tina Zhuk asked Solovyov.

She was not even trying to speak quietly.

'Fine, what do you need from me this time?' Temriukovich asked the academic secretary with irritation, freeing his elbow.

The academic secretary walked around the academician from the opposite side and took him by the other elbow. He was speaking to Temriukovich in an emphatically patient way. Solovyov gathered that he would not be able to get into the library so was now looking for an opportunity to get rid of Tina.

'He barged in on a closed screening at Cinema House where they were only letting in people with membership cards . . .' Zhuk rolled her eyes.

When they reached the men's room, Solovyov excused himself and went in. Tina Zhuk did not come in. Oddly enough, thought Solovyov. Oddly enough. He stopped at a sink and turned on the water. He looked at his reflection in the mirror and wet his hands. Swept the hair off his forehead. Temriukovich raced in as Solovyov was about to leave. Temriukovich rushed for a stall without noticing Solovyov, slamming the door behind himself with a bang.

'The only place at the institute where it's easy to breathe,' carried from the stall.

The end of the sentence was accompanied by furious watery burbling.

Solovyov left the men's room and headed for the institute library. Other than the elderly librarian (how very little she resembled Nadezhda Nikiforovna!), only Murat was sitting in the reading room. He lifted his head when Solovyov appeared and Solovyov greeted him.

'You looking for someone?' asked Murat.

After hesitating, Solovyov told him about the researcher from Moscow.

'There was someone,' confirmed Murat.

The door to the reading room opened and Temriukovich came into sight. He froze silently on the threshold, not letting go of the door handle. The librarian smiled. Temriukovich went out, leaving the door open.

'I heard a good story about him,' said Murat. He took a box of mints out of his pocket. 'Want one?'

'No, thanks.'

'So there was a premiere at Cinema House. Something of a crush at the entrance. Everybody's showing their membership cards and invitations . . . Sure you don't want one?'

Solovyov shook his head. Murat scooped out a few mints with three fat fingers and popped them in his mouth.

'And then, all of a sudden, out of nowhere . . . Anyway, long story short, Temriukovich turns up. Gets in without any explanations whatsoever. "Member at Cinema House?" they ask him as he goes by and he says, "No, I have it with me" . . .'

Solovyov glanced at the librarian—she was laughing. There sure were all kinds of librarians.

'Do you happen to know where that researcher might have gone?' Solovyov asked them both.

Murat shrugged.

'Most likely for lunch,' said the librarian. 'She left her bag here.'

Solovyov stopped as he was nearing the institute café and heard Tina Zhuk's voice. Ultimately, he was not sure he needed to meet with the Moscow researcher. But he went in anyway.

Solovyov saw Tina first. She was sitting and telling a story at a table with an institute guard and two women who worked in the modern history department. The women were laughing hard. Judging from their faces, the history was extremely modern. The guard was sitting half-facing Tina and listening with dignity, as befit a strong person. Every now and then, he brushed crumbs off his camouflage uniform.

The Moscow researcher was drinking tea at the next table. She was the only person in the café that Solovyov did not know. She was around fifty. Wearing a sleeveless jacket. There was an unmotivated bow on her head. When Solovyov approached her table, she herself asked if he was Solovyov. Solovyov confirmed it. The researcher gave her name as Olga Leonidovna (an invitation to sit down) and said she worked at the Rumyantsev Library. She had brought him some materials about the Civil War.

'I left them in the reading room,' Olga Leonidovna smiled. 'I'll just finish my tea, okay?'

'No rush.'

Solovyov smiled, too. Essentially, the bow suited her.

'Leeza Larionova sent them for you. As I understand it, you must know her.'

A chair pulled away from the next table and Solovyov felt like the chair's motion was floating in his eyes now.

'And I have mine with me, too, by the way,' said the guard, standing up.

He straightened his pants and winked at everyone there. Tina Zhuk's other two neighbors got ready to go after him. A window floated slowly along the wall.

'You saw Leeza in Moscow?'

'She and I work in the same department at the library.'

'And . . . how is she?'

'She applied to the philology department last year but didn't get in. She was working at some factory . . .'

'They say it costs eight thousand *green ones* to get into college in Moscow,' said Tina Zhuk. 'Minimum.'

Olga Leonidovna looked at Tina with surprise.

'She obviously didn't have eight thousand.'

'Obviously,' said Tina, putting on lipstick in front of a little mirror, then standing up. 'Greetings, everybody.'

The reading room was empty but Olga Leonidovna switched to a whisper.

'This year Leeza was accepted at the correspondence course division and got a job with us. She sorts through the new acquisitions in the Manuscript Department.' She pulled a plump folder out of a plastic bag and extended it to Solovyov. 'It's a photocopy. A certain something that arrived recently for the collection.'

'Thank you.'

Leeza had held this folder in her hands. Leeza.

Solovyov left the institute and went to the train station. He boarded a trolleybus but then got out at the very first stop and returned to the institute. In the clerical office, he requested a referral letter for the Rumyantsev Library. Just in case. When he got to the station, he learned that the earliest train was leaving in three hours; he bought a ticket. This was a very early train that arrived in Moscow at 4:30 in the morning; the library opened at nine. But Solovyov preferred waiting in Moscow to waiting in Petersburg. Inactivity felt intolerable to him now. On top of that, waiting in Moscow was waiting near Leeza.

At home, Solovyov tossed the most necessary items into

a bag. He thought for a moment, then also put in the folder he had received: he had not even had a chance to open it yet. In memory of his trip to Crimea, he took a can of food. Meat he had bought at a nearby store. For an instant, he had the feeling he was leaving forever. Solovyov looked around. He had everything he needed. He shut the door hard and turned the key in the lock twice. It sounded like two distant gunshots in the echoing stairwell. Like an echo of Solovyov's decisive actions. The clanking of the key had its own significance, even a point of no return, inasmuch, needless to say, as that descriptor could be attached to a key. Solovyov caught a taxi outside. He rode up to the station a half-hour before the train's departure.

He went into the entrance hall and bought a newspaper. As he left the entrance hall, he put it in a trash bin. He took the can from his bag and gave it to a pauper. Went out to the platform. Under bright spotlights, pipes on the carriages were belching smoke. Or steam. Most likely steam: it disappeared instantly over the carriages' roofs, which glistened with ice. Conductors wearing black felt boots stood by the carriage doors. They blew into their mittens from time to time, pressing their lips to their wrists. Sometimes knocking one felt boot against another with a muffled sound. Solovyov showed his ticket and went to his compartment. He greeted the three women who were already sitting there. They answered in chorus. It was nice for him that they were women, not men. The train began moving.

Only after Solovyov had climbed up to the top bunk did he remember the folder. He went back down, got the folder, and crawled back up with it. He turned on the lamp over his head. After getting used to the dim lighting, he opened the folder. He was flabbergasted.

After everything he had heard during the day, he had found something now that was capable of stunning him. There, in the poorly lighted bunk, Solovyov held in his hands the end of the general's memoirs. He could recognize that handwriting in any lighting. Yes, he was stunned. But not surprised.

In the folder was a photocopy of the notebook Filipp had taken at one time and which had suddenly surfaced in the form of *a new acquisition* for the library. It remained unclear if it had been *acquired* from Filipp, where Filipp himself was, and whether he was still on the face of the Earth at all. There were no library markings on the manuscript at all other than the call number.

It was a thick notebook with graph paper. It was too large to copy with facing pages, so each page was copied individually, making for many sheets. Strictly speaking, the notebook could have fit the copier with the pages facing, albeit without the margins: from time to time, the general had made markings in the margins (which he had neatly ruled in pencil). Judging from the various shades of ink, the markings were made at different times. The general had obviously reread his writings more than once and left remarks and additions. 'Dead.' Or: 'Still alive.' Or (facing the words 'It was cold'): 'It was not so much cold as damp.'

It was not so much cold as damp when the remnants of the White Army rolled off toward Chongar. The bulk of the troops had already left Perekop a few days before and were now being loaded onto transports in the ports. The cavalry that remained on the Perekop Peninsula had covered their retreat. The cavalry then held on there until the general received a report one night that his troops were already in the ports. The cavalry soundlessly left Perekop that same night.

The heavy weapons had been disabled. They had removed the locks and left them in position. They had not extinguished their campfires, which Captain Kologrivov's detachment was to watch over until morning. These 150 volunteers had offered to remain until morning. They covered the retreat of Perekop's last defenders.

They led the horses by their bridles for the first several hundred meters. They saddled them before reaching Armyansk and the cavalry moved off at a trot. In the vicinity of Dzhelishay, a small number of the troops turned toward Yevpatoria and the rest continued on toward Yalta and Sevastopol. As he ascended Chongarsky Pass, the general was thinking of those who remained on Perekop. In his mind he asked their forgiveness.

A snowstorm came up on the pass. The huge, wet snowflakes did not drop to the ground. They got caught in the wind and drifted, on a low-altitude flight. Where the pass began to dip, the snowflakes soared upward, as if the hanging, murky clouds were already waiting for them to come back. It slowly grew light.

Sitting motionless in the saddle, the general observed as the remnants of his army laboriously descended from the pass. The horses began slipping on the icy road, scrabbling to keep their balance, sometimes sitting on their haunches. Some fell, trapping their riders beneath them and pinning them to the frozen mud. Shouts and foul language hung over the pass. Many dismounted and carefully led the horses down, holding them by the reins. 'Motion along an inclined plane,' was the general's notation in the margin.

When they arrived in Yalta, the general gave everyone several hours to rest. He headed for evacuation headquarters, stationed in the Oreanda Hotel. The general carefully familiarized himself with the list of evacuated personnel and inventory of vessels. He assigned the transportable wounded to the steamship *Tsesarevich Georgy*. (Bela Kun would shoot the untransportable wounded two days later.) The steamship *Kronshtadt*, on which the Sevastopol Navy Hospital and the Mine and Artillery School were evacuating, took numerous wounded. The rest were loaded on ships with their own troop units.

There were not enough vessels. At the last minute, the transports *Siam*, *Sedzhet*, *Rion*, *Yakut*, and *Almaz* were added to the available tonnage. Under the general's order, everything in the Crimean ports that was capable of staying afloat, including old barges, was made available for the needs of the evacuation. It worked out to 126 large and small vessels. The majority of them were already prepared to sail and stood at outer anchorage.

After noon, a launch was sent directly to the Oreanda and the general, accompanied by his deputy, Admiral Kutepov, headed to the anchorage. The launch went past steamships packed with people. Past barges so laden that their sides nearly dipped into the water. It was frightening to let them set sail. But it was even more frightening to keep them here.

The general climbed up a rope ladder to the cruiser *General Kornilov*. The crowd on deck was so dense that it was almost unable to part when the general made his appearance. As he crossed the deck, he could barely elbow his way behind the Cossacks clearing a path for him. The exact same sort of crowd languished in the hold. At least it was warmer there than on deck, but there was already a palpable stench: there was only one toilet for the entire hold. The hold's largest compartment turned out to be under lock and key.

'What's in there?' asked the general.

'The chief quartermaster's cabin,' said Admiral Kutepov.

'Open it.'

The chief quartermaster held the key but it was already impossible to find him in the crowd. The general nodded to the Cossacks and they peppered the door, hitting it with their rifles' butt ends. A minute later, the lock and the lower hinge had been broken off. The door swung on its upper hinge with a pitiful screech and dropped. The quartermaster's compartment was completely stuffed with expensive furniture. Mahogany cabinets stood pressed against one another. The sides of the cabinets faced those entering, but they were astoundingly beautiful even from the side, gleaming in the porthole's scant light. This light was reflected in several Venetian mirrors arranged along the walls. There were large crates neatly stacked in the corner of the cabin; baled tablecloths lay on them, right under the ceiling.

'Overboard,' said the general.

He came back on deck after finishing his inspection of the cabin. The first of the cabinets had already been delivered there. The sailors rocked the item and tossed it on the count of 'three.' It fell into the water with a fountain of spray and stayed afloat for a time. Then it began heavily sinking, to applause on deck. As it departed for the deep, the cabinet released bubbles as if it were a live being. As the general was making his way down to the launch, two sailors dragged the quartermaster out of the hold.

'Does this one go overboard, too?'

'Let him live,' said the general.

He went ashore after visiting several more ships. He asked about those who had remained on Perekop, but nobody had seen them here yet. Dusk was falling. The general dismissed the Cossacks by the entrance to the Oreanda Hotel. He went up to his room and looked out the window at the sea. He sat at the table, poured himself some cognac from a decanter, and drank it. There was a knock at the door. He had no strength to answer.

'May I?'

Admiral Kutepov entered the room. He laid a hand on the general's shoulder.

'You need to get some rest. We're sailing in the morning.'

'The ones coming from Perekop . . . They still haven't arrived,' said the general.

'The Red artillery will smash us to smithereens if we don't cast off tomorrow . . . May I?' The admiral took the decanter and poured himself some cognac. 'Besides, the ones you're speaking of . . .'

'Yes?'

'I think nothing threatens them any longer.'

The admiral emptied his glass in one gulp and was now thoroughly savoring the drink. Pursing his lips. Closing his eyes. The general drank, too. And also closed his eyes.

When he opened them, Captain Kologrivov was standing before him. The general knew he was dreaming of Kologrivov; he saw in that nothing good for Kologrivov's fate.

'Well, how are you doing out there?' the general asked, looking away.

'Nothing threatens us any longer,' said Kologrivov. He poured himself some cognac without asking permission. 'It's a pity you weren't there. This was the only chance for you to get a genuine feel for Thermopylae after all.'

'But there were only 150 of you.'

'And you aren't Leonidas, either, isn't that right? And so here, you know, it's one thing after another.'

The general woke up shortly before dawn. What he had thought was a firm pillow turned out to be the cuff of his sleeve. He could feel the table's velvet covering under his hand. Lights were flashing to one another in the black motionless sea outside the window; the ships at anchor were ready to sail. The general looked at his watch. A farewell prayer service was to begin on the embankment in an hour.

The commanders of the forces sailing from Yalta came for the prayer. The embankment was packed with people. At the first sounds of the service, the general sank to his knees and all the officers followed suit. The entire huge crowd also knelt. A damp sea wind whipped at the priests' stoles and snapped the tricolored banner against the flagpole. The general attempted to understand each word of the service but was distracted, without realizing it himself. He was thinking that the evacuation could certainly have taken place even without him.

The prayer service was ending. Bestowing his blessing, the bishop sprinkled the general with holy water and several drops fell behind his collar. There was no doubt this had already happened in his life. He had happened to experience so very many unforgettable things. Raindrops running under his tunic. Standing drowsily on the bank of the Zhdanovka River. Semi-darkness. A wind just as wet. Could that water, then, be considered holy? It had fallen straight from the sky. The general fingered a pencil in his overcoat pocket. It would have been better for him to have stayed on Perekop after all. Maybe he had stayed there, though.

The general slowly rose from his knees. From the faces of those standing, he understood they had been waiting only for him.

'Do deign to say a parting word,' Kutepov appealed to the general.

The general watched as the bishop's gray hair whipped in the wind. His hair lashed at his eyes and got into lips opened from shortness of breath, but he made no attempt to remove it. This had happened in the general's life, too. The same elderly bishop and the same gray hair whipping. But he could not remember where. Life had begun repeating itself. The bishop did not look at anyone individually and the pause did not weigh upon him. His face expressed no impatience. The general remembered: it was the violinist from his childhood. He had played right here, by the fence at the Tsar's Garden.

'I have nothing to say.'

Admiral Kutepov smoothed his hair and took several steps toward the crowd. He cleared his throat. A horse began neighing behind those standing.

'We did all that we could . . .'

Kutepov glanced at the general, as if searching for new words. But the general was silent. Kutepov thought a bit, then asked everyone's forgiveness. The general nodded; he found that appropriate. Kutepov cast a look around the crowd, breathed some air into his lungs, and shouted, 'Farewell!'

'Farewell,' the general said to Kutepov. 'My mission has ended.'

'The launch is waiting for us,' said Kutepov, nodding in the direction of the sea.

'I commanded ground operations and now the naval operation is beginning. You're the admiral, not I.'

The admiral looked at his watch.

'We can't linger any longer.' Still acting as if he did not understand, Kutepov took a folder with a two-headed eagle from the general's hands.

'You'll need that in Constantinople,' said the general.

'There's no sense in waiting for them.'

'Including a final statement of the treasury and correspondence about providing asylum.'

'They perished on Perekop and you know it.'

'This is not, really, about them.'

'General, the Reds will not simply kill you, they'll slice you to pieces.'

'It's not worth spending time bickering. There are 145,000 people waiting for you. And that's just according to the lists. I think there are many more of them in reality.'

Admiral Kutepov shifted the folder from his right hand to his left, then put his hand to his peaked cap. He did that so slowly that he had time to inadvertently twist his finger at his temple. Or perhaps it only seemed that way to the general.

The embankment emptied out fairly quickly. There were only horses that had been abandoned during evacuation. Not all their saddles had even been removed. Horses nobody needed dispersed along the neighboring streets. They neighed from hunger. They were returning to the embankment again in expectation of their masters; they rubbed against icy streetlamps. The horses interpreted their abandonment as a misunderstanding.

The wind was flattening flyers against the fence at the Tsar's Garden; they had been scattered around several days ago. The general picked one up. In the flyer, comrade Frunze called upon Yaltans not to put up resistance. He guaranteed universal amnesty for the city's residents. The general unclenched his fingers and the scrap of paper flew off into the empty expanse of the embankment. The city's residents had no intention of putting up resistance.

Yalta was preparing for the Reds' entry in a different way, though. Shop windows were being boarded up. Provisions and table silver were being hidden in houses. The measures were warranted but, as it later turned out, insufficient. When the city froze from horror a day later, both the stores and the table silver seemed like mere details. Yaltans did not even remember those amidst the terror that broke out, just as nobody among the Reds remembered comrade Frunze's flyers.

Captain Kologrivov's detachment entered the city after the smoke of the last steamship had disappeared beyond the horizon. Retreating under the Reds' fire, Kologrivov had managed to save most of his detachment. They were saved that day at dawn by a very strong snowstorm that suddenly came down over Perekop. The blizzard allowed the detachment to leave and disoriented their pursuers. It accompanied the detachment for half the day, hiding it in a solid snowy shroud. Kologrivov's detachment had not perished. They had lost their way.

In the thick snow, the detachment took a mistaken course from the start—to the peninsula's eastern extremity—rather than the Yalta direction that General Larionov had instructed. They did not figure out their mistake until the dead of night, at the Vladislavovka junction railway station. Instead of moving toward the nearest port, Feodosia, and getting on a ship there, the detachment stayed true to the order and turned back, to the west. In order to get to Yalta, they headed along the road they had already traveled, toward the center of the peninsula, not turning south until then. Only toward the evening of the next day did Captain Kologrivov's detachment turn up in Yalta.

When he welcomed the detachment, the general did not consider accommodating them in barracks. He housed them in homes that (according to his information) had been vacated during the evacuation. Rest was a vital necessity for the soldiers after their grueling passage. Burning their military uniforms was just as necessary for them. The general ordered that they begin with that.

He himself went to the city theater. After a brief meeting in the wardrobe room, they brought him all their Tatar costumes (around two dozen) and craftsman costumes (eight). Everything was fine with the Tatar clothing but the craftsman costumes had an ineradicably foreign air to them (they had been sewn in Italy). Furthermore, they were tidy in a nonlocal way. After some thought, the general refused them, instead requesting tuxedoes with top hats; the props for *The Merry Widow* were checked, as well, while searching for those. Several chimneysweeper costumes were found, too, along with ethereal prop-room ladders that the general preferred to refuse: he said he was not encouraging superfluous theatricality. He also asked if the theater had any costumes for paupers but all they found were tatters for a holy fool (*Boris Godunov*); this was unacceptably light-weight for the month of November. The general took individual pieces from the theater's ward-robe—including a dozen sashes and hats—to have in reserve. He ordered that everything he set aside be loaded on a cart and brought to the Oreanda Hotel. Written in the notebook's margin in the general's hand, opposite the story of visiting the theater, was 'a good idea.'

Not everyone, however, thought it was a good idea. That became obvious when the tardy detachment formed up by the Oreanda Hotel at dawn. The soldiers heard out the general's explanations and glumly confirmed their readiness to submit to his orders. These were essentially neither explanations nor orders. The general did not explain anything and, even more so, did not order anything. He simply spoke about what, in his opinion, would be best to do at the given moment. The soldiers understood little of what was happening and one can only guess exactly what thoughts were slinking around in their heads regarding their military commander's condition. Their sullenness was, as the saying goes, written all over their faces, but the inertia of their esteem for the general kept them from insubordination. In the end, they, too, lacked plans for how to save themselves.

The general headed toward the Yalta city limits with a group of horsemen dressed in Tatar costumes. The horsemen swayed beautifully in their saddles, as befits those who grew accustomed to horses in childhood. The general reminisced about how, many years ago, a horse had pawed at the ground, bringing down a rain of pebbles in a gorge.

He then noticed one of his cavalrymen making his horse paw at the ground and he nodded approvingly. He recognized the Petersburg dressage school. Pebbles bounced off ledges in the gorge and flew even better than in the general's childhood. The other horsemen kept to a steady trot and the general listened carefully to their hoofbeats. Resonant clopping on the stony road blended with dull thudding on ivy growing over the road. The rhythm should not betray any anxiety. It was the rhythm of people far from war. Someone needed to fetch kumys from the nearest Tatar village. The general said he wanted them to ride with kumys. He thought he had made provisions for everything, down to the smallest details. They looked at him with undisguised surprise. After the general had ridden off, Captain Kologrivov explained to the soldiers: 'What has occurred once before carries a seal of approval. Do as he orders.'

'One cannot step into the same river twice,' objected warrant officer Sviridov.

He had left his third year of philosophy studies to go to war.

'It doesn't matter what river we're stepping into,' said Captain Kologrivov. 'The main thing now is to not drown.'

Spurring his horse, he galloped off after the general. They had much to accomplish in the day ahead. To begin with, they placed some brand-new shoeshine booths on the corners of several streets (the ones that had stood there previously had been dismantled for firewood by residents during a cold spell). The general ordered that the booth on Morskaya Street be moved fifty meters away from the corner since it had stood on that very spot during his childhood.

Housed in the booths were shoe shiners who mastered

their profession in short order. Remembering his cadet training, the general personally showed them how to shine shoes properly. He urged them not to misapply the polish since too much polish would not allow you to attain the necessary shine. It should be taken from the jar with the very edge of the brush. The general demonstrated to the trainees the proper methods for brush-handling and for rubbing a cleaned shoe with velvet. They shined shoes pretty decently for people who had held nothing but rifles in their hands for two years.

The general placed a group of men on Autskaya Street to repair the roadway. At his request, city officials sent two cartloads of cobblestones to Autskaya (across from the St. Theodor Tiron Church). The general asked that they not send round and rough cobblestones (the kind called *cats' heads*). He ordered the highest quality paving stones: cut granite blocks.

At the city council, they attempted to draw the general's attention to the fact that the roadway in the area around the St. Theodor Tiron Church had recently been repaired; they proposed repairing a lower, thoroughly worn, part of Autskaya Street. The general's childhood memories, however, pointed to his chosen spot, which essentially did not permit him to agree with the city officials' arguments. He recommended pulling up the old stones to install the new ones.

The general also reopened two stores abandoned by their owners: a shoe store and a sweet shop. All told, ten people were dispatched to staff them. Thanks to the breakdown of shoe and sweets production, there was nothing to sell in those stores. Strictly speaking, there was nothing to sell them for, either, since money was swiftly becoming simply paper. In a brief parting address, the general emphasized that the absence of wares was a temporary phenomenon since both sweets and shoes were in demand under any regime. He did not know if there would be money under the new regime. In honor of opening the sweet shop, they gave the general a lollipop that appeared, upon close examination, to be in the shape of a rooster. It was the only ware they discovered in the store. The rooster smelled of burnt sugar and had no color. When the general went outside, he gave it to a newspaper delivery boy.

A barbershop opened up after noon. In giving brief instructions to the future barbers, the general announced to them that under no circumstances should they stop making cutting motions, even when they were lifting the scissors over the client's hair. According to the general's observations, it was customary among genuine barbers to cut air, too. He sharpened a razor on a leather strop and neatly wiped the blade on a towel while shaving one of the trainees. In so doing, he showed several characteristic gestures he had noticed as a child—barbering mastery is judged based upon their accuracy. He cautioned against approximating a barber's actions, saying that every little bit counts in this field. He advised taking a cigarette out of an ashtray with the ring and little fingers because only those fingers remain free of lather. The top of the head should be scratched, if necessary, with those same fingers. He recommended discussing city news during haircuts and shaving, because that is the usual practice in barbershops. He depended on their intuition for everything else.

The general lodged soldiers Shulgin and Nesterenko in

a vacant two-apartment house. He was concerned the soldiers' bachelor life might provoke inquiry into their past and ordered that two women who agreed to simulate marriage be brought to them. On top of all that, the general vaguely recalled that two families truly had lived in a house like this. The families were friends for many years. It was already impossible to decide if it was this house or not because the general remembered nothing but the front stoop.

He and his father had walked up a stoop like this to go into a house at one time. Two men were playing chess in the living room. They represented families on friendly terms. One of them held a knight (the future general could never have mistaken that figure for anything else) in his hands, touching it to his lower lip from time to time. The knight's ears rode fully into the chess player's puffy lip. The other man repeated some phrase, in a reverie. He had uttered the phrase many times but the general could not remember it, try as he might. Had they played here?

The general warned the reestablished families (he was certain of the resemblance between the present and past families) about the emphatic need to be friends. It was noted in the margin across from this statement that friendship did occur, as was to be expected, and eventually both couples had children as a result of simulating marriage. Boys: Shulgin junior and Nesterenko junior.

The general gathered both families in the living room of one of the apartments and proposed that the men play chess. He sat Shulgin and Nesterenko on chairs opposite one another. A chessboard was placed on a stool between them. Shulgin crossed his arms on his chest and Nesterenko was requested to press his hands into his knees. This lent a naturalness to the game that had begun. They played briskly but were not in much of a hurry. Sometimes the women would appear behind the players' backs and cast contented gazes at the board, not understanding anything. The general advised the women to wipe their hands on their aprons during those moments. Or wrap themselves in a shawl, as if chilled. Crockery clinked ever so slightly in the sideboard when the women trod on the plank floors. The general delighted in the coziness that had come about.

'Someone should say,' he requested of the players, '"We're bringing in the minor pieces." That's what they say in similar situations.'

'Is that obligatory?' Shulgin was curious.

The general thought and answered, 'No, it's not obligatory. You can just press the knight to your lower lip and say something of your own. The main thing is to utter it pensively. Several times.'

Then they left for the church, where the general seated paupers in the necessary order. One of them very much resembled Maxim Gorky, which was a definite plus in this particular situation. The similarity was so great that this person later even posed for Yalta's monument to the proletarian writer. Another pauper, who did not resemble Gorky, was ordered to simulate not having a leg. Only this, in the general's opinion, could ensure him certain immunity when the Red Armymen appeared.

The general instructed five musicians by the fence at the Tsar's Garden. One of them could not play any instrument at all but had, so it seemed to the general, a good ear. His task during performances of musical compositions

was to listen carefully, conveying the essence of the performance through facial expressions when possible. This
musician had long gray bangs that he should toss from his
eyes with a sharp head motion. He was also given a violin
and asked to draw the bow near the strings. But not to
touch them.

Toward the end of the day, the general ordered that a
cabinet be taken out of his house. A big oak cabinet with
a two-headed eagle. The general ordered a cart be brought
and he positioned loaders to look after it. The loaders had
just returned from Perekop and did not quite imagine how
they ought to handle such a heavy item. Furthermore, they
still did not understand where or why it should be moved.
Recalling a famous social-democratic slogan, the general
announced to them that the ultimate aim is nothing, but
movement is everything. The cabinet's aimless motion did
not contradict the new ideology, making this pursuit rela-
tively safe. As he was walking away, the general advised the
loaders not to be shy about using coarse language; when in
contact with the Reds this could create an atmosphere of
similarity in social class.

Only late in the evening, when the entire detachment
had jobs, did the general and Captain Kologrivov approach
the pharmacy. The general leaned wearily against an electric
streetlamp (in previous times it had used gas) by the
entrance. He rummaged around in his pockets, fetched the
keys, and began searching for the lock in the dying yellowy
light. A minute later the door opened and a little bell jingled.
The general enjoyed feeling the edges of the beveled glass
on the door. The prisms reflected the evening's last lights.
They reflected the soundness of a previous life. As it

happened, in those November days, it had already been three years since that kind of glass had been made.

The general and Kologrivov entered the pharmacy and looked around. Unlike many abandoned places, the pharmacy had not been ransacked. Everything remained in place there. The general took Kologrivov by the shoulders and sat him down in a chair.

'The main thing is inner calm. Speak in a soft voice. The scrape of a little oak door, the smell of mint drops: nothing more is required here. That is the only way you will be able to exist organically in a pharmacy.'

'I'm calm,' said Kologrivov. 'And I speak in a soft voice.'

The general uncorked one of the little vials and stirred its contents with a glass pestle.

'I placed observers on the Alushtinsk road. They'll shoot a blank from a cannon when they sight the Reds. That will be the signal to start a new life. I won't be able to give further instruction because I'll be busy with my own matters. That, basically, is everything.'

The streetlamp was no longer burning when the general went outside. A cold autumn rain had begun. The pharmacy windows were all that prevented Morskaya Street from plunging into darkness.

The cannon struck at 9:30 in the morning. With that shot, they began playing Oginsky's *Polonaise* by the fence at the Tsar's Garden. A detachment of Tatars rode out to the Alushtinsk Road and energetic paving work began on Autskaya Street by the St. Theodor Tiron Church. Shoeshine booths opened in various parts of Yalta during those same minutes. The quantity of staff as well as the abundance of brushes and polish allowed them to shine shoes for the entire coastline but Yaltans preferred not to leave their homes that day. Even the shops did not open that morning, with the exception of a shoe store and a sweet shop. Yalta was at a standstill, awaiting the entrance of the Reds.

First to enter the city was an armored vehicle with the uneven inscription *Antichrist*. It did not notice the Tatar detachment and drove past at top speed. Shots were fired into the air from the armored vehicle. To the detachment's surprise, the armored vehicle did not notice a curve in the road, either. It did not brake until the place where the road's shoulder turned into a steep slope. The vehicle's front wheels went down and a belated reverse gear could no longer rectify anything. The vehicle rolled into the gorge, topsy-turvy, its armor knocking along the cliff's overhangs. Moans resounded in the gorge after the last echo had finished rumbling. Local residents—simple, god-fearing people—surrounded the vehicle. They had no love for the Reds but they did not plan to refuse them help. The residents began conferring when they saw the inscription on the armored vehicle. They did not know who lay ahead for them to save. Withered grass rustled in the wind. Nobody could bring themselves to come closer to the vehicle with the eschatological inscription. The moaning soon stopped.

The Reds' primary troops entered the city at that same time. Comrades Zhloba, Kun, and Zemlyachka were out front on well-fed horses. They met a Tatar detachment and even received kumys from them. Zemlyachka poured out kumys for representatives of the commanding personnel and passed the leftovers on to rank-and-file Red Armymen. Those entering the city praised the kumys, though they noted its sharp taste. Only Kun did not praise the kumys.

Surprised by his silence, Zemlyachka asked if he liked the kumys. Still on his horse, Kun vomited in answer and stated that this was because he was not accustomed to it. Zhloba jokingly proposed that Kun have his stomach pumped in the city hospital. Everyone laughed so as not to offend Zhloba. Kun blushed and said he was planning to inspect the hospital anyway. Zemlyachka recommended that he record how much blood was in stock. Seeing a shoe shiner, Kun asked the advance guard to wait while he had his spattered boots cleaned. In addition to the kumys, remnants of beet salad and poorly chewed veal were apparent on his boots. Zhloba's boots were not dirty but he dismounted to have his shined, too.

General Larionov was having his boots shined, too. This was happening at the other end of the city, by the St. Theodor Tiron Church. The mezzanine of the Chekhov house was visible about a hundred paces from the church. Maria Pavlovna Chekhova was opening the shutters. As he watched how deftly the brush moved in a shoe shiner's hands, the general said, 'Chekhov died only sixteen years ago but an entirely new epoch has arrived.'

The roadway was being repaired not far from the church. The knocking of wooden tampers, which pressed the paving stones, spread over Autskaya Street. The stones were laid in a fan shape on a sand foundation. The wind was tearing the last leaves from the trees in a front yard. Blackened and crumpled, they rolled along the brand-new paving stone, settling in a gutter.

The general stopped next to one of the houses as he walked down Autskaya Street. The biting November wind had come this far, too. It sounded in a squeaking gate spring

and in a little flapping runner rug that had been flung on
the fence. It was quiet in the house. They were playing chess
there. Two men sitting on bentwood chairs were considering
positions on the board. Their words were inaudible. Their
calm could be sensed. A woman with a pail came down the
front steps. She went behind the corner of the house and
the general could no longer see her. He heard when the
well's door was set aside and the chain began unwinding.
The gurgly dipping, the unhurried path up, the knock of
the full pail against the well house. The general pressed his
cheek to the fence. It was warm, rough wood. The woman
wiped her feet and went out on the porch. Poured some
water into a tank. Someone began coughing behind a
curtain. The bell-like ring of the tank and the patter of
water on the bottom of the basin. Everything was authentic,
nothing was superfluous: a thin trill at the beginning (a little
hysterically), then calmed and muted as it filled. The distant
bark of dogs. The general was not worried about this house.

He turned on Botkinskaya Street and went to the pier
by Alexander Square. Thick snow had begun to fall. It was
wet and not even cold. The sea whipped against the embankment's stones. There was no ice in the sea but it was
hopelessly wintry, from the distant breakers to the splashes
that spread in the snow. The pier's pilings were entwined
in its gray strands. The general sniffed the air—only the
winter sea smelled like this.

He stopped by the gate at the Tsar's Garden when he
caught sight of the musicians. Pensive, he admired how the
snow was coating them, to musical accompaniment. The
general put all his money—several million—in the open
violin case. Occasional pedestrians donated to the musicians,

too. The case gradually filled with snow and multicolored bills that had not yet managed to become old: the snow and the bills already had the same approximate value.

The general picked up another million on the sidewalk by the Frantsia Hotel and gave it to the porter. A horsecab driver bowed to him from the coachman's seat. The wheels turned snow into water to the sound of wet clopping; black furrows stretched sloppily behind the horsecab. A small dark blue spot was forming on the leaden sky. This was the unpredictable Yalta weather. The snowstorm had begun to subside.

The sun peeked out as the general approached the jetty. He stopped, closed his eyes, and the skin of his face felt the sun's warmth. After standing like that for a bit, he turned onto the jetty. The snow that had fallen on the concrete was melting at full speed. The general slowly walked the rest of the way to the lighthouse. A small tree was growing out of a crack in its base. The tree's leaves had fallen so it was difficult to tell what kind of tree it was. The general laid his palm on the base's dirty-gray stones. They were beginning to warm up, barely enough to feel. This was like a return to life. The general closed his eyes again and imagined it was now summer. The sounds of the sea muffling what might have carried from the embankment. The wheels of coaches, shouts of kvass sellers, cries of children. Rustling of palms. Hot weather.

He opened his eyes and saw people walking toward him. They were walking unhurriedly, even somehow peaceably: Zemlyachka, Kun, and a group of sailors. Their faces were not triumphant; they were most likely preoccupied. Expecting a ploy, they were not taking their eyes off the edge of the jetty where the general stood. Those walking realized that the general was one step from the irretrievable and they feared that step. They feared the general would take it on his own.

They exchanged a few words as they drew closer. They were not looking in the general's direction at all now. Their hearts were jumping out of their chests. Zemlyachka was striding ahead of them all. She was holding her half-fastened leather coat with her hand and its hem flapped in the wind. Kun walked a little behind her, his boots cleaned to a shine. His wooden gait gave away his flatfootedness. There was an extinguished cigarette between his teeth. He kicked pebbles as he walked but there was nothing carefree in that. Or in the sailors' feline movements. Those walking were genuine hunters and could not hide that.

The general did not move. He was half-sitting on the base of the lighthouse and watching seagulls stroll along the jetty. They were letting out shrill sounds that were sometimes similar to a duck's quacking, sometimes to a child's screech. The seagulls were searching for something among the wet rocks. They groomed their feathers and raised their heads, pensively examining a sea entirely lacking ships. Never before had they seen a sea like that. The seagulls did not even fly off when the group of people walking along the jetty neared the general. They were not afraid of people.

Zemlyachka was the first to approach the general. She neared him without rushing but it was noticeable even under her leather coat how quickly her breasts were moving. As before, the general was half-sitting on the base of the lighthouse, leaning on his hands. Those walking smelled of horse sweat and unwashed human bodies. The sailors froze, awaiting an order. Kun spat out the cigarette butt. Zemlyachka took out her pen knife and silently drove it into the back of the general's hand. She was overrun with feelings.

A bell struck on Polikurovsky Hill. It was ringing in the St. John Chrysostom bell tower. Zemlyachka and Kun were arguing about something in undertones. The sailors observed the general moving his lips, barely noticeably, and they felt sympathy toward him. His hand was still lying on the base of the lighthouse. A crimson dribble wound through cracks in the rocks. Zemlyachka was insisting that his execution had to be agonizing. Kun objected that the execution should demonstrate the humanism of Soviet power. The striking bell muted Zemlyachka's reply. Its sound floated over the sea, filling Yalta's entire bay. When the argument was over, they led the general to the outer side of the jetty. They placed him on the edge and tied a piece of debris from an anchor to his feet.

'Shoot for the stomach, not the heart,' Kun advised the sailors. 'Then he'll be able to drown after he's shot, too.'

The sailors nodded.

'I'll be the one to shoot,' said Zemlyachka. 'In the groin.'

The sailors nodded again. Far below, brown seaweed undulated in time with the waves. The water had turned emerald green under the bright sun. It no longer had a repulsive wintry look and it seemed warm from a distance. The general decided to look straight ahead so as not to feel dizzy. He could see part of the embankment behind the sailors' heads. Coaches were driving and people were walking. The embankment continued to live its own life but that life was no longer the general's life; they were separated by a short strip of water and a group standing on the jetty. Yalta's cozy amphitheater towered over the embankment. Smoke stretched from the chimneys of some houses. It was rising toward the sky and mixing with clouds at the very top of Ai-Petri. The sailors stepped aside. Nothing else blocked the marvelous picture. The clouds seemed motionless but in actuality they were not. They were slowly drifting toward Ai-Petri. This became particularly noticeable when the shadow of a large triangular cloud began moving along the peak. The cloud itself still did not touch the peak. It was moving more slowly than its shadow. When Zemlyachka's leather coat appeared in front of the general, he thought the cloud would not moor at the peak during his lifetime. That it could have hurried up if, of course, all its spectators were equally important to it. But the cloud was not hurrying. It was obviously imitating the cloud the future military commander had seen from deep within Vorontsov Park in 1889. At approximately 3:00 in the afternoon, when his father, who was keen on photography, decided to take his picture. That time was considered the best for taking a photograph. The sun was still bright but the shadows had already settled prettily on the grass. The boy was standing in a glade between Lebanese cedars. The camera was on a cumbersome wooden stand located a little way below, on a walkway. His father had shortened the legs of the stand so the boy would be photographed against the backdrop of Ai-Petri. A dragonfly froze uneasily over the camera. It was not flying out of the lens; it simply hovered in one place. Its wings were indiscernible and seemed like a light thickening of air. His father needed that peak, suffused with sun, but the shadow of a cloud had already appeared on it. His father kept looking out from under the black cloth but the cloud was not thinking about moving. Only its shadow was migrating. It was creeping ever closer to Ai-Petri, depriving the peak of its last signs of luminescence. Zemlyachka energetically shook her right wrist. Larionov had been posed just as carefully in 1889 as now. Only then he was standing with his back to Ai-Petri. He had been watching the cloud then, looking around the entire time. He saw cedar branches rocking slightly in the wind. Felt the mountain's icy freshness mixing with the aromas of the park among the cedar branches. The boy inhaled that air and his nostrils moved. Caterpillars hung down from trees on thin threads; some were transforming into butterflies. The shrubs were scattered with ripe red berries. Cones dropped slowly from cedar crowns. The cones hit, muted, against the grass, stirring up grasshoppers who jumped together like fountains, then they bounced several times before falling still. The cones had been changing places, unnoticed, when he had turned around. An ant crawled along his knee. Zemlyachka raised the hand with the revolver. The general attempted to see himself from a distance but the image turned out to be a negative. A shot rang out from the opposite side of the jetty. The seagulls began taking off with a shriek but came right back down. The general turned his head and saw Zhloba. Zhloba's meager gestures asked Kun and Zemlyachka to approach him. Zemlyachka expressed dissatisfaction, like a person who has been interrupted at the most interesting part. She jabbed the revolver in the general's direction but Zhloba shook his head in the negative. As if foreseeing disappointment, Kun and

Zemlyachka were in no hurry to make their way to Zhloba. The sailors took sunflower seeds from their pockets and tossed them to the gulls. They liked observing the gulls beating each other with their wings in their struggle for the seeds. Zhloba's conversation with his comrades-in-arms turned out to be anything but simple. Isolated exclamations that the wind carried, and their gestures, spoke to that. Zhloba took a paper folded into quarters from his map case. He unfolded it, showed it to both his conversation partners in turn, and placed it back in the case. The sailors laughed about the birds' basic instincts. This spectacle ennobled them in some way. Zhloba was, perceptibly, beginning to lose patience. He took out the paper once again, pressed it up against Bela Kun's face and held it like that for several seconds. Bela Kun did not resist. Zemlyachka turned around abruptly and left the jetty. The men went after her. The general's gaze followed them but not one of them turned around. The sailors understood nothing. After tossing the rest of the seeds to the seagulls, they began trudging uncertainly after their commanders. One of them returned, untied the general's feet, and bolted off to catch up to the others. The general took several steps away from the edge. The wind was intensifying. The general flung open his overcoat to greet the wind, just as people greet someone they already said goodbye to for the last time, someone who brings joy by simply existing. The general looked at the sun without squinting. Tears welled up from rays that were still bright but already orange. The sun was hanging over the other side of the embankment, illuminating masses of ice that had frozen on the streetlamps after the night's storm. They glistened like a dazzling Christmas garland.

The size of the sun exceeded the boundaries of what is reasonable. Jolting as it moved, the sun disappeared behind the mountain at unexpected speed. The sun was setting in his presence.

ACKNOWLEDGEMENTS

Although *Solovyov and Larionov* is Eugene Vodolazkin's debut novel, it's the third of his books that I've translated for Oneworld. Like Eugene's *Laurus* and *The Aviator*, *Solovyov and Larionov* is a complex novel, both in terms of language, since the narrative voice is very defined, and content, which blends two time periods and includes a fair bit of history. Those complexities mean that Eugene's patient help—reading my manuscript, answering my questions, and simply being his usual humorous and thoughtful self—was more necessary than ever. The three novels fit together so beautifully, forming a sort of triptych, that each one is my favorite in its own right.

Part of the fun of *Solovyov and Larionov* is in the details, which Eugene cleverly plants throughout the novel so they can come together at the end of the book. Eugene often refers to me as his co-author and this book gave me more opportunities than *Laurus* and *The Aviator*, thanks to several passages that we changed significantly, often because translated humor and irony just aren't very funny when they have to be explained. (Fortunately, nearly all Eugene's humor and irony translates very nicely into English.) I also adapted the hundreds of footnotes that appeared in the Russian *Solovyov and Larionov*. Eugene warned me from the start that he was pretty sure I'd need to get rid of them and I confess that I (foolishly) told him most of them could likely stay. That meant it took an epiphany (in the shower) to realize I was wrong and that the novel would maintain its tone, not to mention its continuity, best if I incorporated the footnote information into the text.

Solovyov and Larionov is my fourth book for Oneworld and, as always, I'm grateful to Juliet Mabey for her love of Russian contemporary fiction, and to the team at Oneworld for all their editorial help.

My colleague Liza Prudovskaya read an entire draft of *Solovyov and Larionov*, comparing it to Eugene's original. She also answered hundreds of questions about language, tone, and usage, saving me from dozens and dozens of errors of all kinds. I can never thank her enough for her contributions to my translations. Any blunders are, of course, mine, not hers. Finally, *Solovyov and Larionov* contains quotes from a number of other texts. I'm particularly grateful to Katherine Young, a poet, translator, and friend, who transformed my draft work on lines by Semyon Nadson and Vasily Zhukovsky into real poetry.

Oneworld, Many Voices

Bringing you exceptional writing
from around the world

The Unit by Ninni Holmqvist (Swedish)
Translated by Marlaine Delargy

Twice Born by Margaret Mazzantini (Italian)
Translated by Ann Gagliardi

Things We Left Unsaid by Zoya Pirzad (Persian)
Translated by Franklin Lewis

The Space Between Us by Zoya Pirzad (Persian)
Translated by Amy Motlagh

The Hen Who Dreamed She Could Fly by Sun-mi Hwang
(Korean) Translated by Chi-Young Kim

The Hilltop by Assaf Gavron (Hebrew)
Translated by Steven Cohen

Morning Sea by Margaret Mazzantini (Italian)
Translated by Ann Gagliardi

A Perfect Crime by A Yi (Chinese)
Translated by Anna Holmwood

The Meursault Investigation by Kamel Daoud (French)
Translated by John Cullen

Minus Me by Ingelin Røssland (YA) (Norwegian)
Translated by Deborah Dawkin

Laurus by Eugene Vodolazkin (Russian)
Translated by Lisa C. Hayden

Masha Regina by Vadim Levental (Russian)
Translated by Lisa C. Hayden

French Concession by Xiao Bai (Chinese)
Translated by Chenxin Jiang

The Sky Over Lima by Juan Gómez Bárcena (Spanish)
Translated by Andrea Rosenberg

A Very Special Year by Thomas Montasser (German)
Translated by Jamie Bulloch

Umami by Laia Jufresa (Spanish)
Translated by Sophie Hughes

The Hermit by Thomas Rydahl (Danish)
Translated by K.E. Semmel

The Peculiar Life of a Lonely Postman by Denis Thériault
(French) Translated by Liedewy Hawke

Three Envelopes by Nir Hezroni (Hebrew)
Translated by Steven Cohen

Fever Dream by Samanta Schweblin (Spanish)
Translated by Megan McDowell

The Postman's Fiancée by Denis Thériault (French)
Translated by John Cullen

The Invisible Life of Euridice Gusmao by Martha Batalha
(Brazilian Portuguese) Translated by Eric M. B. Becker

The Temptation to Be Happy by Lorenzo Marone
(Italian) Translated by Shaun Whiteside

Sweet Bean Paste by Durian Sukegawa (Japanese)
Translated by Alison Watts

They Know Not What They Do by Jussi Valtonen (Finnish)
Translated by Kristian London

The Tiger and the Acrobat by Susanna Tamaro (Italian)
Translated by Nicoleugenia Prezzavento and Vicki Satlow

The Woman at 1,000 Degrees by Hallgrímur Helgason
(Icelandic) Translated by Brian FitzGibbon

Frankenstein in Baghdad by Ahmed Saadawi (Arabic)
Translated by Jonathan Wright

Back Up by Paul Colize (French)
Translated by Louise Rogers Lalaurie

Damnation by Peter Beck (German)
Translated by Jamie Bulloch

Oneiron by Laura Lindstedt (Finnish)
Translated by Owen Witesman

The Boy Who Belonged to the Sea by Denis Thériault
(French) Translated by Liedewy Hawke

The Baghdad Clock by Shahad Al Rawi (Arabic)
Translated by Luke Leafgren

The Aviator by Eugene Vodolazkin (Russian)
Translated by Lisa C. Hayden

Lala by Jacek Dehnel (Polish)
Translated by Antonia Lloyd-Jones

Bogotá 39: New Voices from Latin America
(Spanish and Portuguese) Short story anthology

Last Instructions by Nir Hezroni (Hebrew)
Translated by Steven Cohen

The Day I Found You by Pedro Chagas Freitas (Portuguese)
Translated by Daniel Hahn

Solovyov and Larionov by Eugene Vodolazkin (Russian)
Translated by Lisa C. Hayden

In/Half by Jasmin B. Frelih (Slovenian)
Translated by Jason Blake

Winner of the National Big
Book Award and the Yasnaya
Polyana Award

Winner of the Read Russia
Prize 2016

Shortlisted for the Oxford-
Weidenfeld Prize 2016

In fifteenth-century Russia a young healer, skilled in the art of herbs and remedies, finds himself overcome with grief and guilt when he fails to save the one he loves. Leaving behind his village, his possessions and his name, he sets out on a quest for redemption, penniless and alone. But this is no ordinary journey.

Winner of two of the biggest literary prizes in Russia, *Laurus* is a remarkably rich novel about the eternal themes of love, loss, self-sacrifice and faith, from one of the country's most experimental and critically acclaimed novelists.

'At once stylistically ornate and compulsively readable... delivered with great aplomb and narrative charm.'
Times Literary Supplement

'With flavours of Umberto Eco and *The Canterbury Tales,* this affecting, idiosyncratic novel…is an impressive achievement.' *Kirkus*

ONEWORLD

ALSO BY EUGENE VODOLAZKIN

THE AVIATOR

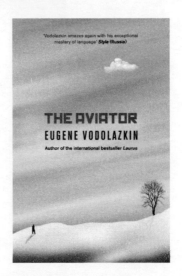

Shortlisted for the Russian Booker Prize

Shortlisted for the National Big Book Award

A man wakes up in a hospital bed, with no idea who he is or how he came to be there. The only information the doctor shares with him is his name: Innokenty Petrovich Platonov.

As memories slowly resurface, Innokenty begins to build a vivid picture of his former life as a young man in Russia in the early twentieth century, living through the turbulence of the Russian Revolution and its aftermath. Soon, only one question remains: how can he remember the start of the twentieth century, when the pills by his bedside were made in 1999?

Reminiscent of the great works of twentieth-century Russian literature, with nods to Dostoevsky's *Crime and Punishment* and Bulgakov's *The White Guard*, *The Aviator* cements Vodolazkin's position as the rising star of Russia's literary scene.

'Vodolazkin's grip on this narrative is iron-tight... We should expect nothing less from an author whose previous novel, *Laurus*, was a barnstorming thriller about medieval virtue.' *Guardian*

ONEWORLD